36

MAY 1 - 2015

Miss Julia Lays Down
the Law

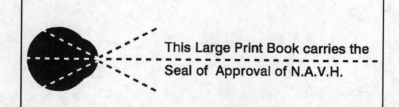

This Large Print Book carries the
Seal of Approval of N.A.V.H.

Miss Julia Lays Down the Law

Ann B. Ross

THORNDIKE PRESS
A part of Gale, Cengage Learning

GALE
CENGAGE Learning·

Farmington Hills, Mich • San Francisco • New York • Waterville, Maine
Meriden, Conn • Mason, Ohio • Chicago

Thorndike Press® Large Print Core.
The text of this Large Print edition is unabridged.
Other aspects of the book may vary from the original edition.
Set in 16 pt. Plantin.

LIBRARY OF CONGRESS CATALOGING-IN-PUBLICATION DATA

Ross, Ann B.
  Miss Julia lays down the law / Ann B. Ross. — Large print edition.
    pages cm. — (Thorndike Press large print core)
    ISBN 978-1-4104-7670-8 (hardcover) — ISBN 1-4104-7670-7 (hardcover)
    1. Springer, Julia (Fictitious character)—Fiction. 2. Murder—Investigation—Fiction. 3. Widows—Fiction. 4. Large type books.
  I. Title.
  PS3568.O84198M5655 2015b
  813'.54—dc23   2015006201

Published in 2015 by arrangement with Viking, an imprint of Penguin Publishing Group, a division of Penguin Random House LLC

Printed in the United States of America
1 2 3 4 5 6 7 19 18 17 16 15

*To all the readers who turned
the first Miss Julia book
into a series, this sixteenth one is for you.*

CHAPTER 1

Holding my coat against the wind, I walked across the brittle grass of the Clayborns' sloping yard to my car, paying no attention to the other women coming out of the house behind me. No one spoke — all the pleasantries and other closing remarks had been said inside, and everyone was anxious to leave, no one more so than I. I bent against the wind as I hurried toward the cars parked in the drive and along the street. The strong November breeze with a nip in it swirled off the mountain — another reason not to linger.

I slid into my car and closed the door, then, with shaking hands, rammed the key into the ignition.

Why hadn't I said something?

Driving a little less carefully than was my wont, I hurried home, shivering occasionally as remnants of the startling lecture flashed in my mind — rural blight, complacent people, unsustainable economy, ugly mismatched storefronts, and on and on, until I'd thought I'd explode with outrage at the tongue lashing.

I hadn't wanted to go to Connie Clayborn's house for coffee, had thought of half a dozen reasons not to go, had almost called that morning to offer my apologies.

Yet I had gone because what else does one do when graciously invited, but graciously accept? As had a dozen or so women — many of whom were my close friends, and others, if not close, well known to me. It should have been a pleasant occasion, full of talk about the approaching holidays, the state of the weather, children, and grandchildren, as well as that of the nation. We were a fairly well-read and well-informed group.

I should've gotten up and left.

During the social hour, I had listened attentively to the comments of almost everyone there over the fact that Sam had lost the election for state senator a few days before. He'd lost, but not by much — he'd given Jimmy Ray Mooney a run for his money — yet a miss is as good as a mile in politics as well as in horseshoes, and we had to live with that. Hearing remarks from some who were sincerely sorry was hard enough, but I'd also had to attend to those pious souls who could hardly bring themselves to offer their regrets, but who had commiserated for the sake of politeness. That was probably why I hadn't wanted to go in the first place, yet better to face it than to avoid it.

They were all eager to see how I was taking the loss — would I be angry, disgusted, bitter? None of the above. I had smiled, even laughed occasionally, saying, "We always deserve whomever we elect, don't you think?" and let them interpret it as they pleased.

After pulling into my own driveway and parking, I strode into a quiet house, recalling that Lillian had said she'd be grocery shopping. With no one to talk to, but still on edge, I immediately went upstairs to change my clothes. I had worn a powder blue woolen princess-style dress with a double strand of pearls under a matching coat with my diamond brooch on the shoulder. After putting the jewelry away, I hung up the outfit and donned an everyday dress and a cardigan. Then, slipping into low-heeled shoes, I sat down in one of the easy chairs in front of a window that looked out over Polk Street, determined to compose myself after enduring a piercingly critical review of my shortcomings, as well as those of every other resident of Abbotsville, North Carolina.

Why had we put up with it?

Connie Clayborn had invited us to a coffee — the term we use for a morning social occasion in which coffee and hot tea are served along with an array of finger food. Such an occasion gave the hostess an opportunity to use her silver, her best or second-best china — depending upon whom she'd invited — and to display by the centerpiece her skill in flower arranging. And, of course, to show off her home.

I had been to hundreds of such gatherings over the years, but never to such a one as I'd been subjected to that morning. Let's get this straight right at the beginning: it had *not* been a social occasion. The invitation to a coffee had been a ruse to get us to attend, and, being polite people, we had accepted even though Connie Clayborn was a newcomer to the town and barely known by most of us.

What had been the matter with us?

In hindsight, though, I realized that she had known us. She'd invited the cream of the crop, so to speak, knowing that if one of us accepted, the others would follow suit. Mildred Allen had been there, and so had

10

LuAnne Conover, Emma Sue Ledbetter, Helen Stroud, Callie Armstrong, Sue Hargrove, and several other leading women of the town. Interestingly, though, neither Hazel Marie Pickens nor Binkie Enloe Bates had been there, perhaps because one was married to a private investigator and the other to a sheriff's deputy — too blue collar for Connie, I supposed.

Which proved that Connie didn't know us quite as well as she thought. Binkie, for instance, was one of the most successful lawyers in town, and Hazel Marie was the mother of Lloyd, the child of my late husband, Wesley Lloyd Springer, which meant that Lloyd and I shared the largest estate ever probated in Abbot County. Neither Binkie nor Hazel Marie would ever go hungry, so Connie Clayborn didn't know everything about us.

As I went over in my mind the ones who had been invited, I realized that Connie had selected the most obviously wealthy and influential women in town either by virtue of their husbands — doctors, lawyers, or executives — or because of inherited wealth, plus one or two who'd made it on their own. But that didn't explain the presence of Emma Sue Ledbetter, the wife of the minister of the First Presbyterian Church of Ab-

11

botsville, because I knew what we paid him. I now realized, however, just why Emma Sue had been invited — it was because she was so *active and involved*. Especially if whatever she did could be counted as another good deed to be chalked up.

I'd also thought that Connie had made a mistake with Helen Stroud because Helen had lost her financial standing when she'd lost her husband. But on second thought, perhaps Helen had not been a mistake, because if anything needed to be organized, supervised, and done right, she was the one who could do it.

But let me tell you about Connie. First of all, she was a little younger than some of us — late forties, I would venture, although about half of the guests had been in that age group. But none, I realized, had young children at home — we could all have been seen as women of leisure.

Connie and her husband, a top executive at the local plant of an international plastics company, had built a glass and stone house in the first and, so far, the only gated community in the county. I didn't know what the plastics company made, but Connie had taken pains to let us know that they had lived in Switzerland, New Jersey, Chicago, and Boston during her husband's climb to the top. It had occurred to me that being transferred to Abbotsville might indicate some slippage from those heights, but who knew?

I can't believe we just sat there and took it.

The first time I'd met Connie, which had been a couple of weeks before at a reading by our local poet at the library, she'd walked up to me, held out her hand, and said, "Did you, by chance, go to Vassar? You look so familiar." A claim that was patently unlikely to begin with, there being such a difference in our ages.

"No," I'd replied, "I went to Winthrop."

"Oh?" she asked with a lift of her eyebrows. "Where is that?"

"Rock Hill." Then as she frowned, I said, "South Carolina."

"Well, that explains it," she'd said. "I don't know the South very well." Meaning, I surmised, that she'd never heard of the school or the town, and I realized that her motive in asking had been to let me know that she was a Vassar graduate. Lot of good that would do her in Abbotsville twenty years later.

Still, it probably explained why she dressed in twin sweater sets and pleated skirts, complete with heavy, clunky shoes. Though quite tall, she was not an unattractive woman, but, then, I wouldn't call her especially attractive, either. She had dark brown hair, deep brown eyes, and an olive complexion that was prone to a sprinkle of dark moles. With her serious demeanor and black-rimmed eyeglasses, she seemed to me to be projecting *intellectual,* which, if she had to work that hard at it, probably meant she wasn't.

She did, however, impress a number of people. Like Emma Sue Ledbetter, for one, who was thrilled to have such a superior being among us.

"Julia," she'd whispered to me at the coffee, "Connie is *unchurched,* can you believe it? I invited her to Sunday services, and she said she's a rationalist who depends on the positive energy of the universe to guide her life. I don't know what that means." Emma Sue added, frowning, "But it really hurt me to hear it. Isn't she just the kind we want to reach? I mean, she's so intelligent that she'll see the truth if it's presented to her. I think she's ripe for evangelizing, so do whatever you can to reach her."

"Well, Emma Sue," I said, balancing a teacup on a dessert plate, "if she asks, I'll be happy to respond. But I'm not much for bringing in the sheaves against their will."

Emma Sue's eyes automatically filled at

that, but she said, "I know you don't mean that, Julia. We must always be on the lookout for the little lost sheep."

Later, as we'd mingled before Connie surprised us by calling us to order, Mildred Allen had sidled up to me and said, "Guess what? I really shocked our hostess by telling her that I, too, went to Vassar. I don't think she knew that any Southern girl had even heard of it." Mildred sipped from her cup, then, with an arched eyebrow, said, "Then I told her I'd left before finishing the first semester. Came back down south where people have manners. I think that makes me one up, if anybody's counting, and I think someone is. She went and stayed. I went and left, having found it lacking."

"Did you mention that you've also been to New York?"

Mildred sputtered, then laughed. For a heavy woman, she had a remarkably light heart.

Just as I was about to head for the guest bedroom to retrieve my coat, Connie began to herd us all into her large vaulted-ceiling living room, saying that she had something important to tell us. Then when we were seated around the room, on sofas, in chairs, on footstools, and on a bench, she stood in the middle and began to tell us what was

wrong with us and what she had planned
that would set us right.

The nerve of the woman!

CHAPTER 2

Hearing Lillian bustling around in the kitchen, I hurried down to discuss the morning's events with her. As soon as I pushed through the door from the dining room, she said, "Miss Binkie call you this mornin' right after you left."

Binkie Enloe Bates was my curly-haired attorney, one of the feistiest lawyers around — anyone who tangled with her came out of it beaten and bedraggled. Married now to Sheriff's Sergeant Coleman Bates, she was the mother of little Gracie, which I kept hoping would serve to domesticate her to some extent.

"Oh, my," I said, suddenly concerned about the state of my finances. Binkie, along with Sam, took care of both halves of Wesley Lloyd Springer's estate that Lloyd and I shared, and every time she called I had visions of stock market crashes, lawsuits, bursting bubbles, and bankruptcies. "What

17

did she want?"

"She don't tell me. Jus' say she gonna be in court most of the day, an' she call back later."

"Well," I said, pulling out a chair at the table, "that makes one more thing to worry about. Not that I don't have enough on my plate already. I declare, Lillian, some people don't have enough sense to come in out of the rain."

She turned, frowning at me. "You talkin' 'bout Miss Binkie?"

"Goodness, no. Binkie has more sense than is good for her, but that's just my opinion. Nothing would do but she had to keep that law practice going, leaving little Gracie to be raised by someone else, and working when Coleman is off, and being off when he's working. I wish she'd put more of that good sense into her home and family." I sighed and rolled my eyes. "Of course if she did, I'd be left high and dry, so I can't wish it too hard."

Just as Lillian was pouring coffee for the two of us, the phone rang. Hoping it was Binkie so I could stop worrying about my economic well-being, I hurried to answer it. It wasn't, but it was a welcome call, nonetheless.

"Julia?" Mildred said, "I'm so mad I'm

18

about to pop. Come over and have lunch with me. I need to vent."

"I'll be right there." And, telling Lillian where I was going, I headed next door to Mildred's large Federal house. I, too, was dealing with a head of steam. Something needed to be done about newcomers who, with nothing but compassion in their hearts for the unenlightened, condescended to instruct us on how everything had been done better in New York, Boston, New Jersey, and Switzerland, and how if we tried harder we might eventually become a beacon in the South to every well-heeled shopper, tourist, and developer looking for a place to spend their money. As if that were what we all longed for.

Mildred met me at the door — a sure indication of her state of mind, for generally her excellent housekeeper, Ida Lee, was the greeter.

"Get in here," Mildred said, "and calm me down." Easier said than done, because she immediately went on. "I have never in my life been so insulted in such an insidious way that I didn't even realize it at the time. What was wrong with us, Julia? Nobody said a word. We just sat there and listened to her run us down, and not only us but the entire town." She took my coat,

19

threw it on a velvet bench in the foyer, and led me into the dining room.

"Tell me about it," I said in agreement. "I've been in a state of shock ever since. I mean, no one has ever criticized a whole group of people *to their faces* like she did." I took the chair that Mildred indicated at the table, and she took her own. Ida Lee had already prepared our lunch, and our filled plates were waiting — open-faced Reuben sandwiches and, as a nod toward Mildred's ongoing diet, tossed salads on the side.

Mildred lifted her fork as a signal to me, took a quick bite, and said, "I was offended as soon as she opened her mouth. She started right in by assuming *we* were the culprits, and it was our fault that the town looks the way it does. Julia," Mildred went on, waving her fork, "none of us is on the town council, and I don't know anyone who *wants* to be. I resented every word that came out of that woman's mouth, and I had a good mind to get up and walk out." She chewed for a minute. "I wish I had."

"I couldn't agree more," I agreed. "But, Mildred, just what did she want us to do? It was such a mixture of criticism on the one hand and rah-rah enthusiasm on the other that I wasn't sure whether she wanted us to

20

hide our heads in shame or organize and take over the town."

"It's all so silly. Our main street is not Fifth Avenue and never will be. Does she not have any idea what it would take to make downtown into a — what did she call it? — a shoppers' mecca or a bustling hive of activity? Where would people park, for one thing?"

"Yes, and how does she expect to get store owners to fall in with her plan? I mean, if she wants to give the street a face-lift — which I admit it could use — who's going to pay for it?"

"Well," Mildred said, pursing her mouth, "she was right about one thing. There're an awful lot of closed and empty shops, but if she expects me to go into the retail business, she can keep expecting. I'm not interested."

"Nor am I. But did you catch it when she said that with the pitiful state the town is in, it wouldn't matter what kind of businesses we had as long as all the storefronts were alike and we had gas streetlamps?"

"I did!" Mildred let her fork fall to the plate. "Tattoo parlors, massage parlors, pool parlors — can you believe it! *Anything* that would draw people downtown. Well, what kind of people, I ask you!"

21

Ida Lee silently pushed open the door from the kitchen to see if we'd finished eating, then just as silently closed it. We were doing more talking than eating.

"What she should do," I said, "is go over to Tennessee and take a look at some of those tourist towns. Every shop is filled with tacky stuff from Taiwan. And after you've bought one Smokey Mountain bear trinket made in Taiwan, who would want another one? And you know that area around the lake at the foot of the mountain — it caters to motorcycle gangs. Sam and I drove down there one Sunday afternoon last summer, and the roads were packed with swarms of motorcycles. And we couldn't even find a place to eat for all the motorcycles in the parking lots. I won't even mention the horrendous noise those things make."

"Oh, I know," Mildred said. "But it stands to reason that a town will draw the kind of people who want what that town has to offer. But what happens when *we* don't want *them*?" Mildred carefully sliced a cherry tomato on her salad plate. Then she said, "Now, she did mention antique shops, which I might could agree to, but that was in the same breath as bars with dance floors. And, Julia, you know as well as I do that we have street dances every Friday night in the summer. That's enough dancing as far as I'm concerned, and if you mix in liquor, you've got problems."

"I know," I said, sighing. "She didn't seem to realize it, but her big ideas couldn't possibly be implemented in a town this size. How in the world could we ever compete with Zurich or Bern or even Gatlinburg, for that matter? Fountains with sprays of water, marble statues, copper flower boxes, and riverboats in the middle of town — how do we do that? Divert Mud Creek so it'll flow through Main Street? It all sounded too grandiose and, frankly, too expensive. I know of only one small town that was completely made over like she was talking about, but it took a Rockefeller to do it. And all we have is a town council that goes into shock at the mention of more trash receptacles."

"Well, that's where we come in, according to Connie. Remember, she said with our combined assets, we could turn this town upside down." Mildred contemplated her plate, then looked up. "I guess that means we should open our pocketbooks. And she said we should organize, put a combined force before the town fathers, and demand they do something to rehabilitate the town. She forgets, or doesn't know, that most of us are past the idealistic age. And the fantasy age, too. But did you catch that about how we should ensure that the town is in harmony with the universe? How're we supposed to do that?"

"I have no idea. I didn't even know that the universe carried a tune. I don't keep up with musical groups, anyway."

Taking a deep breath, I tried to ease my rising temper at the memory of Connie Clayborn's scathing critique of our town and, even worse, of us. "I tell you the truth, Mildred, I'm at the age where I feel I've done my part. I've been to more committee meetings over the years than I can count, and I'm tired. If it wasn't community work, it was church work, and nobody was ever satisfied. They always wanted more — more volunteers, more money, more of your time, more, more, more.

"But," I went on, getting more exercised as I went, "what got to me most was when she scolded us for not using our gifts effectively for the benefit of others. Gifts, ha! What she meant was our time and money, without knowing one thing about what we do or don't do. She called us lazy, self-serving, and burdened with too much leisure."

"Yes," Mildred said, "and I plead guilty to

24

all three. What I do with my *gifts* is my business and not hers."

"Amen to that. And she kept saying that it was our responsibility to *give back*. Give back to whom, I ask you! The only person I could give *back* to is Wesley Lloyd Springer and he's dead. What she meant was simply *give,* not give back."

"You said it, Julia. Just because I don't volunteer for whatever somebody dreams up doesn't mean I'm not contributing in my own way. And contributing *heavily.*"

"Actually," I said, "I've done it all and more in my day. Well, I was never a runner, but nobody else was, either. But there was a time when I volunteered for everything that came along. I worked for the Literacy Council for years. I helped with Vacation Bible School, taught Sunday school classes to kindergartners, brought covered dishes to Wednesday night suppers, collected used clothing for those without and bought new clothes and toys for Christmas, donated to every project that helped children, gave to every fund-raising group that rang my doorbell or sent me a pledge card. And to tell the truth, I've had enough of it."

"It never stopped, did it?" Mildred said, recalling the activities of our younger days. "And now she wants us to take on the town council! Why, Julia, can you imagine what that group of men would do if we showed up and started demanding copper flower boxes? I've got better things to do than cause strokes and heart attacks."

"Well, speaking of better things to do," I said, "you are going to Sue Hargrove's tomorrow night, aren't you?"

"Oh, yes, although my fingers are still sore from last week. I'm not much of a seamstress, but I do enjoy that group, and the ornaments we're making are just lovely. Of course my snowman has bloodstains on it from sticking myself so much. But why don't I pick you up and we'll go together?"

"That'll be fine," I agreed. "I enjoy that group, too, although I expect Connie will be the number one topic. We'd better remind them that the Christmas sale is only a few weeks off, and we have to do more sewing than talking." I took my last bite of salad, thinking of the only fund-raiser I was presently involved with. Every year a compatible group of women — usually the same ones — got together throughout the fall to make felt Christmas ornaments which we then decorated with seed pearls, sequins, and whatever else we could sew or glue on. Some were quite attractive, while others only the makers could love. Yet we sold out every year at the County Christmas Sale because we always chose a widely favored cause to receive the proceeds.

After a brief period of silence in which I had pleasant thoughts of Christmas, images of Connie intruded again. "You know, there was a time when, if you didn't have a nine-to-five job, you were expected to be a full-time volunteer. And we both just about were. So it makes me doubly irate to hear Connie belittle and berate us. There she was, coming in here from up north or Switzerland or wherever, criticizing us when she knows absolutely nothing about us!" At the thought of it, I wanted to grind my teeth. "I'd like to give something back to *her*!"

"That's the thing, Julia," Mildred agreed. "She thinks she *does* know us. In fact, it was her holier-than-thou, know-it-all attitude that got to me the worst. And if somebody has invited her to the sewing group, I'm turning around and leaving. I'd like to snatch that woman bald-headed, and I just might do it if she starts in on us again."

"You and me both," I agreed, but what neither of us had touched on was the awful mortification that I had personally suffered throughout Connie's tirade. Mildred was too careful of my feelings to bring it up, and my feelings were still too tender for me to say anything. But I still burned with resentment, and appreciated the fact that Mildred was letting me know whose side she was on.

CHAPTER 3

I'd barely stepped into my house after my lunch with Mildred when the telephone rang. Hoping it was Binkie, I hurried into the library to answer it, waving to Lillian as I passed. She was scrounging around in the pantry, mumbling about being sure she had another sack of flour somewhere.

As I picked up the phone and almost before the word *hello* was out of my mouth, Emma Sue Ledbetter started talking, and kept talking, hardly taking a breath.

"Julia, I'm so upset. I know I'm the worst of all Christians and I try to do better, I really do. I get up every morning and ask the Lord to lead and guide me, to show me what He wants, to prevent me from doing or saying anything that will hurt my witness, and, you know, to just be with me all day long. I try to watch what I say and what I do, knowing that He has His eye on the sparrow, and other people do, too. Because, as a minister's wife, I'm under special scrutiny, to say nothing of the fact that our Father in heaven sees us as we really are, and . . . and . . . I just don't know what else I can do." Emma Sue began to cry, sobbing piteously over the phone.

"Oh, Emma Sue, please don't cry," I said, uneasy, as always, when she lost control of her emotions. "Listen. Emma Sue, listen a minute. Has something happened? Or are you talking about what happened at Connie Clayborn's this morning?"

"Ye-es," she sobbed. "It just seemed so unfair, because I'm doing the best I can. I go from morning till night every day of my life, except when I have a migraine and can't get out of bed. Oh, Julia, what else am I supposed to do?"

"Not another thing, Emma Sue," I said emphatically. "You already put everybody in the Presbyterian church to shame, and frankly a lot of us wish you'd slow down a little. You drive yourself too hard and take on everybody's problems. It's time you took care of yourself for a change."

"Oh, I do," Emma Sue said, sniffing. "It's just that so many need so much, and I do so little. . . ." And the crying began again. "In fact," she said as the breath caught in her throat, "I've been thinking I should give up working in the city park because I enjoy it so much. I could deliver more Meals on Wheels if I did. But now my heart's just not in anything."

"Emma Sue," I said, almost losing patience, "stop running yourself down. I'm telling you that you don't need to do another thing. Forget Connie Clayborn. And stop worrying about that park. It doesn't need weeding in the wintertime. Mildred and I have already decided that Connie doesn't know what she's talking about. And she has some nerve excoriating us like she did!"

"But, Julia, she's so intelligent. And she's been all over the world, and she's educated, and, and she's, well, I guess she can't help but compare us to other places she's seen. And I know we fall short, especially *me*."

"For goodness sakes, Emma Sue! She thinks she knows it all, but actually she's as ignorant as a post. Just because she's traveled farther than Edneyville doesn't give her any special knowledge about us or what we do — or should do. You can't let her get to you like this. And I'll tell you another thing, I don't think she's so intelligent, because no intelligent person would have done what she did this morning. And I think she'd better watch her step before she really offends somebody. She might get taken down a notch or two."

"Well, I don't know," Emma Sue said. "I think it behooves us to at least listen to criticism and use it to examine ourselves for flaws and ways to improve."

"I've already done that, and I passed with flying colors. And so have you. There is no room for improvement as far as what you do for others. In fact, there's no room for you to do anything else, period. You don't have time for it. You're an example to us all." I said that to make her feel better, but the truth of it was that she made me tired. She was always so busy doing good — often for people who wished she'd leave them alone — that her days were filled with frenzied activity until a migraine struck her down.

"Well," she finally conceded, "I guess I'll just have to pray about it. But, Julia, it really hurt when she called the city park an eyesore, and laughed — *laughed* — at our idea of what a park should look like." Emma Sue had to stop as a sobbing fit overtook her. "I know I'm not a landscaper or a horticulturist, but I try so hard. And what she said was like a knife to my heart, because you know it was my design the garden club used."

"I understand, Emma Sue," I said, trying

to be of comfort, because I did understand — it had hurt me, too. Of all the crushing things Connie had said, her harangue about the city park had been the worst. A few years back, after the town had demolished the old courthouse and built a new one some blocks away, a developer had wanted to construct a high-rise condominium building on the Main Street site. That hadn't worked out so well since the town had an ordinance against high-rises, and nobody could afford his condominiums anyway. I won't go into all the problems we had with that, so suffice it to say that we were left with a huge empty lot, excepting the rubble from the destruction of the old courthouse and a tin replica of Lady Justice salvaged from the top of the dome. That's when the garden club headed by Emma Sue had taken over. The site was now a lovely garden spot, with Lady Justice taking pride of place in the middle of the park in the middle of town.

And it had all been Emma Sue's doing, with a few checks and suggestions from me, because Emma Sue had won the park design contest, and had since been the leading force in the care of the plantings, the paths, the gazebo, and the benches for weary shoppers. That park was the only thing I could think of that Emma Sue did that wasn't first and foremost what one would think of as a purely church-related activity. I thought it was good for her.

"Emma Sue," I said, sharply enough to get her attention, "listen, that park is a jewel. People use it and enjoy it, and it's all because of you. If Connie doesn't like it, she doesn't have to. A lot of other people do."

"Well, but, Julia, she said our Lady Justice is t-t-tacky and ought to be scrapped." And Emma Sue dissolved into tears again. "And everything else, too. And did you hear what she said about spring bulbs? She said they ought to be outlawed because the foliage is so unsightly after they bloom. And I just bought two hundred tulip bulbs to plant along the paths — thanks to your generosity, Julia — and now I don't know what to do with them."

"You're going to plant every one of them and enjoy them when they bloom. The park will be beautiful when the tulips and the pear trees are in bloom, and everybody will thank you."

"Well," Emma Sue said, sniffing, "well, I don't know. I guess it doesn't matter what I do, since Connie thinks it's already so awful. And maybe she's the Lord's way of telling me there are more important things He wants me to do. There're so many lost and needy people in the world, and I've been frittering away my time on weeding and planting and raking and deadheading and first one thing after another, and ignoring my true calling."

"Listen, Emma Sue, think of this. Who was it that gave us flowers and trees and grass? Who gave us gardens, for goodness sakes — think of where Adam and Eve lived! And what were they given to do? Tend the garden, that's what! So it doesn't matter what Connie thinks. You can't let her get to you like this. You are doing the Lord's work every time you put a bulb, annual, or perennial in the ground. And you've put in a lot of them."

"I guess I hadn't thought of it like that." Emma Sue stopped and blew her nose. "Maybe Larry could speak to this in one of his sermons."

I rolled my eyes, but said, "That's a good idea. But, Emma Sue, don't let what Connie said bother you for another minute. She doesn't know it yet, but she has stirred up a hornet's nest. I wouldn't be surprised if she gets stung pretty badly one of these days."

"Oh, I wouldn't want anything bad to happen to her."

"It's just a saying," I said tiredly, because Emma Sue was always so literal. "But it's been my experience that when someone goes out of their way to antagonize people, what's said has a tendency to come back and bite that someone. And in the case of Connie, I'm looking forward to having that happen."

"Oh, no, Julia, we must pray for our enemies, not wish them harm."

"Well, I wouldn't exactly call her an enemy, Emma Sue. It's just that after this morning, I don't care for her company, and I intend to avoid her from now on."

And that started Emma Sue off on our Christian duty to love the unlovely, feed the hungry, visit the sick, and so on. By the time I got off the phone, I felt as if the whole day had been given over to my personal failures and horrendous shortcomings.

I stood for a minute holding the phone after Emma Sue had said good-bye, giving some of Connie's comments serious thought. I hadn't mentioned it to Mildred and had barely touched on it to Emma Sue, but I was not only hurt but also *incensed* by the cavalier way Connie had dismissed the park as an amateurish attempt at beautifying the town. She'd sneered at Lady Justice, unaware that I, along with Etta Mae Wiggins and Poochie Dunn, had risked life and limb to rescue her. Connie had also told us it was time to put aside old antagonisms by removing and discarding the marble marker to the Confederate war dead. Why, what a travesty that would be! And a slap in the face to all the old families in the county whose names were inscribed on it.

And if Connie thought that marker indicated leftover antagonism toward Northern invaders, she had done nothing to lessen it. In fact, for my money, she and her ilk were worse than the original invaders, but we'd all been too polite and *sensitive to her feelings* to have put a stop to the enumeration of our deficiencies.

So I didn't know if my sudden sinking feelings were because I'd not stood up for myself and our town — which I had been too stunned to do — or if they were a result of my having been made aware of my failures.

I wished Sam would get home so I could count my blessings, starting with him.

Chapter 4

Late that afternoon when I heard Sam come through the back door and stop in the kitchen to talk with Lillian, I hurried out to meet him. Lillian was already pouring coffee, asking if we wanted it in the kitchen or served in the library.

"Right here is fine," Sam said, pulling out a chair at the table, then, before sitting, coming over to give me a kiss. "How was your day, sweetheart?"

"Disturbing," I said, taking the chair beside him. "Lillian, join us. I'd like to hear what you think of this."

She put a cream pitcher on the table along with our cups, then said, "I got to finish supper, so I'll jus' listen in."

"Well, feel free to join in, too." Then I turned to my levelheaded, fair, and supremely just husband. "Sam, what do you think of people who move to a town and start excoriating it right off the bat?"

His eyebrows went up. "Haven't given it much thought. Why?"

"Because I went to a coffee this morning at Connie Clayborn's house, and was told that I, and everyone else, should be ashamed to live in a town that doesn't have enough pride in itself to install water fountains, matching shop awnings, and public restrooms on the sidewalks."

Sam smiled. "And who was the city-planning expert who told you such a thing?"

"Why, Connie, of course, and apparently, she herself knows exactly what should be done to draw crowds of spenders from all over who'll boost the economy and put us on the cover of *Southern Living.* The only thing she didn't tell us was how to pay for it. We are up in arms."

"Oh, I doubt it'll come to taking up arms," Sam said soothingly. "The town could use some beautifying, that's a fact. And anything that would draw people downtown couldn't hurt."

"Well, yes, I expect so, if you don't mind motorcycle gangs and tattoo artists and bar-hoppers. I tell you, some of her ideas for updating the town were just plain silly, even outlandish. Why, Sam, she said we ought to get rid of all the grassy areas in our park and spread *gravel* instead. With clumps of swamp grass and huge boulders here and there, and you know how I feel about boulders."

He smiled, for he'd heard me often enough on the subject of big rocks strewn around helter-skelter in a so-called natural landscape. "I do know how you feel, but rocks and gravel would cut down on maintenance costs."

"That's what she said!" I exclaimed. "But that's being penny wise and pound foolish, because who wants a rock-filled park? Where's the beauty in that? How would a rock garden draw shoppers downtown? It wouldn't draw me!" I put my cup in the saucer and looked up at Lillian. "What do you think, Lillian?"

"I think I better stay out of this. I don't have much bus'ness downtown anyway."

"But listen, Lillian. And you, too, Sam. We can all agree that the town could use some help, but who wants a newcomer with no knowledge of our history or our traditions to come in and start telling us how lax and shortsighted we are, and then to tell us that she's the answer to all our prayers?" I took a deep breath. "Except she doesn't believe in prayer, so what can she be an answer to."

Sam grinned. "You have a point. But, Julia, if she wants to approach the town council with a few ideas for improvement, tell her to have at it."

"Well, yes, and I'd say more power to her if that had been all," I said with a dismissive wave. "But it wasn't. According to Connie, it is our moral and civic *duty* to organize, donate, and move the town forward. I mean, she about worked herself into a frenzy of outrage that we were so taken up with our own selfish interests that we'd ignored the needs of the town. And I'd be willing to wager that she has no idea of what she's talking about. She hasn't been here long enough, for one thing, and she doesn't know us well enough, for another. She just assumed that we're self-absorbed and uncaring of others, and that it's her job to lead us forward."

I stopped, recalling the intense anger I'd felt toward Connie as she stood before us and told us how backward we were.

"In fact," I went on, "she as much as told us how she'd dreaded moving here when her husband was transferred. But then she said she realized what a perfect project it would be to fill her time. Don't you just hate it when somebody thinks up a *project*?" I stopped, then thought of something else. "And *then,* on my way out I overheard her say that what she'd really like to do is take a bulldozer to both sides of Main Street! I can't tell you how much that attitude upsets me."

We all thought about that for a few minutes, then in the silence Lillian suddenly said, "I tell you what upset me, an' that lady you tellin' 'bout remind me of it. She sound like somebody I been knowin' for years that went up north an' come back thinkin' she know everything, an' tellin' us we got to quit talkin' like field hands. But I been talkin' like I talk ever since I been born, an' nobody have any trouble understandin' what I say."

"They certainly don't," Sam agreed. "On the other hand, I have real trouble understanding what somebody from, say, New Jersey says."

"Well," I said, "you should've had to sit and listen to Connie this morning. Her voice grated on my nerves so bad that I could hardly sit still. She went on and on until I thought she'd never get through, and, Sam, I'm convinced she, herself, is from New Jersey." I stopped, tilted my coffee cup absentmindedly, then sighed and looked up. "Well, I might as well tell it all. She publicly humiliated me. And Emma Sue, too, who is just devastated. Oh, Sam, you wouldn't believe what Connie said about boxwoods, and you know that I donated a *mint* to buy all those miniature boxwoods to line the paths of the park. And you wouldn't believe what it cost to transplant those big, old ones that make the park look established." I leaned my head on my hand. "And everybody *knew* that the boxwoods were my gift to the town, and everybody *knew* that the design was Emma Sue's. And we had to sit there and listen to Connie tell us that the park is a scraggly, poorly designed mess. And I'm so mad at myself for not speaking up, I don't know what to do. I should've said, 'If you think you can do any better, then do it.' Except we would've ended up with a rock garden edged with wild grasses and reeds. Maybe a puny pond filled with cattails. She likes a natural environment.

"Oh!" I said, sitting up straight, "you won't believe what else she wants to do. Make half the park into a *parking lot*! Can you believe it? Here, we have an entire city block for a green space in the middle of town, and she wants to pour concrete over half of it!"

Sam said, "Well, I'd vote against that."

"Me, too," Lillian said.

"Sorry," I said, "you don't have a vote. Connie's idea is for us — the leading

43

women of the town, according to her — to take the bull by the horns, the bull being the town council, and push the town into the future whether it wants to go or not."

"She won't get far with that," Sam said, smiling, as he patted my hand. "I know who's on the council, and I know at least one leading woman in town."

"Well," I went on, "you haven't heard the rest of it. This just ran all over me. Besides having to endure her scathing personal criticism — although she pretended to speak in generalities — I had to pretend it didn't bother me. But everybody knew who she was talking about when she started in on the park. They kept cutting their eyes at us to see how we were taking it. Poor Emma Sue, I thought she was going to dissolve on the spot, while my face burned and my back got so stiff I couldn't get up and walk out.

"And even worse, it was 'My God' this and 'My God' that until I wanted to slap her silly."

Lillian said, "I thought you say she don't b'lieve in prayin'."

"She wasn't praying, Lillian. She was using *expletives*. You know, like 'My God, that park is awful,' and 'My God, what is wrong with you people to put up with a town like this?' It's bad enough to have to hear it said

44

all over television whenever anybody likes something or when they don't like something. It's 'Oh, my God' this and 'Oh, my God' that, and no one seems to think a thing about it."

Lillian, frowning, gave me a long look.

"Don't be frowning at me, Lillian. I know what you're thinking, but it's a different matter when I say 'Oh, Lord,' or you call on Jesus. What we say is not the same thing at all. They call on God without a thought in the world of getting a response — Connie certainly didn't think she would. That's what taking the Lord's name in vain means. You and I, on the other hand, know we're addressing someone and, furthermore, we *expect* an answer."

Lillian nodded in full agreement. "Yes, ma'am, and amen, we sure do. That's what we askin' for."

And Sam looked from one to the other of us. Then that amused smile of his spread across his face. "If I didn't know better," he said, "I'd think the two of you were trained by Jesuits. You may be doing what I'd call a little hairsplitting."

Hairsplitting or not, I knew what I knew: Connie had done herself in as far as this town was concerned. She might have had the best intentions in the world to be of help to us and to Abbotsville, but one's manner of presentation is everything. Regardless of what she'd intended, she'd ruined it by her strident words and superior attitude. And by holding up Emma Sue, bless her heart — and me — to ridicule.

CHAPTER 5

We'd just finished supper when Binkie finally called back. I had begun to think of calling her, but I always hesitated to disturb her at home — she had so little time there.

"Miss Julia," she said, after a few perfunctory questions about my health, "have you heard about Coleman?"

I stiffened with dread of hearing of some dire accident or disease having happened to Coleman. He had come to Abbotsville not long after Wesley Lloyd's passing, and, at Sam's urging, I had rented my former sunroom to him. Sam had not wanted me to be in the house alone, although, at the time, I'd not known that Sam himself had designs on eventually keeping me company. But that's how I had come to know one of the finest young men in town, and it pleased me that Coleman had met Binkie in my house the day she'd been caught in a rainstorm and had come running in drenched to the skin. Coleman took one look and lost his heart.

"No," I said, fearing the worst, "what's wrong with Coleman?"

"I think he's lost his mind." Binkie giggled just a little. "Or else he's a hero in the making."

"What in the world?"

"Would you believe he's going to do some sign sitting? And I may need your help to get him down."

"He's doing *what*?"

"Sign sitting. He's got a bunch of his buddies helping him build a platform on one of those big outdoor advertising signs out off the MLK Boulevard. And he's going to stay up there until he raises twenty thousand dollars for playground equipment for the elementary school. Says those kids are going to have monkey bars if he has to put them up himself."

"My word, Binkie, doesn't he know it's *November*?"

"Tell me about it," Binkie said, sighing. "But he's looking at the long-range weather forecast and reading the *Farmers' Almanac.* And," she went on with a laugh, "he's consulting some old man on the other side of the mountain who claims to predict the weather a month in advance. Something to do with black gum trees, I think. Anyway, Coleman will have an electric heater hooked up to a generator, and he'll have a thick bedroll. Bought some long johns, too.

"But," she said, taking a breath, "that's why I'm calling around now, asking for pledges. The sooner he reaches his goal, the less time he'll spend up there. See, Miss Julia, I hate asking for a donation, but I don't want my husband freezing to death."

"Good gracious," I mumbled, wondering what the world was coming to — if it wasn't Emma Sue pushing herself to take on more than she could handle, it was Coleman risking his health to sit out in the elements. "Binkie, I'll pledge the whole amount right now. Just keep him off that thing."

"Oh, Miss Julia, thank you, but he won't let you do that. He likes challenging himself, so he *wants* to sit up there. He's hoping everybody in the county will pitch in and get the playground equipped. Right now it only has a couple of seesaws and one of them is broken."

"In that case," I said, resigning myself to the willfulness of some people, "I'll send him a nice check, but, Binkie, if he starts getting frostbite, let me know. I'll put him over the top whether he likes it or not."

Binkie laughed. "I may take you up on

that. And, Miss Julia, thanks for helping me take care of my crazy husband."

With a shake of my head, I hung up the phone and stood there, thinking. Here, I'd worried all day about a financial catastrophe, and all it had been was word of another fund-raiser. Since it was Coleman, though, who was doing the raising, I didn't mind.

The doorbell rang the next morning as I crossed the hall on my way to the kitchen to speak to Lillian. I veered toward the front door, opened it, and stood back as LuAnne Conover rushed in, flapping her hands.

"I'm a mess, Julia," she said, heading straight for the sofa in the living room, where she plopped down, straightened her skirt tail, and kept talking. "I'm so confused, I don't know what to do. Did you understand a word Connie said yesterday? I didn't. First she told us we ought to be proud of our town, then she said we ought to do something about it because it's in the worst shape she's ever seen. How in the world can we do both?"

"Come to think of it," I said, following her into the living room, "that was one thing she didn't tell us. But she pretty much covered everything else we're doing wrong."

"Well, one thing's for sure," LuAnne said,

pulling a sheet of paper from her tote bag and waving it at me. "No matter what she said, I cannot do this."

"What is it, LuAnne?" I asked, sitting across from her in one of the wing chairs by the fireplace. "I can't read it from here."

"It's my instructions — where we're supposed to meet, a town map, and my time to start. Connie gave it to me before we left. Julia," she said plaintively, "I don't know *why* I signed up. I mean, those sign-up papers started coming around and I didn't see a thing I wanted to do, but I felt I should do *something,* so when this one came by, I just signed it and now I'm stuck."

"With what? And, for goodness sakes, why did you sign up for anything?" I recalled my sense of outrage when Connie had handed out five or six sheets of paper to go from person to person around the room, each one of which I'd passed along without delay. A quick glance had told me that they were sign-up pages for assignments to certain committees, like, for instance, the Committee for Listing Derelict Buildings, the Committee for Rejuvenation of Flora, the Committee for Ecological Planning, and, for goodness sakes, the Committee for Town Council Oversight.

LuAnne leaned back against the sofa and

blew out her breath. "I don't know why I did. Everybody else was signing up, so I did, too."

"Everybody else was not signing, I assure you," I said. "I didn't, and neither did Mildred."

"You *didn't*?" LuAnne sat straight up and stared at me. "But how could you not? I mean, Connie was *watching* us, and after she'd cautioned us against being civic donothings — which I don't think I've ever been — I guess I wanted to prove to her how active and willing we are. You know, that we don't live in some backwater without knowing what's going on in the world. And she made it plain that we ought to make ourselves useful for the betterment of everybody." LuAnne frowned in thought as she glanced around the room. "I thought I was already doing that — being useful, I mean."

"You are, and I am, and so are the rest of us. And I will continue to do so, but in my own way," I told her. "And it won't be because somebody has laid a guilt trip on me."

"Well, I wish I'd known you and Mildred weren't signing up for anything," LuAnne said with some resentment. "I felt backed into a corner, so I just put my name down so Connie wouldn't be disappointed in me."

"Oh, LuAnne, who cares if she's disappointed? After she laid us all low yesterday, her feelings shouldn't even be considered. She obviously had no concern for *ours,* the way she criticized us. *Scathingly* criticized us, I might add."

"Well, you're right," LuAnne agreed. "I just wish you'd told me you weren't signing. You know me, I don't like to be the only one holding out."

"What did you sign up for?"

"Oh-h-h," LuAnne wailed, reminded of what she'd let herself in for. "I don't even know what it is! It just seemed like the only thing I could do once and be done with it. Not like signing up for a committee that'll meet two mornings a week for the unforeseeable future or anything. And now, Julia, I can't even do it *once!*"

"Do what?"

"*Run!* She's calling it the Run for Rehab, of all things. What do you think that means?"

"I have no idea, unless she thinks we all need a week at a spa. But, LuAnne, what does a run have to do with beautifying the town?"

"Well, see," LuAnne said, scooting to the edge of the sofa. "She's mapped out our route, and we're supposed to take note of places along the way that need to be torn down and rebuilt — rehabilitated, I guess. But, Julia, how am I going to do that when I may not be able to put one foot in front of the other?"

"I don't know, LuAnne. I didn't even know you were into running."

"I'm *not*! The only good thing about it is that nobody else is, either. See, Connie wants us to be slow enough to take note of the buildings and houses that need to come down. So she's making it an elder run."

"*Elder* run! LuAnne, there'll be bodies dropping all over town."

"I know!" she wailed. "And mine will probably be the first to drop. And here I am, *stuck* with it. What should I do, Julia?"

"Nothing. I just wouldn't do it. Why, LuAnne, you could fall and break something. People who enter these things practice for weeks before the actual run. What kind of shape are you in, anyway?"

"Julia," LuAnne said, sighing, "I'll tell you the truth, I get out of breath just bringing in groceries from the car."

"Then call Connie and tell her you're dropping out, or just don't show up."

"I can't just not show up. She'll be keeping count, I know she will."

I briefly considered my longtime friend —
short in stature, full-breasted, and nervously
energetic as long as she could sit and talk
about something rather than get up and do
it.

"Listen, LuAnne, how far do you think
you can run?"

That stopped her for a minute, then she
said, "I don't know. A block?"

"It's hardly worth going to the trouble of
putting on a running suit for a block."

"That's not the worst of it," LuAnne said.
"I don't even have a running suit. I'll have
to buy one."

"For a block? I wouldn't waste my time or
my money. Besides, I think runners wear
those tight-fitting latex things. You know,
the neon-colored things that reveal everything about you."

"Oh, Lord!" LuAnne wailed. "I can't wear
something like that in public!" Then she sat
up straight and pulled herself together.
"That decides it. I'm going to be sick."

I sat up straight, too. "Right *now*?"

"No, on the day of the run. Thanks, Julia,
I appreciate your help. And I'm glad to
know I'm not the only one who felt run over
and hemmed in by Connie.

"However," LuAnne mused after a moment of silence, "she is going to give out

trophies, and it'd be nice to have one."

"Listen to you! How do you expect to get a trophy for caving in after the first block?"

That stung, I could tell, for LuAnne drew herself up and said, "*Well,* Julia, for your information, it's not just the winner who'll get a trophy. Connie's going to award *participation* trophies, so there'll be no winners or losers, just all of us who *try.* Which apparently neither you nor Mildred is willing to do."

"And I'm glad we aren't," I shot back. "What's the use of expending — and embarrassing — yourself on something you can't do in the first place and which wouldn't mean anything anyway, even if you won? I say, give trophies just for entering!

"I tell you, LuAnne, the woman's a menace. You shouldn't give her or her dime-store trophies another thought."

"Well," LuAnne said, drawing herself up with a little huff, "here's something you don't know. Our running route starts on Main Street and comes right by your house. I'll wave to you as I go by."

"And I'll tell you this: if any of you puts *my* house on that so-called rehab list, you and Connie Clayborn will answer to me. But out of the kindness of my heart, I'll stand on the sidewalk with a cup of water for you."

LuAnne sighed then and rolled her eyes. "If I make it this far."

"No, no."

LuAnne sniffed then and rolled her eyes.

"I'd risk going far."

CHAPTER 6

Saying that she would see me that evening at Sue's for the ornament sewing group, Lu-Anne took herself off, leaving me unsure of whether she'd back out of the run before-hand, just not show up for it, or feel she'd have to give it a try. I hoped she wouldn't do that. She wasn't in any condition to survive the two blocks from Main Street to my house, much less keep at it for a mile. And to have a runner collapse after a couple of blocks would not speak well for rehabili-tating anything, unless it was by way of physical therapy after breaking something. Nor would LuAnne sprawled out on the sidewalk with EMTs in attendance please Connie. And pleasing Connie seemed to be LuAnne's sole motivation.

Thank goodness, I congratulated myself, *I couldn't care less what Connie thinks of me.* And with that, I decided that henceforth she and her multitudinous ideas would be of no concern to me. Let her have at it on her own. As long as, that is, she left that park alone.

As it happened, though, the crusade Connie had started toward civic participation popped back up that evening in an unexpected way.

Sam and I had just gotten up from the supper table on our way to the library when Lloyd came in to spend the night.

"They've all got colds," he said, explaining his appearance at our house, "and I have a paper to write. I can't concentrate with all the crying and sneezing and coughing going on."

"Aren't you about to freeze?" I asked as he came in with a blast of cold air from the open door. "Come in and get warm. Have you had supper?"

"Yes, ma'am. Soup for all the sick and ailing, but it was fine. I'll just go on upstairs and get started on my paper."

We kept Lloyd's room as it had always been, complete with a computer, printer, books, and clothes, because he spent as many nights with us as he did with his mother, Mr. Pickens, and his twin half sisters. Which was fine with me. I liked having him around and always felt content when he was in the house.

Sam and I settled into our favorite places close to the fire in the library, with Sam looking through the paper and me picking up some needlework. Picking it up was as far as I got, though, because it was my first chance to tell Sam how I intended to regain the equilibrium I'd had before Connie Clayborn had thrown me for a loop.

And tell him, I did. But the more I expressed my good intentions, the more incensed I became all over again. Thinking that I'd vented enough to Mildred and Emma Sue to clear the air for good, I was surprised to realize how much fire was still simmering inside.

"And, Sam," I summed up after recounting Connie's lecture again, "Mildred and I are in perfect agreement — Connie has overstepped herself and ruined any possibility of her getting into the garden club or the book club or anything else in town.

"Emma Sue, though," I went on, "I just don't know about her. She takes everything to heart, then it goes straight to her head and down she comes with a migraine. To tell the truth, I'm a little worried about her.

"However," I added, "I intend to put Connie's ranting on a back burner and stay out of her way. I don't want to hear another critical word about the women of Abbots-ville or of the town itself. There're too many other things to occupy my mind and my time. Sewing ornaments, for one, which I guess Hazel Marie can't do tonight with everybody sick at her house. And you know, Sam, it takes a lot of energy to stay mad, and I don't have any to spare on Connie. I'll just put it all behind me so that whatever she thinks of us won't matter a bit as far as I'm concerned. Live and let live, I always say."

"I do, too," Sam said, probably bored to death with the subject by this time. He folded the paper and laid it aside, then opened a book, as one was never far from him.

After a few minutes, I thought of some-thing else I hadn't told him. "Sam?"

He raised his eyebrows as he looked up from his book.

"Have you heard about Coleman?"

He closed the book and put it aside. "What's going on with Coleman?"

"I'm not sure. Binkie thinks he's lost his mind, but she doesn't seem particularly concerned about it." And I went on to tell Sam about Coleman's effort to raise money by sitting on a sign and waving at passing cars. And to do it through rain, sleet, or snow, like a postal worker.

Sam chuckled, shaking his head. "Better him than me."

"Well, I don't think it's a wise thing to do. He could ruin his health."

"Oh, I doubt that," Sam said. "I expect he knows what he's doing. He and Binkie do a lot of camping." He reached for his book again. "By the way, you remember I'm going to Raleigh at the end of the week? You want to go with me?"

"Oh, you'll have old friends to catch up with. Lots of gossip about judges I don't know. I think I'll pass." I smiled at him, for Sam knew how proud I was that he had been named to the governor's Judicial Standards Commission — it had been announced in the newspaper and everything — and that I wanted him to enjoy his time as the governor's representative.

"Mr. Sam?" Lloyd walked in, pen and paper in hand. "Could you help me with my paper?"

"Sure, if I can. What's your topic?"

"Supposed to be on the rehabilitation of economically challenged communities, and I don't even know what that means."

Sam started laughing, and I got to my feet. "I think I've heard enough on that subject," I said, smiling at Lloyd. "I'll leave it with you two to hash out. Sam, Mildred's picking me up in a few minutes, so I'm off to make Christmas ornaments — a far, far better thing I do for my blood pressure than to go through a civics lesson again."

Seven of us sat around Sue Hargrove's dining room table, covered now by a quilt to protect the finish from scratches. Piles of red, green, gold, and white felt squares; boxes of sequins, pearls, and buttons; pin cushions filled with pins and needles; thimbles; scissors of all sizes; hot glue guns; spools and skeins of thread, braid, and piping; and Santa Clauses, snowmen, angels, and stars in various stages of completion were scattered across the table. An urn of hot spiced tea and a plate of shortbread were on the sideboard, available to anyone who wanted a break. Our rule was to not get bogged down with entertaining as such, nor with visiting with one another, but to *work*. We'd started, as usual, in early September, and our goal was for each member to complete an ornament at each weekly meeting. Mildred was far behind, but she was good company.

Roberta Smith, who'd started out some years before with flowing red hair that was now a weekly tended coif of rust-colored waves and wisps, shifted her chair as Mildred and I took our places at the table. Roberta was an angular woman of a fairly young but uncertain age, one — well, two — prominent assets, and a generally quiet demeanor — so appropriate in a librarian. She looked up from her sewing, blinked several times, and asked, "Does anyone know where Mrs. Ledbetter is? I hope she's not ill like Hazel Marie and her family."

I, too, had wondered about Emma Sue's absence. She rarely missed any kind of meeting. "I spoke to her on the phone yesterday, and she seemed fine." That wasn't exactly true, but I wasn't about to repeat the conversation I'd had with Emma Sue. The less said about Connie Clayborn, the better. "Actually," I went on, "we're short several others tonight, so something may be going around." I stopped and looked under the table. "Where's that box of odds and ends? I need some fur for this Santa Claus."

"Here it is," Helen Stroud said, reaching behind her chair and sliding a box toward me. "There's fur in there somewhere. I used some on that elf I made."

"An elf!" LuAnne said. "Do elves wear fur?"

"Mine do," Helen said complacently. "I put a knob of it on his cap and on the

64

turned-up toes of his shoes."

"Oh, I saw that," Sue said, "and it's darling. I think we should ask ten dollars for it.

"Which brings up another thing," Sue went on. "We need to decide where our proceeds will go. We only have about five weeks before the county sale, and they'll be after me to turn in our advertising copy. I need to be able to say who or what we're supporting this year."

"Well," LuAnne said, "I still think Meals on Wheels is what we should support."

"We did them year before last," Callie Armstrong said, "and I thought we'd agreed to spread the wealth around." Callie was a plump, pleasant woman with a houseful of children and a husband who'd agreed to put them to bed one night a week. Callie made the most of it, always being the last one to leave.

"What wealth?" Mildred said, laughing. "If anybody buys this snowman I'll be surprised. Ida Lee said she can get bloodstains out, but I just put another one on it."

"What're some of the other groups supporting?" Helen asked, referring to the several groups around the county that contributed handmade items every year to the County Christmas Sale. Some groups were making Christmas placemats and

65

napkins, others were making stuffed toys, topiary trees using artificial greenery, wreaths using real greenery, and, of course, Christmas cookies, cakes, and candy. And this year we'd heard that some retired men had decided to join us by making birdhouses to sell. The County Christmas Sale was always well attended because so many people throughout the county were involved in making sale items. We counted on their families and friends, at least, to feel obligated to support us.

"Oh, I have an idea!" I said, suddenly remembering Binkie's concerns. "What about playground equipment for the elementary school?" And I went on to tell them about Coleman's cold weather sign-sitting project. "We must all go out on the boulevard and wave at him. That may be the only way he keeps warm."

"He's crazy," Mildred pronounced.

"That's what Binkie thinks, too," I said. "But we do have some mild days in November, so the weather's on my prayer list."

"You better pray hard," Callie said, always seeing the gloomy side. "We usually have at least one snow in November."

"Oh," Roberta said, almost moaning, "I hope he won't get cold. But what a heroic thing to do! He's such a fine man. Officer of the law, I mean. 'Protect and serve' — that's what *hero* means, you know, and that's their motto. He came to the library and spoke to the children's reading group. They were simply fascinated with him and all his accouterments."

Accouterments? I had to give full attention to my Santa ornament so I wouldn't laugh. Miss Roberta Smith was given to sudden emotional outbursts, usually announced in a decidedly loud voice when she wasn't in the library. She was, of course, quite well read and often referred in rapturous tones to any number of her favorite characters, most especially Mr. Darcy.

"Well," Sue said, bringing us back to the subject at hand since she wasn't quite so fascinated by Coleman. "I say we choose playground equipment to sponsor this year. It's certainly a worthwhile cause, and we'd be helping Coleman out, too. Maybe he won't have to sit up there so long."

That proposal was met with general approval, but I hoped Coleman would have long been off that sign and back in his warm house by the time of the Christmas sale. If he had to stay up there in the weather until the second week of December, the poor man would be frozen solid.

■ ■ ■ ■

On our way home that evening, Mildred said, "I've about decided that Roberta has had a breast enhancement."

"What? Mildred, she's a librarian. She wouldn't do that, although I will admit that she's somewhat out of proportion."

Mildred laughed. "More than somewhat, I'd say. She's as skinny as a rail except up top, and the only way you get that kind of figure is surgically. But who knows? I guess they could be genetic."

"I think they are," I said. "Haven't you noticed that she always wears open jackets or cardigans, sort of like she wants to make them less, well, outstanding?"

"You may be right. You'd think if she paid out good money, she wouldn't want to hide them.

"But listen," Mildred went on, glancing at me, "do you realize that Connie wasn't brought up even once tonight? I thought she'd be the main topic."

"I did notice, and I, for one, am glad she wasn't. To tell the truth, I was afraid somebody had invited her to join us. Thank goodness they didn't."

"I wasn't worried about it."

"You weren't?"

"No," Mildred said, squinching in the dark car as bright headlights flashed across the windshield. "Because I called Sue this afternoon and told her that if Connie was coming, I wasn't."

"Oh, Mildred," I said, laughing, "you didn't."

"I certainly did. I know I didn't exactly exhibit the proper Christmas spirit, but neither did Sue. She said she hadn't even thought of inviting Connie because she wanted us to enjoy the evening, not be castigated again for our shortcomings. And speaking of that, wasn't that shortbread good?"

CHAPTER 7

True to my intentions of discounting Connie and the black marks she'd given us, as well as keeping other, more uplifting things foremost in my mind, I was able to put aside the whole miserable mess she'd created. Several days of peaceful routine calmed me down considerably, although I admit that every passing thought of Connie brought out my ill feelings again. It was her arrogance in presuming to lecture us — *me* — that rankled. Who was she to set herself up as our instructor in civic responsibility? We volunteered, we voted, we contributed, we pitched in when need was apparent. And what had she done? Criticized and debased all our efforts, and that was it.

No one, to my knowledge, had ever moved to Abbotsville and immediately set themselves up as judge and jury of everyone in the entire town. And, I mean, doing so before she even *knew* us. It was her assumption of our ignorance while being utterly ignorant of us that irritated me more than anything. What insolence!

"Just ignore it," Sam counseled as we sat at the table finishing breakfast. "And her. If she wants to organize volunteers, let her. Maybe she'll do some good. And if she wants to whip the councilmen into shape, let her do that, too. You don't have to participate. More coffee?"

"Yes, thank you," I said, holding out my cup. "I know I don't, and I won't. But it just galls me that she's acting as if she's not a newcomer. Newcomers are supposed to allow us to get to know them gradually, standing back and letting us come to them. Of course, joining a church doesn't hurt in becoming known around town. But has Connie done that? No, she hasn't. She believes in *reason,* or maybe in energy or something. But there's not one thing rational in her behavior. Any normal person would not have done what she did, and, worst of all, I have no doubt that she's proud of herself for having given us the benefit of her superior knowledge."

"Just stay out of her way, honey. If she upsets you this much, you should avoid her. From what you say about the reaction of the other ladies, it's unlikely she'll be invited to anything you normally attend, so it'll be easy to do."

"Yes, probably so. Except it's so tacky to ask a hostess beforehand who else she's inviting, then to decline when a particular name is mentioned." I stirred my coffee absentmindedly. "Of course, do that often enough and hostesses will get the message — it's either Connie or me, take your pick."

Sam laughed. "From what you say, not many hostesses will be eager to entertain her."

"You're right, and maybe I should set the example. I'll just not invite her to my annual Christmas tea. Everybody will know that I owe her because I accepted her invitation, and they'll know I'm deliberately not returning the compliment. And if anybody has the nerve to ask why, I'll tell them that I'm not in the habit of turning my home into a lecture hall, as some people have done. And hope it gets back to her."

Sam grinned. "That'll fix her."

"On second thought," I said later that evening, as Sam and I sat in the library in companionable silence with the television turned low and a fire flickering in the fireplace.

"On second thought, what?" Sam asked,

lowering the *Abbotsville Times.*

"On second thought, I *am* going to invite Connie. I'm going to give her some instructions for a change. Let her see how things should be done, and if she's as smart as Emma Sue thinks she is, she might learn something."

"Sounds like a good idea. I think you should. At least," Sam said with a smile, "you'll have paid her back for inviting you, and you'll have no further obligation to her."

"Exactly. And furthermore, she's so intent on teaching us how to be ecologically correct, I'll just teach her how to be *socially* correct."

"And she couldn't have a better instructor."

"That's right," I agreed with some complacency, for I knew my way around Abbotsville's social scene. "I just hope she has the sense to learn from it."

To that end, quite early the following morning I began making out my invitation list. It wasn't too soon to make plans — the hectic Christmas season began earlier every year, and the wise hostess had her invitations in the mail a good two weeks or more before the designated date.

Of course, no one ever declined my invitations other than for the direst reasons, like a sudden illness or a scheduled surgery they couldn't change. Simply having accepted another invitation on the same date never stopped a soul from attending my affairs — if something had to give, it wouldn't be my invitation. I was justifiably proud of that and made every effort to make my guests happy that they'd chosen correctly.

But this year I was determined that my Christmas party would exceed all previous ones — even as satisfying as they had been in the past. As my list grew longer, I began to think of dividing the guest list into two sections. The first group could be invited from two to three P.M., and the second group from three till four. Some overlap could be expected — there always were some who overstayed their time and others who would come early. And some who would simply come early and stay late. Still, it was a way to attempt to accommodate a large crowd.

And with that, I put down my pen and began to think of building a new house, one that would comfortably contain as many guests as Sam and I wanted to entertain. Maybe a house with our bedroom on the first floor. Bedroom *suite,* I mentally corrected myself, and thought of how nice it would be as the years went on to have no stairs to climb.

A small, well-appointed two-bedroom house, I thought as I began to visualize how it would look. Then changed my mind. We'd need three bedrooms — the second one for Lloyd, of course, and the third for guests. No, why not a guesthouse for guests, with Lloyd's in the main house with ours? And we'd have to have a library, modeled on the one we already had. And a working office for Sam. And an up-to-date, thoroughly modernized kitchen. And, oh, another bedroom for Lillian and Latisha for the nights they spent with us. And, of course, a bathroom for each bedroom.

Then there were what I would call the public rooms — maybe a double living room with facing fireplaces and a dining room large enough for my table to be fully extended, both with plenty of room to receive any number of guests. And a foyer and halls — there would have to be space for that. I just hate dark, narrow hallways, so they should be at least five or so feet wide upstairs and down-, wherever we needed hallways.

How many square feet, I wondered, would a house have to be to accommodate all the rooms I would want? I had no idea. I knew only that if we were to build something, it should be exactly what we wanted. No need to go to the trouble and the expense to end up with anything less.

I sighed, put aside my daydreaming, and picked up my pen. I had a party to give. As I looked at the lengthening guest list, I had an inspiration — not a party but a soiree! Put them on notice right at the beginning that it would be special. Now, of course, I knew that, strictly speaking, a soiree is an evening affair, but I also knew that people in New Orleans called almost everything — morning, noon, or night — a soiree. So what I could do was to change the times to, say, from four to five for the first group and from five to six for the second, which would be close enough to qualify as an evening affair. And if anybody wanted to stay the whole two hours, why, that would be fine, too.

Music, I thought. A soiree would require background music, and something more than the FM radio or the Christmas tape Lloyd had put together. Then I thought of Sara O'Neill — she played the harp when the Episcopal church had special musical programs, and I'm talking about one of those huge instruments, which required her to wear a long dress so she could straddle it, not one of those mouth organs. Or was I mixing it up with a cello, which I was sure required an unladylike position?

Sara would know how she was to sit, and with her name, she was undoubtedly of Irish descent, and weren't they great harp players? Or was I stereotyping her? Another thing Connie accused us of doing.

Well, whatever.

The music would be beautiful, all in the background, of course. I wasn't looking for a recital, where people would have to sit and listen instead of talk and mingle.

But where to put her? Those harps were quite large, and just one of them with Sara next to it would take up a fourth of my living room. The back hall? Maybe close off the kitchen door and stick Sara and her harp back there under the stairs. People would see her as they moved from the living room to the library, where I would put a red felt floor-length cloth over the mahogany desk with another punch bowl on it along with a couple of trays of finger food.

Of course, putting Sara and her harp in the back hall might interfere with access to the downstairs bathroom, which could be a problem with so many ladies in the house. They'd have to go upstairs, which would be fine for everybody except Miss Mattie

Freeman, who'd never make the climb in time. I sighed, knowing I couldn't make it perfect for everyone. Another reason, I thought, with some justifiable pleasure, to consider building a new house.

With a sudden intake of breath it came to me that I might be in the process of falling in with what Connie had recommended — doing away with the old and building the new.

That decided it, right then and there, my old house suited me just fine. I wasn't in the mood to rehabilitate anything and daydreaming wasn't getting my soiree planned.

So to get myself back into a party mood, I wrote out "A Christmas Soiree" to see how it would look on an invitation. I liked it, and if Connie Clayborn wasn't impressed with the way we did things in Abbotsville, she could go back to Boston. Or to Switzerland, which would be even better.

CHAPTER 8

I put down my pen again when I heard the front doorbell ring, wondering who could be calling at eight-thirty on a Tuesday morning. Listening carefully so I'd know if I wanted to be available, I heard the scuffle of Lillian's shoes with the run-over heels as she walked to the door, then the low rumble of a male voice. Who in the world?

"Miss Julia?" Lillian said as she appeared in the library doorway. "The Reverend Mr. Ledbetter come callin'."

"Well, for goodness sakes," I murmured, considering, then deciding against, a correction to the Reverend *Dr.* Ledbetter by virtue of an honorary degree. "What does he want?"

It was a rhetorical question, but Lillian answered. "He don't tell me, but he waitin' in the livin' room."

"Ah, well," I said, putting aside my notes and preparing to go in and be as gracious as possible while turning down whatever committee on which he wanted me to serve. In spite of Connie's rant about *giving back,* I'd about had my fill of giving either to or back to church committees. Besides, Connie didn't support any church at all, and I'd spent my life taking on one church-related job, project, or program after another. "Thank you, Lillian."

I walked down the hall to the living room, where I found Pastor Ledbetter standing in the middle of the room.

"Have a seat, Pastor," I said. "How nice to see you. I hope you're well."

He looked up, surprising me with the lines of strain on his face. "Is there a place we can talk?" he asked. "Somewhere a little more private?"

I started to tell him that Lillian was the only one who could possibly hear us, and she wasn't at all interested in what he had to say, and that I'd probably tell her whatever it was, anyway. The anxious look on his face stopped me.

"Why, yes," I said. "Let's go into the library."

He followed me back to the library, stood back as I entered, then pulled the door closed behind us.

Whatever was on his mind seemed serious

enough to warrant a soothing fire in the fireplace, so I turned up the gas until a small blaze began to warm the room. I motioned to one of the wing chairs beside the fireplace, but he took a seat on the leather sofa on the other side. I took the wing chair facing him, and waited.

"Well, Pastor," I finally said, since he seemed reluctant to begin, "is there something I can do for you? Although I will tell you now that my calendar is full and I simply can't take on another thing, at least before Christmas." Of next year, I mentally added.

He shot a quick look at me, then darted his eyes around the room. Sitting there in a typical male position — legs a-spraddle with hands clasped between his knees — he looked as if he'd rather be anywhere than where he was. Whatever proposition he had to present, it was looking more and more likely that I wouldn't want it.

"Miss Julia," he said, looking past his hands toward the floor and ignoring my attempt at cutting him off, "I must ask you to keep this conversation confidential. I considered asking you to my office, where confidentiality is assured, but I couldn't sit still long enough to wait for you. I'm in a desperate situation, and I need help."

I knew it, I thought as I fought to prevent my eyes from rolling back in my head. *Somebody has had to drop out, and he needs a Sunday school teacher or a committee chairman or a representative to the General Assembly for a week somewhere in Texas.* No, no, and no again.

"I hate to turn you down, Pastor," I said, although I didn't really mind at all, "but, as I've said, I can't accept another thing, and besides . . ."

"No," he said, holding up a hand, "this has nothing to do with the church. I mean, it does, but not directly. I mean, it affects the church in that my ability to lead and minister to our members is badly hindered. But . . ." He stopped and looked directly at me. "This must not get around, Miss Julia. I'm trying to mitigate the consequences of it as much as I can."

This *did* sound serious, and I wondered why he had come to me and not to Sam or to one of his elders.

"I assure you, Pastor, that I'm not in the habit of telling everything I know, and you may trust my word on that."

"And I must ask you to give it," he said, staring at me. "I must ask you not even to discuss it with Sam — not that I distrust him, but someone might overhear. You have lots of people coming in and out here, and they could pick up something that could, well, be damaging."

Not only was it sounding serious, it was beginning to sound weird, but I gave my word.

"I will not discuss whatever it is with anyone," I said, knowing full well how difficult it would be to keep anything from Sam. Especially something that sounded so tellable, as this was beginning to sound. "Now, for goodness sakes, Pastor, tell me what's troubling you so."

He unclasped his hands, leaned back against the sofa, blew out a long breath, and said, "Emma Sue."

I blinked in surprise. "Emma Sue?"

"Emma Sue," he affirmed, then sat up straight as if ready to face the problem. "She's in a bad way, and I thought you might be the one to help."

"Why, what's wrong with her? Is she ill?"

"I'm beginning to think it's more than that. I tell you, Miss Julia, I'm at my wit's end. I've talked to her till I'm blue in the face, and everything just rolls right off."

I could understand that. Most of what he said in the pulpit rolled right off me, too.

"My goodness," I murmured. "Perhaps she needs a complete medical checkup. She may have low thyroid or something."

He breathed deeply and, as if finally conceding a sorry conclusion, said, "Worse than that. She admits that it's a spiritual sickness, but I'm thinking it's a willful disregard of her duties and responsibilities to me. First Timothy three tells us that any man who desires to hold a church office must first rule his own house. Yet she won't listen to me, and that, in turn, affects my authority in the church. I'm beginning to think that my influence over her has waned. That's why I thought of you."

I heard him and hearing, wondered about whom he was most concerned — Emma Sue or himself. But I knew the one I cared about, so I said, "I'll be glad to help if I can, but, Pastor, it sounds as if she may need more help than I can give. Professional help, I'm referring to."

"Possibly so," he admitted, which was a giant step for him and proved to me that he was indeed up against something he couldn't handle. "But it would have to be someone who's a Christian, and even then, I hesitate because she's so suggestible. To everyone but me, that is. But she's suffering, and so am I. That's why I'm turning to you. I don't know what else to do."

"Well, I'm not sure that I'd be much of a

substitute for a counselor. Even a Christian one, but I'll certainly do what I can. I care about Emma Sue. But tell me, Pastor, just what is she doing? I mean, to distress you so much. I know she suffers from migraines, but usually they're over in a day or so."

"Oh, it all started with a migraine," he said with another deep breath. "A bad one. I had to put off writing my sermon to take her to the doctor for an injection. That usually puts her right quickly enough, but not this time. She's been in bed since Friday — missed Sunday services, too. She hasn't bathed or washed her hair, and she's hardly eaten a bite. She . . . she just cries. And looks off in the distance. I am sick with worry. Something has to be done."

"It certainly seems so," I said, feeling great sympathy for Emma Sue, although I'd long thought that she put too much pressure on herself. "But Emma Sue is so capable and so energetic, I can't imagine what could have brought her to such a pass."

"Oh, I know what instigated it, but after much prayer and long consideration, I've come to the conclusion that I shouldn't attempt to resolve the problem myself."

"You mean you can pinpoint it?" I was surprised, because I'd assumed that Emma Sue suffered from a general dissatisfaction with her life — which she was unable to admit, even to herself — and from overwork while trying to make up for whatever was missing.

"Yes," he said as his voice hardened. "It was that woman, that Clayborn woman."

"Connie? Why, Pastor, Emma Sue and I discussed her on the phone the other day, and we decided that Connie has ruined herself in this town. But now that I think of it," I mused aloud, "Emma Sue was more upset than usual, taking what Connie said as a personal criticism and even as a direct scolding from the Lord. I thought I'd talked her out of that, but I guess I didn't if things are as bad as you say."

"They're bad, all right. She hasn't combed her hair in four days."

"That is bad," I agreed, my hand going to my hair to make sure it was behaving. "What can I do to help, Pastor? I'm not very good at bedside nursing, or reading to people, and so forth. But if you need food, I can bring supper tonight."

"No, that's not what's called for. Miss Julia, I want you to go see that woman. I know," he went on softly, as if he hated to admit to any failing on his part, "I'm asking a lot. It should really be my responsibility, but from all I've heard about Ms. Clayborn, a minister of the Gospel is the last person she would listen to — much less take instruction from. But if you would talk to her, explain to her how sensitive Emma Sue is to criticism — even unintended criticism — she might listen. Let her know the kind of damage she's done, and see if she'll call on Emma Sue to reassure and encourage her. A positively constructed visit from that woman — with you to listen in so she doesn't do more damage — might be enough to show Emma Sue that the Lord is not chastising her."

I did some leaning back and deep breathing of my own. "I don't know, Pastor. For one thing, I don't know Connie Clayborn well enough to predict how she'd respond. There was something about her that was . . ."

"Evil? I was afraid of that."

"Oh, I wouldn't go that far. I was going to say *different,* but that may've been because she's never lived in a small town and doesn't know how to conduct herself."

"Well, I've had to consider the possibility that there's something evil about her — Satan does use people, you know, especially people who don't believe he exists." Pastor Ledbetter bowed his head in despair. "Miss Julia, if the Clayborn woman is involved in

Satanism, she can do more mischief than we can imagine. My greatest fear is that she's started with Emma Sue and that park that Emma Sue has put her heart and soul into."

Lord, he was so serious, cold chills ran down my back. Getting mixed up with Satan was the last thing I wanted to do, but I shook myself back to a sane consideration of what the pastor wanted from me.

"Frankly, Pastor, I think Connie is less Satan-influenced than just plain lacking in common sense. To say nothing of common courtesy. So I don't mind talking to Connie. In fact, I'd like to give her a piece of my mind, especially now that she's distressed Emma Sue so badly. But I have to warn you — I have my doubts as to how much good it'll do. In fact, the woman was so determined to lambast us that it might take a stick of stove wood to cut her down to size." I smiled as I repeated one of Lillian's favorite threats toward anyone who gave her grief.

Pastor Ledbetter didn't return my smile. "Just try, Miss Julia. Knowing that you'll try gives me hope." He stopped and looked around the room, then hung his head. "It's beyond me to understand why the Clayborn woman's opinion means so much to Emma

Sue. You'd think that my opinion would outweigh anybody else's, but nothing I say sinks in. If you could get that woman to take back whatever she said, or to apologize, or to just say that she didn't have Emma Sue in mind when she said whatever it was. I don't know what else to do. So then," he said, suddenly standing up, "I have to leave it with you, but be in prayer while you talk to her and especially if you take her to see Emma Sue. Gird yourself with the whole armor of God and with unceasing prayer, and keep it all to yourself."

I assured him that I would, walked with him to the door, bade him a good day, closed the door, and collapsed in a chair, wishing mightily that I could discuss this unexpected and burdensome job with Sam. Or with Lillian. One needs all the help one can get when given such a mission, even if Connie Clayborn was a Vassar graduate who thought that such an accomplishment translated into an overweening conviction of her own superior knowledge on every subject known to man.

CHAPTER 9

Connie Clayborn, evil? No, I wouldn't go that far. But pushy, rude, and totally insensitive, any of which was enough to strike her off my dance card. Such thoughts were running through my mind as I walked back to the library, wondering what I'd gotten myself into.

I sat by the fire for a few minutes, all plans for my Christmas soiree put on hold, while the conversation with the pastor played over and over in my mind. Why had I agreed to such a thing? Well, for one thing, I was worried about Emma Sue and wanted to help. But this kind of help? Getting in the middle of two women — one deeply hurt and the other oblivious? I, or anybody who tried that, could make the situation worse. For all I knew, Emma Sue's response was exactly what Connie wanted from all of us, forcing us to take stock and recalibrate the way we viewed the world. But if so, what, then, for

Emma Sue? Would she sink further into depression or would she suddenly accept Connie's admonitions and redouble her efforts to help others, run the church, collect more money, cover more dishes, pull more weeds, and on and on until she finally ran out of steam and caved in for good?

No, not if I had anything to do with it, and that, I decided, was why I'd agreed to mediate between the two women. And in addition, I realized with some anticipation, doing so would give me the perfect opportunity to release some of my own antagonism toward Connie. Putting her in her place by letting her know the damage she'd caused was a righteous reason for anyone to step in.

I hoped that giving Connie a piece of my mind — in a nice, rational way, of course — wasn't the sole reason I was eager to take on the pastor's mission. But it was part of the reason, I conceded, because I always try to understand my own motivations for whatever I do. So I was quite pleased with myself that I could recognize my own stake in this opportunity. I was, however, completely satisfied that it was primarily for Emma Sue's sake that I would do it.

But, oh, how I longed to ask Sam's advice. Or Lillian's. Or even Hazel Marie's. Actually, though, I didn't need to ask — I knew what they'd say. Every one of them would tell me to stay out of it. I could just hear Lillian already: "Won't do no good you meddlin' in the middle of them two ladies. It be like two cats a-fightin', an' you the one gonna get scratched." And she'd be right, except that Emma Sue wasn't fighting. She was taking a beating, and shouldn't I take up for her?

And Sam? What would he advise? I could just see the kind concern in his eyes as he'd tell me to be a friend to Emma Sue, but to stay away from Connie. "Nothing good can come of it, Julia," he'd say. "Ledbetter is asking you to do something he can't or won't do himself, and it's too much to ask of anybody."

Hazel Marie would get teary-eyed at the thought of Emma Sue's suffering and angry at the one who'd caused it. But, like Sam, she would warn me against getting involved for fear that I, too, would be hurt.

So with all that advice against doing what I'd been asked to do, what did I do? I began planning my strategy, because I'm not one to turn down a cry for help, especially since it was my pastor doing the crying. He so rarely asked for help, be it for increased tithes, over and above giving, teaching a

Sunday school class, standing for a church office, or putting up a missionary's family for a week or so. He simply announced his needs, expecting them to be met before he had to ask.

But before jumping in with both feet, it occurred to me that I'd do well to talk again with Emma Sue. For all I knew, she could be on an uphill climb out of her depression or whatever it was, so that nothing more was needed than to give her a little time. Of course that would mean I'd lose the chance to express my own righteous anger at and to Connie — something I would dearly love to do. I clenched my fist — how I wanted to put that woman in her place! Cut her down to size. Take her down a few notches. Wipe that know-it-all smirk off her face.

I shook myself free of all such unchristian thoughts. No, if I could get Connie to realize what she'd done, to show her a better way, wouldn't that be a helpful thing to do? Of course it would. Therefore my walking into the fray wouldn't be meddling at all. It would be of benefit to both Emma Sue and Connie.

I picked up the phone to call Emma Sue, then put it back down. No need to ask in her present state if she'd like a visitor — she'd say no. Especially if she hadn't combed her hair in days.

I went to the kitchen, calling Lillian as I went. "Lillian, what do we have that I could take to Mrs. Ledbetter? She's not feeling well, so I don't want to go empty-handed."

Lillian looked up from the potatoes she was peeling. "I got some of them teeny little chicken pot pies in the freezer, if you think she like that. Or I could make her some soup."

"If the pot pies are the ones you make, I'll take two of them. Soup would take too long, and I need to go on now."

"She that bad off?" Lillian dried her hands on a dish towel and went to the freezer. "She such a nice lady, I don't like to hear that."

"Well," I said, stifling a great urge to tell what I knew I couldn't tell, "she has migraines, you know, and this is a particularly long-lasting one. I'll just drop off the pies for their dinner and see if she needs anything. I don't plan to linger."

I slipped into my coat while Lillian wrapped the frozen miniature pot pies in foil and newspaper, then stuffed them into a sack. On my way out the door, I remembered to pick up my cell phone — something I rarely did because I was sick and tired of seeing people walking down the street with one attached to their ears and giving everyone around the benefit of their day's progress. I saw no need to broadcast my business to everyone within earshot.

Pulling into the Ledbetters' driveway, I brought the car to a stop, then called Emma Sue on the cell phone. It took her forever to answer — exactly what I thought would happen if I had rung the doorbell. But this way, I could sit in the warm car while I let the phone ring as long as it took. Sooner or later, she'd pick it up, whereas she could've ignored the doorbell.

I hardly recognized her voice when she finally answered.

"Emma Sue," I said, "it's Julia, and I'm in your driveway with two of Lillian's wonderful chicken pot pies. They're frozen and need to be in the freezer. Come to the door, and let me in."

"Oh, Julia," she said, her voice muted and ragged. "Thank you, but . . ."

"But nothing. Open the door, Emma Sue. You need to eat something. I'm getting out of the car, so don't let me stand out here and freeze." Sometimes you have to be firm with people who're reluctant to accept help.

She murmured okay, or at least I think she did. I clicked off, grabbed the sack, and headed for her front door. She opened it a bare inch or so. One eye looked at me while one hand reached out for the sack.

I pushed gently on the door, feeling it give as she stepped back. "I'm coming in, Emma Sue. I've brought you something for dinner, and I need to give you directions for heating it up." I stepped into the hall, muffled a gasp at her dishevelment — a much-washed flannel gown, pale face, bare feet, and stringy hair — and proceeded to her kitchen.

It was a mess. The remains of a single breakfast were on the table, stacks of unwashed dishes in the sink, coffee grounds on the counter, and an overflowing trash can in the corner.

"Julia," Emma Sue said, sounding as if she could barely get the words out. "I've been too sick to get my work done. But, well, I'm sorry you have to see this."

"*You're* sorry? Emma Sue, for goodness sakes, there's a grown man who lives here, too. Anybody who's old enough to feed himself is old enough to clean up afterward."

"It's my job," she murmured.

"Well, now it's mine. Have you had any breakfast? No, I guess you haven't. Sit down, and I'll put on the coffee. You want some cereal? Never mind, you're getting some."

It took awhile to fill the dishwasher, clean off the table and the counters, wipe up drippings on the stovetop, empty the trash can, sweep the floor, and encourage Emma Sue to eat a bowl of Frosted Flakes — the only cereal I could find.

I poured a glass of orange juice for Emma Sue, a cup of coffee for myself, and sat at the table with her.

"Drink up, Emma Sue. You need the vitamins." I sipped the coffee, longing for a dash of cream but fearful of the dregs I'd found in the refrigerator. "Now listen," I began, "you've got to pull yourself out of this. If you need to go back to the doctor, I'll take you, and if you need me to talk to the pastor, I'll do that, too. There's no reason in the world for you to suffer while he's not turning his hands to anything in this house. And don't tell me it's your job — that's not only ridiculous, it's out of date. *Everybody* — man, woman, or child — helps when somebody's sick."

"Well, Larry," she said, picking at her flannel gown. "Larry thinks I'll get well faster if the house gets bad enough."

"Then *Larry* thinks wrong," I said. "I declare, even J. D. Pickens changes a diaper now and then. It wouldn't hurt the pastor to clean this house, cook something for you to eat, and take care of things around here."

Emma Sue started crying, not sobbing, just two lines of tears began rolling down her face. "He has a lot to put up with," she said, her head hanging down. "I'm not the wife he needs and deserves. And he has the burden of so many people on his shoulders, and, and I just pile on more." Her own shoulders began to heave.

I reached over and put my hand on her arm. "Emma Sue, you are his *wife*. You should come first."

Her reddened eyes glanced up at me. "Oh, no. The Lord comes first."

"Okay, second, then, but not the last in line." I sat and looked at her for a minute. "But listen, I really came over to encourage you to forget about Connie — she's not worth getting sick over. She'll get her come-uppance sooner or later, and you don't have to give her another thought. Drink your juice."

Well, Emma Sue really started crying then, sobbing and heaving and gasping. I got up and gave her a paper towel. She grasped it and covered her face.

"Oh, Julia," she finally managed, "Connie just put a terrible icing on the cake, making me see what a poor Christian I am, and a poor church member and a poor citizen of the community and a poor wife. Larry is right — I am a burden he has to bear, and I . . . I know I am." Her shoulders hunched over as she shrunk into herself. "I can hardly bear the thought of it."

Well, my Lord, I thought, leaning back in my chair, just done in by what I'd heard — and not for the first time from her. I didn't know who needed horsewhipping more — Connie Clayborn or Pastor Larry Ledbetter. Or Emma Sue herself for believing such claptrap.

CHAPTER 10

Well, I thought to myself on my way home, *that's two more who need a good talking-to.* And if I had to take on one at the urging of the other, the pastor couldn't complain if he was next in line. *The burden he had to bear!* I'd never heard such foolishness in my life. Actually it wasn't just foolish, it was cruel, and I could just shake Emma Sue for sitting still for it.

Of course, she wasn't sitting still, she was lying in bed. And no wonder. If Sam said such a thing to me, I'd probably crumple up and die. But I wouldn't stay that way. No, sir, I'd be up and out before he could turn around good.

Yet as I thought about the highly unlikely prospect of my kind husband ever thinking, much less saying, such a thing, I realized with a swift pang that it wasn't inconceivable that Wesley Lloyd Springer had thought it of me.

Well, so what if he had? His load had been lifted when he suddenly passed over the great divide in the front seat of his new Buick Park Avenue, gray with power steering and surround-sound stereo, while parked in our driveway some years ago. That's one way to be relieved of a burden.

I put those thoughts behind me and began thinking of how best to approach Connie. Dropping in on her wasn't an option — one doesn't do that when one is intent on setting a socially correct example. I'd have to call first and say I'd like to talk with her. Then she'd invite me over. At least, that's the way it worked in Abbotsville, except Connie didn't know how anything worked in Abbotsville. For all I knew, she'd demand my reason for wanting to visit, or she'd tell me she preferred to talk over the phone, or perhaps not talk at all.

I should be prepared for whatever response she gave. She was so abrupt and blunt that she would render me speechless or else stumbling around for a reason to visit. I didn't want to be put off. Face-to-face was the way to get through to her, so I didn't want her to know my purpose beforehand — she'd be ready to talk me under the table before I could get a word out.

The more I thought about it, though, the

more I dreaded having anything to do with Connie. She was so far from the kind of woman I was accustomed to that she intimidated me even from afar. No telling what she'd do up front and eye to eye, especially since my purpose would be to criticize and rebuke. And, of course, to offer a better way of doing things. She ought to appreciate that, although I doubted she would.

Have you ever noticed that the very people who like to tell others what to do don't like the tables to be turned? So I needed to be prepared to talk over her if need be and to say what needed to be said, specifically where Emma Sue was concerned.

What are friends for if not to defend when defense is called for?

"Connie?" I asked, when she answered the call I'd made as soon as I got home. "It's Julia Murdoch. I'm calling to thank you for that lovely coffee you had, and to compliment you on your beautiful home."

Well, see, right there I started off with dishonesty. The coffee was anything but lovely, and her home was so stark and cold that I could never feel comfortable in it. Not to my taste, at all.

She thanked me in return, then said, "I'm glad you called. I've been thinking that the two of us should get to know each other better. I need to learn more about the local customs so I'll know what I'm up against. And you've lived here so long that I'm sure you know them all."

"How interesting," I said, stung that she would refer to my age. "I've been thinking the same thing." *More than you know,* I thought. "And I'd be delighted to sit down with you and have a long talk. When would be convenient?"

"Well," she said with a patronizing laugh, "you're nothing if not eager, aren't you?" Which flew all over me, but I held my tongue. "But that's good," she went on. "I'm sure you need something to fill the time. The days get long with nothing to do, don't they?"

"Oh, Connie, you wouldn't believe," I replied, carefully holding down the sarcasm. "I'd be so grateful to hear your ideas, and, in return, I may have a few for you."

She laughed outright at that. "Maybe so. But I don't mind your coming by about four this afternoon since you're so eager. I am simply swamped till then, unpacking boxes that have just gotten here from Europe, and the front hall is crammed full. I'll be working in the kitchen, so just park in the drive and come around to the back door."

After agreeing to that, I put down the phone with a growing sense of unease. How would I ever get through to such a woman? She wouldn't *mind* my coming by, but she had no intention of interrupting her work in order to visit with me. If it hadn't been for Emma Sue's dire circumstances, I would've told Connie what she could do with a visit.

Well, in fact, if not for Emma Sue, it would never have occurred to me to want a visit with Connie, much less to actually ask for a moment of her time.

As four o'clock approached, I became more and more nervous. I admit it, and kept thinking as I prepared to leave that I should just sit down and stay home. But in the end, I told Lillian I was going to a meeting that would be short and sweet, which was all I could say, not wanting to divulge the pastor's mission. Though the closer it got to four o'clock, the more I dreaded what could turn out to be a long and bitter meeting.

I wished I could take Mildred with me. She tolerated no nonsense or silliness from anyone, and certainly would not put up with Connie's brand of self-importance. But I didn't have her, and furthermore, I couldn't even have gotten her advice. Pastor Ledbetter had strapped me in tight, and I rued the promise I had made not to confide in anyone.

Not even Sam, not even Lillian, who told me as I went out the door, "If you goin' out this time of day, you better wrap up good. That wind go right through you." I'd just nodded, told her I didn't plan to be out in it long, and left.

But let this be a lesson: don't ever promise not to tell something without first considering the possibility that you might need to tell someone.

As I drove the few miles out of town to the gated community known as Grand View Estates — a name more suited to a cemetery, if you ask me — I could feel the blustery wind against the car and hoped, for Coleman's sake, that this would be a quickly passing cold front. The gray, lowering clouds and the fall time change had turned the afternoon dark earlier than usual — a good excuse to make this a short visit.

I turned in at the gate near the golf course that was surrounded by hills dotted here and there with newly built homes, made mostly of stone and glass with hints of Tudor design. The security guard started to wave me through, then opened the window in the kiosk.

"Ma'am, we're gettin' some limbs down on the roads. High winds, you know, so be careful."

Thanking him, I said I wasn't going far, then continued on as the winding street gradually rose to the first level of scenic view lots, where the Clayborns' house was located.

I pulled up the steep drive and parked near the closed garage, set the emergency brake, and got out of the car, pausing a moment to survey the sweeping view as well as the leaf-strewn front yard. Holding my hair as I looked around, I could barely make out the side of another house some distance away through the thick growth of trees that bounded the yard. I realized that if one wished to build in the area, one would have to carve out a lot by cutting trees and removing stumps. A mint would have to be spent before laying a foundation, and from the looks of the place, not many people had been willing to tackle it. I turned to look at Connie's house, noting the lonely, isolated feel it had, the dearth of neighbors, the lack of cars on the street, the swaying of the treetops in the wind, and the darkness of the late afternoon edging in on it from the woods.

106

The view would be nice to have, but not at the cost of getting it. Not for me, I decided. If Sam and I built another house, it would be on a level lot with streetlights on the corner.

The isolation of the place made me edgy, so I locked the car, dropped the keys in my purse, and stepped up on the stone walkway that led around to the back of the house. Pushing through a gate in the decorative fence that connected the house to the garage, I walked to the back patio — more stone. The house was large, but much wider than deep. The back was lined mostly with full-length windows that looked out over a tightly covered, winterized swimming pool so close to the house that Connie could probably roll right out of bed and into the water if she wanted to. I wouldn't, if it were me.

I paused to survey the yard, taken aback by all the tile and concrete — the whole area was paved with something. There was not one speck of green — not even one box-wood — until you looked across the long, narrow pool to the retaining wall on the far side, where a hillside thickly covered with laurel bushes, pine trees, and rhododen-drons rose above the house. If this was Con-nie's idea of a garden, the town park was in bad trouble.

Picking up my pace, I took note of the many full-length windows and sliding-glass doors facing the pool as I tried to determine which door led to the kitchen. Ah, I thought, where the light is, of course, noting also that only the row of short windows — above the sink, I assumed — and a glass door were lit. No other lights were on in the house, nor, I suddenly realized, on the patio or over the back door.

Was Connie not expecting me? Had she forgotten I was coming? Or did she not care if I stumbled around her backyard, fell, and broke my neck?

A gust of wind that bent the trees and raised my skirt hurried me along as I strode toward the lighted glass door. Pressing the doorbell, I looked into the large, white kitchen filled with stainless steel appliances and granite countertops, just as every house-hunting couple wanted. A chair with metal legs and leather strips in place of a back and a seat — the kind I always avoided for fear of it folding up on me — was upended by the island counter. Across from that, I saw an empty cardboard box lying on its side on the floor, a dust mop under a table, and a flapping newspaper on the center island.

What in the world, I wondered, then saw the ceiling fan whirling at full speed over head. Connie must have been working hard to need a fan on this chilly November day, but maybe she had a high metabolism. Or something.

Shivering, I rang the bell again, thinking that Connie might be in the front of the house. Maybe in the bathroom. No one came. Everything was still. Except the wind. And the fan. And the newspaper.

Enough of this, I thought with some indignation, and turned to leave. Then I stopped, a glimpse of something just registering in my mind — a shoe. Pressing my face to the glass in the door, I saw the sole of a clunky shoe sticking out beside a cabinet. Whatever it was attached to was beyond my view.

"Connie!" I called, rapping hard on the glass. Nothing.

"Connie, are you in there?" I called again, raising my voice over the rustle of the trees. "Are you all right?"

I rattled the doorknob, then felt it turn in my hand. I pushed it open and hurried inside.

My Lord! The shoe was attached to Connie. To her foot, I mean. She was lying half on her stomach, stretched out on the floor in front of the dishwasher and the sink

109

cabinet. In a stunned flash, I took in the overturned chair, several pots and pans strewn across the floor, a broken cup, the stench of burned coffee, the expanse of black granite countertops, and the glistening puddle of blood under Connie's head.

CHAPTER 11

Strange how the mind can take in so much at once, while thoughtless impulse focuses on some minor thing. That's what happened to me as I slung my pocketbook over my shoulder and took action. Stepping over Connie's outstretched arm that was lying across the pool of blood, I ran to the coffeepot and unplugged it. Don't ask me why. I don't know. Just didn't want the bottom to burn out.

Then I turned back to Connie. One arm was under her body, one eye stared at nothing, and one leg was hiked up so that her pink bloomers were showing. Squatting down beside her, I pulled down her skirt, thinking as I did that I would not have thought her the pink bloomer type.

"Connie!" I called, putting my hand on her shoulder. It was soft to my touch, yet as I gently shook her, it felt hard and cold

x

111

underneath — sort of like a half-thawed roast.

Telephone! Still sitting on my heels, I strained to look around for it. Then called her again. "Connie!" The only sound was the rapid whirling of the fan overhead.

Deep down, I realized from her ungainly position and the glazed look in the one eye I could see that she wouldn't answer, couldn't answer, and never would. Besides the blood under her head, there were spatters of it on the sink cabinet and dotting the kitchen floor. *Be careful where you step,* I told myself.

But I wasn't able to step anywhere. Squatting there, stunned and shocked, I was as stiff and frozen in place as Connie was. I had a great urge to straighten her into a more comfortable position, but I couldn't bring myself to touch her again. I wanted to leave, but couldn't just walk off and leave her. That wasn't much of an option anyway because I couldn't get up.

Then the power went out — lights and all.

I stiffened in my squat, listening as the fan softly decelerated. That was the only sound until . . . *Good Lord! Is somebody in the house?*

Trying to rise, my stiff knees failed me.

Ten years ago, even five, I could've sprung to my feet and been out the door without a second thought. As it was, though, I was stuck in a squat and might've stayed that way if I hadn't been scared to death. Stretching up over Connie — without touching her — I reached with one hand for the edge of the counter over the dishwasher and used the other hand to push off the floor. Between the ungainly pull and push of both hands, I finally struggled to my feet.

Almost tripping over Connie's shoe, I ran for the door. Get out! Get help! *Get out, get out!*

It was all I could think of as I ran across the stone patio and along the stone path, humming with each breath.

When I reached the car, I stopped running, but not humming, and began rummaging in my purse for the car keys.

It was lighter outside than inside the house, but not by much. The wind, filled now with flecks of rain, swirled through my hair, but I didn't care. I kept feeling for the keys in the bottom of my bag, but when I finally brought them out, I nearly dropped them. The palm of my hand was smeared with blood — Connie's blood — and so was my purse.

Without thinking, I wiped my hand on the

front of my coat, then unlocked the car and fell inside. Quickly relocking the door, I jabbed the key into the ignition, my hand shaking so badly that I could hardly turn the thing.

Let me say at this point that I don't drive very well in reverse. Which means that I zigzagged the car down the steep driveway and would've backed into the ditch across the street if I hadn't left the emergency brake on.

Get help! That's all I could think of as I released the brake and drove toward the gate at the entrance, hoping to see lights from a house or from an oncoming car or even from a flashlight. But there were no other cars on the street, no lights in the few houses I passed, and no one on the golf course.

I didn't even try to avoid the small branches blown into the street by the wind — just went right through and over them.

Screeching to a stop at the gatehouse, still humming with each breath, I rammed the car into park, jumped out, and banged on the window. The security guard threw down his newspaper and came to open the window.

"Ma'am?"

"Call the sheriff! Call an ambulance! She's

on the floor and she can't get up! Hurry, hurry!" I had to lean against the gatehouse, so drained that I could hardly stand.

"What?" the guard asked, frowning. "Ma'am, are you all right?" He opened the door and stepped out.

"No! I'm not all right. And she's not, either. Mrs. Clayborn! She needs help. Call somebody. Call somebody now!"

"Yes, ma'am, right away." He turned to pick up a phone in the gatehouse. "The Clayborn house, you say?"

"Yes! Straight up this road, on the left. Glass and stone, you can't miss it. But the lights are out so be careful. Somebody might be inside. Besides her, I mean."

He spoke quickly on the phone, then came outside, locking the door behind him. "They're on the way, but I'll go on up and check it out." Then he stopped and gave me a close look. "Ma'am, are you hurt?"

I glanced down at a smear of blood on my coat and the dried remains of it on my hand. "I just needed help getting up. I was beside her, see, and, well, it's her blood, not mine."

"Huh," he said. "Guess I better hurry, then." He hustled over to the golf cart parked behind the gatehouse, jumped in it, and puttered away toward the Clayborn house, leaving me standing alone with my coat and hair blowing in the wind.

I didn't know what to do next. One thing was for sure, though, I was not going back to Connie's house. He could check it out by his lonesome. Yet I couldn't stand around in the growing dark outside a locked gatehouse, either, so I got in my car and went home.

I don't know how I got there. Images of what I'd seen, the fear I'd felt at the thought of another person lurking in the house, and the revulsion of having Connie's blood on my hand washed through me in waves. At the sound of approaching sirens, I slowed and pulled over to the side of the road, waiting for the convoy of emergency vehicles to pass. Briefly thinking that perhaps I should return to the scene of the crime, I decided I'd only be in the way.

So I stayed the course, still humming, breathing in gasps, and hurrying home, where there were lights and safety.

"Lillian! Lillian!" I started calling her before I was halfway out of the car.

Running across the yard, I banged through the kitchen door and met her on her way to me.

"What's the matter? What's the matter?" Lillian grabbed me, stopping my headlong rush. "Lord help us, what happen to you? Lemme close this door." She leaned away and slammed the door. "Set down, Miss Julia. Lemme see what's wrong."

I collapsed toward a chair and would've missed it if she hadn't guided me down. "Oh, Lillian, it was awful. And I think somebody was in there with me, and Connie . . . It was awful, and all I could think to do was unplug the coffeepot." I think I began to cry. "Sam, where's Sam?"

"He on his way. He jus' call an' tell me." Lillian squatted beside my chair, crooning, "What happened, Miss Julia? You have a accident? You get hurt?"

"No, no, I'm all right," I said, trying for a deep breath. "Just scared to death. Oh, Lillian, it was awful, she was just lying there, and when the lights went out, well, I thought I'd be next."

"Be next for what? What kinda meetin' you go to, anyway?"

"Well, I was only doing what I was asked to do, but I'm not supposed to tell that. Oh, Lillian," I moaned as a shudder went through me, "she was dead. I couldn't believe it, but she was. Is, I mean."

"Dead? Oh, my Jesus, Miss Julia, how she

117

get that way?" Lillian clasped my hand, then quickly unhanded it. "What you got on you?"

"Blood, Lillian. *Her* blood." I jumped to my feet and headed for the sink. "Got to get it off. Get it off. Brush, Lillian, a Brillo pad or something. I can't stand this."

Lillian grabbed me by the wrist, held my hand over the sink, and doused it with a blue liquid. "This here Dawn'll do the trick. Least it do with ducks." Turning the water on full blast, she went on. "Rub both them hands together, then wrench 'em off. An' gimme that coat while you at it."

I slid out of my stained coat, then proceeded to rub and scrub my hands under running water. I didn't remember putting my hand in Connie's blood, but the evidence was certainly there that I had. Getting it off even with a scrub brush wasn't easy, especially around my thumbnail, where it had soaked in.

"Oh, Lillian," I moaned, "this is making me ill. I can't get it off. I'll be scrubbing forever, just like Lady Macbeth, but with far less reason."

"Lady who?"

CHAPTER 12

"They'll need to talk to you, Julia," Sam said. He had just come in and we were sitting close together at the kitchen table. Sam's arm was around me as I recounted, in between full body shivers, the day's events. "So the sooner you call, the better."

"I know, and I'm going to," I said, nodding unhappily at the thought of going over it all again to someone in a uniform. "I'm just trying to get myself together. Of course, the sheriff already knows, so I don't know what I can tell them. I just found her like that."

"I know, but you were the first to . . ."

"We don't know that," I interrupted. "No telling how long she'd been there or who else had dropped in."

"True," Sam agreed, pulling me closer. "But you have to let them know. They'll get around to you eventually anyway."

I wasn't so sure about that. Who even

knew I was going to visit Connie? I hadn't told anybody, not even Sam or Lillian. Well, the pastor knew, but he didn't know *when* I was going. And the security guard at the gatehouse didn't know who I was. He might be able to pick me out of a lineup, but only if my hair was in the wild state it had been, and, believe me, I would have it combed and properly arranged if it came to that.

"I just hate the thought of going public," I said in defense of my hesitancy. "Like, you know, I was trying to get on television so somebody could ask me how it *felt* to find a dead person. The less people know my business, the better I like it, because it'll spread all over town." Everybody would want to know why I had been visiting Connie in the first place, and, after my promise to the pastor, how would I answer that?

"Miss Julia," Lillian said, hovering over me with a hot water bottle she wanted to put at my feet. "Miss Julia, you better do what Mr. Sam say. They swear out a warrant on you, you'll wisht you had."

"Honey," Sam said with some urgency, "from what you've told me, you left fingerprints, handprints, and footprints all over that kitchen. Now, let's call Coleman and tell him you found her."

"That's a good idea," I said, getting to my

feet. "He'll listen to me without jumping to any unwarranted conclusions. I just hope he's not about to climb a sign anytime soon."

Then I stopped on my way to the telephone. "He won't be on duty. He's off somewhere with half the deputies on the force working on that platform he intends to sit on."

"Just talk to the dispatcher," Sam said, taking my arm and walking me to the counter. He handed the phone to me. "You don't want them to waste investigative time tracking you down."

"Track me down? Will they do that?" Of course they would — I knew that. I knew I couldn't bury my head and pretend I had no knowledge of Connie's death. I mean, I *didn't* have any knowledge of it, but they might think differently, especially with my prints on the coffeepot, the edge of the counter, Connie's shoulder, and apparently in a puddle of her blood. Only I didn't remember doing that.

"All right," I said, taking the phone. "I'm just putting off the inevitable. I'll call, but we better prepare ourselves for gossip to run rampant."

Just as I began to dial the number, the front doorbell rang.

"Saved by the bell," I said with a weak smile. "At least for a little while."

Well, not exactly saved by anything. When Sam answered the door, in walked a looming and glowering Lieutenant Wayne Peavey — my longtime nemesis.

I stopped short there in the middle of the hall, mesmerized again by his sheer size. Well over six feet tall with a corresponding width of body mass, clad in an official navy blue puffy cold-weather jacket, he filled whatever room he entered. And right at that moment he was doing it in our front hall.

"Come in, Lieutenant," Sam said as he held the door open. "We were just about to call you."

Ignoring these welcoming words, the lieutenant's eyes lit on me as I stood behind Sam. "Mrs. Murdoch, we'd like you to come down to the sheriff's office and give a statement concerning your activities today. Would you be willing to do that?"

He couched his words in a question, but I knew I had little choice in the matter. But that didn't stop me from trying.

I cleared my throat. "I'll be happy to give a statement, but I'd prefer to do it here if it's all the same to you. I mean, since you're already here. Would you like some refreshments, Lieutenant? Hot cocoa? Coffee? It's cold out tonight."

"We need to get this done right away," he said, paying no attention to my courteous offer. "And it's best to do it at the station."

"Sam?" I turned to my retired-from-the-practice-of-law husband, expecting a vigorous defense on my behalf.

"Come on in, Lieutenant," Sam said. "We'll get our coats."

"I'll wait here," the lieutenant said firmly. "And you're welcome to come down anytime, Mr. Murdoch, but your wife shouldn't delay any longer than she already has."

"Are you arresting me?" I quavered. "I had every intention of contacting you."

"No, honey," Sam said before the lieutenant could respond. "It's just routine to get statements from everybody who might know something about a crime."

"But I don't know anything."

Lieutenant Peavey was having none of it. "We know you were there. A witness has come forward."

"*Who?*" I demanded. I *knew* there'd been somebody in the house besides me. And Connie. "Who was it?"

Lieutenant Peavey's mouth tightened, as if he hated giving out any information. "The security guard at the gate. He takes down the tag number of every visitor. You were there, and he saw you going and coming."

Why, that tattletale, I thought.

"Sam?" I said again, feeling surrounded and trapped even though I'd only been doing a good deed at the request of my pastor. Now look where I was.

"It's all right, Julia," Sam said. "I'll call Binkie and she'll meet us there."

"Binkie? Why? I don't need a lawyer. I mean, I have you. Don't I?"

"Better to have Binkie," he said. "I'm not in active practice, and we're too close. Lieutenant," he went on, turning to him, "could you give us a minute to call her attorney?"

"I thought her attorney would've already been here," Lieutenant Peavey said, lasering his eyes at me again. "Considering the fact that Mrs. Murdoch has delayed reporting the crime."

"Well, not for all that long," I said. "I've only been home barely thirty minutes, and I had to wash my hands and . . ." I started, but Sam interrupted me.

"Hold on," he said, turning toward the library. "I'm calling her attorney now."

He left me alone with Lieutenant Peavey, while tremors ran up and down my body and Lieutenant Peavey shifted from one foot to the other. I was anxious to stay and he was anxious to go.

"Listen, Lieutenant," Sam said as he came back into the hall. He was exhibiting a little anxiety himself. "Ms. Enloe Bates doesn't answer. Can you give us a little more time so I can track her down?"

Well, no, he couldn't, although he was nice enough about it, suggesting that I ride with him while Sam followed along with Binkie — if he could find her. So, feeling outside myself, I allowed Sam to help with my coat, permitted Lieutenant Peavey to take my elbow and guide me down the front steps into the cold night, and let him usher me into the front seat of his patrol car.

At least he didn't put me in the back behind the wire cage, so that everybody who saw me would think I was a hardened criminal.

I scrunched back into a corner of the seat, hoping no one would see me and holding on to Sam's last words to me, "Don't worry, honey, you'll be back home in no time. I'll get Binkie and we'll be right behind you. In fact, I'll go pick her up."

It was dark inside the car except for the glow of the rows of flashing red and green lights of electronic equipment on and under the dashboard. Lieutenant Peavey mumbled something into a microphone about a female in the car at 5:25 P.M.

I didn't think it incumbent on me to engage him in conversation, so I looked out the window at the night lights on the street corners and in closed shops, thinking how I'd failed to appreciate my freedom when I had it. People were home safe and comfortable, unshaken by having found a dead acquaintance and being subsequently questioned about their complicity in same, while I was caught up in a web of suspicion and uncertainty.

I cleared my throat. "Lieutenant Peavey?" I ventured.

"Yes?"

"Aren't you supposed to read me my rights?"

He gave me a quick glance. "Only when we arrest you."

"I thought that's what you'd just done."

"Not yet. You'll give us a statement, answer a few questions, and that'll be it. Unless we find further evidence that implicates you."

Prints! I thought — *finger, hand, and foot,* just as Sam had said. I was in big trouble, unless . . . *unless* they find somebody else's prints as well. And surely they would, I assured myself, because I most certainly was not the only person who'd been there.

"How long before you know if there's more evidence?" It flashed through my mind to wonder if I'd have enough time to abscond to a faraway location.

"We're still collecting it from the scene," Lieutenant Peavey said, being, I suddenly realized, uncommonly communicative. Did that have a sinister meaning? Did they become nicer once they had you in their grasp? "There'll be some people we can exclude and some we'll have an interest in."

Have an interest in? That didn't sound good.

I needed to know what category I was in. "Does that mean I'm one of those persons of interest?"

"We don't use that term," Lieutenant Peavey said.

"Well, what do you use?"

"Suspects."

CHAPTER 13

Lieutenant Peavey led me inside the sheriff's department, down a hall, and into a small room about the size of my kitchen pantry. The word INTERVIEW was on a plaque beside the door, which was better than CELL BLOCK. The decor, however, left a lot to be desired, there being only a mirror on the wall and no pictures. The only furnishings were a table with one chair on the far side and two chairs on the near side. He directed me to the single chair.

"Detective Ellis will be right in," the lieutenant said as he turned to leave. He stopped at the door as if he'd just thought of something. "Can I get you anything? Coffee? A cold drink? What would you like?"

"I'd like to go home."

He shook his head, either to deny my request or in disgust at my recalcitrance. With no other response, he shut the door behind him and left me. And left me.

I thought they'd forgotten I was there, but just as I was about to get up and remind them, the door opened and a man some inches shorter than Lieutenant Peavey but equally as wide entered with a warm smile.

"Sorry to keep you waiting," he said, drawing out one of the chairs opposite me and taking a seat. "Busy night. Now, Mrs. Murdoch, I know you're anxious to get home, so all we want from you is an account of what happened this afternoon. Oh, by the way," he went on with a warm smile, "I'm Detective Ellis, and my job is to make you as comfortable as possible, get your statement, then send you on home."

"I'm glad to hear that, because I'm more than ready to go." Actually, it was a great relief to deal with a man of some refinement, rather than the uncivil lieutenant.

"Okay, then. Just look this over," he said, sliding a pen and a page of closely typed sentences toward me. "And sign at the bottom. All it does is give us permission to take your statement. It'll save you a little time and get you home quicker. Although," he said, then paused as he searched my face, "I know you've asked for your lawyer, so we can continue to wait for her if that's what you want to do."

"I don't know what could be keeping her,"

I said, looking around with some anxiety, "but I don't want to stay here any longer than I have to." I scanned the page, found the blank for my signature, and signed my name. I slid it back across the table.

"I don't blame you," Detective Ellis said, implying that he would've done the same. "We'll be through here before you know it. Now, for your protection and with your permission, I'm going to record our interview." Then with an easy grin, he said, "That'll keep us law enforcement types on our toes." He put a small recording machine on the table, turned it on, and stated my name, his name, the date, and the time.

"Is this legal?" I asked, fearful of having every word I said recorded for posterity and anybody else who wanted to listen. I could possibly change my mind at some point in the proceedings, or my memory could fail me, or I might just wish I'd worded something differently. "I mean, I thought we were just going to talk. Maybe I should wait for my lawyer after all."

"It's entirely your decision, ma'am," Detective Ellis said, clicking off the recorder and getting to his feet. "I just thought you'd rather go ahead and get this done so you could leave. But we'll wait if that's what you want."

"Well, I don't know. I thought she'd be here by now, but I don't want to drag this out half the night. Let's just go ahead and get it over with."

"That's the ticket," he said with an approving smile as he clicked the recorder on again. He was such a nice man that it pleased me to please him. "We'll have ourselves a little chat, and then you'll be through.

"Now, in your own words, Mrs. Murdoch," he went on, settling back in his chair, "why don't you start by telling me when and why you went to the Clayborn house this afternoon?"

"Well," I said, my mind racing to determine what and how much to tell. I was still committed to the promise I'd made to Pastor Ledbetter, so I couldn't reveal that my visit to Connie had been an effort toward home missions outreach. "Well," I said again, "I didn't know Connie Clayborn well, but I called her this morning . . ."

"Hold right there," Detective Ellis said, sitting up. "You made the first contact?"

"Well, yes," I said, not understanding his need to clarify such a minor matter. "The first contact *today*. But she started it all last week when she had a social event for a dozen or so local women, of whom I was

131

one. So I called to thank her for the invitation she'd extended to me, and she invited me to come over this afternoon about four o'clock. To talk, you know. She said she wanted to get to know me better, but she'd just received a large shipment from Europe — I don't know what it was, furniture and so on, I suppose — they'd just recently moved here, you know. Anyway, she said she'd be busy until late afternoon." I paused, thinking rapidly. "I almost suggested another day because the weather was so threatening, and I wish I had. But she encouraged me to come, and to come to the back door because her front hall was full of crates and boxes. The shipment from Europe, you know."

"Uh-huh," Detective Ellis said. "And did you go to the back door?"

"Yes, I did, and almost left because no one answered the door — another thing I wish I'd done. The lights were on in the kitchen, but nowhere else in the house. That I could see, that is. And it was getting dark and the wind was picking up, so after ringing the bell and rapping on the window, I was about to leave."

"Did it upset you that she'd invited you, then didn't answer the door?"

I thought for a minute. "No, I don't think

it did. I think I was relieved to forgo a visit so I could get back home before dark. I thought maybe she was in the bathroom or maybe in the front of the house where she couldn't hear me. See, Detective Ellis, when you pay a visit to someone, just showing up when you're supposed to counts as a visit made. Doesn't matter whether the hostess is there or not, so I figured I'd done my duty and started to leave. I would've left a calling card if I'd had any with me."

"But you didn't leave."

"No, because I saw the shoe."

"The shoe? Where? Outside?"

"Oh, no, it was inside. I saw it through the window. It was a clunky shoe like the ones Connie wears. Wore, I mean. Like she wore. It was lying sideways on the floor. The heel and the sole were sticking out beyond the counter — that's all I could see from the window."

"So you were looking through the window. Over the sink?"

I looked at him, wondering what he could be thinking. "No, Detective, I did not climb up on anything to look through a high window. If you've been to her house, you'll know that the back door is half window, the top half. I was looking through that."

"Oh, right. Just trying to get the full

picture. So what did you think when you saw the shoe?"

"I'm not sure I thought anything. Just reacted, I guess. No, wait a minute. I guess I thought she'd fallen and was hurt. Anyway, I knocked louder and rattled the doorknob. That's when I found that the door wasn't locked, so I went in to be of help if I could. And there she was — sprawled out on the kitchen floor right up next to the row of sink cabinets with that one foot — with the shoe on it — sticking out just where I or anyone could see it from outside."

"Okay, so what did you do?"

"Well, and this was the strangest thing, Detective, and I have no explanation for it. It was like I took it all in at once — Connie just lying there, blood puddles and spatters all over the place, that fan whirling overhead as hard as it could go, pots and pans scattered around, a dust mop under the table, a chair lying on its back with its legs up in the air — and, see, that wasn't like Connie at all. As far as I'd been able to determine during my previous visit, she was a meticulous housekeeper.

"Anyway," I went on, brushing back my hair from the heat in the room, "the first, and seemingly the most important, thing I noticed was the heavy smell of burned coffee, and, see, Detective Ellis, that's what I can't explain. The first thing I did was walk right past Connie and unplug the coffeepot. That's what was so strange. I mean, except for finding her unconscious on the floor, which is what I thought she was. At first."

"Uh-huh, so then what?"

"Then I squatted down beside her, called her name, then shook her shoulder." I shuddered. "I wish I hadn't done that, either, because that's when I realized that she wasn't just unconscious." I paused, recalling the feel of Connie's shoulder. "That, and the one eye staring out over the puddle of blood under her head."

"So you moved her head out of the blood, right?"

"No! Where are you getting this, Detective? No, I did not touch her again. Oh, wait, yes, I did. I pulled her skirt tail down. It was hiked up over her hips, and I knew she'd be embarrassed to death to know that her underclothes were on display. And just as I was about to get up — see, I was still crouched down beside her — that's when the lights went out and I heard a noise somewhere in the front of the house." I really shuddered then, just thinking of it.

"What kind of noise?"

"I don't know, just something, a shuffle or

135

movement of some kind, and I had to get out of there. I was terrified, and of course I wanted to get help for Connie. I couldn't stay in that house alone, by myself, with the corpse of somebody I barely knew for another minute."

"So you called somebody?"

"What? No, I didn't have my cell phone, and I certainly wasn't about to go looking around that dark house with strange noises emanating from deep within while I looked for a telephone. So, no, all I could do was go where I knew someone was — the security guard at the gate. And that's what I did, because I didn't see another soul all the way from Connie's house to the gate. Now," I said firmly, relieved that I'd done my duty, "you'll have to get the rest of the story from him because when he left to go to the house, I left, too. And that's all I know, and that's all I have to say."

"And you didn't go back to the house? Just left the crime scene and went home."

"I'd already left the crime scene, Detective Ellis. To get help. So I'd gotten it, and after urging the guard to call you folks, there was nothing else for me to do. Besides, I was cold, hungry, and scared out of my mind."

"Okay, then. Is there anything else you'd

like to add to your statement? You want it to be full and complete."

"I can't think of anything, but I might later on. Oh, wait, one other thing if you want it full and complete. Connie's step-ins were pink, if that makes a difference."

He stared at me for a minute, then he frowned. "You think it does?"

"I have no idea. Just trying to cover everything, but I will say that pink nylon step-ins surprised me. I'd have thought that Connie Clayborn was more your basic, traditional white cotton type."

Detective Ellis's frown would've gotten deeper if the door hadn't banged open and Binkie Enloe Bates, my curly-headed lawyer, hadn't barreled in full of sound and fury.

Wearing jeans, lace-up hiking boots, and a fleece pullover sprinkled with sawdust, the curls on her head shaking with outrage, she slammed the door closed in Lieutenant Peavey's face.

"This interview is over!" she announced, glaring at Detective Ellis. "I'm surprised at you, Detective. You knew I was on the way. You had no right to interrogate my client after she'd asked for an attorney."

"I didn't . . ." he began, getting to his feet.

Binkie whirled toward me. "Did he give you a waiver to sign? Did you sign it?"

"I, well, I signed something. A permission slip or something." I looked at Detective Ellis for help. "What was it that I signed?"

Binkie didn't give him a chance to answer. She clenched her fists and yelled right in his face, "Insupportable! This whole interview is insupportable. You ought to be ashamed of yourself, Detective!"

"It's all right, Binkie," I said, wanting to soothe her. "I just told him what happened, that's all."

"Right," Detective Ellis said, regaining a tinge of authority as he picked up the recorder. "I'll just have this typed up, Mrs. Murdoch, then you can read it over, sign it, and that'll be all. We appreciate your cooperation in getting to the bottom of this horrific crime. We wish all our citizens were as helpful. Evening, Ms. Bates." And out he went, hurriedly.

"Miss Julia," Binkie said as she slid into the chair that Detective Ellis had just vacated, "what did you tell him?"

"The truth, Binkie. That's all I told him, and he really didn't question me. We just had a little chat about what I did and what I saw, and that was it."

"Oh, me," Binkie said, folding her arms on the table and leaning over them. "Never, ever just have a little chat with a police officer or a sheriff's deputy without your lawyer at your side."

"Even to tell the truth?"

"Honey," she said, half smiling, as she reached across the table to pat my arm, "especially when you tell the truth."

Chapter 14

After Binkie looked over my typed statement, questioned me about a few details, and gave me the okay to sign it, we left, collecting Sam on our way. He'd been waiting in the tiny reception area, pacing the whole time, from the looks of him.

"Julia," he said, rushing up to me, "are you all right?"

"I'm fine, Sam. There was really nothing to it, so, Binkie, I'm sorry we bothered you on such a minor matter."

Binkie and Sam looked at each other, then at me. "Not so minor, Julia," Sam said. "A murder investigation — if that's what it is — is extremely serious, and I hate that you've been caught up in it."

"But I'm not caught up in it, and now they know I'm not."

Binkie's eyes rolled just a little. "Okay, but let me tell you right now that you are not to say one other word to anybody — friend, foe, or family. If they come back to you about anything, whether it's to clarify something or to get more details, you are to call me before you say anything." She shook her finger at me. "Understand?"

"Well, if you put it that way, of course I will. But, Binkie, we tried to call you before I left home and couldn't get you."

"I know," she said, resignedly. "I took Gracie to watch the guys work on Coleman's platform. Some of their children were there, and she was so excited about playing with them and watching her daddy hammer and saw that I left my cell phone in the car."

"Oh, that's too bad," I said. "I was hoping Coleman had gotten over his strange urge to climb a billboard."

"Not a chance," Binkie said with a wry laugh. "I think he's going up later this week when old man Carver says we'll have a few balmy days in the sixties. If you believe in black gum trees."

By this time we'd left the sheriff's office and gotten into Sam's car. He had, indeed, gone to pick up Binkie when he'd been unable to reach her by phone and, luckily, got there just as they returned home from their carpentry workshop. Which I later learned had been in the garage of a K9 officer who made furniture as a hobby.

"Well," Binkie said as she leaned up from the backseat, "that cell phone's going to be glued to my body until this mess is cleared up. So don't hesitate to call me day or night if you hear from anyone official. Be sure, both of you, that my number is in your contacts list."

"But, Binkie," I said, shivering as I turned the heat dial up, "I think it's all over as far as I'm concerned. I've told them all I know, so now they'll be looking for whoever actually attacked Connie. But I'll tell you both," I went on, reaching for Sam's free hand, "it's just really hitting me that someone I know has been a victim of something so awful. I mean, things like that just don't happen in Abbotsville."

Neither Sam nor Binkie replied, and I realized that in their line of work, they knew that such things did happen in Abbotsville.

"Binkie?" I asked, to clear my mind of images of blood and coffee and pink bloomers. "Will Coleman take enough food with him for four days? How's he going to eat?"

"Oh, he'll eat, all right. Probably better than at home. Some of the restaurants on the boulevard want to feed him — they've worked out a schedule. FATZ one day, KFC another, and Outback another — he'll probably gain weight."

"That's only three days. Let us have a day
— maybe Sunday? But how would we get it
to him? Does he come down to eat?"

"Oh, no, he'll have a pulley system. He'll
lower a box for food and a bucket when
anybody stops to donate. And thanks, Miss
Julia, but the First Baptist ladies already
have Sunday." Binkie laughed. "He says he
can't wait. Those Baptist ladies can *cook*!"

"Well, let's don't tell Lillian. I expect she'll
want to send him some snacks or a dessert
or two."

"He'll love it. Listen, if you take him
anything, just park right there on the side of
the boulevard. There's a little path from
there to the foot of the sign. He'll see you
and lower the bucket or the box or whatever." Binkie stopped, then went on. "Only
thing is, you have to climb over the guardrail. It's not high — couple of feet, maybe,
so wear something suitable or, even better,
send Lloyd."

Sam said, "How's he going to get his
platform up there, Binkie? That sign's pretty
high off the ground."

"They'll use a ladder truck from the fire
department," Binkie said. "Coleman's got
his generator, TV, DVD player, some con-
cert speakers, and a heater that they'll set
up at the same time."

"My goodness," I said, somewhat in awe at all the preparations.

"All the comforts of home," Sam said.

"Not quite," Binkie said, laughing. "He won't have me."

With profuse thanks and good wishes for Coleman's survival if he stayed his course, we dropped Binkie off at her house, then proceeded home in silence. There was so much to talk about, yet neither Sam nor I seemed able to start a conversation. I was tired, for one thing. It was past my bedtime, and I was anxious to close my mind to the events of the last few hours and sleep.

But to tell the truth, the memory of finding Connie had receded to the point that it was almost as if I'd seen it on a television show. Come to think of it, I probably had. Not with Connie in it, of course, but a similar, yet made-up, crime scene.

What was much closer and more clear in my mind was having been in the clutches of the law. Did they really suspect me? I understood the need to eliminate all the possibilities until only one was left standing, but who could ever believe that could be me?

"Sam," I said as we walked into the house,

"I wish I'd pointed out to Detective Ellis the age and size differences between Connie and me. They couldn't possibly think that I could — even if I'd wanted to, which I didn't — do what was done to her. I'd be the one lying on the kitchen floor if that had happened. Not that I'm in the habit of fighting with anyone, especially to the death." Then, without warning, tears filled my eyes, my nose began to drip, and I wanted to bawl my head off. Finding Connie had been bad enough, but to be suspected of causing great bodily harm to another human being was beyond my ability to handle.

"Sweetheart," Sam said. He came over, put his hands on my shoulders, then drew me close. "They know that. But they have to consider all the possibilities from an accident to a home invasion to a domestic dispute to . . ."

"That could be it!" I jerked my head off Sam's shoulder, aware now that there was another, more likely suspect. "Her husband! Where is he? Nobody around here has ever even seen him. Maybe they had an argument, maybe it escalated and he killed her. Listen, Sam, it stands to reason because the door was unlocked, meaning that somebody just opened it, or unlocked it with his own key, then went in, did what he did, and left. There was no break-in, because none of the windows were broken. None that I saw, I mean. Of course," I said, slowing down, "I didn't specifically *look* for a broken window. But I would've noticed if a pane in the door had been broken."

"I'm sure you would've. But, Julia, why did you go out there, anyway? All I've heard this week has been Connie this and Connie that, and none of it good. What possessed you to call on her?"

"Well," I said, temporizing as I realized how imperative it was that I be released from the promise made to Pastor Ledbetter. And he'd better release me, too, because this was getting sticky. Even Sam was questioning my motivation, and I did not like being less than open with him. To say nothing of withholding information from Detective Ellis.

"She asked me to," I said. "I didn't just show up and knock on her door without being invited. And I so wish I hadn't accepted."

"I'm a little surprised that you did," Sam said as we walked into the library and sat together on the sofa. "You've been ambivalent about her all week — first deciding that you wanted nothing to do with her, then changing your mind by adding her to your party list just to demonstrate some local social customs."

I nodded. He was right. "I guess that was part of my reason for going out there. I was feeling bad about all the negative feelings I'd had toward her — you know, after she'd criticized us so roundly. I thought a one-on-one conversation would help her fit in a little better. Sam," I said, looking directly at him, "I promise you that I went out there with the best of intentions, hoping to be helpful to a newcomer and to, well, some others as well."

There. I'd come as close as I could to revealing the real reason for visiting Connie. But, come morning, I was going to make another visit and Pastor Ledbetter had better be prepared.

"So," I went on, hoping to change the subject, "I guess that brings up another question. Should I cancel my Christmas soiree? I mean, out of respect for Connie?"

"Soiree?" Sam said with a smile.

"Oh, I guess I haven't told you. I decided to make this year's tea special and invite a large group and have live music — that would be Sara O'Neill and her harp — and, you know, just go all out. Which, I remind you, was mostly for Connie's benefit. So she'd learn something. Now I don't know what to do."

"When're you having this wingding?"

"About a week before Christmas."

"Honey," Sam said, almost laughing at me, "it's not even the middle of November, and it's not as if Mrs. Clayborn were a close friend. I think you'd be perfectly correct to go ahead with your plans if you want to."

"Well, I do and I don't. But I may feel better about it after some time has passed. Of course, there'd be no question about canceling if it had been somebody close to me. Which I can't even imagine." But I could, for Emma Sue came immediately to mind. Not because I feared an attack on her but because now, with Connie unable to reassure her, she might simply shrivel up and fade away.

"Speaking of canceling plans," Sam said, "I've decided not to go to Raleigh. With things so unsettled here, I'd feel better staying here with you."

"Oh, you shouldn't do that, Sam. It'll be your first meeting and it's only for a few days. Besides, the governor might regret appointing you if you don't show up."

Sam gave me a wry smile. "I doubt he'll know, either way. But I'll see how things go, then decide."

I nodded, but I would encourage him to go. The sooner things got back to normal, the better I'd feel.

But just as I thought that I could begin to think of other matters — like Coleman's climb and Sam's trip to the capitol — the image of Connie's broken body returned to mind in sharp relief. "Will they be able to tell what killed her?" I asked. "I mean, exactly how she died?"

"I expect they will," Sam said, nodding. "They'll do an autopsy, probably not here since foul play may be involved. They'll send the body to Chapel Hill most likely, so it'll be some days before they get a report back." Then, as if his experience with criminals of all kinds from his years in the practice of law suddenly emerged, he calmly asked, "Was she shot or bludgeoned? Could you tell?"

"My word, Sam, I don't know," I said, drawing back from him. "I didn't *examine* her! But I can say that most of the blood came from her head. I mean, that's where the biggest puddle was. But from the way she was lying, I couldn't see the wound."

"Well, the autopsy will show what kind of weapon or object was used to strike her — if that's what happened. The size and shape of it, that is. And if she was shot, they'll probably be able to identify the type of firearm."

"My goodness," I murmured, trying to visualize what had been in Connie's kitchen. "I didn't see a firearm anywhere — I would've noticed that. And I don't think I saw a thing that could've done that kind of damage. Certainly not a dust mop or any of the pots and pans on the floor — they all looked like the lightweight aluminum kind. Not like an iron skillet or anything like that, which could do some damage. Of course, I didn't look around, so something could've been there."

"Listen," Sam said, clasping my hand, "the thing to do is try not to dwell on it. The experts will figure it out, and if it was a random attack, whoever it was probably took the weapon with him. Certainly would've if it had been planned in advance."

"Oh, don't say that," I said, my hand going to my mouth. "She hadn't been here long enough for anybody to dislike her enough to *plan* anything. Unless it *was* her husband — I guess he'd known her long enough. Actually, I don't like thinking of either one — random or planned. None of us would be safe."

"I know," Sam said soothingly, "and we shouldn't even be discussing it. In the meantime, though, at least until we know more, we should be careful to keep the doors locked, especially when you and Lillian are here alone during the day."

"Don't worry, we will. I'd hate for anybody to walk in and find what I found at Connie's house." Especially if it was Lillian or me they found on the floor.

CHAPTER 15

"Sam?" I said. We were in bed, nestled close, and from his breathing I knew he was close to sleep while I stared wide-eyed at the ceiling.

"Hm-m?"

"You know what my problem is?"

"Julia," he said with a muffled laugh as he raised his head from the pillow. "I wouldn't touch that with a ten-foot pole."

"Oh, you," I said, giving him a nudge. "I'm serious, because I've just realized that I really don't like change. I don't like change in any way, shape, or form. That's why I was so upset with Connie. She came in here telling us we should change everything — tear down and demolish, then refurbish, rehabilitate, or rebuild. And I didn't like it one little bit. I mean, who gave her the authority to demand such a thing? Just thinking of such arrogance bothers me all over again. And now, right at this minute, she's in a hearse on her way to an autopsy table. And I feel so bad, I don't know what to do. It's almost as if my anger at her had something to do with what happened, and when I think of how terrified she must've been when somebody — well, I wish I'd gotten there earlier and maybe protected her in some way. The whole thing just tears me up."

"I know," Sam said soothingly. "But I'm glad you didn't get there earlier — you might've been hurt, too. Listen, Julia, we don't know what happened, but I want you to stop going over and over it in your mind. We can't change anything, we can only change our reaction to it. You had nothing to do with it, whether you were there to find her or whether you'd stayed home all afternoon. And certainly your feelings about her had nothing to do with it. Now let's leave it to the investigators to figure out and to the Lord to give us peace of mind."

Good advice, and I was almost asleep by the time he gave it. But come daylight, I intended to see my pastor and get out from under the rule of silence he'd imposed on me.

My eyes suddenly flew open — the *pastor*! Of all the people who'd expressed anger toward Connie — and I'd include Mildred,

LuAnne, Emma Sue, and me as well in those who had — Pastor Ledbetter was the one who held the most against her.

No, impossible, I assured myself. But Pastor Ledbetter had considered the possibility that Connie was a tool of Satan. Could such a belief give him justification to harm her?

No, it was so incredible to ponder that I decided not to wake Sam again to run it past him. But now that it had occurred to me, I knew it would stay in the back of my mind until the actual cause and perpetrator of Connie's death were determined. And it would certainly flit through my mind as I talked to the pastor on the morrow.

One can't help but entertain a thought once it has popped into one's mind. It's a settled fact that it can't be *un*thought, and my restless night was witness to that.

After breakfast the next morning, Sam went upstairs to his working office in the remodeled sunroom, giving me the opportunity to prepare myself to visit Pastor Ledbetter's office at the church across the street. I hadn't mentioned my intention to Sam, because then I would've had to tell him what I had promised not to tell, which was that I had been *sent* to Connie Clayborn's house. Otherwise, I wouldn't have been within a mile of that crime scene, therefore it was up to the pastor to get me out of the messy situation in which I found myself and for which I was under constraint to give no explanation.

The pastor usually made a quick visit to any ailing Presbyterians in the hospital, then got to his office by nine or so. I kept watch through the front window for his car to enter the parking area behind the church, after which I intended to march over there and demand that he release me from the promise I had so rashly given him.

My intended march to the church was severely delayed by the telephone. A little before eight it started ringing, and as soon as I hung up from one call, another came in. LuAnne was the first.

"Julia!" she yelled, then began rattling off questions too quickly to be answered. "What is going on? I just heard about it. The paper didn't have the details — happened too late to get in, I guess. But you were there? *Why?* What were you doing at Connie's house, anyway? I can't believe this, it's too horrible. And to think you were the last person to see her alive!"

"No, LuAnne, *no*! I wasn't the last one —

whoever killed her was the last one to see her alive. Don't be saying it was me — that's wrong! I just found her *after* she was dead. Lord, LuAnne, don't go around saying something like that. I'll be in more trouble than I already am."

"Oh," she said, lowering her voice in expectation of hearing something new. "Do they think you did it?"

"Absolutely not, because I didn't. How can you ask such a thing?"

"Well, I know you didn't like her. Not," she quickly added, "that anybody else did, either. But you were outspoken about it. You called her a menace to society."

Well, that just flew all over me. How many of us like having our own words thrown back at us?

"No, I did not, LuAnne," I said. "I may have said she was a menace, but not to society as a whole. And if we're going to bring up private conversations between *friends,* I can recall some less than complimentary things *you* said about her."

"Well," she huffed, *"I'm* not the one being questioned by the authorities. But I see you're in a bad mood this morning, so I'll let you go. Call me if I can be of any help."

I hung up the phone, thinking, *Call her for help?* She'd have me under the jail before I turned around good.

With my hand still on the phone, it rang again. Without thinking, I answered it.

Mildred said, "Julia, what in the world is going on? There was just a brief paragraph in the paper about Connie being dead, which was shocking enough. But when it mentioned you, I couldn't believe it. Are you all right?"

"I'm as well as can be expected under the circumstances," I said wearily. "Oh, Mildred, it was awful. I just found her, that's all. But what did the paper say? I haven't seen it yet."

"Nothing, really," Mildred said. "Just one sentence saying you were being questioned."

"Oh, my Lord," I moaned, "that sounds as if I had something to do with it. Mildred," I continued with renewed firmness, "I'm going to sue that paper. See if I don't. The very idea! I just happened to drop by and just happened to find her."

"But *why*? Why were you there at all? Everybody knows you didn't want to have anything to do with her. You really raked her over the coals when we had lunch together, remember?"

You, too, Mildred?

"Yes, and I remember that you threatened

157

to snatch her baldheaded, too. So if we're all going to be held responsible for what we say, you're in trouble along with me."

"Oh, Julia," Mildred said lightly, "don't be so defensive. I can quote chapter and verse of what a number of other people have said about Connie, and, believe me, it wouldn't be pretty."

"That's a good point, Mildred, and if that detective comes back at me, I'm going to tell him he ought to question every woman in town. We *all* had something against her, which does *not* mean we wanted her dead."

Mildred chuckled. "Well, go ahead and give him my name. I'll give him an earful. But, Julia, why *did* you go see her?"

"I can't discuss it, Mildred — Binkie's orders. Just trust me that I had a good reason for going, and it certainly wasn't to kill her. How anybody could even think . . ."

"Well, Julia, of course I don't. But you really ought to make the paper print a retraction or something. What they printed today certainly gives the wrong impression. It lets readers jump to the wrong conclusion, and if I were you, I'd go down there and snatch a few reporters and editors baldheaded." She laughed, then said, "I'll help you if you want."

■ ■ ■ ■

After hanging up, I looked out the window again just in time to see the pastor's yellow car turn into the parking lot across the street. Taking up my coat for the walk over to the church, I was stopped by the ringing of the phone. Hesitating, I almost left it for Lillian to answer. I was glad I didn't.

When I answered, Sergeant Coleman Bates said, "Miss Julia, I'm just calling to see how you are this morning. Anything you need? Anything I can do?"

"Oh, Coleman, how nice of you to call, but are you calling officially or out of the goodness of your heart? After last evening, I don't know who to trust anymore."

He gave a little laugh. "I hear you. But I'm calling to reassure you. I just looked over your statement, and if everything checks out, you'll be all right."

"Do you have all that evidence that Lieutenant Peavey mentioned? I mean, any evidence of who attacked Connie? Because, Coleman, it was not me."

"I know that, Miss Julia," he said, his voice warm with assurance. "But, no, it'll take some time for the forensic evidence to be processed, get the autopsy report back, and for us to question everybody."

"Who?" I demanded. "Who else is being questioned? Because somebody else *had* been there, and might still have been when I left."

"You know I can't discuss that, but I want you to know I'm here for you. And to tell you that I'm going up on the sign tomorrow. My weather guy says we'll have a few mild days before a cold front comes in, so if he's right, I'll be up there till Sunday evening. But if you need anything, you let me know."

I thanked him and hung up, wondering how he thought he could help me if he was going to be sitting up on an outdoor advertising sign. Still, I appreciated the thought.

"Lillian," I called, putting on my coat. "I'm going over to the church. I shouldn't be long."

The phone rang again as I went out the door. I kept going.

CHAPTER 16

Going through the back door of the church, I followed the hall to the group of rooms that made up the business office, the pastor's office, and the office of Norma Cantrell, the pastor's gatekeeper. Prim, precise, and too precious for words, Norma took her job as guardian of the inner sanctum seriously. She and I had had run-ins on previous occasions, but I was in no mood to get into it with her on this day.

"Good morning, Norma," I said, breezing into her office as if I had an appointment. She turned her carefully frosted and teased head of hair toward me, lifted her eyebrows, and tried to smile. She'd been told that members of the church were to be welcomed at all times whether or not they had appointments.

"I have to see the pastor," I said, before she could speak. "He's here, isn't he?"

She sniffed. "He just left."

"Norma, I saw his car pull in just a few minutes ago, so please tell him I'm here on a matter of some urgency."

"He came in to pick up some papers, but he had to go back out."

"Look," I said, standing in front of her desk, "if he went back out, why didn't I meet him in the hall on my way in?"

"Be*cause,*" she said, as if I needed to have it spelled out, "he went up through the sanctuary to check on the sound system, then he went out the front door." And concluding with some satisfaction, she said, "I'm sure he's already left the parking lot by now."

Foiled and distressed, I asked, "Well, when will he be back?"

"I have no idea. He has a luncheon engagement and several meetings this afternoon. It'd be best to make an appointment. Would you care to make one?" She pulled a desk calendar over, covered it with one arm, and began to study it. "Let's see. This week looks full. What about a week from today? Would that work?"

"Norma," I said, putting my hands on the desk and leaning toward her. "This will not wait a week. Now, you find a time for him to see me, and find it today."

"Well!" she said, drawing back, pulling the

calendar with her. "You don't have to get snippy. *I'm* not the one who makes the rules around here. I just do as I'm told."

I stood up straight and looked long and hard at her, realizing that she had just let the cat out of the bag. "He's avoiding me, isn't he? He told you to put me off, didn't he?"

"I just work here, Mrs. Murdoch. That's all I do."

"All right, I understand. But I want you to give the pastor a message. Tell him that if I don't hear from him *in person* as soon as humanly possible *today,* then all bets are off, all promises revoked, and all you-know-what will break loose."

Fuming with anger, I went home, completely incensed that Pastor Ledbetter was sneaking in and out of the church so he wouldn't have to see me. I knew why he was doing it — he didn't want to release me from my promise. He would let me face questions and suspicions without doing one thing to help. What did that say about a Christian minister? Well, what did it say about a Christian, period?

Nothing good, I can tell you that. And I couldn't even unload on Sam or Lillian, much less on Lieutenant Peavey, Detective Ellis, Binkie, Coleman, or the local newspaper. I would remain under a cloud of suspicion until I could explain my heretofore unexplained presence at Connie's house on the day of her death.

As I walked up onto the front porch of my house, my steps slowed as the thought that I'd tried to unthink came back to haunt me. No, and no again, the pastor could not have committed such a crime. All he was trying to do was protect his suffering wife, who was proving less than able to weather a spiritual crisis. And, as he had practically admitted to me, he was trying to protect his reputation as a serene and capable leader who was in full control of his own family. Because it is a fact that no matter how well a man — maybe a woman, too — manages his professional life, any prestige or authority he has is lost if his personal life is in chaos.

But that didn't excuse him or help me, and I intended to have it out with him if I had to camp on the church doorstep from here on out. Maybe I should take some camping-out lessons from Coleman.

"Oh, there you are," Sam said as I walked into the house, shedding the coat that I hadn't needed. "I was looking for you. Where were you?"

"Oh . . . around," I mumbled. "Why, what's going on?"

"I just got a call from Raleigh, and I'll have to go to that meeting after all. The National Weather Service is predicting icy weather across the state the first of next week, so the meeting's been moved to tomorrow. Seems there's a bad situation with a judge in one of the eastern counties that has to be dealt with. I'm sorry, Julia, but it puts me on the spot and I'll have to go."

"How long will you be gone?"

"Honey, I could be back tomorrow night — it all depends on how quickly we can come to terms. But I'll certainly be home Sunday at the latest, especially if an ice storm is on its way." He reached for my hand. "I hate to leave with all that's going on here."

"I'll be fine, Sam. You do what you have to do, and I'll be all right. Just get back before the weather moves in — it's too risky a drive if it's icy. Come on," I said as I headed for the stairs, "I'll help you pack. Oh, by the way, get back early if you can so you can see Coleman on his sign. He's taking advantage of the mild weather to go up tomorrow and stay till Sunday evening. You don't want to miss that."

Sam laughed. "I'll tell the committee I have a friend in dire need of having his head examined."

Still hesitant about leaving, hemming and hawing about it, Sam finally set off on his five-hour trip right after an early lunch. His reluctance almost made me think I could be in more trouble than I'd been led to believe.

"Lillian," I said as I pulled out a chair at the kitchen table, "I declare, I hate that Sam has to be away. I didn't want him to know it, but I'm still so upset about what's already happened and about what else could possibly happen."

Lillian put two cups of coffee on the table and sat down across from me. "You know he be right back here if something else come up. An' it don't look like anything else could happen worse than what already happen, could it?"

"Oh," I said as airily as I could manage, "maybe only a few trivial things. Like somebody else being attacked, or the newspaper saying I'm the prime suspect, or the sheriff deciding to arrest me. Nothing very important."

Lillian laughed. "Miss Julia, you worry too much. Nobody gonna arrest you, an' ev'ry door in this house is stayin' locked, an' nobody b'lieve the newspaper anyway." She stirred sugar into her coffee, then leaned forward. "But I tell you what worryin' me. That's that nice Coleman settin' up there on that big sign, even if he doin' it for the little chil'ren." She stopped, then went on. "But I guess that lady friend you tole about won't like me sayin' he ought not do it 'cause he's doin' it for somebody else's good."

"She won't care. That's the lady I found dead yesterday."

"No!" Lillian cried, her eyes going wide. "Is that the truth? Law, I didn't mean to say something bad about a dead lady."

"You didn't, Lillian. But I'm having the same problem. I know we shouldn't speak ill of the dead, but I didn't know her well enough or long enough to find anything good to say."

"Well, I don't even wanta think about it no more. I got enough worries with Coleman settin' up there, gettin' cold an' hungry an' wishin' he home in bed with Miss Binkie. Miss Julia," she said, hunching over the table, "you tell him if it gets frosty up there, he better not be puttin' his tongue on any of them metal poles holdin' up that sign."

"What? Why?"

"I always hear 'bout people puttin' they tongue on a frosty ax blade an' it takin' the skin off."

"My word. Who would do such a thing?"

"Crazy people don't know no better, an' people campin' out in the wintertime."

"Oh, well. I'll pass that along to Coleman. But, Lillian, let me ask you something, and if it doesn't suit you, please say so. But would you and Latisha come spend the night here while Sam's away?"

She smiled. "I was wonderin' 'bout that. An' I don't blame you. We be glad to."

CHAPTER 17

It was a long afternoon with Sam away, Lloyd in school, Hazel Marie and family down with colds, and no one I dared talk to. Even the telephone had stopped ringing — a bad sign. It probably meant that no one wanted to be associated with me, much less be tainted by conversing with me.

I almost wore a path on the Oriental in my living room, going back and forth to the front window to watch for Pastor Ledbetter's car turning into the church parking lot. By late afternoon he still hadn't shown up, and it occurred to me that if he absented himself from his office all week, we were in for a poorly prepared sermon come Sunday. But I had laid the law down to him, via Norma, so he knew I was just before telling what I'd promised not to tell — officially released or not. Binkie would be most interested in hearing what I had to say, and so would Detective Ellis. Lieutenant Peavey probably wouldn't care one way or the other.

Then I thought that maybe the pastor wanted to sneak over to see me under the cover of darkness. Which didn't make much sense, because as soon as he released me from my promise I was going to talk my head off to anybody who'd listen, anyway. *But I told Norma he had today,* I thought, *so I'll give him till midnight.* It was going to be a long wait.

Hearing Lillian and Latisha come in through the kitchen, I hurried to meet them. Latisha, talking constantly, had her little suitcase in one hand and three dolls in the other.

"Go on upstairs an' put them doll babies in our room," Lillian was telling her as I came in.

"Hey, Miss Lady," Latisha said in her high, piercing voice. "We're spendin' the night with you, did you know that? Great-granny said you ast us, so here we are."

"And I'm so happy to see you, Latisha. You're doing me a great favor by keeping me company while Mr. Sam is away."

"Well, let me ast you something," Latisha said, standing beside Lillian and looking me over. "I wanta know when the police comin' to 'rest you. 'Cause I been wantin' to see

170

something like that."

"Latisha!" Lillian cried. "What you talkin' about! Nobody gonna get arrested 'round here. Miss Julia, I'm sorry. I don't know where she hear such a thing. I sure didn't tell her."

Before I could reassure Lillian, Latisha said, "No'm, Great-granny don't never tell me nothin', 'cept, 'Latisha, go to bed,' 'Latisha, go to school,' 'Latisha, go to sleep,' 'Latisha, go to church,' till I get tired of all that goin'. But she don't have to tell me, 'cause I hear it all over school today. Everybody real sorry, Miss Lady."

"It's all right, Latisha," I said, trying not to moan at learning that I was the current event topic for the first grade. "But I'm not going to be arrested, because I haven't done anything to be arrested for. So that'll be something you can tell all your classmates tomorrow."

"Well, that'll be good," she said, heading toward the hall. "I'm gonna put all this stuff upstairs, but if the police change they minds, call me. I really wanta see somebody get 'rested."

"My Jesus," Lillian said, mopping her face with her hand. "What they learnin' in school, anyway?"

"There's no telling. But don't worry about

it, Lillian. I know there'll be rumors and gossip flying around. I'll just have to put up with it." *But not for long,* I thought, and went back to the living room to check the church parking lot again.

That evening, the three of us sat around the kitchen table after eating, Lillian and I occasionally talking but mostly listening to Latisha. Sam had called just as we'd gotten to the table to say he was safely in Raleigh, checked into the hotel, and getting ready to meet an old friend for dinner.

Although I'd watched all afternoon, I'd not seen hide nor hair of the pastor, but now that it was getting dark, I had hopes that he'd soon show himself.

"Lillian," I said, "I may have a visitor sometime this evening, and if so, he'll probably want to slip in and slip out without anybody seeing him."

Lillian frowned as she looked at me, one eyebrow arching up. "Do Mr. Sam know 'bout this?"

I smiled. "Not yet, but he will. It all has to do with my current situation, Lillian, and as soon as I can, I'll tell you about it."

Latisha opened her mouth to say something, but the front doorbell diverted her. "That pro'bly him," she said.

172

"Who?" Lillian asked.

"That man Miss Lady waitin' on."

"I certainly hope so," I said, getting to my feet, eager to put an end to my uncertain status in the eyes of the law.

Lillian stood up as well. "It could be anybody. I better go with you."

"No, I don't want to scare him off. You and Latisha, finish your dinner. This shouldn't take but a minute."

I hurried through the dining room with a lighter heart, already planning what I'd do as soon as the pastor left. Binkie would be my first call, then Sam as soon as he got back to the hotel. Then I would call Mildred and LuAnne to put their suspicions to rest, and after that I'd call Detective Ellis and tell him to take my name off the suspect list — I had a legitimate reason for having been at the Clayborn house and a respected religious leader who could attest to it.

Thinking that this was one time I could honestly say I was happy to see Pastor Ledbetter, I flipped on the porch light, flung open the door, and opened my mouth to welcome him.

It wasn't the pastor. It was, instead, a tall, thin man in a Burberry raincoat, the only thing I recognized about him.

Sliding behind the door and holding on to

it, I said, "Yes?" as visions of Connie's kitchen and Connie's body danced in my head.

"Mrs. Murdoch," he said, "I apologize for not calling before coming by, but I'm Stan Clayborn, Connie's husband. I'd like to speak with you, if I could have a few minutes of your time. Just a question or two to help me understand." He had to pause as his voice broke. "I won't keep you long."

Were homicidal maniacs so well spoken? Or, as I noted the fine woolen suit and silk tie under the raincoat, so well dressed?

"Well," I temporized, "I'm expecting my, ah, my sewing group in a few minutes — about a dozen ladies all with needles and scissors, and there're people waiting for me in the kitchen. But I know this is a stressful time for you, so . . ." I stopped, looked behind me to see if Lillian was near. "I don't want to be inconsiderate at such a time, so come in, Mr. Clayborn. And may I say that I am very sorry for your loss."

I opened the door wider and he stepped inside, allowing me a closer look at him. I declare, the lines on his thin face were etched with grief, his eyes somber and deep in his head, and his cheekbones stood out in sharp relief. I was moved with pity for this suffering man.

174

But not quite enough for me to forget that I might be in the presence of a psychopathic wife killer. I gestured to the sofa, which he took, while I eschewed my usual seat in the wingback next to the fireplace in favor of a straight Chippendale chair near the door to the hall. Just in case.

Sitting stiffly on the sofa, his feet firmly planted, Mr. Clayborn lifted his haggard face and said, "This may be difficult for you, Mrs. Murdoch, but I can't rest until I know what Connie's last words were. Would you be kind enough to tell me what they were?"

My mouth opened as I stared at him. What? What was he talking about? "I'm sorry?" I said, as if I were hard of hearing.

"Her last words. Did she by chance mention me before she died? Or did she say anything that I could treasure and remember her by?"

"Mr. Clayborn," I said, standing because I couldn't sit still while he labored under such a misconception. "The last words that your wife said to me were said over the telephone early yesterday morning. I think they were something like, 'I'll see you about four.' I'm sorry to tell you that when I arrived about four — give or take a few minutes — she was in no condition to say anything. I found her *body,* Mr. Clayborn, and the only words spoken were my own as I tried to rouse her." I glanced behind me, hoping that Lillian was in the hall. "I can understand your wanting to hold on to her last words, but I assure you, I was not there to hear them."

"Ah, well," he said, his head dropping low, "I was afraid it was too much to hope for. But when I learned that you'd been there . . . well, I just hoped."

"Be assured, Mr. Clayborn, that I would tell you if I had anything to tell. Whoever told you I was there gave you wrong information. I mean, I was there, but she was not. That's as kindly as I can put it."

"Well," he said again, suddenly springing to his feet. "Thank you for trying to help her. I must go. I've missed my daily run and I'm not myself if I don't get in five or six miles every day."

He strode past me toward the door, and I had to hop to it to let him out. Locking the door behind him, I leaned against it, my mind in a whirl. What I'd thought were signs of grief — the lanky body, the gaunt face — weren't that at all. He was an emaciated long-distance *runner.*

And why had he thought that I'd heard Connie's last words? Did he think *I'd* killed her? *Or* — and here I almost sank to the floor — was he making sure that Connie had not identified her killer to me?

"Miss Julia?" Lillian said, taking my arm and leading me away from the door. "You all right? You look like you seen a ghost."

"No, not a ghost, Lillian, but maybe a ghost maker."

CHAPTER 18

The first thing I did Thursday morning —
well, not the very first because I had to wait
till eight-thirty — was to call Norma at the
church office. I hadn't heard one word from
the pastor, so my full confession of why I
went to Connie's was on hold, and I was
still up in the air as to what to do. I'd
threatened to tell on him even without a
formal release, but I hadn't been able to
bring myself to actually do it. So far.

"Norma," I said as soon as she finished
her lilting telephonic spiel of "First Presbyterian Church of Abbotsville. This is Norma
speaking. How may I help you?" "Did the
pastor get my message?"

"He did. I gave it to him when he came in
at five o'clock yesterday just as I was getting
ready to leave. It was the first time he'd
come back all day."

"Well, what did he say? I haven't heard
from him, and it's imperative that I do.

Believe me, he won't like the consequences if I don't."

There was dead silence on her end for a few seconds, then she said, "I think making threatening phone calls is against the law, Mrs. Murdoch, especially against a minister of the Gospel."

"Don't think, Norma, it'll get you in trouble because I'm not making threats. I'm just telling you — and you can pass it along to him — exactly what's going to happen if he keeps avoiding me. Now, what did he say?"

"Well," she huffed. "He said to tell you that he's taking Mrs. Ledbetter to a specialist at Bowman Gray School of Medicine in Winston-Salem today, and he'll see you when he gets back. You won't be able to catch him — they were leaving about six this morning." She paused, then went on. "I was going to call and tell you."

"Thank you for passing it along so promptly," I said, heavy on the sarcasm as I thought of my sleepless night. "But you could've told me yesterday afternoon and spared me some concern."

"It was after five."

My eyes rolled so far back I was afraid they'd never line up again. But what can you expect from someone like Norma Cantrell, who treated church members as if they were nuisances who impinged on her time and the pastor's.

There was nothing more I could do, so there I was, hanging by a thread held by Pastor Ledbetter. I could go ahead and tell what I knew — as I'd indeed threatened to do. But now there was Emma Sue to worry about, because she must have gotten worse or, at least, not gotten any better. I had to concede that taking her to a specialist was certainly reason enough for the pastor to have something other than my quandary on his mind. It looked as if I would have to give him a pass — a temporary pass — and wait for his return before making a clean breast of it.

I walked through the house looking for Lillian and found her changing the sheets on Lloyd's bed.

"There you are," I said, going to the far side to catch the sheet that she flapped across the bed. "Talk to me, Lillian. I need something to do besides think about what I'm thinking about."

"I guess you worryin' 'bout Coleman like me. Miss Julia, he got no bus'ness livin' out in the open like that. I wish Miss Binkie'd straighten him out."

180

"She can't do a thing with him, you know that." I handed her a pillowcase, then said, "But that's what we can do! Let's pick up Latisha and Lloyd when school's out, then ride out there and see him."

"An' I can take him something to keep up his strength. Le's get this bed made so I can make some brownies. I'm glad you think of that, Miss Julia. I feel better when I see how he doin'."

"You may not see much, Lillian. You know that sign is setting in marshland on the low side of the boulevard, but Coleman said there's a dry path to walk on. Only thing is, you have to climb over the guardrail to get to the path. I doubt you'll want to attempt it — I sure don't. Lloyd will, though."

"Latisha, too," Lillian said, laughing. "If it's somethin' a little risky, she be the first one to try it."

I laughed with her, thinking of how impetuous Latisha was. "I can finish up here if you want to start those brownies."

"I'm 'bout through, but, Miss Julia, I been thinkin' maybe Mr. Sam or Mr. J.D. ought to talk to Lloyd a little bit."

I straightened up from spreading out a blanket. "What about?"

"Well, you know I don't mind doin' the cleanin'. I cleaned a many of 'em in my day, but Lloyd might need to be told 'fore he marry somebody. Wives don't much like it."

"Married? Why, Lillian, he's nowhere near old enough to think of marrying. What does he need to be told, anyway? I can tell him whatever it is."

"No'm, he need a man to tell him, somebody that can show him how."

"How what?"

"Aim better. Miss Julia, he gettin' up at night without wakin' up good, an' he missin' what he oughta be hittin'."

"Oh, for goodness sakes," I said as we laughed together. "You're right, that's not for me to bring up. I'd embarrass him to death. And myself, too. I'll get Sam to talk to him. No way in the world would I speak to Mr. Pickens about that."

When the phone rang later that morning, I nearly broke my neck getting to it. At last, somebody wanted to speak to me.

"Miss Julia? It's Sue," Dr. Hargrove's wife said when I answered. "Do you know anything about Emma Sue? I just heard that the pastor's taken her to a specialist in Winston-Salem, and I'm concerned about her."

"I am, too, Sue. And, yes, I've heard about it, but I don't know any more than that.

I've been hoping to hear from the pastor with some details about her condition." About a few other things as well, but I didn't mention those. "If I hear anything more, I'll let you know."

"Please do. Everybody's worried about her," Sue said. "But listen, with Emma Sue out for a while, and Hazel Marie, too, we're going to be pushed to get our ornaments made in time. I'm thinking that we ought to meet twice a week, or at least a few extra times, so we'll have enough to sell."

"That's a good idea. We're already behind compared to this time last year. When do you want to meet?"

"Well, tonight? Except I can't have it at my house — several of Marsha's friends are coming over to make cookies for the team." Marsha was Sue's popular, volleyball-playing teenage daughter. "But I've spoken to Mildred and she says we can meet at her house."

"That's perfect for me. Sam's out of town, and it'll give me something to do."

"Oh, good. I'll bring everything with me and see you there."

So my day and evening schedules were now filled, leaving little time to grapple with worrisome matters like suspicious detectives, slippery preachers, and daring sheriff's

deputies hanging out on windswept bill-
boards.

CHAPTER 19

It wasn't a simple matter to pick up the children and drive through town to Coleman's sign. First, I had to call Hazel Marie so she'd know Lloyd wouldn't be home on time. She was so hoarse with a cold that I could barely understand her, but she said she'd text Lloyd so he'd know to look for my car.

"He can't use his phone in school, can he?" I asked, not wanting to get the boy in trouble.

"No," she croaked, "but it'll be the first thing he looks at when the bell rings."

Then, while I waited with car keys in hand, Lillian couldn't make up her mind about how to transport a plate of brownies.

"I don't guess a silver plate would do, would it?" she said.

"No, we might never get it back. Just put them in a sack, Lillian, and let's go. The

185

children will be standing outside waiting on us."

She fiddled around with a brown paper sack, decided against that, then tried a plastic bag and didn't like that, either. Finally, she placed a stack of brownies on a paper plate and covered it tightly with plastic wrap. "That'll do it," she said, finally satisfied, and out we went.

We drove through the pickup line at school and stopped for Latisha and Lloyd to get in. They piled into the backseat, slinging book bags, coats, and Latisha's artwork all over the place. Lillian made sure they buckled their seat belts and then we were off.

"I sure am glad somebody thought of this," Latisha said. "I been worryin' 'bout Coleman all day long. 'Cept when we went through the lunch line, an' I saw what they put on my tray. All I could worry 'bout then was starvin' to death."

His mind on our destination, Lloyd asked, "Miss Julia, do we know where we're going? I mean, which sign Coleman's on?"

"No, but we shouldn't have any trouble finding him. He'll be the only person sitting on one. But there're a lot of signs on both sides of the boulevard, so you and Latisha watch for him. You, too, Lillian, because I have to watch the traffic, and there's more of it than I like."

We were heading east out of town toward what passed for a mall in Abbotsville on the Martin Luther King Jr. Boulevard, the four-lane highway that led to the interstate. There was a speed limit, but whatever it was was too fast for me if I had to drive and look for Coleman at the same time. As a result, there seemed to be an uncommonly long line of cars behind me, with any number of them blowing their horns and streaking past us.

Just as I saw an Abbot County Sheriff's car parked on the paved shoulder just ahead of us, Latisha screamed, *"There he is!"*

"Where?" Lloyd yelled.

"Right there! See?" Latisha bounced up and down, pointing and yelling.

"I see him! Stop, Miss Julia, stop!"

"I can't," I said, as two more impatient drivers whizzed by.

A wash of fresh air and the blare of loud music swept through the car as Latisha's window came down.

"Lord help us," Lillian said, struggling to unbuckle herself to turn and see what Latisha was doing.

She was yelling at the top of her voice,

"Hey, Coleman, hey! Look over here, Coleman! It's us, it's us!"

I risked a quick look back and saw Latisha hanging halfway out the window, waving both hands. "Grab her, Lloyd! Get her back in here.

"And close that window," I said, speeding up to accommodate certain people who were too impatient to sightsee.

"Oh-h-h," Latisha wailed. "We gone on by, an' I can't see him no more."

"Couldn't nobody see him," Lillian said, "what with you 'bout to jump outta the window. Latisha, you got to put that seat belt back on and stay in your seat."

"Well, that's what my teacher always say, 'cept she don't put a seat belt on me."

"Listen now," I said, "I'm going to pull off up here at the service station. Then we'll turn around and go back past him."

"Won't do no good," Latisha said. "We'll be on the other side of the road."

"I know, but I'll turn around again, and we'll come back on his side. And now that we know where he is, we'll pull over and stop."

"Well, now," Latisha said, "that makes sense." Lloyd started laughing, while Lillian tried not to.

So we did the sensible thing and finally

got parked on the side of the boulevard, some yards from the occupied sign that advertised a rest home: LOVING CARE FOR YOUR LOVED ONES, complete with three meals a day and light housekeeping. Adorning the corners of the sign were pictures of smiling white-haired couples — some playing golf and others looking as if they'd found true love, though somewhat late in life.

And sitting in a webbed lawn chair on the wooden platform about twenty or so feet above the marsh, Coleman saw us. He leaned over and turned down the loud, driving music that was entertaining most, but not all, passersby. One man, leaning out a car window, yelled, *"Play on, Willie Nelson, you sonofagun!"* Coleman stood and waved at us and, I guess, at all the other waving hands from passing cars.

Lloyd had the back door open, and he and Latisha were scrambling out. "Hold on to her, Lloyd," I called, "and stay by the guardrail." Then at the blast of more horns from passing cars, I said, "Lillian, I'm afraid to open my door. Somebody'll take it right off. I'm going to stay right here."

"Yes'm, and now I see that railin' and how far down the path is, I am, too. Lloyd, you an' Latisha wanta take these brownies to

189

Coleman?"

"Yeah, yeah!" Latisha said, hopping up and down. "We'll take 'em, won't we, Lloyd? Maybe Coleman let us climb up there with him. Come on, le's go see."

Lillian handed the brownies to Lloyd, then walked over to the guardrail to watch as the children climbed over and slid down the incline to the path below. She came and sat back down sideways in the open door as we watched them wend their way to Coleman's sign.

He leaned over the side of the platform to talk to them, but with the cars passing and horns blowing, we couldn't hear what he was saying. But we watched as he lowered a box with the pulley and as Lloyd placed the brownies in it. Up it went, eliciting a huge grin and a wave from Coleman when he saw what Lillian had sent.

Then Latisha turned and dashed back up the path. "Great-granny! Great-granny! I need some money. Quick, throw me some money! I got to help fill up Coleman's money bucket!"

Lillian and I both started scrounging in our pocketbooks to make a donation for a good cause. "I should've thought this out a little better," I said. "The wind will blow paper money away, and Latisha can't catch a handful of change. She'll be searching the swamp for hours."

"Here," Lillian said, pulling out a small pouch from her large tapestry handbag. "Le's put our money in this, and Latisha can bring it back. I hope, 'cause that's what I keep my hair pick in."

While we waited for the children to dump money from pouch to bucket, then watched it go back up to Coleman, I took note of what I could see on the platform. Besides the lawn chair, I saw that he had a small tent — sort of a miniature Quonset hut — at one end, some kind of metal-looking canister that I hoped was a heat source, a stack of magazines that the wind was playing havoc with, and what looked like a boom box with speakers large enough to entertain the entire county. And he had three more days and three nights to go in such rugged circumstances.

After calling the children several times, Lillian finally got them up the path, over the rail, and back in the car. While I waited behind the wheel, I was appeased to realize that all the horn blowing had not been aimed at me but was to draw Coleman's attention. Just as we drove off, two cars pulled onto the paved shoulder that we'd just vacated. A woman in a head scarf got out of one, carefully carrying a sack as she edged between the cars to the guardrail. More goodies for Coleman and maybe more donations, too. Monkey bars couldn't be too far in the future.

"Great-granny," Latisha said in a rush, "you know what that Coleman had on? A big ole sweater an' shorts an' flip-flops! If I put them kinda things on, you'd say, 'Latisha, you not goin' outta the house lookin' like that.'"

Lillian agreed that she would say exactly that, and for a few minutes as we drove a couple of blocks before turning around for home, there was quiet in the car.

Then Latisha said, "I don't guess he goin' anywhere, so he can wear what he wants to. But what I want to know is where's he goin' to the bathroom."

Lillian said, "That's not something you need to worry about."

I said, "I expect he's thought up some arrangement, Latisha."

I glanced up at the rearview mirror and saw Lloyd lean over and whisper in Latisha's ear. She jerked back in disbelief and, staring wide-eyed at him, yelled, *"Over the side?"*

Still thinking about Coleman's personal hygiene situation, Latisha was mostly quiet on the way home. She became more animated, though, when I suggested to Lloyd that he stay over to keep her and Lillian company while I went to the sewing group that evening.

Later, as Lillian was preparing supper, I heard Latisha whispering to him. Busy with the mail, I caught only the occasional "But *how*?" and *"Why?"* Finally, Lloyd had had enough, or maybe he had told all he was willing to tell, for I heard him say, "Latisha, you'll have to figure that out yourself. I've got homework to do."

Having had no experience in explaining certain anatomical differences, I was glad she hadn't come to me.

CHAPTER 20

After the evening meal and taking a long, interesting call from Sam, I walked next door to Mildred's. Staying as long as I could within the light from the streetlamp on the corner, I occasionally sidestepped into the street to keep my footing. The darkest place was at the line between our lots, filled as it was with boundary plantings of dogwoods, azaleas, forsythia, and laurels on both our sides. The area was glorious in the spring, but a little spooky in the early November night.

I made my way easily toward the flickering gaslit sconces flanking Mildred's front door, although walking up her curved drive was somewhat hazardous. Several cars were already parked there, which meant that I was late. I didn't mind, because talking with Sam and hearing his comments about a senile judge who'd just won reelection were worth being the last one to arrive.

Ida Lee welcomed me and led me into Mildred's double living room, where Sue, Roberta, Callie, LuAnne, and, of course, Mildred were already delving into the sewing boxes. *Leave it to Mildred,* I thought, as I saw that she had rearranged her fine French furniture to form a circle in front of the fireplace, where a small fire fluttered around ceramic logs.

Well, of course I don't mean that *she* had done the moving, but she'd directed it.

"It's just chilly enough to warrant a fire," she said as she patted the chair next to her. "Come on, Julia, you're late and we need to get some work done."

"Sorry," I said, taking the chair. "We took the children out to see Coleman this afternoon, so supper was later than usual." I laughed. "I think Latisha would've stayed if Lillian had let her."

"Oh," Roberta moaned, "aren't you all worried sick about Coleman? When the temperature started going down as it got dark, all I could think of was how he must be *suffering.*"

"He'll be all right," Mildred said, unconcerned, as she snipped off a length of embroidery thread. "If he gets cold enough, he'll come down."

"I do hope so," Roberta said as she clasped

a felt Christmas tree to her bosom. "He's such a *giving* person that he could do himself harm by living so much for others as he does."

Hm-m, I thought as I glanced at Roberta in the throes of hero worship, *I hadn't noticed that.* Not that Coleman wasn't a kind, thoughtful person, of which I had long been aware, but I seriously doubted his desire for martyrdom.

"Okay, ladies," Callie said, holding up her ornament, "I've finally finished this reindeer and it's the last one I'm making. I've sewn his horns on three times, and they're still crooked. I'm switching to something easier this time."

Roberta bent over her ornament. "Antlers," she said.

"Antlers, horns, who cares?" Callie said. "They both grow out of his head, and I'm through making either one."

"Do a star," LuAnne said. "They're easy, and there're several already cut out."

"Hand 'em here, then. And the yarn box, too."

The muted ring of a telephone somewhere in the depths of the house made us all look at Mildred, expecting her to answer it, as we would've done in our homes. She didn't stir, just kept on sewing, then shrugged in

196

response, and said, "Ida Lee will get it."

I straightened to ease my back, then glanced around the circle. "Mildred, we're going to have bits of thread and yarn all over this beautiful Aubusson. You should've put us at the kitchen table."

"I don't mind," Mildred said, laughing, "and neither does Ida Lee. Besides, I just finished having the old elevator refurbished, so we'll be doing a thorough housecleaning anyway."

"Good gracious," LuAnne said. "I didn't know you had an elevator."

"Oh, it's back yonder," Mildred said with a wave of her hand. "We haven't used it in years. But I got tired of trudging up and down stairs all day long just because I thought I needed the exercise."

Roberta, off in space somewhere, held up her Santa ornament to see how it looked. "Did you get any?"

"Roberta!" We all glared at her, because Mildred's generous size was never referred to by any of us.

Roberta looked up, blinking. "What?"

Mildred, bless her heart, laughed. "Well, not enough, obviously. Anyway, it was getting too hard to get up the stairs, so I thought, why have an elevator and not use it? So we do."

None of us had anything to say to that, so we stayed pretty much on target by working steadily on our ornaments. We finished several and started on others by the time Ida Lee served tea, finger sandwiches, and biscotti — more extras as only Mildred would do.

"Has anyone heard anything from Emma Sue?" LuAnne asked as she took two of the tiny sandwiches from Ida Lee's tray. "Sue, do you know anything?" Sue Hargrove, the doctor's wife, was our go-to person when any medical question came up.

"Not a word," Sue said, shaking her head. "But they may not know anything yet. I'm sure they'll do a battery of tests, so it could be several days before we hear." She threaded an embroidery needle. "I just wonder who'll be preaching Sunday. They left in such a hurry that the pastor might not've had time to get a substitute."

Startled to think that the pastor could leave me hanging for several days, I said, "Surely he'll be back tomorrow."

"Well, I don't know," Sue said. "If they admit her, he'll probably stay for a while. I expect he'll call one of the elders to take the service on Sunday."

Mildred smiled and said, "Y'all can to come to the Episcopal church. We'll be happy to have you."

I may just do that, I thought, but got sidetracked before I could say anything.

"What's wrong with her, anyway?" Callie asked. "I mean, why did she have to go to a specialist?"

"Migraines," Sue answered in a tone that invited no further questions. Her husband had been treating Emma Sue, but now had apparently been judged insufficient.

"Well," LuAnne said, "what's happening in this town is enough to give anybody a migraine."

"What?" Roberta asked, suddenly interested. "What's going on besides Coleman's sacrificial outing?"

"Roberta," LuAnne said, "don't you hear anything at that library? I'm talking about Connie Clayborn being killed in her own kitchen, and I think it's strange that nobody is talking about it. I mean, how often is a prominent woman found dead in this town? And everybody just goes on about their business like it happens every week. But I'll tell you, it's been a real shock to my system. Although," she said after a pause, "I am relieved I won't have to enter that run next week."

"Nobody's talking about it," Mildred said, coming to my rescue so that the conversation wouldn't turn to my involvement, "because nobody knows anything. Obviously, it's under investigation, so it doesn't help for us to be speculating."

"I wonder, though," Roberta said, gazing off into the distance, "how they'll manage without Coleman. You'd think the sheriff would want him on that assignment."

Mildred's eyes rolled just a little. "I expect the sheriff has it well in hand. But has anybody met Connie's husband? He's been strangely out of the picture, it seems to me."

That could've been my cue to say that I had met him, but before I made up my mind to do so, Roberta went back to her favorite subject.

"Well," she said, "I went out there today, you know, to drop a donation in his bucket and to take him some hot doughnuts. I know how he likes them, and I asked him . . ."

"Who?" Callie asked. "Connie's husband?"

"No, Coleman. I asked Coleman if he knew who'd killed her."

"What'd he say?" LuAnne asked eagerly.

"He said he didn't know, because he'd been off duty. As, of course, I knew, him being where he is. But he was so sweet, thanking me over and over for the doughnuts. He loves doughnuts."

Really rolling her eyes this time, Mildred said, "*All* cops do," as if she knew the gastronomic preferences of every law enforcement unit in the country.

As the ladies got into their cars and began to pull out of Mildred's driveway, I lingered by the door for a few minutes. I was feeling I'd been somewhat dishonest by letting everyone assume that, like them, I had not met Connie's husband. Of them all, Mildred was the only one I felt I could trust, so I was about to tell her about my visitor the evening before. Before I could bring it up, though, she took my breath away with something else entirely.

"I think Roberta has a crush on Coleman, don't you?"

"What? Oh, surely not, she just gets these little enthusiasms now and then, and she, well, she's Roberta. Don't you remember how she ordered all six videos of *Pride and Prejudice* just so she could have Mr. Darcy on her shelf?"

"Well, that's true," Mildred conceded, laughing. "Bless her heart, we need to find her a husband."

"Maybe so," I said, laughing with her, "but, believe me, it won't be Coleman. I

201

shudder to think what Binkie would do if she thought somebody was after him. This town would never be the same."

Still smiling at the thought, I thanked Mildred for her hospitality and started down the drive toward my house. Calling after me to scream if anybody got me, Mildred closed the door and left me to it.

CHAPTER 21

With the cars gone, the drive was wide and well lit by the light from Mildred's sconces — easy walking. Through the branches of the now leafless trees, I could see my own porch light and the streetlamp beyond it.

It was a matter of only a minute or two to step up to my own door, where Lillian would be waiting for me.

As I reached the sidewalk at the foot of Mildred's drive, I became aware of a soft but steady thumping sound. Looking around, I saw only the empty street — no cars, no walkers, not even a swirling leaf. Moving right along, I tried to place the source of the sound and vaguely thought that someone blocks away was running a generator. Then the sound conjured an image, and I knew what I was hearing — the measured thump of a runner's feet pounding on pavement.

I stopped halfway home, wondering if I

should go back to Mildred's or hurry on to my house. As I vacillated, the sound of running shoes beating rhythmically against concrete was coming ever closer.

Without thinking, I slid in between two large boxwoods, scraping my hand against a forsythia branch, and melted behind an azalea bush — an evergreen one, thank goodness. A running figure sprang into the light at the corner of my front yard, crossed Polk Street, and turned to run down Polk right across the street from me.

It was a man, tall and thin, churning away in latex and large running shoes with neon patches. He wore a shiny jacket, but nothing below the tight-fitting running shorts, so that his white legs looked like a pair of scissors zipping along the sidewalk. I strained to see who it was, but the visored ball cap he wore low on his brow shielded his face. He didn't pause, slow down, or turn his head, just loped along as the streetlight behind him stretched his shadow ever longer down the sidewalk until he looked like a thin-legged stork high stepping in front of me. He soon passed out of my sight into the darkness beyond, as the soft thumps of his shoes dwindled in the night air.

I slid out of the bushes and hurried home, trembling and on edge. I hadn't been able to get a good look at the runner's face, but the first thought that had entered my head as he passed by began to form more clearly in my mind. The figure had looked an awful lot like the man I'd met the night before — minus a woolen suit and a silk tie, but a self-confessed runner.

If so, though, what was he doing in this part of town late at night? The Clayborn house was some five miles from Polk Street. Why would he choose this street to run on? Was he watching my house? Or watching me?

"I'm sorry I'm so late, Lillian," I said as she met me at the door. "But thank you for waiting up." I turned and locked the door, deciding that I would not mention the runner. He was probably a perfectly innocent man out for exercise, although he'd chosen a strange time and place to get it.

"You're not so late," Lillian said. "The news not even on yet."

"I know, but it feels late. And you've had a long day. Did the children get to bed all right?"

"Yes'm," Lillian said, smiling. "And it been real peaceful ever since."

We went around the house, making sure that all the doors were locked, then, turning out lights as we went, we started up the stairs together.

"Oh, Miss Julia, I almost forget to tell you. But I write it all down." She pulled a piece of notepaper from her pocket and handed it to me. "He say he a detective, an' he want you to call him first thing in the morning."

I took the paper, saw that Lillian had jotted down the time of the call — eight-thirty that evening. In her scratchy writing, she had written: *Call detetive Ellie early tomorow.*

"Oh, my," I said, my heart sinking. "What could he want?"

"He don't tell me. I tole him where you went, but he say no need to bother you tonight."

"Well, I wish he had. Now he'll be bothering me all night long, worrying about what he wants."

And worry I did, getting up several times in the night, each time looking through the blinds down onto the street. Except for the occasional car, it was always empty. I saw no runners, which should've reassured me, but didn't.

And if that wasn't enough to disrupt my rest, there was the phone call from Detective Ellis to worry about.

What could he want with me a second time? Why call so late in the day, then say it wasn't important enough to call me at Mildred's? And with Pastor Ledbetter out of town — obviously avoiding me, although he had a good excuse in Emma Sue — should I go ahead and tell Detective Ellis why I'd gone to Connie's?

And if even that wasn't enough to trouble me, I missed Sam. The bed was too wide and empty without him. It was one of the longest nights I'd ever spent.

The phone started ringing the next morning before I'd had my first cup of coffee, and the first call indicated the way the day would go.

"Julia!" LuAnne demanded, as if something were my fault. "What does Detective Ellis want with *me*?"

"I don't know, LuAnne. Why?"

"He called last night while we were at Mildred's, and Leonard didn't give me the message until just now. And would you believe that detective wants me at the sheriff's office at nine o'clock this morning! What's going on?"

"I have no idea, LuAnne. But maybe he's interviewing Connie's friends."

"Well, I wouldn't exactly call myself a *friend*. I barely knew the woman."

"Then that's all you have to say." And I

207

went on trying to reassure her, and all the while, I, too, was wondering what Detective Ellis was up to.

It didn't get any better when Callie called as soon as I put the phone down. "Julia, did you get a phone call from the sheriff's office last night? What in the world do they want with us? I just talked to Sue, and they've called her, too. I'm supposed to be there at ten, and she's going at eleven."

"Oh, my," I said, "they're running us in every hour on the hour. LuAnne's going at nine, but I don't know when he wants me. I haven't called him back yet."

"Well, you better go ahead and do it. Sounds like they're calling in everybody who knew Connie, but I'd never met her before she had that coffee. I don't know why they want to interview me."

"Me, either," I said, "but, Callie, I better get off this phone and see when he wants me."

"You know what I've a good mind to do? Take all five children with me. I'd probably have the shortest interview on record."

Glad that at least one of my friends could face an official interview with humor, I hung up the phone, stood there a few minutes, then answered it when it rang again.

"Julia, it's Mildred. I haven't been up this

208

early in ages, but Ida Lee woke me because some detective called last night and wants me at the sheriff's office at twelve noon. Who makes an appointment right at lunchtime? I could have a drop in my sugar level and faint dead away. Did you get a call?"

"I did, but I haven't returned it yet. But LuAnne, Sue, and Callie have to go in this morning, too. I don't know what's going on, Mildred, but it's beginning to look as if they're interviewing everybody who was at Connie's coffee."

"That's right! That's exactly what they're doing, because Helen just called me, and she has to go at one this afternoon. What do they expect to find out from a bunch of women who did nothing but stand around and drink coffee?"

I hated to think what they'd find out, because I well remembered the anger and outrage I'd felt — and not only me but everybody else, too — after Connie had criticized us up one side and down the other. Detective Ellis was well titled, for he was undoubtedly detecting into a possible source of extreme umbrage toward Connie Clayborn.

CHAPTER 22

"Binkie?" I said when I was finally able to stop answering calls from worried friends and dial her number. "I'm sorry for calling so early, but I wanted to catch you before you left for the office."

"It's all right, Miss Julia. I've been up for a while. What's going on?"

I told her about the interviewees that Detective Ellis had lined up and told her that I also had a message to call him.

"He's interviewing all of us, Binkie, but I've already been through that. What should I do?"

"Call him back," she said. "Call him right now, and if he's not in, call me back. I have his home number."

"Oh, Binkie, I can't call him at home."

"Yes, you can. He called you at home, didn't he?"

Somehow that didn't seem to be quite the same, but I didn't argue. Sam had told me that the law was an adversarial process, and with Binkie, I was seeing it in action.

Binkie's last command to me was to call her back and let her know what the detective wanted.

So I did, for I had no trouble reaching the detective at the sheriff's department, and was able to call her back just as she was leaving for work.

"He does want to interview me again," I told her, my voice revealing the agitation I was feeling. "Can he do that?"

"Only if you agree to it," she said. "And I advise you to agree for one reason only, and that's to find out how the investigation is going. If he wants to go back over your first interview, I'll put a stop to it. But if there's something new, I want to know it. We'll be able to tell what he's up to by his questions."

"You'll be there with me?"

"Absolutely. When does he want you?"

"This afternoon, about three. I'm way down on the list, so maybe that's a good sign."

"I'll call and tell him we'll be there at four."

"It doesn't matter, Binkie. Three, four, if I have to do it, either one is fine with me."

Binkie laughed. "We don't want to be too

accommodating. Let him wait. Four is soon enough. I'll meet you there a few minutes before."

Goodness, I thought as I hung up. Adversarial might have been the correct description, but it was sounding more like a game between Detective Ellis and Binkie, although, to tell the truth, I didn't feel much like playing.

By the time I readied myself to make a return trip to the sheriff's office, I'd heard from all those who had been interviewed before me. Not that I hadn't thought of them all day long, wondering what they were saying and what conclusions Detective Ellis was drawing.

One after the other, Mildred, LuAnne, Callie, Helen, and Sue called to tell me how their interviews had gone.

"I was right," Mildred had said. "He wanted to know all about the coffee — who was there, what was said, and especially if there'd been any spats with Connie."

"Spats? What does that mean?"

"Fusses, fights, arguments, and the like, I guess. I told him I didn't know what kind of social life he led, but we weren't accustomed to such unpleasant occurrences in ours, and nobody *spatted* with anybody."

"That's true," I said, "but none of us was happy by the time we left."

"Believe me, Julia," she said with a sigh, "he knew all about that by the time he got to me. I don't know what LuAnne and Callie and whoever else he interviewed said, but he already knew that Connie had upset us all. I just spoke to LuAnne, and she swore that she'd not said a word. Just told him that she was devastated that such a kind and far-seeing woman had been struck down. *Then,* Julia, do you know what she said?"

"What?"

"She told me that she was disappointed that the Run for Rehab had been canceled, and then she said she'd asked Detective Ellis if they'd found any trophies in Connie's house. She thinks that everybody who'd signed up — all three of them, I expect — ought to get them because they'd *tried* to run!"

The only bright spot of the day had been when I'd called Norma Cantrell to ask if there'd been any word from the pastor about his return. Couching my question in terms of concern for Emma Sue, I was relieved to learn that they were on their way home as we spoke. So if, during the approaching interview, I could avoid answering a direct question as to the reason for my second visit to Connie's house, I would get my release from the pastor and make a full and complete confession soon enough.

Sitting in the same small room where they'd put me before, I waited with Binkie for my second interview. We were sitting side by side, for Binkie had moved one of the two chairs to my side of the table — something I was not bold enough to do. But Binkie was not intimidated and thought nothing of rearranging the sheriff's furniture.

"Binkie," I said, trying mightily to hide my dread of what was to come. "How's Coleman doing on his sign today?"

She grinned. "Well, he's decided that flip-flops aren't ideal for the weather — so he's wearing his wool socks and hiking boots. Put on his long johns, too. He's been lucky so far since we've not been below freezing. But," she said, laughing, "he didn't get much sleep last night. Said he was all snuggled up in his sleeping bag when about three o'clock, one of the youth groups from church came by with a water balloon launcher."

"My goodness, I hope he wasn't hurt. Did he arrest them?"

"Oh, no, it was in good fun, and he didn't care. Except, that is, when he crawled out of the tent, one of the balloons hit the sign above his head and almost drowned him."

After an abrupt knock, Detective Ellis strode in, smiling his let's-all-pretend-we-like-each-other smile. I knew better by now, but he could still take me in with the patient, yet concerned, expression that came over his face with each question. That expression now seemed somewhat strained, and from his wrinkled shirt I figured he'd had a long and grueling day interviewing the likes of the women I knew.

"Ms. Bates," he said, nodding at Binkie. "Glad you could join us."

Binkie grinned. "I bet. But thank you for inviting me."

He grinned back at her, while I realized that this wasn't the first time those two had been legal opponents.

"And, Mrs. Murdoch," he went on, "thank you for coming down again. I only have a few things to go over, just to get a better picture of what may've led to the attack on Ms. Clayborn." He put a legal pad and a recording machine on the table, scooted his chair up close, and gave me a warm smile.

"This won't take long, but I do have to record our conversation. Is that all right with you? Like I told you before, it's really for your protection."

After looking at Binkie, who nodded, I nodded at Detective Ellis, and he went through the recitation of names, dates, and so forth, as he'd done at my previous visit.

As I stiffened in anticipation of his questions, he turned a few pages on his pad, looked up at me, and said, "What I'd like to talk about today is that morning when you and some other ladies were invited by Ms. Clayborn to her house. Tell me about that."

Well, I happened to know that he'd asked the very same question of everyone he'd seen that day, so what more could I tell him? I suspected that he was looking for discrepancies among the accounts, but he didn't realize how many notes had been compared through a series of telephone calls.

So I told it from my perspective — that I'd almost not accepted the invitation, went only for the sake of politeness, and to visit with friends, and hadn't particularly liked Connie's house.

"Uh-huh, uh-huh," Detective Ellis said, nodding encouragement throughout my narrative. "Now tell me what you heard Ms. Clayborn say about the town and what she'd like to do to it."

"Pretty much what everybody else heard,

I expect."

"Oh, we always hear things differently, don't you think? I'd like to know what you thought was important in what she said."

"Well," I said, and began reeling off Connie's plans for rehabilitating the town — Main Street especially, and the old courthouse park specifically — even as I glanced now and then at Binkie to be sure I was not missing any signals from her.

"Okay," the detective said. He flipped another page on his pad, then went on. "How did you ladies respond to her suggestions?"

"We listened."

"I know, but did anybody say they didn't like her ideas?"

"Nobody said anything."

"Well, then give me some specifics. What exactly did she want to do?"

"Bulldoze both sides of Main Street, for one thing, and most of the houses in town, for another."

Detective Ellis's eyebrows went straight up. "Really?" He scribbled that down. "And nobody objected?"

"She said it later, as we were leaving, so not everybody heard it."

"But you heard it."

"*Over*heard it, because she wasn't speaking to me." I glanced at Binkie, who was watching Detective Ellis with squinched-up eyes.

"How did the ladies respond to this grand rehabilitation scheme? Were they for it? Against it? Was there any discussion about it later? Did anybody say anything to you?"

"I try not to repeat what's told to me, Detective. Things tend to get muddled when they're told over and over."

"I understand," he said, sounding as if he really did, "but you realize that you could help solve a shocking crime. So let's take it as a given that you don't engage in gossip, but there might be something you can share with me that'll help the investigation."

I should've known that when anyone uses the word *share,* it's time to look out. They want to unload on you, or, more likely, want you to unload on them. Binkie was staying quiet, so I gingerly recalled a few things I felt safe in *sharing.*

"Well, Mrs. Conover thought she'd been tricked into participating in the Run for Rehab. She was fairly hot about it, until Connie said there'd be trophies for everybody. She was fine with it after that. And my friend Mrs. Allen just laughed at the idea of tearing down and rebuilding Main Street. I can't recall anything else. Oh, wait," I said, wanting to prove to Detective Ellis that I could be open and aboveboard, but without tattling on my friends. "I think a few people came down with headaches afterward, but I wouldn't necessarily say it was because of what Connie wanted us to do. A lot of people get headaches when jobs are being handed out."

"Uh-huh. Okay, you've told me how some responded, but, Mrs. Murdoch, how about yourself? Did you say anything in rebuttal? You know, stand up and say something like, 'We like our town the way it is,' or, 'This sounds like more than we can take on'?"

I shook my head. "No, it wasn't the time or the place. I figured she'd find out soon enough that she was biting off more than she could chew. Besides, there wasn't time for a long discussion. People had things to do, so we were getting ready to leave."

"Sounds like y'all were anxious to go. Why was that? Was there a problem?"

"No, we'd been there a couple of hours. We'd eaten, we'd socialized, we'd listened to Connie's ideas, and it was time to go. See, Detective Ellis, if we'd stayed any longer, the hostess would've felt obligated to offer us lunch. And that's not the way we do things in Abbotsville."

"I see," he said, although I wasn't sure he

did, it being highly unlikely that he'd ever been to a ladies' coffee. He tapped his pen against his pad as he studied me intently. "But tell me this, Mrs. Murdoch, what did you really think about Ms. Clayborn's proposals? How did you feel when you had to listen to what sounds to me like pretty ruthless criticism, not just of the town but of each one of you personally?"

Detective Ellis *did* understand, I thought, and opened my mouth to tell him how white-faced with anger I'd been at Connie and her arrogance in condemning us for being slack, lazy, and unwilling to lift our hands for the betterment of those who would come after us. Then I closed my mouth, afraid of what would come out if I ever started.

Detective Ellis waited for my reply, then to encourage me, he said, "I know Ms. Clayborn was pretty hard on you ladies, and probably accused you of some things you had every right to resent. I'd just like to know your reaction, what you thought as you sat there listening to her."

He waited patiently for my response, a look of understanding and concern softening his face. "I know this is difficult for you, Mrs. Murdoch. But it's important for me to know if there were any hard feelings toward her — on anybody's part. Was anybody angry or upset about what she'd said?"

"I can't speak for everyone."

"I understand. But what about yourself? I'd really like to know how you felt?"

And, again, I almost let it all spew out — how I'd felt and what I'd thought and why I'd taken myself to Connie's house a second time, even though I hadn't wanted to go even the first time. It was all I could do to contain it all, but years of restraint stood me in good stead.

"Binkie," I said, turning to her, "I believe I'll take the Fifth on that."

Chapter 23

"You did fine, Miss Julia." Binkie and I were standing outside the sheriff's brick building before going our separate ways. Then she peered closely at me. "Are you all right? You look a little peaked."

"I feel a little peaked," I said. "Binkie, did I do myself in by taking the Fifth?"

She smiled and patted my shoulder. "You didn't take the Fifth. I didn't give you time."

And she hadn't. Before the words were out of my mouth good, up she'd popped from her chair, talking over me. "Mrs. Murdoch is tired, Detective. Let's continue this another time. I think you've quite overtaxed her."

I remembered thinking as she urged me to my feet that she was right — he should've seen my tax bill last year. Of course, at the same time I knew that Detective Ellis had had nothing to do with that, and I'd begun laughing at my own errant thoughts.

"See, Detective," Binkie had said as she shoved my pocketbook at me and urged me toward the door, "my client needs to rest. She missed her nap today."

Detective Ellis hadn't been sympathetic because he'd said, "I have one last question." He looked kindly at me. "If you don't mind, Mrs. Murdoch, let's go over your actions one more time after you found Ms. Clayborn on the floor. You squatted beside her, shook her shoulder, called her name, pulled down her skirt, and about that time the lights went out. Describe for me in detail what you did then."

"Well," I said, hating to mentally put myself back in that place. "Well, first of all, I was too scared to do anything, as I told you. Then when I heard something somewhere in the house, I knew I had to get out. So I stood up . . ."

"Just like that?" Detective Ellis asked. "You jumped up and ran out?"

"Hardly, Detective. I couldn't just spring up without help. When you get to be my age and your knees give out on you, you'll know what I'm talking about. No, I had to struggle to get to my feet, just as I have to do when I work in the yard, so I was able to push myself up with my hands. See, when you're as scared as I was, you can do what you think you can't do. But I was very careful not to disturb Connie — even with the lights out, I could see well enough to get up without touching her. Then I ran out."

"But you had to put your hands in some of the blood on the floor?"

"No!" I said, shocked at first, but after thinking for a minute, went on. "At least, not on purpose. But when I got outside, there was blood on one hand — the left one, I think." My voice was quavering by this time, and I was feeling teary as I tried to remember where I'd put my hands when I'd pushed myself off the floor. "But, Detective Ellis, whichever it was, I didn't mean to."

"Okay," Binkie said, moving toward the door. "That's enough for today."

"She has to be fingerprinted," Detective Ellis said. "Let's get that done before you leave."

"Binkie?" I said, trembling. They really did suspect me, because none of the other ladies had said they'd been fingerprinted.

"It's just routine, Miss Julia," she said soothingly, although Binkie didn't do soothing so well. "You were there, and you touched things. They need your prints so they can distinguish them from whoever else was there."

"Well, put that way . . ." And we'd followed Detective Ellis to another room, where my finger-, thumb-, and palm prints were taken and probably entered into some database on file in the bowels of the government to be accessible to every law officer in the nation. I could be a future suspect in a crime committed in, say, Idaho. Or New Jersey, even.

As we left the room and walked down the hall to the exit, I recalled Binkie's remark about my being tired and overtaxed by the detective's questions — and missing my nap. I removed my arm from her clasp and glared at her. "Now, Binkie, I'll have you know that I don't appreciate your implying that I'm senile."

"Sh-h-h," she said, grinning as she glanced behind us. "Nobody knows better how sharp you are than I, Miss Julia. But I wanted you out of there before Detective Ellis thought you were hiding something. Which is what it sounded like when you mentioned the Fifth."

So then there we were standing out in the weak November sunshine in front of the sheriff's office, as she explained that she'd rather the detective think I'd lost some of my marbles than that I was hiding something important to his investigation.

"I guess I was hiding something, Binkie. See, it was like this. I . . ."

"Don't tell me. I don't need to know."

"Well, somebody needs to know, because it's bothering me. So just listen. I *was* angry at Connie Clayborn. I was so mad, I could hardly see straight — mad at her arrogance, mad at her insolence in presuming that she knew everything, and mad that some one of us hadn't slapped her cross-eyed. But, Binkie, I did not hurt her."

"Miss Julia, I know that." Binkie took my arm as we began walking toward our cars. "But I wanted you out of there before Detective Ellis knew how angry you'd been at her."

"Well, but I wasn't the only one. We all were, and now all I can do is wonder who, *among my friends,* might've been mad enough to do what was done. It's a terrible thing to live with."

We'd reached our cars by that time, and still we lingered on the sidewalk. "I know," Binkie said with sympathy. "But I can't believe that any of them had a thing to do with it, and I can't believe that Detective Ellis does, either.

"But, Miss Julia, you shouldn't be discussing this with anybody. It doesn't matter if everybody else felt the way you did. If you're now having suspicions about them, you can bet that they're having the same about you. So just keep everything to yourself." She stopped, looked closely at me again, and said, "Are you all right to drive home?"

"I'm fine. All I need is a little rest. I missed my nap today."

I had to stop and pull to the side of the road before I got halfway home, and home was only eight blocks away. It had suddenly come to me that I'd admitted to Binkie something I'd not been able to face myself.

All along, ever since I'd walked into Connie's kitchen and found her on the floor, I'd been wondering, way back where vague, unformed thoughts begin, about my friends — running each of them through my mind and questioning their hidden capabilities.

I'd heard them — Mildred had been furious at Connie, LuAnne had felt tricked and compelled to do something she couldn't do, and Emma Sue couldn't do anything but turn her anger against herself, as she usually did. But even though I was loathe to remind myself — which I did anyway — Emma Sue's aggressive husband didn't work that way.

And who knew the level of anger among

the others who'd been trapped into listening to Connie's sneering rant against all we held dear? No wonder Detective Ellis had looked so tired and strained — he had too many suspects.

I rubbed my eyes, trying to think clearly even as I castigated myself for considering the possibility that people I'd known most of my life were capable of causing what I'd found in that kitchen.

How I longed for Sam, so much so that it crossed my mind to turn around and drive to Raleigh. Accost him in his hotel room and bare my soul so he could assure me that there was no way in the world that what was flickering in my mind could actually have happened. Why, I'd even wondered about that lovely Sue Hargrove, who'd spent weeks designing and stitching angels' wings and sprinkling them with gold glitter.

How could I suspect any one of us? Well, maybe because I had no other options. Except, I thought, Connie's husband — Stan, the night runner. So where was he in Detective Ellis's investigation? How many times had he been interviewed?

Those were the things that I so wanted to discuss with Sam, who wasn't there to discuss anything. With him, I wouldn't have had to watch my words, weigh my opinions, or withhold anything. I could express myself fully, and, I suddenly realized, I could feel perfectly free and justified to tell him exactly why I visited Connie that awful day when I found myself at the wrong place at the wrong time.

If Sam had been home, I could've told it all for I would've no longer felt constrained by my promise to the pastor. Too much had happened since I'd made it, and after he'd taken Emma Sue out of town — thereby avoiding me — he could no longer, in conscience, hold me to it.

So I quickly drove home, hoping and half praying that Sam would be there or that he'd left word he'd be home the next day. Instead, Lillian was frying chicken — jumping back each time the grease popped — Lloyd was in the library watching television while doing homework on the floor, and Latisha was running back and forth between them, talking and talking.

"Has Sam called?" I asked as soon as I got in the door.

"No'm, 'less he call while Latisha talkin', an' I didn't hear it."

At a burst of laughter from Latisha, I said, "I'm going upstairs to put my feet up for a while. If the phone rings, I'll get it."

I'd barely settled myself in the easy chair

in our bedroom when the phone rang. I snatched it up before one of the children answered it.

"Julia," Sam said, and I felt the tension in my body begin to ease away. "How are you, honey?"

"Oh, Sam," I said, as tears sprang to my eyes in relief at the sound of his voice. "I'm fine, but how are you? Have you decided what to do about that senile judge?"

Of course I wasn't fine, but I didn't want to inundate him with my problems before expressing my interest in his.

He laughed. "I tell you, Julia, when you're part of a committee or board or whatever we are, you have to listen to every member's opinion. Then everybody has an opinion about that opinion. But I'm enjoying it, more than I thought I would. Everybody's congenial — of course, I knew several before I got here, went to law school with a couple — so we all get along.

"But the best times, Julia, are at dinner. You'd think we'd get enough of each other during the day, but we don't. We sit around a table in a restaurant and talk and talk, tell tall tales, and laugh our heads off. Then we fall into bed and get up the next day and do it all over again. It would be perfect if you were here. I miss you, sweetheart."

That was thoughtful of him to say, but I knew he wouldn't have felt free to go and come with his friends if I'd been there.

Unhappily for me, he sounded so light-hearted and enthusiastic about what he was doing that I could not bring myself to unload a pile of worries on him. I could wait until he got home.

"When will you be home, Sam?"

"Maybe tomorrow, late. We'll definitely finish up tomorrow if we can agree on the wording of the report we have to submit to the governor. If we can't, it'll be Sunday, for sure. We're watching the weather channel, and we all want to be home by Sunday afternoon before that storm moves in."

I could do nothing but accept that, even though it meant continuing to carry my worrisome burden alone for another long day. Which, I reminded myself, is what good wives do.

CHAPTER 24

That wasn't the end of the telephone calls on that busy day. Just as Lillian announced supper, the phone rang again.

"Julia, it's Sue Hargrove," she said. "I know we've all had a hard day and you probably have plans, but my house is empty tonight. Everybody's off doing one thing or another, and I thought a few of us might get together to work on ornaments."

"You may be a lifesaver, Sue," I said. "Sam's away, too, and my house is full of children — loud ones. Actually, only two, but it sounds like more. I'd love to get away for a while. I'll see if Mildred wants a ride."

"I just spoke to her, and she thinks she's getting a cold, so she's going to stay in. Helen has plans so she can't come. It'll just be Roberta, LuAnne, Callie, and you and me. We'll get started about seven, if that's not too early for you."

"Not at all. See you then."

Learning that Mildred was coming down with a cold, I thought of Hazel Marie, realizing that I had not checked on her lately. So even though the phone had rarely been left alone that day, I used it again.

"Hazel Marie," I began as soon as she answered, "I apologize for not calling you before this, but I've been keeping up with you through Lloyd. And, by the way, thank you for letting him stay with us — he's been wonderful with Latisha. And of course I always love having him. But how is everybody at your house?"

"I think we'll live, but it's been touch and go. As soon as one of us begins to feel better, somebody else gets worse."

A coughing fit overtook her, so I waited until it was over.

"Miss Julia," she was finally able to say, although her voice was raspy, "I was shocked to read about Connie Clayborn. I didn't know her, but I know you did. You must be devastated."

"I was. I mean, I am."

"But you *found* her? How awful for you!"

Before I could respond, Hazel Marie was convulsed with more coughing. It went on so long that I said, "Why don't we talk when you're feeling better." Gasping for breath, she agreed. So, hoping that she had a good supply of Robitussin, I hung up and went to the kitchen for dinner.

Gathering my pocketbook and car keys, I told Lillian where I was going and urged her not to wait up for me.

"Just leave a lot of lights on downstairs," I said. "It'll look as if somebody's up." That dark figure running by our house was still on my mind.

As I drove to Sue's almost authentic Cape Cod house, it occurred to me that getting together tonight might not be such a good idea. We were certainly behind with our sale items — reason enough for a sewing session — but I had a feeling that after the day we'd all had, there'd be more on our minds than Christmas ornaments.

I knew I wanted to talk, or rather to listen — we'd all been interviewed by Detective Ellis and I wanted to know what he'd asked and, more important, how they'd answered. Well, Roberta wouldn't have been interviewed. At least, I assumed she hadn't because she'd not been invited to Connie's coffee.

And thinking of Roberta made me think of Coleman. We should've gone out to see him again, but, I declare, I'd had too much on my mind that day. But then I thought,

Coleman. Wouldn't he be a perfect stand-in for Sam? Binkie hadn't wanted to hear about my inner turmoil, which was understandable. She was my lawyer and couldn't put herself in the position of defending the indefensible, if I happened to fall into that category. No way could I talk to Lillian that night, either, because nothing could be said that would be out of Lloyd's hearing, much less Latisha's.

So I was about to explode, needing to release some of the stress I was under. But no one knew better than I that I would have to hold my tongue in the presence of a bunch of women who were also under stress and who couldn't be trusted, even in the best of times, not to tell everything they heard to everybody they knew.

I determined to keep a tight rein on my mouth. I would listen, learn what I could, but I wouldn't say one thing that could be repeated, and likely repeated incorrectly.

Sue had us around her quilt-covered dining room table again, and for a while the conversation was, if somewhat subdued, pleasant enough. We worked on our ornaments and confined our talk to how one color worked with another and the like.

Finally, LuAnne could stand it no longer.

"Well, I don't know why we're not talking about those interviews we had. That's the main reason I came tonight, but we've been sitting around here like being questioned by the police is an everyday occurrence. But, I tell you, it's not for me. Where're the scissors?" She looked around, found them, and snipped a thread. "I don't even know why they had me come in in the first place. I'd only met her that one time."

Roberta looked up, blinking. "Who?"

"Connie Clayborn," LuAnne said. "It was in the paper, Roberta."

"I think they wanted to know what we thought of her," Sue said in her calm way. "Particularly if anybody had any hard feelings toward her."

"Well," LuAnne said, "*I* certainly had no hard feelings toward her."

I couldn't hold my tongue. "Why, Lu-Anne, you were beside yourself because she'd trapped you into signing up for that Run for Rehab, or whatever it was."

"Well, Julia, it was you who said Connie would get what was coming to her sooner or later."

"I most certainly did not!" I said. "How could you say such a thing? Did you tell that to Detective Ellis?"

"I had to tell the truth. When he asked me

236

if anybody'd been mad at Connie for telling us all her wonderful plans for Abbotsville, what else could I do?"

"Ladies," Sue said, putting down her angel, "let's stop for a while and have some coffee. It's decaf."

I struggled to keep my composure. I had known full well that LuAnne would tell everything she knew and a few things she only thought she knew. Still, it was shocking to learn that she had repeated my words to Detective Ellis, except I didn't think I'd said those exact words. At least to her.

Callie said, "That detective asked me the same thing — who was mad at her and if anybody had been upset at Connie's coffee, and I told him the truth, too. I told him we'd all been upset, but, LuAnne, I didn't quote anybody directly. You need to be careful about that."

I could've hugged Callie.

"Well, what I think," Sue said, "is that they're looking into her background, and talking to anybody who'd known her. We just happened to be part of that."

"I think you're right, Sue," I said. "And that brings up a lot of possibilities. We don't know who all she knew before she moved here. With all the places they'd lived, who knows how many unsavory people she'd come across? Somebody could've been tracking her or following her till they found her. We just don't know anything about her or her husband."

Roberta had been listening to the various opinions, looking from one to the other of us. She said, "Maybe they were in the drug trade."

"Roberta!" we all cried.

"Well," she said, immediately on the defensive, "I heard their house was full of unopened boxes and crates and cartons. Does anybody know what was in them?"

"Furniture," I said. "At least that's what Connie told me." But I couldn't help but wonder — had that been true? If they'd brought something back from, say, Switzerland that shouldn't have been brought, could it have also brought big-time trouble, too?

"Well, see, Julia," LuAnne said, "you had more contact with her than any of us. No wonder the detective was so interested in you. So don't blame me if he asked about you."

"LuAnne," Callie said, rolling her eyes, "even my three-year-old knows not to tell on people. You know good and well that Julia did not kill Connie, so why you have to blab everything you know is beyond me."

"Well," LuAnne said, taking immediate umbrage, "I certainly didn't *say* Julia had anything to do with it. I just don't like being questioned by the police like a common criminal."

"Sheriff's deputy," Roberta corrected.

"Oh, quit being so picky," LuAnne snapped. "Police, sheriff, deputy, what's the difference? I just think that none of us would be involved at all if Julia hadn't gone out there by herself and found her body."

"Believe me," I said, "I wish I hadn't."

"Then why did you?"

Well, there it was, the one question I couldn't truthfully answer. I bit my lip, very nearly on the verge of telling about Emma Sue's extreme reaction to Connie's plans, the pastor's unusual request of me, and my intense desire to speak up for my friend while justifiably giving Connie a piece of my mind.

I thought better of it and clamped down on the urge to let it all out.

"She invited me," I replied, calmly enough. "That was the reason I went. I made a social call at her invitation, and, Lu-Anne, I would appreciate it if you would not quote me to Detective Ellis again. Or to anybody else."

Roberta said, "If Coleman was on duty

and working on this, he'd probably have it all figured out by now."

Several pairs of eyes began rolling, but nobody responded to her. I mean, what could you say?

"When's the funeral?" Callie asked. "Anybody know?"

"Whose funeral?" Roberta asked.

"*Connie Clayborn's,* Roberta!" Callie said. "Who do you think we're talking about?"

"That's a good question," Sue said, responding to Callie. "There's not been an obituary in the paper yet, but it should tell us a lot about her when it gets in. You know, where she's from, who her family is, where she went to school, and so on."

"Vassar," I said. "That's all I know, and I only know that because she asked me if I went there."

"Well, see, Julia," LuAnne said, "that shows you knew her better than any of us."

"No, it doesn't, because she asked Mildred the same thing, and I don't hear you accusing her. And, LuAnne, I'm getting tired of all the implications you've been making."

Roberta said, "I think you mean insinuations."

"No, I don't," I snapped. "I want her to stop *implying* that I had something to do with it."

Quite calmly, Callie said, "It's impolite to correct your elders, Roberta." Which should've made me feel better, but didn't.

Sue jumped up and grabbed the coffeepot. "More coffee? Have some cookies. Anybody?"

Roberta, her mind lost in some dreamworld, held out her cup. "I just hope Coleman has a good thermos. I worry about him not being warm enough."

We all left at about the same time, cranking cars and driving off on our separate ways. LuAnne had me so uptight, my jaws were aching from keeping them clamped together. I didn't know why I put up with her. She just had no discretion whatsoever, and the more she talked, the worse it got. And when anybody called her on it, she immediately got defensive and dug herself into a deeper hole.

One of these days, I told myself, *I'll be able to explain everything, and I hope LuAnne will be ashamed of herself for doubting me.*

I turned onto Summit Avenue, a straight thoroughfare lined with bare-branched pear trees that ran for eight or so blocks, crossed Polk, and kept on going. Although it wasn't late, about ten-thirty or so, mine was the only car on the street. I could see almost all the way to my house on the corner of Polk and Summit. The streetlamps cast cones of light down to the pavement, and way ahead of me, a lone, lanky-legged runner flitted in and out of the darkness between them.

Oh, Lord, I thought, and slowed the car. Although I was too far away to see the face, I had no trouble recognizing the long, skinny legs making the same loping strides I'd seen the night before.

Not wanting to pass so that he'd know I was out on a lonely street by myself, I acted on a self-protective impulse and took a right toward busy Main Street. My plan was to drive up and down it a few times — teen-agers did it all the time — until the runner was long past my house and I could get inside unaccosted.

But this was Abbotsville, and Main Street was almost as deserted as Summit, so I took another right and headed away from town on MLK Boulevard.

I'd been thinking of talking to Coleman anyway, and this could be just the time to do it.

CHAPTER 25

Lit by tall sodium streetlights, MLK Boulevard was almost as light as day, giving me an immediate feeling of safety — no shadows for a dark figure to slip through. Up ahead, I saw Coleman's patrol car parked alone on the side, so I carefully guided my car onto the shoulder and stopped behind it.

The long blast of a horn froze me in my seat as a car with arms waving out the windows to Coleman whizzed past. Leaning over to look up out the passenger window, I saw him sitting in his lawn chair under the three long-armed spotlights at the top of the sign. He was alone, and nobody was on the path with money in hand to drop in his bucket.

As I got out of the car, Coleman stood up and waved. There was too much traffic noise for me to attempt calling out to him, so I walked over to the railing and looked down the slanted bank to the path. In between passing cars, I vaguely heard Coleman calling my name. I didn't respond, just swung one leg over the rail, straddled it, then pulled the other leg over until I was at the top of the bank, where I saw that some thoughtful soul had dug five steps leading to the bottom.

The steps didn't keep me from sliding part of the way down, but, holding on to my pocketbook, I made it in one piece and walked over to the sign, where the racket from a generator almost blocked the noise from the street. I looked up to see Coleman, fully winterized in padded coat and pants, and a watch cap on his head, leaning over the edge of the platform.

"Hey, Miss Julia, what brings you here? Is everything all right?"

"No, everything's not all right. I need to talk to you, Coleman, so either come down here or I'm coming up there."

"Hey, Coleman! Hey, you idjit, don't you know it's wintertime?"

We both looked toward the street as the rude words were yelled from a speeding pickup. And from another one right behind it, a head leaned out a window with more yelling.

"Hey, you needin' a womern up there?"

Coleman said, "Come on around to the back of the sign, Miss Julia." He motioned the way, and I stumbled through weeds to the side away from the boulevard, where it was dark.

Coleman lowered a ladder, then pushed on it to stanch it firmly in the ground. "Think you can crawl up here? Just come halfway and I'll grab you." He lay full length on the platform, his top half hanging down the ladder, waiting for me.

The platform wasn't anywhere near as high off the ground as the dome of the courthouse, and I'd climbed that. So, placing my pocketbook over my shoulder, I clasped both sides of the ladder, put one foot after the other on the rungs, and felt Coleman's steadying hands clasp my arms and pull me over the edge. I was up.

"Scoot over here," Coleman said as a big truck's air horn blasted the air. He lifted the flap of his tent and grinned at me. "Crawl in where it's warm."

And it was. In fact, the inside of the tent was insulated with a down-filled lining — walls and floor. A small heater, fed by the generator, purred on one side. Roberta, if I had a mind to tell her, would be reassured as to Coleman's comfort.

"Sit a little way back from the flap,"

Coleman said, "and nobody'll know you're here. If it gets out that there's a way up, I'll have half the town camping out with me. Use the bedroll to wrap up in if you get cold." He moved his lawn chair over to the open flap and sat down, ready to listen or talk or whatever I'd made that perilous journey to do.

"What's going on, Miss Julia?"

"Well, it's like this: Sam's in Raleigh so I can't talk to him, and Binkie doesn't want to hear what I have to say, and Detective Ellis *does* want to hear, but I can't tell him. And my friends are asking too many questions, which means they're wondering about me, and Pastor Ledbetter left town and who knows when he'll be back, and that strange runner keeps showing up around my house, and I keep thinking about finding Connie dead on the floor, and I want to know when something's going to be done so I can sleep at night."

"Okay, that's a good start," Coleman said, and scooted his chair closer to the open flap. He leaned over, his arms on his thighs, looking in at me as I sat with my limbs curled up in his little warm tent. "What can I do to help?"

"Well, Coleman," I went on, "I know you're officially on the other side of this,

246

being a sheriff's deputy and all, but I need to know what kind of spot I'm in. And I know you're off duty and not part of the investigation, but you must know something, and I want to know just how much Detective Ellis and Lieutenant Peavey suspect me. And who else are they looking at and who all are they investigating, because there're all kinds of possibilities that are more worthy of suspicion than I am.

"Because, Coleman, I did not do it."

"That's pretty much confirmed," Coleman said, as my heart leaped in my breast. "The autopsy report came back today, and you can thank the gatekeeper for keeping a time sheet on who came and went — just visitors, though. Not the residents." He stopped and looked down at his hands. Then he lifted his head. "But I do have to caution you, Miss Julia, because time of death — anybody's death — is hard to pinpoint. It's an estimate, at best, but from the amount of rigor, lividity, the state of the cornea, the body temperature, and the stomach contents, it looks like Ms. Clayborn had been dead an hour or more before you got there."

"Oh, my word," I said, limp with relief, even though I could've done without all the details. Then a rush of outrage surged through me. "Why hasn't somebody told

247

me? I've been left hanging out to dry, worried sick about being falsely accused, and all this while they *knew* I couldn't have done it."

"All this while," Coleman said with a smile, "has just been since late this afternoon when the report came in. But you're right, they probably won't tell you — mainly because you're the only one they know was there. And there's some question that you could've gotten in earlier without being seen. But they'll put you on the back burner for a while and turn the investigation in another direction."

"I ought to sue them for loss of sleep," I grumbled, then latched on to what he'd said. "And how in the world could I have gotten in earlier without being seen? That gatekeeper was right there all day scribbling in his little book, wasn't he?"

Coleman nodded. "As far as I know. But realize that I've been off duty for a couple of days, so I'm not up on the evidence they have."

"Well," I said, discouraged now that Coleman didn't have all the answers. "Sam said the autopsy would determine how she died. Did it?"

Coleman's mouth twisted with irony. "Our favorite cause of death: blunt force trauma.

Which could mean anything. A blow of some kind. Whatever weapon was used fractured the skull and cut the scalp near the temple. And there was a large bruise on the forehead. The cut on the scalp bled a lot. . . ."

"I noticed."

"Death was caused by the blow across the temple, so the question is: what kind of weapon would be sharp enough to cut the scalp and heavy enough to depress the skull? Or were there two weapons? Or two assailants? Identifying and finding the weapon or weapons is where the investigation is focused now."

"Well, I hope they look that house over good — it's huge and full of boxes and crates and who-knows-what-else. And what about the woods around it? There're a million places on those undeveloped lots to throw something or to bury something."

Coleman smiled. "They're looking, and they've called in the big dogs, too. The SBI is sending a forensic team to double-check us."

Hearing that the State Bureau of Investigation would be on the job made me feel better. Of course it might mean that I'd be interviewed again, but if they had proof — even though the exact time of Connie's death was iffy — that I could not have committed that crime, then I might enjoy it. Or at least not mind it so much.

"Now tell me about that runner you mentioned," Coleman said.

So I told him how Stan Clayborn had shown up at my house the other night wanting to know what Connie's last words were. "He was adamantly convinced that she had said something to me before she died, Coleman. I kept telling him that she was in no condition to say anything when I found her. But, see, I've been thinking about that, and it seems to me that he either thinks that I was the last one to see her alive because I killed her, or maybe *he* did it, and he's afraid she was still alive enough when I found her to tell on him.

"And twice now I've seen a man running by my house late at night. It's been too dark for me to see his face, but the rest of him looks an awful lot like Connie's husband — tall and skinny. Of course, I could be wrong. I've never seen her husband with his pants off. His long pants, I mean."

"So you're not sure it was him?"

"No, not really. It could've been anybody of that particular build, but I've never seen anybody running past my house at that time of night before. Then again," I said, and paused to consider what I'd said, "I've never had reason to look out the window at ten-thirty or eleven o'clock at night, so for all I know, it's a common running route for people who work all day."

"Okay," Coleman said, "that's something to look into. The Clayborn house is still a crime scene, so the husband may be staying somewhere close to you. Running past your house could just be a convenient way to go."

"That's true, I guess. But, see, when he came to my house, he mentioned that he was a runner, so that's why — besides looking like Mr. Clayborn — I thought it was him."

"Did you tell Detective Ellis about this?"

"No, he didn't ask. I just answered his questions as briefly as I could. To tell the truth, I was so nervous that I didn't even think about adding anything extra."

"All right," Coleman said, "I'll let him know. Now tell me about Larry Ledbetter. What's he got to do with this?"

I took a deep breath, prayed to be forgiven for breaking a promise not to tell, and opened my mouth to tell it.

"Yoo-hoo, Coleman!"

We both looked toward the street. At the sight of Roberta Smith waving as she stood at the railing beside her car, Coleman got to his feet.

"Close the flap, Miss Julia," he said. "She's brought me a midnight snack. She won't stay long."

A midnight snack? I thought as I lowered the flap. *Every* midnight? Then, *Does Binkie know about this?*

CHAPTER 26

I lowered the tent flap and scrooched up tighter, feeling the platform give with each of Coleman's steps as he walked to the end nearest the street. Through the noise of traffic and the generator, I could barely hear him call down to Roberta, who was now apparently standing below the platform.

"You didn't need to do this, Roberta," Coleman said, as I pictured him leaning over the edge to look at her. "But I sure do appreciate it. Hold on, and I'll winch the bucket down."

I heard the sound of her voice yelling up to him, but I couldn't make out the words. I was too busy worrying that she would recognize my car and want to know where I was. But as the conversation went on and no one demanded my appearance, I gradually relaxed. Roberta — bless her heart — was so otherworldly that she probably didn't even notice the car.

Then I began thinking she might see the ladder. And if she did, she'd find me and want to know what I was doing and why I was hiding in a tent. Well, that was easy to answer — I didn't want anybody to know I was there. And Coleman didn't want anybody to know I was there, either, because maybe he didn't want Roberta to know there was an easy climb to his side. And maybe it was a good thing I was there — Coleman might have need of a chaperone.

I eased the flap open to a tiny slit and peeked out to see Coleman squatting on the far edge of the platform, looking down. A McDonald's sack — easily identified by the golden arches printed on it — sat beside him, and the bucket in which it had ascended was dangling from the pulley. Roberta had completed her good deed and, to my mind, it was time for her to go.

Besides, my limbs were beginning to cramp up — I needed to straighten them out, I needed to stand up, I needed to get out of that tiny tent and go home. What could Roberta be talking about for so long?

I continued to pick up the odd word here and there, as I watched Coleman nod his head and thank her over and over. Finally, though, he stood, McDonald's sack in hand, and watched as Roberta apparently walked away toward the street. Then I saw the back of her head rise into view as she climbed the bank toward the railing.

My word, I thought with a gasp, as I watched her straddle the railing with her skirt hiked up on her thighs. I couldn't believe it, but she'd gone home from Sue's and changed clothes. In this chilly weather, made colder by the wind of passing cars, Roberta was wearing a tight-fitting, V-necked pink mohair sweater — I could see the little fuzzy fibers blowing in the breeze.

Coleman came back to his chair, opened the sack, and, rummaging around in it, said, "Let's see what we have here." Pulling out a large cup, he uncapped it, then said, "Oh, man, hot chocolate. Want some, Miss Julia?"

"No, Coleman, I don't. But I do want to know if this is an everyday, or rather an every night, occurrence. What is Roberta doing bringing midnight snacks to you?"

"She's just being nice. Hey, and look here, two hot apple pies."

"Just being nice, my foot. You're playing with fire, Coleman."

He turned toward the street, gave a big wave as a horn tooted. "There she goes," he said. "Back toward town. You can open up now, Miss Julia. She's gone."

I did, and I was mightily disturbed. There he was, happily eating away at a hot apple pie and sipping from a steaming Styrofoam cup of hot chocolate without one thought of how it looked for a romantically inclined woman like Roberta Smith, who had a tendency to fall for bodice-ripping literary characters, to have brought them to him.

"Coleman, this is not any of my business, but have you thought of how this looks?"

"What? You being here? That's why I told you to stay in the tent."

"No, not *my* being here. Who would think a thing about that? I'm talking about you wanting me to hide from Roberta, for one thing."

He stopped chewing long enough to say, "I thought you didn't want anybody to know you were here."

"Well, I guess I didn't. But you didn't, either."

He grinned. "Miss Julia, if Roberta had known I have a ladder and that you had used it, what do you think would've happened?"

"She'd be up here, too?"

"Yep, she's already said she'd like to see the view from up here. And I told her there was no way except to shimmy up one of the

256

poles on the sign. So far, she hasn't tried that."

"Oh, my goodness. Well, Coleman, all I can say is that you'd better nip that in the bud while you can. Roberta is losing her head."

"It's the uniform," he said, shrugging, as he happily chewed away on a warm apple pie, seemingly unaware of what he brought to a uniform. "She'll get over it."

"I hope you're right," I said, and began struggling to crawl out of the tent. "I've got to get on home, Coleman, but, my gracious, I'm as stiff as a board."

I reached for the arm of his chair to pull myself up and out, just as he started to rise to help me.

"Wait, don't get up!" Pulling on the weighted chair with one hand and pushing myself off with the other, I said, "I need you for ballast."

He kept his seat, but started laughing. "I've been called a lot of things, but ballast is a new one. Miss Julia, let me help you."

"Just sit still. I can manage." And I did, finally. But the effort of leveraging myself upright was beginning to tell on me, and I decided that I would stay on my feet from then on.

Standing, now that I was, too, Coleman

grinned and said, "I've always admired your management style, and I've just seen another instance of it."

I straightened my coat and, still panting from the strain on my system, said, "I intend to fend for myself for as long as I can."

Just as Coleman took my arm to walk me to the ladder, a voice too near to be on the ground said, "Hey, there, Sergeant. Want some comp'ny?"

Startled, Coleman released me. I quickly dropped back down into the tent as we both turned to see a man's head top the ladder. Then the rest of him leaped out onto the platform.

"Oh, 'scuse me. You already got some."

"Lamar!" Coleman said. "Where'd you come from?"

"That gas station over yonder." He pointed toward the east. "I come 'round the back way to check on you. Man, it's *nice* up here."

Uneasily, because I hadn't intended to do it again, I eased back into a crouch, not to hide, because I'd already been seen, but because the tent was the warmest place on the platform and the only place to keep from being seen from the street. No telling what would happen if people in passing cars thought Coleman was holding a council or having a party instead of a solitary sign sitting for a charitable cause.

Coleman said, "What kind of trouble are you in now, Lamar?"

"Ain't in no trouble," the intruder said, grinning. "Not now, anyway. Jus' wanted to see how you doin'."

I'd recognized the voice by this time and the two plastic grocery bags tied together and run through the belt loops of his jeans. He was the man Sam and I had picked up last summer, the one who had promised as many votes as Sam needed, and the one who practiced outlaw justice.

"Say, Sergeant," he said, "you don't have another one of them pies, do you? Looks mighty good."

"Just happen to have one. Here you go." Coleman drew out the second of Roberta's McDonald's apple pies, which undoubtedly was not as hot as advertised by now.

Lamar unwrapped it, and as he began eating it, he squatted down beside the tent flap. Looking in, he said, "I 'member you. You took me to the gas station on a hot-as-hell day last summer. Sergeant, this here's a nice lady, an' I hope you ain't arrestin' her."

Coleman snorted. "No, Lamar. This is Mrs. Murdoch, a friend of mine. Miss Julia, this is Lamar Owens, a frequent guest of

259

the Abbot County jail."

"Got that right," Lamar said, unruffled, as he stuffed the last of the pie into his mouth. "You boys look after me when my unemployment runs out."

"Okay," Coleman said, "time for you to take off, Lamar. I appreciate the visit, but Mrs. Murdoch is leaving and I'm going to bed."

Lamar didn't move, just kept staring at me through the tent flap. Then, as if he'd just put a few things together, he said, "I hear the cops been givin' you grief, an' I know how that is." He hunched in closer. "If you want my advice, ma'am, this ain't a good place for you to be." He jabbed his thumb in Coleman's direction, then whispered, "He's one of 'em."

Coleman tried not to laugh. "She knows that. Now, Lamar, it's time for you to boogie on outa here. Let's go."

"Okay, okay. Jus' wanted to see how you're makin' out. I got to git back, anyways." He stood up and headed toward the ladder, calling behind him, "Nice seein' you, Miz Murdoch."

"You, too," I murmured.

Then I heard Coleman say, "Here, go get something to eat. But if I hear you went to the liquor store, I'm gonna run you in again."

Coleman came back to the tent, leaned down, and said, "It's clear, Miss Julia. We'd better get you down and on your way before anybody else shows up. I need to get that ladder out of sight."

"And to think I worried about you being lonely up here," I said as I crawled out again, but this time gratefully accepting Coleman's help. Stepping behind the tent to avoid eyes from the street, I asked, "Do many like Mr. Owens come by to see you?"

"Oh, yeah. At one time or another, we've arrested about half the county, seems like, and they take a personal interest in what we do. And they all come out at night. In fact, you'd be surprised at what goes on around town at night." Coleman laughed. "Believe me, who you see at three P.M. is a whole lot different from who's out at three in the morning, and right now, I'm their number one attraction."

"Hey, Officer! Look over here!"

Turning toward the street, I couldn't believe my eyes. A car filled with yelling and hollering men was creeping along the street. A young woman, completely unclothed, hung out the back window, exposing herself

to the whole world, and to Coleman specifically.

"My Lord," I said, feeling slightly faint
and mortally embarrassed. "Get me down
from here, Coleman. This is worse than an
unknown runner zipping past my house."

Coleman laughed as he walked me to the
ladder. "At least he has clothes on, skimpy
though they are."

I stopped at the head of the ladder, un-
slung my pocketbook, and opened it. "Here,
put this in your bucket and let us hope that
you'll soon be down from here and back
home where Binkie can look after you." And
I emptied my wallet, thrust the bills in his
hand, and took my leave.

But halfway down the ladder, I was as-
sailed by the most horrendous, ear-splitting
racket, wailing and shrieking loud enough
to wake the dead. Struck dumb, I slipped
and almost fell. Frightened half to death
and holding on for dear life, I yelled, "What
is it? What is it?"

Looking up at Coleman's grinning face, I
had a mind to climb back up and dress him
down good. But finally as the din faded
away in the distance, he said, "It's just some
of my buddies using their sirens to tell me
good night."

"Oh, for goodness sakes, my hearing will

never be the same again. Coleman, do you ever get any sleep?"

"Not much," he admitted. "The town vagrants'll be creeping around pretty soon."

"Then I'm getting out of here. Thank you, Coleman, for making me feel better."

But not all that much better, because with all the interruptions and distractions, I hadn't been able to tell him everything. Which may have been a good thing after all.

CHAPTER 27

I crawled into bed some hours later than I normally retired, grateful for the peace and quiet — Latisha was asleep and no sirens went off — and hoped that Coleman would get some rest before the vagrants showed up. I declare, I didn't know that so much went on during the night hours when I thought everybody was home in bed. There seemed to be a culture of nocturnal roamers who came awake and began their days only when the sun went down. I was glad to be home and out of it.

Yet as tired as I was, I couldn't turn off the roiling thoughts in my mind. I'd gone to Coleman to lay them all out to him, but there'd been too many interruptions to have spread them out fully. I'd not gotten anywhere close to telling him of my concern about Pastor Ledbetter and Emma Sue. But, oh, how I longed to tell somebody, then have that somebody tell me and show me

264

how wrong I was. As it was, I could say only
— to myself — that the situation with the
Ledbetters was getting more and more
muddled.

After turning over for the umpteenth time,
I sat up in bed, propped up by a pillow, and
went over what I knew:

Number one: Emma Sue had been laid
low by Connie's criticism of the courthouse
park, specifically the design, implementa-
tion, and upkeep of the plants and care of
the statue — all of which were of Emma
Sue's doing. And Emma Sue had taken
every censuring word that came out of Connie's mouth personally.

Number two: When I say that Emma Sue
had been laid low, I mean really done in.
I'd never seen her in such a state as she'd
been and apparently was still in. Why, she'd
not even called or written a thank-you note
for the chicken pot pies and for cleaning
her kitchen. That was not at all like Emma
Sue, and was as good an indicator of her
state of mind as anything I could think of.

Number three: Pastor Ledbetter had been
more concerned about Emma Sue's reaction to Connie's criticism than I'd ever
known him to be about anything that had
ever happened to his wife. Normally, when
she suffered the occasional migraine, he

took it in stride with only a hint of martyr-dom for having a susceptible wife. This time, though, he'd been noticeably and deeply worried, and, even worse, he had come to *me* for help. Right then and there, my guard should've gone up with red flags flying. When had he ever done that before?

Number four: He had effectively silenced me by inveigling a promise I was having trouble keeping — and not only *having* trouble keeping, but deep *in* trouble for keeping.

Number five: He had taken Emma Sue and himself out of town, thereby making himself unavailable to release me from my promise, and thereby also making them both unavailable to be interviewed. And as far as I knew, Emma Sue was the only one who'd been at Connie's coffee who had not been treated to an hour's session with Detective Ellis.

Wasn't that strange in itself? Wouldn't innocent parties be eager to help solve a crime? And as I thought about it, even worse was . . .

Number six: Pastor Ledbetter had told Norma that he was taking Emma Sue to a specialist in Winston-Salem, yet, according to Norma, they'd barely spent one night there before they were on their way back.

Now, don't tell me that you can get an appointment with a specialist, have an examination, then get a diagnosis and a treatment plan all in one day — that's beyond belief. It would take that long to draw enough blood for all the tests that would be ordered.

So something was wrong somewhere, and even though I could not bring myself to actually suspect either Ledbetter, I couldn't shut down the questions that were engendered by their actions, either.

I got out of bed, put on a robe and slippers, and left the room — too edgy to sleep. Stopped at the top of the stairs by the sound of a mumbling voice, I stood for a minute, listening.

Ah, Latisha, talking away in her sleep. That child never stopped. So I continued on down the stairs to the first floor, which was dimly lit by the glow from the streetlight on the corner. I didn't turn on any lamps, just needing to move around a little to bring my erratic thoughts under control.

Walking to the front window, I looked out at Polk Street to check on the weather. I had no fear of seeing a runner — it was much too late for even the most ardent exerciser.

Still, I was wary, leaning sideways to glance out the window, and as I did, *a face looked back at me*! Lord, I nearly fainted, until I realized it was my own reflection in the glass.

I sat down, breathing heavily and trying to get a grip on my nerves. I could not go on this way — suspecting a man of God and/ or his meek wife of something so horrendous as the taking of a life, and, on top of that, being frightened half to death by runners and reflections. And, on top of *that*, knowingly misleading Detective Ellis by not telling him why I'd gone to Connie's on that fateful day.

To tell or not to tell — that was the question. Whether it was better to break a solemn promise, thereby turning the investigation in a startlingly new direction, or to keep my mouth shut, thereby protecting those who perhaps should be investigated?

It was beyond me to decide what to do, so I determined then and there to do nothing until Sam got home. And I determined — promise or no promise — to give him an earful when he did get home. Then I got up and went back to bed.

"You better look at the paper," Lillian said, as I, bleary eyed, entered the kitchen the following morning. She poured a cup of coffee and handed it to me. "Set down while I fix your eggs."

"Where're the children?" I asked as I sat at the table and picked up the newspaper, which she'd left by my place. "It's awfully quiet for a Saturday morning."

"They over at Miss Hazel Marie's. Nothin' would do but Latisha had to go see them little girls, so Lloyd took her. I tole 'em not to get too close — just say 'hey,' then come on home. You see the paper yet?"

"What's in it, Lillian? More about the investigation? I hope to goodness they've left my name out of it."

"That lady's death notice in it, an' it's the worst one I ever see. It don't say a thing about her that folks want to know, like where she come from an' what she do in her life. They oughta be 'shamed to put such a say-nothing notice in the paper."

I opened the newspaper and turned to the obituary page. My eyes were drawn to a small paragraph at the bottom. It read:

Constance "Connie" Clayborn, 51, the only daughter of the late Harriett and Thomas Warren, died unexpectedly at her home on Tuesday, November 12. She is survived by her husband, Stanford H. Clayborn, of the home. Arrangements for a private interment will be made by the Holloway

Funeral Home and Crematorium in Tren-
ton, New Jersey.

"Why, this doesn't say anything," I said.

"That's what I been sayin'," Lillian said.
"People want to know more'n that, an' I
don't know why they leave out so much."

"Well, Lillian, maybe it tells us more than
you'd think. First of all, I expect her griev-
ing husband did this for the paper. I mean,
who else would have written it? Her parents
aren't around, and apparently she had no
children. But, my goodness, it doesn't even
mention that she was a Vassar graduate, and
she was so proud of that. I agree with you,
Lillian. I'd like to know more than this."

"Yes'm, an' it don't even say she survived
by her *lovin'* husband, an' everybody say
that whether they the lovin' kind or not.
And it don't say where to send flowers,
either."

"You're right, and it doesn't name a
favorite charity of the deceased for people
to donate to, either."

"Yes'm, an' it don't say nothin' 'bout a
visitation time. People kinda 'spect that so
they can view the body."

"Not me, Lillian. I've already seen it."

"Well, but what about a memorial service?
It don't say a word about havin' one of

270

them, an' that's what peoples do when they have the burial somewhere else."

"Maybe Mr. Clayborn felt they hadn't lived here long enough to have a good attendance. Of course, he doesn't know small Southern towns — we would've all turned out for a service. Then again," I said, sighing, "they weren't churchgoing people, so I guess he didn't see the need. I declare, Lillian, how in the world do people live through pain and grief without the comfort of faith?"

"Yes'm, they's got to be something more an' better'n this world, but lotsa people live like this one's all they is. It's pitiful, is what it is."

"I feel so sorry for them both."

Lillian walked over and put a plate of scrambled eggs and grits in front of me. "Quit readin' the paper now, an' eat 'fore it gets cold. But I tell you what's a fact. If I didn't know my sweet Jesus be waitin' for me on the other side, I don't know what I'd do."

"Me, either, Lillian," I said, my heart heavy for Connie and, I'll admit, for her husband as well — in spite of his propensity for running around half-naked at night.

Chapter 28

"Lillian," I said, putting aside the paper and rising from the table, "I really appreciate your staying with me, but Sam will be home late today. You must have things to do at home, so why don't you and Latisha go on? There's no need to stay here all day and the night, too."

"You be all right by yourself? What if Mr. Sam don't get home?"

"I'll have Lloyd, so I won't be alone. You run on, I'll be all right."

"Well, if you sure. I do need to get some washin' done, an' go to the grocery store, an' get Latisha ready for Sunday school, an' fix supper for Miss Lula. That's my neighbor I been helpin' out. So soon's I get this kitchen clean, I'll pick up Latisha at Miss Hazel Marie's an' go on. I been wantin' to see them baby girls, myself."

"Then I'll see you Monday morning." And thanking her again, I walked across the hall to the new library and began to consider my next moves. For one thing, Mr. Pickens had come to mind. I mean, here I had a private investigator at hand, so why hadn't I thought to use him? I wasn't sure how much attention Detective Ellis was giving to Connie's husband, especially since the detective didn't know that Connie's husband was occupying his evenings by running around my house. The thing for me to do was to take up the slack by employing Mr. Pickens for a stakeout on Polk Street. He could watch for the runner and at least identify him so I'd know for sure who I was dealing with.

And for another thing, I, myself, intended to stake out Pastor Ledbetter until I cornered him at the church, his home, or wherever I could find him. And when I did, I was going to let him know what was what. I intended to tell, not ask, but *tell* him that my promise was henceforth null and void, and that he'd better prepare himself for a few official interviews by Detective Ellis. And for all I knew, by Lieutenant Peavey, too.

And *then* — I stopped with a gasp. Why in the world had I not thought of this! My breath caught in my throat as I realized how dense I'd been. Lieutenant Peavey had tracked me down because the gatekeeper had kept a list of the license plate numbers of all visitors to Grand View Estates. So if either the pastor or Emma Sue had been there before me — as I'd been fearing — his or her tag number would've been in the hands of the law at the same time mine had gotten there.

Now, whether or not — given the Ledbetters' apparent ability to avoid people they didn't want to see — Detective Ellis had ever been able to follow up on that information was another question altogether. But that was his problem, not mine. My problem was partially solved — I could stop fearing that one Ledbetter or the other had taken matters into his or her own hands and gone to Connie's before me. Neither could've gotten past the gatekeeper without being noted and reported.

I'd always heard of feeling as if a load had been lifted, and now I knew what it was like. My horrible suspicions were allayed, and all I had to be concerned with was my own status in the eyes of the law for withholding the reason I'd paid a visit to Connie. If she had had no visitors other than me that day, then I could still be in their sights. Well, and so would her husband — he'd certainly been there as well.

■ ■ ■ ■

I waited until Lillian told me she was leaving, then gave her time to pick up Latisha and visit with Hazel Marie before I lifted the telephone.

"Hazel Marie?" I said when she answered. "How're you feeling today?"

"Much better, Miss Julia. I may even live, especially since the girls are all but well. How are you?"

"Oh, I'm making it. And Sam should be back tonight, so I'm looking forward to that. We've missed you at the sewing group, Hazel Marie. I hope you'll be there next week."

"I don't know if I can or not. I'll see if Granny Wiggins can babysit. J.D. left this morning on a case, and who knows when he'll be back."

My renewed spirits grew old in a hurry. "He's gone?"

"Yes, he's in Louisville, I think. He never knows where a case will take him. But let me know when the group will meet and I'll try to make it. Oh, and by the way," Hazel Marie said, "since Mr. Sam's on his way back, I'd like to have Lloyd home tonight. I just feel safer with all of us here together when J.D.'s gone. Will that be all right with you?"

"Oh, of course, Hazel Marie. I just appreciate having had him for the last couple of nights."

After a few more minutes of idle chatter, I hung up and wondered how I'd get through the night if Sam didn't get home. Being without either Lillian or Lloyd for the short run or Mr. Pickens for the long run, I was suddenly on my own. Instead of having things worked out, all I'd succeeded in doing was to work myself into having no help at all. And if Sam didn't get home, it was going to be a long, lonely night for me.

Well, there was one thing I could do on my own, so I put on a coat, took up my pocketbook, locked the house, and went to the car. If Pastor Ledbetter was in Abbotsville, I intended to find him.

The first thing I did, of course, was to check the church parking lot across the street. As it was Saturday, the pastor's car would be easily visible in the lot, if it was there. But it wasn't, nor was anybody else's.

So I drove to the Ledbetter house, slowing down as I passed to see if there were any signs of life. No car in the driveway, no lights on in the house, the garage doors down, and the curtains closed. I drove to the end of the block, turned around, and went past the house again. And that time I saw a rolled newspaper still in its plastic sleeve lying to the side of the front door.

As I drove on past, I deduced that the uncollected paper meant the Ledbetters had not returned from Winston-Salem, or it meant that the pastor had left home early and Emma Sue was still too depressed to care about the news. For all I knew, she was inside the house, curled up in bed with the covers over her head, while the pastor visited the sick and ailing in the hospital.

I considered turning around and going to the door. I could ring the doorbell until it irritated Emma Sue so much that she would drag herself out of bed to put a stop to it. Maybe I should call first, but of course I'd not brought my cell phone with me.

So I drove to the hospital and, ignoring the signs that limited parking to doctors and the clergy, drove in, through, and out of the various lots, looking for Pastor Ledbetter's large car. It would be easily recognizable if it were there — there were no other ten-year-old yellow Mercedeses in town. I didn't find it there, and I didn't find it when I cruised the lots open to the general public.

Maybe they hadn't returned from

Winston-Salem. Maybe Emma Sue had been admitted to the hospital there. She could be lying on a bed in a psychiatric ward a hundred miles away, for all I knew. Of course, I was assuming the worst, as I usually did, although it was entirely possible that Emma Sue's condition hadn't been caused by Connie's criticism at all. She could be suffering from low blood sugar, for one thing, or some strange clinical condition, for another.

I couldn't think where else to look for Pastor Ledbetter, not knowing his favorite hangouts if he had any, like the Bluebird Cafe or the bagel place, nor did I know where he got his hair cut or his shoes re-soled.

So I went home, planning to phone Emma Sue and sit while it rang for as long as it took. And if I got her answering machine, I would tell Emma Sue in no uncertain terms that if she was there she'd better talk to me before I was morally compelled to tell Detective Ellis all I knew. If that didn't get her out of bed, I'd know she wasn't home.

Once more I surveyed the church parking lot as I neared my driveway. Then on impulse, I continued on, turning left on Summit and circling the block on which the church was built. Several cars were parked on both sides of Taft Street — the one that ran parallel to Polk.

And there it was. Pastor Ledbetter's car nestled in a space half a block from the front of the church. I should've thought of that! Hadn't he avoided me once before by going up through the sanctuary and out the double front doors? It made perfect sense that he would go inside the same way, thereby giving the impression that he was not at the church.

Now to get inside, myself.

CHAPTER 29

I left the car in my own driveway and walked across the street. The back door to the church was a common entrance because it was the most convenient to the parking area. Not only did church members use it on a regular basis but so did Norma Cantrell, the janitor, the occasional vagrant, and anybody who needed help from the pastor's discretionary fund. For the convenience of members, the door was unlocked during Sunday services, but it didn't stay that way during the week. It was kept locked to prevent just anybody from walking in at will. There was a loud buzzing doorbell for the purpose of summoning help.

And I used it. I *knew* Pastor Ledbetter was in there — his car parked partially hidden out front proved that. But did he answer it? No, he did not.

Looking through the glass panes in the door, I felt a chill run down my back. The last time I'd looked through the glass panes of a door, I'd seen what I never wanted to see again. This time, though, I saw no shoes and no movement anywhere inside. What could he be doing? Nobody could concentrate on writing a sermon with the racket the doorbell was making. Because I didn't let up on it. In fact, my finger was about to give out from pressing on the bell. You'd think nobody could ignore the urgency of it. What if there was a fire? What if someone desperately needed help? What if that someone was suffering a spiritual crisis? How could he ignore it?

Well, I thought as I finally turned away, maybe he'd slipped out the front again and was gone. I didn't believe it.

So I walked with purpose back across the street, got in my car, and drove back to Taft Street. There was no sign of the pastor, but his car was still there. And, fortunately, so were two empty parking spaces three cars behind the yellow Mercedes.

I avoid parallel parking whenever I can, but with two spaces right together I was able to drive straight in and had to back up only twice to fit nicely into one of them.

Turning off the ignition, I made myself comfortable, thankful that the day was clear and moderately warm. I settled in to await the appearance of the pastor. Then it occurred to me that someone might walk by and ask what I was doing just sitting there. They might even wonder if I'd lost my way home, and then word would get out that I was showing signs of dementia — the instant accusation for every misunderstood word or action at the first emergence of gray hair on one's head. I didn't care. I was going to sit there until the pastor showed himself, and, unless he walked home, he would have to come to his car sooner or later.

I glanced at my watch and wished I'd thought to bring a snack or the newspaper or a book. A stakeout is not the most constructive way to spend one's time.

Fast becoming bored with checking my watch every two minutes, I began to wonder if Pastor Ledbetter would stay in the church all afternoon. If he did, I was in big trouble. My kidneys were already giving notice that they were ticking along quite normally, even though there was no relief in sight. Plenty of bushes were around, but it was broad daylight so they were out. Plenty of houses, too, occupied by people I knew, but how would I explain knocking on a door and asking for the use of a bathroom when everybody knew I lived only a block and a half away? I'd really be accused of dementia then.

I gasped as a car pulled up beside me and stopped. Glancing through two car windows, I saw a man put his arm across the back of the seat, turn to look out the rear window, then back his car into the space behind me. That car slipped into the space as slick as you please — no backing up and pulling forward, it just nestled in there like a piece of a jigsaw puzzle.

Watching through the mirrors, I saw a middle-aged man get out, slam the door, and walk purposefully down the sidewalk, swinging a briefcase. Selling insurance, I thought, and breathed easier because he was headed away from the church. He'd paid no attention to me, may not even have noticed I was there.

So I continued to sit and watch, squirming occasionally as I wondered how long I'd be able to hold off the increasing pressure. Images of my bathroom danced in my head.

Then the front door of the church opened. I sat up in a hurry, staring hard through the windshield. For a minute or so, no one appeared. Then a black-clad figure slid through the door, closed and seemed to lock it, then disappeared again.

I squinched up my eyes, wondering where he'd gone. Then he reappeared from behind one of the columns on the front of the church. Looking right, then left, the pastor — for it was him — quickly came down the few steps, turned hurriedly, and fast-walked to his yellow car.

Fearing he would see me, I flung myself across the console, then thought, *Why in the world?* Here, I'd been waiting a solid hour or more, and there he was. Why didn't I get out and accost him on the street?

I don't know why I hid — it was just an unthinking reaction to his appearance. Maybe I didn't want to be accused of spying on him. But I was completely within my rights to pursue him, given his efforts to avoid me, yet I felt guilty for doing it. Although I intended to give the pastor a piece of my mind, I am averse to creating a public spectacle. To confront him on the sidewalk and have it out with him where any number of people could watch and listen was simply not my way. I wanted to corner him inside somewhere so I could freely vent everything I had against him, demand to know why he was making himself scarce, and tell him in no uncertain terms that I was going to make a clean breast of everything I knew to Detective Ellis. One just doesn't do all that in public.

Well, no more hiding. I'd follow him until he was cornered in a place more suitable for the showdown I intended to have. But by the time I regained my resolve to face him down and had sat up, he was in his car and cranking it.

I turned on my ignition, put the car into reverse, and backed into the car behind me — not hard, but enough to let me know that I was not in an extralong parking space. Ramming the gear into drive, I pulled up and nudged the car in front. Pastor Ledbetter's car eased onto the street and drove off, while I cut my wheel to the right and reversed until I felt a tiny bump. Then I turned the wheels to the left and pulled forward to another tiny bump. After a few more tiny bumps, front and rear, I was finally able to pull out into the street.

Perhaps I should've stopped and checked for any damage, but the nudges hadn't been hard — just little bumps. Which is why cars have bumpers, isn't it?

There was no sign of the yellow Mercedes, but I'd seen it cross Summit, heading toward Main Street. So that's the way I went, looking left and right at each intersection, and didn't see even a flash of yellow. Around and around I went, looking and watching until I could stand it no longer. I headed back down Polk Street, pulled into my own driveway, and ran inside to the bathroom. Even though I'd lost the pastor and, for all I knew, he was on the run, it was a great relief because some things are more urgent than others.

I quickly fixed a sandwich, and sat at the kitchen table to eat it while I listened to the quiet house. It wasn't often that I was alone in it, so I entertained myself by picturing Sam leaving Raleigh and turning west to head for home. He had not called, for I'd checked the answering machine, but I held tight to his semipromise to be home by nightfall.

But what was I to do about Pastor Ledbetter? I didn't know where else to look for him, although I suspected that by now he was closed up in his house — he and Emma Sue both — with no intention of answering either the door or the phone. That told me, right there, that they had something to hide, but what? If either of them had visited Connie on the day of her death, Detective Ellis already knew it — so why would they hide from him? But lots of luck if that's what they were doing, because the sheriff had a SWAT team that loved to batter down doors.

But maybe it was just me who the pastor was hiding from. But why? The promise he'd required of me was of trivial importance in the scheme of things — I mean, in the present circumstances, who would look down on Emma Sue for having her feelings hurt and getting a severe headache because of it? A woman was dead, killed in her own home. We should all be eager to cooperate with Detective Ellis. We should all be telling everything we knew and letting the cards fall where they may.

That's why I decided to do just that. I'd already planned to tell Sam everything as soon as he got home, so I'd do that, then I'd call Binkie and Detective Ellis and tell them. No more withholding of information, I decided, although what good it would do the investigators to know that the reason I'd visited Connie was at the pastor's urging, I didn't know.

Still, my duty would have been done, and if Pastor Ledbetter showed up in the pulpit the next morning, I'd waylay him as he shook hands with departing members afterward and tell him what I'd done. It would serve him right.

Chapter 30

All those decisions flew out the window before suppertime. Sam called just as the afternoon began to fade, apologizing as he told me he wouldn't be home until the following afternoon. And all afternoon I'd been mentally following him along I-40 West, picturing him drawing nearer and nearer home.

"I'm sorry, Julia," he'd said. "We just can't come to terms on what to do, and rather than leave and have to come back, we've decided to stay another day." Then he'd added, "At least."

"But what about the storm? You could get snowed in down there and have to stay for who-knows-how-long."

"We're watching the weather. It's coming in from the south and will either head up the coast to New England — and get us on the way — or go on out to sea. Parts of Alabama and Georgia are already iced over.

But we're watching it, don't worry."

After a little more conversation in which I assured him that all was well on the home front, we hung up. Of course, all was not well with me, but what good would it have done to moan and groan about my worries, the biggest and most pressing of which was the fact that I'd be spending the night alone?

You're a grown woman, I told myself as I lingered by the phone, *and the doors are strong and the locks are new and nobody's after you anyway.*

I wasn't so sure about that, but I kept saying it until I was almost convinced. The thing to do was to check all the avenues of ingress to the house, make a little supper, check the doors again, go upstairs, get in bed, and read until I was good and sleepy, maybe come down and check the doors — and windows — one last time, then go to sleep. Before I knew it, it would be morning and I could laugh at being so unnerved by an empty house.

So I kept myself busy as the night began to close in. I turned on all the lights downstairs and a few upstairs as well, intending the house to look full and busy. I felt a noticeable chill as night fell, and, as I turned up the thermostat, spared a few minutes of concern for Coleman. But surely he had enough sense to come in out of the cold if the temperature dropped too low.

Opening the refrigerator door, I looked in to see if Lillian had left anything that looked like supper. She had, but a leftover pork chop and sauerkraut just didn't appeal. I decided that a little cooking would keep me busy and make the time pass as well. So I got out a skillet and began to fry a few strips of bacon, which almost immediately burned and had to be thrown out.

A few more strips went into a cool skillet and I made sure the eye was on low heat. I sliced a tomato, washed some lettuce, and put bread in the toaster. Opening a can of tomato soup, I congratulated myself on being able to feed myself with little trouble.

I sat down at the table with a fine-looking bacon, lettuce, and tomato sandwich, along with a bowl of tomato soup. I had successfully passed one hour of the night with no mishaps — well, I had burned some bacon, but besides that, I was managing to move the lonely night along quite well.

As I finished eating, I began to think over what I could do to move it along even further until it was time to go to bed. That's the problem with changing back to standard time — night comes so early, but actual time doesn't correspond to it. So it looked like bedtime, but it was barely six o'clock and I was through with supper, with a long, empty evening in front of me.

I cleaned up the kitchen, checked the doors, then walked across the hall to our new library. The lamps were lit and a small fire flickered across the gas logs, so that the room looked warm and welcoming. I turned on the television for company, and took an unaccustomed seat in a wing chair facing the door to the hall so I wouldn't worry about someone coming up behind me.

I was spooked, no doubt about that. But who wouldn't be after what I'd been going through — suspected of a brutal crime, stalked by a shadowy runner, stymied by a slippery preacher, and on high alert for anything happening out of the ordinary.

Then the doorbell rang.

I thought my heart had stopped. I know my breathing did. I sat absolutely still, while my mind whirled with visions of who would be at the front door in the dead of the night. Except it wasn't that late, it just felt that late. Still, who would be visiting on a storm-threatened Saturday night?

Lloyd? No, he'd come to the back door and use his key.

Sam? No, he was still in Raleigh.

Hazel Marie? With all three children? No,

she would've called first.

Mildred? Ha, not a chance. Mildred would not walk next door uninvited and unannounced.

Lillian and Latisha? No, they, too, would use a key to come through the back door. Besides, Lillian knew not to scare me half to death.

Coleman? Binkie? Unlikely. They'd both call first.

Stan Clayborn, dressed in Burberry or half-dressed in latex? A good possibility, but did I want to see him? Should I let him in since I was here alone? Not hardly. Visions of what I'd found in the kitchen of his house flashed through my mind.

And still I sat, hardly daring to move. Maybe whoever it was would go away. But whoever it was didn't. The doorbell sounded again, insisting I get up and see who was ringing it.

Ah, of course! My breathing settled down and so did my heart rate. Who had I been looking for all day? Who had finally gotten my messages that I needed to see him?

Why, Pastor Larry Ledbetter, of course. At last, he was ready to face me. I put aside a magazine, gathered myself to go to the door, and wondered why I had no fear of someone to whom I had so recently attributed a murderous intent toward his wife's tormentor.

Well, the answer to that was as clear as day. Who kept the church in the black, the budget balanced, and the pastor well housed and well fed? No matter his state of mind, he would no more endanger the church's major contributor than he would dance in the street.

I walked with confidence down the hall to the front door. At last, I would have it out with Pastor Ledbetter, maybe learn how Emma Sue was doing, and have him out of here in plenty of time for me to call Binkie and Detective Ellis before they went to bed, thereby having the burden of silence that had been imposed on me lifted for good.

I didn't turn on the hall lights. Every lamp in the living room was on, and so was the chandelier in the dining room. I had plenty of light. As an indication of welcome, I switched on the exterior sconces that lit the porch.

My front door had three small windows high enough that I almost had to stand on tiptoe to see through them — not at all like Connie's door, which was half glass paned and half paneled.

So as I unlocked the deadbolt, I strained upward to assure myself that it was the pastor outside my door. But perhaps he'd stepped to the side, for I didn't see even the top of his head, which I usually could when he visited.

I hesitated, thinking that I might've been mistaken in deciding who was there. One thing was sure: it couldn't be Stan Clayborn. He was tall enough to have looked straight into the hall through the little high windows.

After another moment of hesitation, I comforted myself with the knowledge that a strongly locked storm door would stand between me and whoever was there. I opened the front door.

Nobody was there. My heart went into its stop-flutter-and-go mode again, and I quickly stepped back. Swinging the door closed, the possibility of a prankster flashed through my mind. I didn't care. If it was a child having fun or a teenager bent on wrapping my house with toilet paper, I was calling the cops.

"Miz Murdoch?" a voice from a mouth I couldn't locate called out.

"Who's there?" I demanded, clinging to the almost closed door.

"It's just me." And Lamar Owens hopped down from the fern table, empty now for the winter, which was beside the front door.

"Beg your pardon, ma'am, I'm kinda wore out. Been walkin' from over at McDonald's all the way here. I had to set down awhile."

"Mr. Owens? Is that you?" I patted my chest in relief, but left the storm door locked. "My goodness, you gave me a fright."

He stood on the other side of the storm door, looking cold and peaked in an oily-looking barn jacket that was about two sizes too large for him. His battered tennis shoes turned up at the toes — nothing he wore seemed to be sized for him, as he wasn't a large man by any means. Actually, he was a wizened little man, malnourished and poorly cared for, and the dirt-streaked, tattered Burberry scarf wrapped around his head didn't improve his looks. Scotch clad or not, he was certainly no Stan Clayborn.

I couldn't just stand there all night, as he seemed willing to do. So in the absence of any further word from him, I asked, "What can I do for you?"

"Well, see, you done me a good turn one time, so I wanta do you one, too. That's why I walked all the way over here — my ole car's give out again. Had to ask where you lived a coupla times, but everybody knows you, so I didn't have no trouble gettin' here." He shifted his feet, looked down, then back up at me. "See, Miz Murdoch, I heard something you might orta know, seein' as how the cops already got you on their list. I tole Sergeant Bates you couldna done it, an' he believed me, but, see, I don't know as how the other'uns do."

"What? You mean they really think that I . . . ?"

"Yeah. I mean, yes, ma'am, some of 'em. I heard some of 'em talkin' in the Bluebird an' I spent the night in jail last night an' heard some more. 'Course they don't know I was listenin', but that's how I learn a lot of things. I figgered I owed it to you to warn you. I can help you with some alibis, if you need 'em. I pretty much know which of 'em work an' which of 'em don't."

I was both frightened anew by the possibility that I was back in Lieutenant Peavey's sights and moved by Mr. Owens's offer of help. Who else, I ask you, had cared enough to gather a few tried-and-true alibis for my use, free of charge?

"Won't you come in, Mr. Owens?" I said, opening the storm door. "I was just about to put on a pot of coffee."

CHAPTER 31

I closed and locked the door behind us and led Mr. Owens through the hall and into the kitchen, all the while wondering why I, the most fearful of women, felt perfectly at ease with this unkempt stranger. Enough at ease that I brushed aside the thought that I was locked inside my house with a habitual ne'er-do-well who was apparently more at home in a jail cell than in his own house, if he had one.

"Just put your coat over there, Mr. Owens," I said, pointing to a chair against the wall, "and have a seat at the table. I'll have the coffee on in a few minutes."

He came out of his coat, folded it, and laid it across the chair. Then he unwrapped the scarf from his head and neck, and laid it neatly on the coat. The scarf had hidden a mop of hair that needed washing, combing, and cutting, but from the scarf's ragged condition, it looked as if it had been retrieved from a Goodwill bin.

Hm-m, I thought, *two visitors in Burberry.* Did that mean anything?

Mr. Owens sat, carefully and uneasily, where I indicated at the table, then looked around. "Sure smells good in here. Kinda like bacon."

I laughed. "Yes, and unfortunately I burned most of it." Then, on impulse, I added, "Mr. Owens, could you eat a pork chop, already cooked, and just needing heating up?"

"Why, yes'm, I b'lieve I could. Don't go to no trouble, though."

"It's no trouble at all." I took the chop from the refrigerator, dumped it and the sauerkraut onto a square of tin foil, wrapped it up, and placed it on a baking sheet. Into the oven it went, along with a square of cornbread. Without asking, I poured a container of leftover black-eyed peas into a pan and set it on the stove, turned low to heat up.

Then I directed him to the downstairs bathroom to wash his hands. No one comes to my table with dirty hands, although I had to close my eyes to the fact that they would be the only clean bodily parts on the man.

While he was gone, I had a sudden urge to do something nice and offer to wash that filthy scarf. I picked it up to check the label, noting that I had not been wrong in identifying the maker. But when I turned the label over, I saw "Dry Clean Only" and got over my urge to do something nice.

To say that I was anxious to hear what he had to say is putting it mildly. I could hardly contain myself and had to struggle to keep from demanding what he knew and when he'd known it. Could I believe him? Well, why not? People, even officers of the law, often discuss important matters among themselves, unaware that others are listening.

To my way of thinking, Mr. Owens was a sudden and unexpected pipeline into the thinking of the investigators who were looking into Connie's death, and I was just before learning how high on their suspect list I was — something they wouldn't tell me until they snapped the handcuffs on.

Still, I could not bring myself to believe that they could actually suspect me. I mean, how *could* they, given that I had a lifetime of following the rules and walking the straight and narrow behind me? Plus being a faithful Presbyterian every step of the way?

Except, I reminded myself, they had nobody else to suspect. By the gatekeeper's written record, I was the only visitor that day to the Clayborn house — unless he had abandoned his post long enough for someone to get in unseen, which, from what Coleman had said, was a possibility they were looking into.

Back at the table, Mr. Owens seemed to marvel at the placemat, napkin, and utensils I'd put at his place. I quickly turned out the heated food on a plate and set it before him. Then I poured two cups of coffee and took a chair at the table, myself.

"Sure looks good," he said, and dug in.

He must have been half starved, for I got no further word from him until he'd cleaned his plate, emptied three cups of coffee, and sat back with a beatific smile on his face.

"That's the best I et in a long time," he said, almost in a state of bliss.

"I'm glad you enjoyed it. But now, Mr. Owens, tell me what you heard the deputies say. Tell me everything."

"Well, see, they was talkin' about how they got nobody else to pin it on 'cept you. So they're lookin' for something to make a case."

"But Coleman, I mean Sergeant Bates, said that the evidence proved I couldn't have done it. They know when and how long I was there, and all the evidence points to an earlier time of death."

"I don't know nothin' 'bout that, but I tell you, Miz Murdoch, them boys is all fine an' good, but if they need some evidence, they'll find it. One way or t'other."

I didn't believe what he so evidently did. The sheriff's department and the district attorney surely would not manufacture evidence. It frightened me, though, to realize that Mr. Owens had a great deal more experience in what they would and would not do than I did.

"I just don't understand," I said, leaning toward him. "How in the world could they think I did it? I wasn't there more than fifteen minutes, maybe twenty, from gatehouse to gatehouse, where my presence was duly noted both times. Coleman said she had been dead at least an hour or more. So that proves that somebody else got there before I did." I sighed and sat back. "Except there's no record of anybody else visiting her. But somebody *had* to, because she was dead when I got there."

"Well, see," Mr. Owens said as he pushed his plate away, "that's what they fin'lly figgered out. One of 'em said — this was while I was gettin' booked — he said you coulda come in the back way, killed her, then later on, come back in the front way so you'd have yourself a alibi. An' it's a pretty good one, 'cause if you come in the back way, nobody'd see you."

"The back way?" I sat up straight at the thought. "There's a back way into Grand View Estates?"

"Yes'm, it's real easy. Well, not so easy on foot, 'cause it's longer, but you go in on a fire lane back off New Hope Church Road, wiggle 'round up there on the mountain awhile, an' pretty soon you come right close to where they built them houses. You can look right down on 'em. But if you keep on a-goin', you come out on the Greenville Highway, an' by that time, you're just another car toolin' along. Nobody'd know the difference." He nodded his head in conclusion, then said, " 'Course it could be so overgrown by now, couldn't nobody get through on it."

"Oh, my goodness," I said, leaning back in my chair, just about done in. Not because his information put me in greater jeopardy — I could account for my time that entire day, and Lillian and Mildred and Ida Lee could confirm where I was every minute of it. No, in fact, if anything, a previously unknown access road into Grand View Estates opened up a certain can of worms I thought I'd sealed up for good.

Anybody could've gotten to the Clayborn

house, unseen by human eyes, by the back way. Certainly a random attack by an unknown person who just happened to be wandering through the woods would have to be seriously considered. A lone woman working in her kitchen, seen through a window, might've been a tempting sight to a criminally inclined stranger.

It also opened up the possibility that her husband could've left for work that morning, then snuck back home without being seen. As a homeowner, he would surely know about the fire lane.

There was also another possibility — that certain aforesaid can of worms. Either of the Ledbetters could've gotten in that way as well. Although, as I thought about it, I had to discount Emma Sue — she'd been in no physical or emotional state when I saw her to make that trek. And how would she know about it in the first place? But the pastor could've known — he'd grown up in Abbot County. Granted, he'd left to go to college and seminary at a fairly young age and had served a couple of small churches before being called by the First Presbyterian of Abbotsville, where he'd been for the past twenty years or so. During that much time, though, he could've easily reacquainted himself with the highways and byways of the county.

I could've cried. It made so much sense, especially in the face of the pastor's strange evasive actions over the past several days. But I didn't want to even think what I was thinking. I may have silently disagreed with Pastor Ledbetter on a few theological issues and vocally disagreed on a number of his high-handed methods, but it hurt me to the quick to raise the possibility that he could've done what had so obviously been done in Connie Clayborn's kitchen.

"Mr. Owens," I said, breaking the long silence that had ensued as I considered this new information and while Mr. Owens's stomach continued to greet the sudden influx of food, "I need to see that fire lane. I need to see how close it comes to the Clayborn house and how difficult it would be to get from one to the other. You know where it is and how to get there, so will you show me?"

"Anytime, ma'am, anytime. I know 'zactly where it is. I used to hunt back up in there. Did a little trappin', too. So I can show you anytime you wanta go."

"Right now?"

"Now?" Mr. Owens straightened up, causing an internal growl, as his eyes widened. "Ma'am, it's dark out there. You can't see

304

your hand in front of your face."

"Oh, come now, Mr. Owens, it's a little cloudy out, but the moon is up and I have a flashlight."

"Yes'm, but you can see a lot better in the daytime."

"Quite true," I agreed, "but the deputies — if they're still investigating the scene — can see *us* a lot better in the daytime, too. I'm hoping nobody'll be out there at night."

"Maybe not, but they'll have a patrol drive by ever' once in a while to make sure nobody's monkeyin' around out there."

"On the fire lane, too?"

He considered for a minute. "It ain't likely. Even if the fire lane's open, they don't have enough radio cars to cover the county, much less tackin' that on, too."

"Then it's more likely that the best time to go is in the dark of the night. You see, Mr. Owens, I trust your superior knowledge of the patrol circuits and so forth of the sheriff's department."

"Well, I sure have rid with 'em enough times," Mr. Owens said, quite modestly for one who had so much experience with law enforcement personnel. "I orta know what they're up to and where they go and how many times they do it."

"Then," I said, getting to my feet, "you're

just the man I need. Let me get my coat and a flashlight. I hope, though, that we'll be able to stay in the car and see what I need to see. I'm not all that eager to be tromping through the woods at night."

Looking somewhat stunned by my sudden decision, he kept his seat and watched as I searched a drawer for the flashlight and went into the hall for my coat.

Finally he stood, picked up his empty plate, and carried it to the sink. Then he mumbled, almost under his breath, "Me neither."

CHAPTER 32

Putting on my coat and finally locating a flashlight that worked, I led the way out the back door, then turned and locked it behind us. Mr. Owens had taken his time putting on his coat, then, following me, he moved slowly around the car to the passenger side then, as if reconsidering the wisdom of our expedition, seemed to hesitate before sliding in.

I was behind the wheel with the car cranked and running before he got his door closed. He was telling me without saying a word that what we were about to do might not be the best idea anybody'd ever had. I didn't care. Anything was better than sitting around waiting for something to happen. And wondering if, when it did, it would involve me.

"It'll warm up in a minute," I said, adjusting the heat vents, then beginning to back out of the driveway.

"It ain't too cold," Mr. Owens said, although he commenced wrapping his head with the scarf again.

"Which way, Mr. Owens?" I asked as we reached the street.

"Go west on the highway till you start up the mountain. Then take a left on Pisgah Road. Stay on it for a few miles, then turn on New Hope Church Road. I'll have to look for the next turn."

I shot him a sharp look. "You do know the way, don't you?"

"Yes'm, I do. But that fire lane ain't used much and, ma'am, it is dark."

Yes, it was, in spite of a low-hanging moon barely visible above the treetops. Strips of cloud streamed across it. Harbingers, I supposed, of the storm coming up from the south.

"Well, I'm in your hands, Mr. Owens, and I'm depending on you to get us there without getting lost."

"No'm, I won't do that."

But he shrank back against the seat, huddling down in his outsized coat. As the car warmed up, I began to get some whiffs of a musty odor. Mr. Owens needed more than a washing of hands, but, as he had spent the previous night in jail, I couldn't fault him. The sheriff's hotel, as I'd heard it

308

called, lacked a number of amenities.

I drove and drove, following Mr. Owens's directions, until I began to wonder if we'd end up in Tennessee or South Carolina. Gradually, though, I realized that we were making a wide circle through the county, all the while closing in on the back of Grand View Estates.

"Okay," Mr. Owens said, sitting up to look out the windshield. "Better slow down now. It'll be up here a little ways."

We'd been driving some thirty minutes or so, and I'd seen farmhouses, barns, and lonely clapboard churches that I'd never seen before. I'd had no call to be in the southwestern part of the county in a long while and, let me tell you, there wasn't that much to see. The occasional car passed us, heading toward town, but none was behind us. It was a lonely place, which was all to the good for what I had in mind.

"Right there!" Mr. Owens yelled, startling me after his long silence. "New Hope Church Road. Turn left."

Easy enough, because left was the only way to turn. New Hope Church Road either began or ended, depending on which way you were going, at Pisgah Road. It wasn't much of a road, narrow with crumbling pavement and no shoulders, obviously little used by travelers and forgotten by the Department of Transportation. And no wonder. All I could see were a few cleared fields interspersed with timbered tracts along the roadsides. I could feel the car shift down as the road began to rise along the side of the rounded mountain.

Mr. Owens still sat forward, peering out the windshield, on the alert for the fire lane. "I don't know as how you wanta take this fancy car on that fire lane. They may notta cleared it in a while."

Now you're telling me? I thought it, but didn't say it.

"Right yonder!" he suddenly yelled. "See that big rock? Turn left right there."

I slowed, peered at the huge boulder on the left side of the road, then asked, "Before or after it?"

"Um-m, lemme think."

"It makes a difference, Mr. Owens."

"Yes'm. Right after. Yeah, that's it. Turn left after you pass it. I used to come at it from t'other side. That's why I got mixed up. And, uh . . ." He stopped, thought a minute, then said, "I don't hardly know who you're talkin' to, so you can call me Lamar if you want to."

"Why, thank you, Lamar," I said, with a quick glance at him. "That's kind of you and easier for me." But I did not make the same offer to him, nor, I thought, did he expect it of me. Distinctions must be made for the comfort of all.

I carefully passed the boulder on the left side of an unpaved track consisting of two shallow ruts with weeds growing between them. I could hear them swish against the undercarriage of my car. I stopped and sat for a few minutes, gazing through the tunnel of my headlights into more weeds, bushes, and, on each side of the track, tall pines swaying slightly in the wind.

"You think the road'll get any worse? I don't want to get stuck."

"Oh, no'm. It looks in pretty good shape — better'n I thought it'd be. They have to keep it passable — fire laws or something."

"Let us hope," I murmured and began to creep along the track as pine trees on each side converged overhead. But I'd begun to doubt that it was a fire lane — too narrow for the department's huge trucks, for one thing. Of course it didn't matter to me what it was or how it was used if it gave access to the Clayborn house.

At one point, I thought I saw the gleam of metal to the right of the lane in a clump of bushes. I kept driving. "Lamar, did you see that?"

"See what?"

"There might've been a car parked back there."

"Could be," he said with no noticeable concern. "Lotsa people park up in here. Hunters an' the like. An' people who don't want nobody to know what they're up to."

"Oh," I said, and kept maneuvering along the uneven road.

We bumped along at a slow pace, the car listing now and then as it went in and out of dips in the road, but on the whole, it could've been worse. It was likely that the road had started as an animal path, then used by the Indians who had once roamed the mountains, as many paved and heavily used arteries in our area had been.

Mr. Owens, I mean Lamar, fully alert now, sat forward in his seat, watching the road in front, but more often gazing off to the left.

"You might orta turn off your lights," he said. "I'm thinkin' we're pretty close to some houses. They'll be down on the side of the hill a little ways."

"On my side?"

"Yes'm. They cut ledges in the hill to make a place to build on. So we'll be lookin' down on whichever house you wanta see."

I turned off the headlights and came to a full stop. It was so dark that I wondered what I'd been thinking to believe I could pick out Connie's house from the back, through the trees, and by its roof, which I'd never seen.

"It's too dark," I said. "I can't see a thing."

"Yes'm, but I got eyes like a cat. I'll find what you're lookin' for." Then with a wave of his hand, Lamar said, "Ease on up, but don't make no noise. I see a light down there a ways. Somebody's up and stirrin'."

That made sense, because it wasn't all that late. But I knew that the houses in the area were far apart, so I hoped that we could glide on by and no nosy neighbor would wonder at the sound of a heavy motor going past in the night.

"Lamar," I said, whispering because it just seemed the thing to do in the dark that surrounded us. "If I hit a tree, what're we going to do?"

"Aw, you won't hit no tree. But, if you do, it won't matter. We'll just get out and walk."

I rolled my eyes at the thought of walking all the miles we'd just driven and leaving my car as more evidence to be used against me. And as my eyes rolled, I realized that my vision was improving enough to make out the trees on either side and, glancing out of my window, to also see a cleared area where a large structure stretched out several yards below us. Lights were on in the house, as was one yard light over what appeared to be a garage.

"That it?" Lamar asked, whispering as I had done.

"No, I don't think so. The Clayborn house had a neighboring house on either side, but they were quite far apart. The next house may be it." And I eased the car along, trying to keep it quiet. I even turned off the heater fan to cut down on the noise.

Then I saw it. Or thought I did. We'd traveled what I deemed the width of two or three sizable lots from the first house when I saw the structure below us. No lights were on, but the lot was cleared enough for the moon to give us a clear view of the house I'd hoped never to go near again.

I stopped the car. "That's it," I said, really whispering this time. "See the walkway there running along the back of the house? And the swimming pool. They could walk right out of the house, take about two steps, and dive in."

Lamar was leaning awfully close to me so he could see out my window. I held my breath, while he said, "Don't see no swimming pool."

"Oh, it's under the tarp, the cover, whatever it is. See that long, dark rectangle right behind the house? That's it. You see any lights anywhere?"

"No'm. Might see some way over yonder," he said, pointing farther along the access road. "But it's just a flicker."

"That would be about right. When I was here in the daytime, I noticed that she had neighbors on both sides, but they weren't close at all."

I reached down and turned off the ignition, planning to sit there until I was sure I was looking at Connie's house and until I was sure no one else was watching it.

"Can you see the driveway," I asked, "and what about the street in front of the house?"

"Yeah, pretty well. What you want me to look for?"

"Patrol cars, Lamar."

"Oh, yeah."

"Actually, see if there're any kind of vehicles anywhere around. It may be, if they've released the crime scene, that the husband's there. I wouldn't want to run into him."

Lamar gave me a long, searching look, then mumbled, "Well, me neither."

CHAPTER 33

We sat there in the dark long enough for Lamar to get tired of leaning over to look out my window. He settled back in his seat, willing, it seemed, to stay there doing nothing for as long as I wanted.

I, however, was doing plenty. I was reliving that afternoon when I'd parked in Connie's drive, walked up onto the stone pathway, around to the back of the house, and on to the kitchen door. I could almost see myself ring the doorbell, rap on the window in the door, then, with an exasperated sigh, turn to leave. *Oh, if I'd only kept going.*

One thing was for sure, if I'd left without seeing that shoe, I wouldn't be sitting now on a dark lane in the woods, wondering what to do next.

But, with a mental shake, I turned my mind to do what I'd come to do — determine if Connie's house was accessible from the back. And, without a doubt, it was, one

way or the other. Oh, the fire lane hadn't
been the easiest to drive, but we'd done it,
and there were trees and laurel bushes on
the slope between the lane and the house.
But looking down on Connie's concrete
backyard, the growth didn't seem that thick
or the slope that steep, and it wasn't that
far — maybe fifty yards or so — from one
to the other. Anyone with a mind to could
make it with little trouble, and surely the
investigators knew that.

The one worrisome factor was that it
looked to be such an easy trek that even my
age and physical condition might not take
me out of consideration. Maybe I should
start using a cane.

"Looka there!" Lamar sat up with a start,
pointing down toward the house. "See
that?"

"What? Where?"

"Somebody's in there," he said in a raspy
whisper. "Watch that last winder at the end
of the house. Somebody's got a light on."

I peered through the windshield, straining
to see what I assumed was a bedroom
window, but even though I thought I could
see a bluish glow, I couldn't be certain I
was seeing anything.

"Are you sure?" I asked. "It may be a
reflection from something."

"I'm sure," he said. "My eyes is the onli-est things that work good. I can see in the dark."

"Like a cat," I said.

"Yes'm, jus' like a cat, an' that's some kinda light comin' from that winder. And it wadn't on a few minutes ago, meanin' somebody in there jus' turned it on."

"Oh, my goodness, Lamar," I said as a line of chills ran up my back. "It couldn't be a deputy, could it? I mean, we'd see a patrol car, wouldn't we?"

"Yes'm, there'd be a car, all right. They don't never hide 'less they're watchin' for speeders."

We watched in silence for several minutes in which the glow neither faded nor grew in brightness. No shadows passed in front of it, so it probably wasn't a lamp, even a lamp with one of those corkscrew bulbs that give such a pitiful amount of light.

"You think it's somebody with a flash-light?" I whispered.

"No'm, it'd be movin' around if it was a flashlight."

"What about a television set?"

"Don't think so. I seen enough of 'em when I'm walkin' by houses to know that light from them changes — kinda flickers, you know, goin' from light to dark, depen-

318

din' on what's goin' on."

"You're right, especially when there're no other lights on. So what could it be, Lamar, and who could've turned it on?"

"Maybe it's something on a timer."

The mention of a timer relieved my anxiety, but not for long. "If it's something on a timer, I'd think they'd have used a decent light. I mean, that's what timers are for — to make it look as if somebody's home. That little glow wouldn't deter anybody."

"Could be a clock."

I stared at him. "A clock?"

"Yeah, you know, one of them that throws the time up on the ceiling so you don't have to get out of bed."

I recalled the clock that Sam had given Lloyd one Christmas and how much he'd enjoyed waking in the middle of the night to see what time it was on the ceiling.

"Yes, but somebody has to press a button before it'll work, then I think it goes off by itself. And what we're seeing is still on." I let the minutes go by, then said, "But it wasn't on when we first got here, was it?"

"No'm. I'da seen it if it'd been on, but that whole house was dark as the grave when we got here."

"Oh, don't say that! I'm about to jump out of my skin as it is."

We sat in silence for a long few minutes, our eyes fixed on the dim block of light emanating from the room at the end of the house.

Then I blinked, stared again, and blinked some more. "It went off, Lamar! Didn't it? Can you see it?"

"No'm, it's off all right. Wonder what it was."

I leaned back, tired of staring into the dark. "Probably what you suggested — something on a timer. Maybe some electronic thing that automatically comes on and backs itself up." I didn't know what I was talking about, but I knew Lloyd had any number of in-boxes and out-boxes and Firefoxes and Zip drives and flash drives — none of which I understood nor wanted to understand.

Breaking the silence, I said, "Lamar?"

"Yes'm?"

"I need to go down that hill. Will you go with me in case I fall and break my neck?"

He waited so long to answer that I began to think he wasn't going to. Then he said, "Why you need to go?"

"To see if somebody could've approached the house this way. And left this way, too. If I can do it, anybody could." Even an out-of-shape pastor who had to stop and catch

320

his breath after climbing three steps to the podium.

"Yes'm, but the cops're already figuring you could. All you'd be doin' now is provin' it."

"Well," I said with some asperity, "I wouldn't *tell* them I'd proved it." I looked him straight in the eye. "Would you?"

"Oh, no, ma'am, me, neither. I wouldn't tell."

"Then let's go." I stuffed the car keys deep in my coat pocket, then crammed my pocketbook under the seat, feeling slightly off-kilter without it.

After unwrapping the scarf from around his head, Lamar carefully draped it across his shoulders. I started to open my door, then stopped.

"The car lights'll come on, won't they?"

"Yes'm, but I might can fix 'em." He twisted around and stretched for the overhead lights. He popped off the covers and unscrewed a couple of bulbs. "That might not be all of 'em. These new cars got lights all over the place."

"Then let's be quick getting out, but don't slam the door. A flash of light might be missed, but the sound of two car doors slamming will carry."

We both got out, quietly pressing on our

doors so they'd close enough to turn off a few interior lights that came on.

A thick row of laurel or some kind of bushes interspersed with pines ran along the edge of the road. We walked carefully beside them, looking for a break in the undergrowth. I was surprised at how well I could see — maybe the clouds had passed on. The lane was clearly visible, as was the roof of Connie's house below us, but deep in the thicket beneath the trees, it was as dark as pitch.

"Here's a place," Lamar said, jumping the shallow ditch and diving between two laurels.

I hesitated, then followed him, expecting to be able to stand on the other side. Instead, limbs and leaves surrounded me and it was all I could do to push on through, hunched over and sliding on the pine needle-covered ground.

"Wait, Lamar," I gasped, pushing a branch out of my face and getting scratched in the process. "Don't go so fast."

He squatted down and waited. "It's pretty thick in here," he said as I caught up with him. "Not as easy as it looks."

"Should we go back?"

"Not 'less you just want to. I bet it'll clear out closer to the house."

He was right. The Clayborns had cleared some of the undergrowth immediately above the house, which would've made for an easier descent if they hadn't left the pine needles. We slipped and slid, grabbing trees, branches, and each other to stay reasonably upright. Finally we reached the top of a retaining wall and squatted down behind a row of evenly planted shrubs — azaleas, maybe. We stopped to survey the house and the concrete yard that featured the dark cover over the pool. Then I looked down — it was at least a man's height to the pool deck. I discarded the idea of jumping.

"You could break a leg gettin' down from here," Lamar whispered. "We better go back."

"Not yet. Let's slide down to the end of this wall. See if there's a way to get into the yard without jumping."

He didn't say anything, just kept squatting as he thought for a while. "Okay." And we began moving along the top of the retaining wall, staying low behind the shrubs, to the far corner, where, lo and behold, we found a set of steps that led down to the pool deck.

When we got to the bottom of the steps, we both stopped, crouched down low behind some deck chairs, and looked across the pool to the back of the house.

Holding my breath, I leaned close to Lamar's ear and whispered, "Think we ought to see if we can tell where that light came from? Maybe see if anybody's in there?"

"No'm. I think we oughta go back up."

But we were so close, and by this time I had about convinced myself that no one was in the house. Surely if there was, we would've heard something or seen some movement by this time. Besides, there was another possibility to consider. If someone *was* rummaging around in the house and we could make an identification, Detective Ellis would have a much better suspect than he now had. Which was me.

CHAPTER 34

"Scoot around these chairs," I whispered, giving him a nudge with my shoulder. "If anybody's looking, they won't see us. We're beyond the end of the house."

He grunted, hesitated, then moved, and so did I. We stayed out of a direct line from any window and crept around a metal table, minus its umbrella, and several large terra-cotta pots.

Reaching the corner of the house, I edged one eye to the window and looked into total darkness. Lamar was right on my heels, scrooched up next to me and clinging to the siding.

"Don't make no noise," he whispered.

I nodded my head, trying to pierce the dark of the room and see something that would make this perilous trek worth the risks. And worth the stinging scratches on my hands and face as well.

Trying to see inside, I pressed my forehead

against a pane of glass and nearly died of shock. Every light in the world — inside and out — came on, and a siren shrieked like a banshee, echoing and bouncing around the hills of Grand View Estates. My heart jumped a mile, and my nerves went haywire. Lamar yelled and pushed at me as he scrambled to get away.

I was screaming, too — I think. I couldn't hear anything but the wailing blasts of noise summoning every neighbor, gatekeeper, and deputy sheriff within miles of the place.

Lamar grabbed my arm, pulled, and as I turned to run, my feet tangled with his and, tripping each other, down we went. Expecting to hit the concrete pavement, I braced myself for a hard landing. Instead, I bounced — and so did Lamar, first on top of me, then onto the pool cover, as water sloshed under us.

Hoping we weren't over the deep end, I pushed at Lamar. "Hurry!" I panted, getting my knees under me in an effort to rise. "Get up, Lamar! Run!"

Struggling to his feet, he set the water undulating under us and I went sprawling again. He kept moving, and the last I saw of him was his high-stepping, bouncing run across the roiling pool cover, a jump to the deck, and a sprint up the steps into the laurel thicket.

I had to move, leave, get out of there, as far away as I could get from the ear-splitting noise of the siren and the eye-watering glare of the lights. But every effort to stand tipped me over and down again. So I crawled. I crawled to the edge of the pool, rolled onto the deck, finally got to my feet, and ran to the steps, panting and heaving, frightened half to death.

Up the hill I scrambled on hands and knees, grabbing on to roots and branches, pushing and pulling myself up the slippery incline, ignoring vines and branches and briars. Lord, they even had spotlights in the trees! Keeping low — well, I had to — it was too steep to stand up — I finally reached the ditch at the top, coming out a good bit farther along than where we'd gone in.

I saw the car, darkly gleaming from the glare below. It was right where I'd left it, and nothing had ever looked so good. Hardly able to get my breath, I ran toward it, feeling for the keys in my pocket. No matter if the interior lights came on now — who would notice in the several thousand watts already burning?

I jerked the door open, tumbled in, jabbed the key into the ignition, and took off, bumping and rocking back and forth on the little-used lane. I couldn't turn the car around — the lane was too narrow — and I didn't know where I was going. I just drove wherever it went — it didn't matter as long as I ended up far from where I was.

And Lamar? Who knew? I'd thought he'd be waiting in the car, but there was no sign of him.

Maybe I'd come up on him walking or running along the lane, but I didn't. As I put some distance between me and the Clayborn house, with all its lights and the racket still echoing and bouncing around the hills, I began to worry about him.

What if the deputies found him and arrested him? What if he was hiding in the woods, only to freeze to death during the night? Well, it wasn't that cold, but that didn't ease my concern for him.

Finally I reached an intersection where the lane led onto a decent paved road with curbs and stop signs and cars with lights on. That's when I remembered to turn mine on. I'd been driving half blind for who-knew-how-long. That's what happens when your mind is on leaving in a hurry.

Who would've thought that the Clayborn house was wired to the gills? I shivered and shook at how close we'd come to being caught sneaking around a crime scene, and, for all I knew, Lamar had been or was about to be. I didn't know what to do but to keep on going. So I did.

Turning onto the highway, I headed toward town, my eyes peeled for a small, huddled figure trudging along the side. I didn't see anybody, huddled or not, and now that I was reasonably safe, regret and a sense of loss swept over me. He'd been so helpful and so considerate, and I'd just gone off and left him. If the deputies found him in the vicinity of the Clayborn house, what would they think? That he'd been there before? Maybe, but I consoled myself by recalling that he'd seemed well armed with alibis, some of which might actually hold up.

But I couldn't shake the awful feeling that I'd thought only of myself, without one thought of his safety. Then, as I neared Main Street, I had another thought that gave me considerable relief — he'd left me first, hadn't he?

I almost turned for home, but thought better of it. I needed an alibi. I didn't like the thought of Lieutenant Peavey showing up at my house and demanding an account of my recent activities. What could I say? *Oh, I've been home all evening, Lieutenant, but, no, there's no one who can confirm it.*

How well would that go over? And if they caught Lamar anywhere near the Clayborn house, how long would he hold out before telling it all? I'd be nabbed for attempted breaking and entering — although I'd not been close to getting in nor had I even wanted to — and caught in a lie as well. My goose was just before being thoroughly cooked.

Well, you do the best you can, so I turned off Main Street but not toward home. I'd go see Coleman again on his last night of sign sitting. He'd be able to testify to the fact that I had visited him at least part of the evening. Maybe he wouldn't notice the time, so he could be wishy-washy about how long I was with him. Some things have to be left to chance, but what better alibi can you have than one from a deputy sergeant of the sheriff's department?

Driving out on the boulevard, I glanced at the clock on the dashboard — barely nine o'clock. Where was Lamar Owens? I couldn't shake the feeling of responsibility for him, but I didn't know what to do about it. It certainly wouldn't have helped either of us if I'd lingered at the Clayborn house until the deputies got there.

And to depress me further, I had seen for

myself that the gatekeeper's record of visitors didn't amount to a hill of beans. *Anyone* could have gotten to that house without being seen and could've left the same way if they didn't mind scrambling up and down a bush-covered hillside. And, of course, Lieutenant Peavey and Detective Ellis would include me in that *anyone*. Until, that is, I presented them with a list of iron-clad alibis for the entire day of Connie's death up to and including the time I entered Grand View Estates and the time I reported what I'd found.

But that *anyone* could include Pastor Ledbetter, as unlikely and unthinkable as that was. He wasn't in the best of shape, constantly fighting the battle of the bulge and rarely exercising. A large man to begin with, he had reached the age when any extra pounds went to his midsection and stayed there. It wouldn't have been easy for him to have gotten to and from Connie's house the back way, but it could've been done and no one would've been the wiser.

I didn't want to even think that. I *hated* thinking it. I couldn't bring myself to believe it, but there was no getting around the fact that he was acting in unusually strange ways — even for him.

I put it all out of my mind as I saw

Coleman's car parked on the wide shoulder of the boulevard. Pulling in behind it and parking, I was thankful there were no other visitors, specifically a certain ditzy librarian. I had enough on my mind without adding her romantic enthusiasm for a married man, and a younger one, at that.

CHAPTER 35

I pulled down the visor to check my stinging face in the mirror. Finding a Kleenex, I
wet it with my tongue to clean the long briar
scratch across my forehead. Then pulling a
few wisps of hair down to cover it, I hoped
Coleman wouldn't notice. No need to give
him a reason to question how I'd gotten it.

There was enough light from the streetlamps on the boulevard to give me pause
when I saw the state of my hands. Shocked
at the scratches on them and the dirt under
my nails — the ones that weren't broken —
I did my best to clean them, then gave up. I
didn't have that much saliva. Instead, I
found a pair of gloves in the car and put
them on. It was November, after all.

Then I made the climb over the railing,
down the little slope — which was nothing
compared to the one I'd recently been on
— and along the path, waving merrily to
Coleman as I went. He had the ladder wait-

ing for me on the far side of the platform.

"What're you doing here, Miss Julia?" Coleman called down as I began the climb to the platform. But he was smiling and seemed glad to see me. I had a feeling that he'd about had enough of solitary sign sitting in spite of all the horn blowing, catcalls, and eye-popping spectacles that kept him company.

"Oh, I just got lonely at home, and thought you wouldn't mind some company." I caught my breath as he helped me off the ladder. Then, brushing leaves and twigs, undoubtedly from the Clayborn property, from my coat, I made light of my dishevelment. "My goodness, Coleman," I said, laughing, "if you do this again, you should clear out that path down there."

"Don't want it too clear," he said, leading me over to his tent. "It keeps down the riffraff." He helped me crawl into the tent, which I had promised myself not to get stuck in again, but there I was, folded into a limb-cramping position from which I dreaded the pain of getting out. Coleman brought his lawn chair over and sat beside the open flap of the tent. "Mr. Sam didn't get back?"

"No, and I'm worried he'll get caught in that ice storm. Have you heard the weather forecast lately?"

"The storm's still on the way, but it may miss us — might be too far to the east. Raleigh's in its path, though, so he better keep an eye on it." Coleman's hands dangled between his knees as he leaned over to talk with me. "You heard anything more about the investigation?"

"No. Well, not directly. But I have heard that there might be a back way into Grand View Estates. And that means that anybody using it wouldn't show up on the gatekeeper's record. Which could put me back in contention for the prime suspect spot. Although," I said, laughing in a disparaging way, "how anybody could think *I* would've known about it is beyond me. I can hardly find my way downtown."

"I'll be back on duty Monday morning, so I'll see what's going on."

"That'll be good," I said, then wondered how to get off that subject before I said too much. "Oh, Coleman, I'm sorry. I should've brought you something to eat. Or a hot drink, at least. I don't know where my mind is."

He smiled. "Don't worry about it. I don't need anything. Besides, Roberta will be by in a little while."

"Then I better be gone before she gets

335

here." I began to gather myself to leave the tent. "I just dropped by to see how you're doing, and, I admit, to pass the time while Sam's away."

"Uh, Miss Julia," Coleman said, looking down at his hands. "Before you go . . . I think I might have a problem, and I don't much know what to do about it. But you mentioned it, so I thought . . ."

"Roberta?"

He looked up with a rueful grin. "Yeah."

The long blast of a car horn drew our attention to the street, and Coleman turned to wave. Then, turning back with a frown, he said, "It's gotten so bad that I was thinking of going on home tonight. You know, to avoid her. But tomorrow will be my best day with people coming by after church to donate. And I sure do want to collect enough for that playground equipment."

"Coleman, I . . ."

"Nope." He shook his head. "This is my thing, and I'm going to see it through. I thank you for the offer, though." He grinned. "If that's what you were going to do."

"It was, and the offer will stay open if you change your mind. But, Coleman, what is Roberta doing? I mean, other than bringing hot chocolate and hot apple pies?"

"Well, that and hamburgers and home-made cake and fudge and coffee, and this morning she brought sausage biscuits, ham biscuits, and sausage and egg biscuits — so I'd have a choice. And for lunch she brought Kentucky Fried Chicken and more biscuits, and said she'd have a surprise for me tonight. And, see," he said, with a tinge of exasperation, "it was okay when she was coming once a day, but today's Saturday and she was off. She was here, bearing gifts, every time I turned around, and she's off again tomorrow. Only thing, though, so is Binkie."

"My word," I said, addressing the smallest problem first. "How do you eat all that, along with what other people bring?"

"I don't. I give it away, or throw it out. Hate to do it, but . . ." He turned up his hands. "And she doesn't just bring food and leave. She's staying longer and longer each time, asking my favorite color and when my birthday is and what I like to do for fun. I tell you, Miss Julia, I about get a crick in my neck from looking down at her and talking so long."

I almost laughed at the worried look on his face. Yet it was plain that Coleman didn't think it a laughing matter, so I responded in a sympathetic manner.

"I don't suppose you could be busy with something? Too busy to talk, I mean."

"I've tried that," he said, "but it doesn't work. She says she'll wait till I'm through. I can't even hide and pretend I'm not here."

There was no getting around it — Roberta was making a nuisance of herself, and I marveled at how she could throw herself at an indifferent man the way she was doing. Most women could take a hint, but Roberta was off in some vague dreamworld populated by heroic men and pre-Raphaelite women. And, come to think of it, if she'd brush out her hair, she'd look just like one of those women.

"Let me study on this, Coleman," I said. "I have an idea or two, although I expect she'll calm down when you're not as available as you are now. Roberta is prone to going off on tangents, then veering off in other directions before you know it."

"Well," Coleman said with a laugh, "I hope she veers off before Binkie knows it. I'd never hear the end of it."

"Yoo-hoo!"

Coleman straightened up and turned to look toward the street. "Oh, Lord, here she comes."

"Binkie?"

"No, Roberta. Just stay in the tent, Miss

338

Julia. I'll get rid of her as soon as I can."

Soon wasn't soon enough for me. My limbs began to tremble from my position in the tight quarters, and after several minutes, during which I could catch only a few words of the prolonged conversation at the other end of the platform, I'd had enough. Roberta needed a good talking-to, and I decided to give her one.

With no leverage and no ballast in Coleman's chair, I had no option but to crawl out on my hands and knees, and keep crawling to the head of the ladder. Once there, I quickly descended to the ground. Well, as quickly as I could manage, because I'd become so stiff and sore from all the unaccustomed exercise I'd gotten on a certain hillside, I could barely straighten up.

But I reached the ground in reasonable shape and proceeded to march under the platform to Roberta's side before either of them noticed me. I stood in the dark for a minute, watching and listening, and while I did, I was moved with pity for a lonely woman looking for love in all the wrong places.

Roberta's head was tilted back so she could look up at Coleman, as she rattled on and on about the courage and heroism of warrior kings, medieval knights, and deputy sheriffs. No wonder he didn't want Binkie to know what was going on — she'd laugh her head off.

I walked right up to Roberta, put my hand on her arm, and said, "Roberta."

She screamed and jumped a mile.

"It's just me," I said. "Now, come on. It's time to go."

"But . . . what're you doing here? I mean, where did you come from? Oh, my goodness, Miss Julia," she said, patting her heaving chest, "you scared me to death."

"Sorry, but I need you to walk me to the car."

"Oh, of course. Are you all right?" Then, with a wave behind her, she called, "See you later, Coleman. Miss Julia needs some help." Roberta had a good heart — she was just as willing to offer assistance to me as she was to stand around talking to Coleman half the night.

After asking her to sit with me awhile, she got into the passenger seat of my car, as, avoiding passing cars, I took my life in my hands and made my way to the driver's side.

"I'm so glad you came along, Roberta," I said. "Like you, I was concerned about Coleman's welfare, then found the trek through the weeds more arduous than I'd thought."

"I'm just happy I was here to help," she said, as I felt a smidgen of guilt for taking advantage of her good heart. "Is there anything else I can do? Can I take you home?"

"I'm all right now, thank you. As one grows older, you know, one must learn to slow down." I paused to allow her to consider the limitations of age, then went on. "But there is one thing I've been wanting to ask you. I hate to admit this, Roberta, but I've never seen *Pride and Prejudice,* and I know you have the videos. Could you, would you . . . ?"

"Oh, Miss Julia, of course!" she said, waving her hands in excitement. "You must see it — it's a classic, and you'll love it. Then we can talk about it. Don't you just love to discuss a book or a movie with someone who really understands? Whenever you want to watch it, just let me know. I'll bring it to you."

"Well, Sam won't be home till late tomorrow, and I was thinking what a long day it was going to be. I do have a problem, though. I don't know how to work the video player or whatever you call it, so I was wondering if you and I could watch it together at your house. Maybe tomorrow? You could give me all the historical background and so forth that would make it more meaningful for me."

"Oh, I would *love* to! What time can you come? Right after church? I could fix some sandwiches." She stopped as if remembering something. "I was planning to bring some for Coleman's lunch. . . ."

"Don't worry about that, Roberta. The Baptist ladies are bringing an absolute spread — a full hot meal, I've heard. Believe me, he won't starve."

"Well . . ."

"Thank you so much for giving me such a treat. I have *longed* to see that movie, especially the wonderful Mr. Darcy. After hearing you speak of him so often, he must be quite special."

"Oh, he is! I can't wait to share him with you."

My eyebrows went up at that, but I let it pass. After deciding that I would come calling as soon after church as I could manage, she hopped out of my car and, flapping her hands, hurried to her own.

Well, I thought, as I pulled away from the curb to head for home, that was a successful diversion of the attention she'd been showering on Coleman. Of course, it meant my entire Sunday afternoon would be taken up with watching videos one after the other for hours on end. But those would be hours that would keep Roberta home and out of Coleman's hair, so I could view them as a reasonable sacrifice for his benefit.

If there's one thing I've learned, it's this: if there's something you really need to do — like locate a certain pastor — but you're thwarted at every turn, then go to the next item on your list and get that done in its place. In other words, use the time judiciously, which was what I was doing.

As I drove up the boulevard to the gas station to turn around for home, I began to plan my Sunday. As soon as I got out of bed, I would call Roberta and ask her out for breakfast. Then we'd go to church together — that would take care of any morning visits to Coleman.

After church, I'd send her on home to set up the viewing, while I lingered to waylay Pastor Ledbetter — if he showed up to preach. If he didn't, I'd have to track him down some other way. Or just go ahead and tell Detective Ellis what I knew and be done with it. Then we'd see just how adroit the pastor was at avoiding an all points bulletin.

I was about to work up another round of anger at the position that both Connie — although she couldn't really be blamed — and Pastor Ledbetter had put me in. And to make it worse, I'd put my own self into the position of having to endure a long, boring afternoon watching a two-hundred-year-old romance and listening to Roberta's raptures over a make-believe Mr. Darcy.

My goodness, I thought with a touch of self-congratulation, *what I'm willing to do for my friends!*

As I crossed Main Street to head toward Polk, I noticed how little traffic was out and about. Abbotsville rolled up the sidewalks fairly early on a winter's night, and, though it was barely past my usual bedtime, a great, lonely feeling swept over me. Especially since I knew I'd have to enter a dark and empty house all by myself.

Shivering at the thought, I felt a wisp of air blow across the back of my neck and heard a soft whisper.

"Hey, Miz Murdoch."

CHAPTER 36

I screamed. Shock, like an electric charge, zipped through my system and I went stiff as a board, my hands locking onto the steering wheel. *Kidnapping! Carjacking! Robbery! Assault and battery! Murder!* Or worse.

I slammed on the brakes, screeching to a stop in the middle of the street, snatched up my pocketbook, and flailed away at whoever was behind me.

"Whoa," Lamar Owens yelled, cringing from the onslaught. "Hold on, it's me! It's me!"

"Oh, *Lord,*" I moaned, sagging over the steering wheel, as limp as a rag with relief. "Lord, Lamar, you took ten years off my life, and I don't have that many to lose. Where have you *been*?"

"Back here on the floorboard."

"What!" I said, turning to stare at him. "You've been in my car all this time? While I was looking for you and worrying about you, you were on the floorboard all along?"

"Well, no'm, not all along. I hightailed it when that siren went off and all the lights come on, and I didn't stop till I got to the highway. Uh, ma'am?" Lamar pointed at the street in front of us. "You gonna hit something."

It helps when one brakes a car to then put the gear into park, which I quickly did. On second thought, I reengaged the gear and pulled the car out of the middle of the street and parked on the side. I was in no condition to be driving, anyway.

My nerves still twanging away, I turned back to Lamar and, patting my chest, said, "I'm still hyperventilating from you creeping up on me like that." Then, catching my breath, I demanded, "So what else did you do? How did you get here from there?"

"Well, I started walkin' when I got to the highway — didn't wanta look like I was runnin' away from something. An' you won't believe the luck! A deputy on patrol stopped an' picked me up. Took me right to the Mc-Donald's on the MLK an' give me some money for a hamburger an' a milkshake. Some of them deputies is good boys."

"Oh, Lord," I groaned, realizing that I was calling on Him an inordinate number of times, but I was in great need of His help.

"Lamar, didn't it occur to you that the deputy might put two and two together with you so close to the house with all the alarms going off?"

"Well, I thought about it, 'cause his radio was about to send him right back where I come from, but then it changed its mind and sent him to the MLK to check on a drunk driver. When we got to McDonald's, he about throwed me outta the car, he was in such a hurry. So he didn't think nothin' of it."

I blew out my breath and tried to slow my heart rate. "So how'd you get in my car? And weren't you concerned about me? I mean, Lamar, you just *left* me!"

"Yes'm, an' I feel kinda bad about that. But, see, I figgered they was no use both us gettin' caught. An' you had a better chance of talkin' your way out of it if I wadn't around. I mean, some of them boys is bad about lookin' up my record."

"I see what you mean," I said tiredly. What else could I say? "All right, you've explained that. Now explain how and when you got in my car."

"Well, I was pretty much stuck at the Mc-Donald's, an' I'd already thought about spending the night at the mission 'cause it's gettin' cold at night. You noticed how cold it's gettin' at night? Downright freezin'."

"No. I mean yes, of course I have. But that's beside the point. I want to know how and why you got from McDonald's to the back floorboard of my car."

"Oh, well, yes, ma'am. I set out to walk to the mission, which to get there you have to take the MLK, so I was goin' along there an' the cars was whizzing past an' I was about to freeze, 'cause, see, I lost my scarf somewheres an' my ears was about to fall off. So when I seen your car parked right where I had to pass by, I just said to myself, 'Lamar, there's a warm place just a-settin' there.' An' I crawled in while you was talkin' to Sergeant Bates. I mean, I guess that's what you was doin'. I didn't try to listen in or nothin'."

"They Lord," I mumbled, giving up, because it all made a warped kind of sense the way he told it. "Well, I'm glad you're all right, and I'm glad neither of us is in jail."

"Oh, it ain't so bad. They treat you pretty good."

I rolled my eyes without dissent, conceding the point to one more experienced than I in such matters. Starting the car and pulling carefully out into the street, I had a brief, crazed impulse to invite him to stay the night at my house. I quickly suppressed

348

it, even though I was not looking forward to facing my empty house alone. Besides, how would it look?

"I'm going to take you to the mission, Lamar. I expect you've had enough walking for one night."

"Yes, ma'am, I sure have. I'll be glad to crawl in bed after all we done tonight."

"That reminds me," I said, glancing in the rearview mirror. "I hope, Lamar, that you'll keep everything we've done to yourself. Nobody, and I mean *nobody,* needs to know that we were anywhere within miles of that house. If it got out, we could be in trouble the likes of which neither of us has ever seen. You understand?"

"Uh-huh. I mean, no'm, I won't tell nobody."

"Actually," I went on, then stopped. I wanted to impress on him the importance of keeping our activities secret, but recognizing how unlikely that was, I decided to give him the right way to tell it. "Actually," I said again, "we didn't do anything wrong — we didn't damage anything and we didn't interfere with a crime scene. We were just seeing if it was possible to access the house the back way. Right?"

"Yes'm, that's what we did and we could."

I glanced again in the rearview mirror

and, to test him, asked, "Could what?"

"Assess the house."

"No, Lamar, no! Not as*sess* the house, but *acc*ess it — to get to it. We were seeing if anyone could *get to it* from the back way."

"Yes, ma'am, an' they could."

"That's right." I blew out my breath, realizing how close I'd come to letting him tell a roomful of deputies that we'd been casing the Clayborn house with intent to break, enter, and commit mayhem. That could put us *under* the jail, because I had little doubt that he would eventually tell somebody something. I just hoped he'd be able to hold off until the true criminal had been tried and convicted, and what Lamar might say no longer mattered.

A red light stopped me, even though there were no other cars in sight. But I obey the rules, traffic or no traffic. I was so tired I could hardly see straight and was happy to wait the minute or so for a green light. Lamar sat in silence behind me, seemingly content to be in a warm place without feeling the need to talk. I heard him yawn, his jaws creaking with the effort.

Then it hit me.

"*Lamar!* Oh, my goodness, Lamar!"

"What? What?"

"*Where* did you lose that scarf?"

"Um, well, I don't know. I guess if I did, it wouldn't be lost."

Well, that made sense, but it didn't help.

"Think back," I urged. "When was the last time you remember having it? Where were you? What were you doing?"

"Lemme think a minute. I prob'ly can come up with it in a minute. Uh, ma'am? Light's green."

I pulled to the side of the street again and parked. At this rate, I'd never get home.

"Let me help you remember, Lamar. You had it on when we left my house. I saw you wrap it around your head."

"Yes'm, my ears get cold."

"Okay, when did you . . . Oh, I remember! You unwrapped it when we parked in the fire lane. It was right before we got out of the car. Did you leave it in here?" I brushed my hand across the front seat where he'd been sitting, then felt around the floorboard.

"No'm, I 'member having it after that. It got hung up on a bush one time when we was goin' down that hill. It mighta got outta kilter then, 'cause I 'member stumblin' on the long end when I went down them steps."

"Okay, what did you do with it when you stumbled? Did you wrap it back around your neck?"

"Yes'm, I kinda think I did. I wouldna left

it, I know that."

So then I asked the question whose answer I feared to hear. "When the deputy picked you up on the highway, did you still have it?"

There was a long silence from the backseat. "No'm, I guess I didn't 'cause my ears was about to freeze off."

Oh, me. I leaned my head against the steering wheel, feeling another testy interview with Detective Ellis coming on.

Then I sat up, stiffening my spine and accepting my fate. "That means, Lamar, that you lost it at the house or when you went back up the hill or on the access road when you were running to the highway. And, that being the case, I can tell you exactly where it is now."

"Where?" Lamar asked eagerly. "I sure do need it."

"You won't get it anytime soon. The deputies would've searched every inch of that place after the alarms went off. So if you lost it anywhere around there, you can bet they have it. And they'll be looking for the owner."

Another long silence ensued as he processed that information. Then he said, "That don't sound too good."

Well, no, it didn't.

"How long had you had the scarf, Lamar?" I asked, wondering if the distinctive plaid design and filthy condition would immediately identify its owner, especially since its owner made frequent use of the sheriff's department's taxi service.

"I ain't had it a whole year yet!" he said, suddenly realizing, it seemed, the value of what he'd lost. "Best thing I ever found at the mission, and now it's gone. I don't know what I'm gonna wrap up in, an' it's gettin' on to wintertime when I'll need it worser'n I do now."

"We'll find you something else. Don't worry about it." What was done was done, I thought with a despairing sigh, and I had to accept it. Our fate, in the form of a recycled Burberry scarf, was now in the hands of the sheriff's forensic evidence team.

I edged the car back into the street and drove to the mission on Railroad Avenue. "Here we are," I said, drawing up near the door. A single light burned over the door, indicating, I hoped, that beds were still available. I turned toward the backseat. "Look, Lamar, I'd never encourage anyone to tell an untruth, so if anybody asks, you must answer. But keep in mind that you don't have to add anything extra."

He opened the door, put one foot out of

the car, and turned to me. "Yes, ma'am, but don't you worry. Them boys don't half believe anything I say, anyway."

"Well then, thank you for all your help tonight. I couldn't have done it without you." Although by that time, I was wishing I had.

CHAPTER 37

By the time I got home, I was no longer concerned about entering an empty house. I was too tired to care. If anybody was waiting to get me, they could just have me.

That thought didn't keep me from turning on lights as I went through each room, looking behind the sofa and into the hall closet — the pantry, too — and making sure all the doors were locked. Trudging up the stairs, I firmly put out of my mind all the possible future ramifications of the night's activities. There was nothing I could do to forestall any of them. All I wanted was a bath and a bed.

And when I'd gotten both, I lay in bed, all but asleep with only two questions running through my mind — could fingerprints be detected on Scottish wool, and how in the world was I going to get through a whole day in Roberta's company?

Maybe Sam would be home early and save

me. If he left Raleigh about sunup, he'd be home by noon or so. That would give me a good excuse to forgo Mr. Darcy, but it wouldn't help Coleman. He'd have to put up with Roberta's visits all afternoon.

Then I began thinking, as I turned over in bed, about the matter of fingerprints on Lamar's scarf. I wasn't concerned about Lamar's prints — obviously they'd be on it. But mine would be, too. I'd picked up the dirty thing with an eye to putting it in the washing machine and had refrained only after reading the label.

It occurred to me that if I'd ignored the cleaning instructions and washed it anyway, I wouldn't be worried about fingerprints now. Of course, Lamar might've ended up with a Burberry handkerchief instead of a scarf, but his loss could've been rectified by the purchase of a hat with earflaps.

Then with a sudden eye-opening thought, it came to me that cloth might not be the ideal conveyer of print evidence. I mean, imprints of fingertips might not adhere to cloth as they would to more solid surfaces, so the investigators would have nothing to work with. But what did I know? Still, it was something to be devoutly wished, and I fell asleep with that hopeful thought.

■ ■ ■ ■

I woke that Sunday morning so stiff and sore I could barely crawl out of bed. Hunched over and shambling along, I made it to the shower stall and stood under a hot spray until things loosened up enough to return me to a semblance of normality. Then I took two aspirins.

And all along, a cloud of dread hovered over my head. *I don't want to do it. How can I get out of it? Think of a good excuse not to do it.* Maybe I could get sick.

I sighed, giving in to the inevitable, as I finished dressing and headed for the telephone to put my plan of giving Coleman a full day's peace into action.

"Roberta?" I said when she answered. "It's Julia. I hope I'm not calling too early, but I wondered if you'd like to have breakfast with me. We could go on to church together afterward."

"Oooh, that sounds delightful," Roberta said with an eagerness that put me to shame. "But, you know, I was going to take some banana nut bread to Coleman this morning. I'd hate for him to miss that."

"I expect Binkie and little Gracie are taking care of his breakfast, don't you think?"

"I guess so, but I am so torn. I'd love to have breakfast with you, Julia, but I don't want him to go without."

"I promise you, he won't."

"Well, if we do it, what about Sunday school?"

I declare, I didn't think it would be so hard to do something nice.

"I say we bypass it. I want to have enough time for you to give me the background of *Pride and Prejudice* so I can appreciate it as it deserves."

"Oh, Julia, that's exactly what I was thinking. You are such a perceptive reader and I know how you love good literature. That decides it, I would love to share breakfast and that most wonderful eighteenth century with you!"

Telling her that I would pick her up and that we'd go to the country club grill, I hung up, feeling virtuous after working so hard to do a good deed for Coleman's benefit. And, come to think of it, for Roberta's benefit, too — she didn't need to be displaying such a juvenile infatuation so publicly. I mean, she was a *librarian,* for goodness sakes.

Still, I dreaded being tied up all day for I had counted on being able to corner Pastor Ledbetter after church — the only time and place it looked as if I'd be able to catch him.

So it wasn't that I didn't appreciate Roberta's company, it was just that I wasn't looking forward to being in it all day.

After having a quick cup of coffee, I prepared to leave the house. I didn't fear missing a call from Sam — he'd know I'd be at church — but it would've been comforting to know that he was on his way home. Especially when I walked out to the car and felt the damp cold from dark, low-hanging clouds. Abbotsville might not be in the direct path of the oncoming storm, but we might well be on the sidelines of it.

Roberta started talking as soon as she got in the car, and she talked through her scanty breakfast of oatmeal and fruit and continued talking until we got out of the car in the church parking lot. I learned more than I ever wanted to know about comedies of manners, making good marriages, and the perils of having too many daughters in the eighteenth century.

Entering the church a minute or two late, I quickly settled into my usual pew with Roberta attached to my side. With a quick glance around, I determined that the Pickens family, including Lloyd, had not made it to church. Maybe the weather was too raw for the little girls with their bad colds, or maybe they were enjoying a leisurely breakfast. I caught sight of LuAnne sitting across the aisle — she was almost hidden beside Leonard, who would make about three of her. And Callie and some of her brood of children were near the front, but I didn't see Emma Sue. Her usual place was in the second row of pews next to the aisle on the far side. That way she could be seen by the congregation to be in attendance, as well as being conveniently positioned to offer smiles, frowns, and nods as called for by the various points made by the pastor.

But what I was really interested in was who was going to occupy the pulpit that morning. Somebody was waiting, for I could see black-robe-clad knees jutting out from the chair behind the podium. Who those knees belonged to was the question.

Finally, after the assistant pastor, Rob Timmons, read the Scripture passages and drew attention to the notices in the bulletin and led us in two hymns and the responsive reading, those knees stood up and I was at last able to set my eyes on Pastor Ledbetter.

I squinched them up and glared at him, thinking to myself, *You won't get away from me this time.* Not once, *not once,* though, throughout the entire sermon did he look at my side of the sanctuary. His gaze swept the far side of the congregation and the middle of it, then back again — just as an orator should do to keep the attention of his listeners — but it was as if the side where I sat were blocked from his view.

I didn't care. I understood it. He couldn't meet my eyes, but I kept them fixed on him. He knew he was in for it, and I intended to set him straight before he could get away from me again.

I was so wrapped up in what I aimed to say to him that I almost missed what he was saying to us — something I often did, as my mind tended to wander during the hour of the Sunday morning service. You won't believe what the man preached on. As soon as his words began to penetrate, I almost got up and walked out.

Taking his text from several verses in the Book of Proverbs, the pastor warned us of the dire consequences of letting our tongues run loose. "He that refraineth his lips is wise," he began, then went on for twenty minutes or so on the perils of talking too much, talking out of school, and telling everything one knows, risking disbelief in one's listeners because they get tired of hearing you go on and on, and risking the loss of one's witness as well, because people avoid gossipy chatterboxes like the plague.

And finally, he summed up by citing another proverb. "Even a fool, when he holdeth his peace, is counted wise; and he that shuteth his lips is esteemed a man of understanding," he intoned, and made particular note that the word *man* actually meant "person," man *or* woman. With that, he darted a quick glance in my direction, and if I hadn't already figured out to whom he was addressing his sermon about not telling everything one knows, I would've caught on then.

I was infuriated, absolutely beside myself, squirming in the pew to keep from springing to my feet and making a public spectacle of myself. Even Roberta, whose mind wanders worse than mine, looked concerned and, whispering, asked if I needed to go to the bathroom.

Even a fool, he'd said, *appears wise when he — or she — keeps his — or her — mouth shut.* That was what he thought of me, a fool who would be deemed wise only if I kept silent. As far as I was concerned, he'd stopped preaching and gone to meddling. He had just made it personal, calling my character and my intellect into question.

"Roberta," I whispered as we stood for the closing hymn, "I want to ask the pastor about Emma Sue, but there's no sense in you waiting around here. Why don't you run on over to my house and wait for me there? Then we'll go on to your house." I handed the door keys to her. "Just make yourself at home."

She nodded and whispered back, "Okay, I need to go to the bathroom anyway."

So I impatiently bided my time during the final prayer, the doxology, and the recessional. Then, dodging and sidling between others as they rose from the pews and congregated in the aisles, I edged my way down the central aisle and out into the narthex, where I intended to plant myself behind Pastor Ledbetter until he'd shaken the hand of every parishioner who was lining up to get out the door. I would wait till the last one was gone, then I'd have it out with him. He wouldn't escape me this time.

But he already had. Instead of Pastor Ledbetter shaking hands with church members swarming at the door, it was Rob Timmons, smiling and accepting compliments on the way he'd moved the service along by making short work of announcements, hymns, and the benediction, keeping it all within the allotted hour and fifteen minutes and not a minute longer. Presbyterians are known to appreciate timeliness.

CHAPTER 38

I dashed down the front staircase from the narthex to the basement, which housed the Fellowship Hall, the pastor's office, the kitchen, and the robing room of the choir. Stopping briefly to rattle the locked door of the pastor's office, I hurried on to the room where the choir members were divesting themselves.

"Have you seen the pastor?" I asked the first tenor I came to. "Did he come down with you?"

"Uh, well, I think so. You might ask one of the basses. They're the last in the recessional, so they might've seen him."

That made sense, for at the close of the services, Pastor Ledbetter always followed the choir down the center aisle of the sanctuary, hymnbook in hand and singing lustily, as the congregation stood, watching and feebly mouthing the words until the choir dispersed in the narthex. Then it was every member for him- or herself.

Dodging the swirls of maroon polyester as the choir quickly disrobed, I accosted the tallest bass. "Jim, did the pastor follow you down here?"

"Yes, he came down the stairs right behind me."

"Where did he go? I really need to speak to him."

"Marsha?" Jim said, turning to the lead soprano. "Did you see where Mr. Ledbetter went?"

"Straight out the back door. He handed me his robe to hang up for him. Said he had to get home to Emma Sue."

I flew out of the choir room, pushed through the back door, and surveyed the parking lot. The preacher's space was empty.

Foiled again! And not only that but I couldn't even follow him — Roberta was waiting. I stood there, mortally tempted to abandon her and make my apologies later.

But turning aside, I sighed. *Maybe it isn't meant to be today,* I thought, trying to take comfort in my Presbyterian predestinarian views. I drew my coat closed, huddled down against the cold, and proceeded across the parking lot toward my house. Church members were hurrying to their cars, doors opening and closing as motors roared to life and cars pulled out onto Polk Street. I waved to several as I went on my way, but no one, including me, was eager to stand around and talk. I was distraught to have missed the pastor again, angry that he was so obviously avoiding me, and finally resigned to my fate of watching television all afternoon. One good thing, though, I now knew where to find him, closed-up house or not.

As I crossed Polk Street, I tried to console myself by planning to take advantage of the captive afternoon to think through my next moves. Surely, the hours of boredom ahead could be put to good use. For one thing, I now knew that the fire lane — the access road — made the gatekeeper's record of visitors of little value in narrowing down the list of suspects. Anybody could've gotten to Connie's house with no one the wiser, as indeed Lamar and I had done until I learned the hard way that the house was wired from one end to the other.

But, and at that point I stopped on the steps of my front porch. Going over in my mind what we had done, I recalled why Lamar and I had ventured down the hillside and up to the side of the house in the first place — we had seen something strange going on inside the house. I pictured that eerie, bluish block of light glowing in the dark without illuminating anything in the back room. We had seen it come on and go out, then come on again — had it been a sleeping and waking up again computer screen like the one Lloyd had? I knew that his needed a tap on a key to rouse it from slumber, which meant that someone had been in the house doing the tapping. Which also meant that all the while that we were creeping closer and closer, someone had been watching us.

But, I thought again as I went up another step and stopped again, if someone had gotten into the house before us, why hadn't that someone set off the alarms?

My breath caught in my throat — only one person would know how to set the alarms and how to turn them off, and only one person would know how to get out of the house and away while Lamar and I floundered on the bouncing cover of the swimming pool and scrambled back up the hillside — Connie's husband, owner of the house and keeper of its keys.

"Roberta?" I called as I opened the front door and went inside. "It's me."

"Oh, there you are," she said, coming into the hall from the library. "I just love your home, Julia. It's so warm and comfortable, and you have some beautiful pieces. The Hepplewhite sideboard in the dining room is magnificent. Where did you get it?" Roberta had a tendency to ask inappropriate questions.

"Thank you, Roberta. It was Wesley Lloyd Springer's mother's sideboard, which at one time I thought of getting rid of. I'm glad I didn't." There was no need to share with Roberta my past fury toward my first husband. "Are you ready to go?"

"Oh, yes. I'm anxious to get started. You're in for a treat, Julia." She turned back to the library. "Let me get my coat. Oh, and, Julia, you have a message on your machine. The light's blinking."

I hurried to the kitchen, thinking, *Sam.* And it was. I listened carefully as his warm voice rolled off the tape.

"Julia, honey, I'm sorry, but I'm going to be later getting home than I thought. The governor has invited the committee to lunch so we can talk over some judicial appointments. It's a real compliment to want our input, and I'd hate to miss it. But don't worry. I'm planning to leave right after lunch, and I should be home around eight or so." He paused, then went on. "And don't worry about the weather. There's a light rain here, but the temperature's stuck in the midthirties. No freezing." He chuck-led. "At least not yet. Take care, sweetheart. I miss you and can't wait to get home."

"Huh," I said, half smiling. "Can't wait to get home? Doesn't much sound like it." I was disappointed, but at the same time pleased that Sam was being recognized and feted by the governor. Who knew where it would lead?

Leaving a note for him as to my where-abouts, I sighed. No escape from the after-noon. "Roberta? I'm ready to go."

Roberta's house was a partially remodeled summer cottage, meaning that at some point in its long life, a furnace had been installed. Her decor was what I thought might be called country chic — lots of ruffles, flounces, whitewashed walls, dried flowers and shells, peeling painted furniture, and several shades of pink in checks, plaids, and stripes everywhere you looked. It was not to my taste, but it was cozy and comfort-able, especially when she turned on the lamps and lit the coal in the small grated fireplace.

I praised her decorating skill as I took a seat on the wicker sofa and sank into the multitude of pillows on it. The little house, every part of it decorated to within an inch of its life, was attractive in its way and perfectly in tune with Roberta's romantic inclinations.

"I've made a quiche," she said as she hung up our coats. "But it has to bake. Why don't we go ahead and watch the first video, then we'll eat."

I agreed, although I wondered how I'd be able to wait another hour for lunch. But Roberta had thought of that, and she brought out cheese, crackers, and grapes to hold off starvation until the first video had run its course.

And I'll have to say that by the time it was over, the story had taken me in. I was entranced with the four daughters — one sweet, one sensible, one scandalous, and one silly. The mother, as outrageous as she was, was the only one who recognized the urgency of getting her girls married. I mean, who would want four old maids on their hands? Excuse me, I mean four spinster ladies.

The afternoon wore on, but I barely noticed. Roberta turned on more lamps, added a few lumps of coal to the fire, and offered an afghan to ward off the chill. In the hours after lunch, she hastily served coffee and pound cake when a video had to be changed, both of us caught up in the antics of the Bennet family. She and I were transported to another century, so much so that, contrary to my fears, Roberta refrained from explaining every little word, nuance, or cocked eyebrow on the screen. She made up for it, though, during the few minutes it took to rewind and change videos, talking nonstop about the authentic costumes and the stately estates and the handsome, but haughty, Mr. Darcy.

At the end of the fourth video and the fourth hour of viewing, I desperately had to excuse myself to visit Roberta's bathroom, where I found more flounces even on the toilet seat. On my return to the living room, I glanced out the window, then went closer for a better look.

"Roberta," I called, noting the drooping tree limbs and power lines. "I think it's icing up out there. Come look."

She did. "Oh, no," she wailed, "if we lose power we won't be able to finish watching."

"Not only that," I said, somewhat wryly, "I won't be able to get home." *And neither will Sam,* I thought with a sinking heart as I hoped that he wasn't already on the road. "We'll have to finish another time, Roberta. I need to go on before it gets worse."

"I guess so," she conceded as she opened

the closet to get my coat. "But I'm really disappointed. The story is so much better when you see it all at one sitting."

"We should plan it better next time," I said, hurriedly putting on my coat. "I didn't realize how quickly the afternoon would pass. It's been a real imposition on you to have a visitor stay so long."

"Oh, not at all, Julia. I've loved having you. You're perfect to watch *Pride and Prejudice* with. You don't distract from the story by commenting on everything. Don't you just hate it when people talk all the time?"

I nodded, then thanked her for a lovely afternoon and a lovely lunch, then reached for the doorknob.

"Julia!" Roberta screeched, scaring me half to death.

"What?"

"Coleman's out in all this! Oh, my goodness, I'd forgotten the danger he's in. He could get frostbite and lose his fingers and toes. Oh, Julia, what are we to do?"

"Not one thing, Roberta. Coleman's not a fool, and I expect he's already home, lying on the sofa by the fire, watching a football game."

"Oh, I hope so. But he's such a moral person and he made a promise to stay on that sign until this evening and it would be just like him to stick it out and harm himself. Oh, I'll never forgive myself if that happens. Here, I've been so wrapped up with Mr. Darcy that I've not given one thought to Coleman, who is being so heroic in braving this weather." She jerked her coat off the hanger. "I've got to go see about him."

"Roberta," I said, holding the doorknob as I decided that a little law needed to be laid down. "Listen, my dear. Coleman does not need your help, nor does Binkie. You should stay home where you belong and not out driving on icy streets just to see about Coleman. First of all, it's not your place, and second of all, how would it look to have your name in the paper if you had a wreck?"

"Well," she said, as if the wind had been taken out of her sails, "not good, I guess. But I do worry so about him."

"I know you do, but remember that he has a wife, who, I assure you, would not appreciate your help. And remember this, too. Miss Elizabeth Bennet had too much pride to go chasing after any man, no matter how heroic. Now you stay home and don't go risking life and limb in pursuit of a married one."

"Well, maybe I should. My tires are kind of slick, anyway. I'll just have to try not to worry about him. But, Julia," she said, her eyes lighting up, "when can we get together again? We have two more videos to go and the best is yet to come."

"Just as soon as I can spare two more hours, Roberta. I'll let you know."

CHAPTER 39

In spite of the ice-covered lines, limbs, leaves, and the questionable condition of the streets, I had little trouble getting home. I crept along at less than ten miles an hour to avoid slipping and sliding and got there in one piece. *Thank you, Mildred,* I thought, recalling how she'd insisted that I get a self-starting generator like the one she had. "You may need it only once a year, Julia," she'd said, "but you'll be glad you have it on that once." So, congratulating myself for having listened to her, I had no worries about losing power.

But I did have worries about Sam, wondering if he was on the interstate — or off it in a ditch. My heart skipped a beat when I saw the message light blinking on the phone the minute I walked through the door.

It was Sam again. "Julia, where are you? I keep missing you. Call me, honey. I'm worried about you."

Well, I was worried about him, so I immediately dialed his cell phone and was relieved when he immediately answered.

"Sam! I'm so glad to reach you. Where are you? Are you all right?"

"I'm fine, honey. I'm still at the hotel because Raleigh is iced in. The temperature dropped below freezing while we were at lunch, and from the looks of it, there's no telling when I'll be able to get out. It's coming down hard and fast."

"Oh, my goodness, and I was so worried that you'd be caught on the road. Abbotsville is icing over, too, so please don't try to get here until it melts."

After several more minutes of catching up with each other and my promising that I would not spend an entire afternoon away from home without telling him where I'd be, we hung up. Then, still in my coat, I called Hazel Marie to tell her to bring her family to my house if she lost power.

Then, having brought some of Roberta's concerns about Coleman home with me, I called Binkie.

"It's me, Binkie," I said when she answered. "I hope Coleman is not still out there icing over on that sign."

She giggled. "No, I got him home about three, just as it started freezing. He wouldn't leave till the Baptist ladies brought lunch. He's stretched out now in the recliner with Gracie. They're both sound asleep."

After hanging up, thinking, *So far, so good,* as to the state of those I cared for, I dialed Lillian's number to tell her to bring Latisha and come to my house if the power went out. "I was plannin' to, anyway," she said. "This ole house get mighty cold when the furnace quits."

All messages having been given and received, I removed my coat, turned on lights throughout the house and the gas logs in the library. It was full dark outside and barely four-thirty in the afternoon.

I had nothing else to do but decide what I'd have for supper. And decide what I should do as soon as the ice melted and I could get out and around. Connie's death still hung over me, and I had no idea where the investigation was or where it was going. No one had seen fit to inform me, which one would think would be a priority, seeing that my name seemed to be uppermost on their suspect list.

Maybe tomorrow, I thought, *I'll hear something.* Coleman would be going back on duty, so surely he'd learn something and be willing to pass it along to me. Although I conceded that I probably couldn't count on that — he was, after all, sworn to uphold the law, and probably also sworn not to tell civilians anything.

I went to the kitchen and rummaged around in the freezer until I found one of Lillian's individual chicken pot pies. I put it on a cookie sheet and stuck it in the oven. It would take a while to cook, being frozen and all, but it would taste all the better for the wait.

And being reminded by what I'd just done, I recalled taking two of the individual pies to the Ledbetters, and I began thinking again of the pastor and his wife. For the first time in several days, I knew exactly where Larry Ledbetter was — I just couldn't get to him. But, then, he couldn't get away, either. The Ledbetters were pretty much trapped in their own house by the weather, and I was pretty much trapped in mine. How ironic to know at last where he was, only to be stymied by the whims of the weather.

I turned on the lights in the backyard and was shocked at the amount of ice bearing down on the tree limbs. The grass was white with ice or snow or something. We were getting more than the sidelines of the storm, and that was confirmed for me as the lights flickered. I quickly turned off the yard lights and looked for a flashlight in case the generator I'd been counting on left me in the lurch.

Then I laughed. Laughed at the sudden urge I'd had to call the Ledbetters and invite them to come over if they lost power. After all his evasive actions, would the pastor accept? Maybe, I thought grimly, if it came to a choice between facing me and freezing.

Still, having thought of it, I couldn't easily dismiss the idea. Emma Sue was ill and probably not making good decisions — how would she cope with no lights, no heat, and a rapidly cooling house?

The lights flickered again, so before I could think better of it, I dialed the Ledbetters' number. Knowing that neither of them was likely to answer, I mentally prepared myself to speak into thin air.

And so I did. "Emma Sue?" I said when the taped voice invited me to leave a message. "You know I had a generator installed last year? And it looks as if it's going to come in handy any minute now. So I just wanted you to know that you and the pastor are welcome to come over if you lose power. Just be careful on the streets. It's bad out there, and, well, that's all I wanted to say, so bye. Come on if you want to."

There, I thought, if that wasn't a Christian in action, I didn't know what was. I didn't expect the pastor to accept the invitation, but I had done what was right by extending it and that was all I could do. Of course, if we all got into dire straits — like several counties without power and not enough linemen to correct the problem for days on end — well, accepting my hospitality might appear the lesser evil to the pastor.

Too on edge to do much more than keep looking in the oven to see if my supper was ready — it wasn't — I set a place at the table and fiddled around in the kitchen. Just as I'd found a plastic container of mixed fruit in the refrigerator and prepared a salad, the front doorbell rang.

Smiling at the thought of having company, but wondering who had ventured out on such an evening, I dried my hands and hurried to the door. It would probably be Lillian and Latisha, or maybe Hazel Marie and her children. Although, I thought with a frown, either of them would've used a cell phone to let me know they were coming.

I opened the door to see the last person I expected to see. He stood there looking cold and bedraggled, in spite of the long, padded, and quilted coat he was wearing — another prize from the mission bin, I assumed. His neck was scrooched down into the turned-up collar and his hands were deep inside his pockets.

"Lamar! What're you doing out in this weather? Where did you come from?"

"Jail," he said, shuffling his feet. "They come an' got me at the mission, an' they just let me out."

"Well, come in before you freeze." I held open the storm door, hearing, as I did so, the creaking of tree limbs from their burden of a coating of ice.

He followed me, sniffling as he went, as I led him to the kitchen.

"Have a seat at the table, Lamar," I said, handing him a handful of Kleenex. "Are you hungry?"

He nodded. "I pro'bly could eat."

I'd thought as much and took another frozen pot pie out of the freezer. Exchanging it for the one already nicely browned in the oven, I resigned myself to another hour of waiting for my own supper.

After putting on a pot of coffee, I dumped the pot pie onto a plate and took it and my salad to Lamar at the table, along with a glass of milk.

I sat down beside him, ready to hear the bad news. "Now tell me why the deputies came to get you. How did they know where you were? What did they want? They found your scarf, didn't they?"

"This here hits the spot." He was shoveling it in faster than he could chew.

"Thank you, but tell me, Lamar. What did they ask you, but even more important, what did you tell them?"

"Nothin', I didn't tell 'em nothin'. You got any white bread? It sure would go good."

"Oh," I said, rising, "yes, of course." And I brought the whole loaf of bread and the butter dish to the table. Then, in spite of my rising anxiety, I resigned myself to wait until his hunger was assuaged before questioning him further.

And just as I settled down to wait out his feeding frenzy, the lights flickered and went out.

CHAPTER 40

Lamar yelped and dropped his fork. "The lights is out!" he yelled, as if I hadn't noticed. Appliance motors and the furnace fan whined down as we sat immobile in the black silence.

"It's all right," I assured him. "The generator'll come on in a few seconds." *I hoped.*

And it did, the reassuring sound of the motor doing exactly what it was supposed to do lifted my heart and turned on the lights. The furnace rumbled on, and checking the oven, I saw that it, too, was picking up where it had left off. Maybe I would eat, eventually.

"I hope you got plenty of gas to keep that thing goin'," Lamar said. "I can fill it for you when it runs out."

"That's very nice of you, but it's hooked up to the underground gas line. We don't need to worry about it."

"Well, by golly," he said in some wonder. "What won't they think of next?"

"Listen now, Lamar, forget about the power. I need to know what happened after I left you at the mission."

"Well, they come . . ." He stopped to wipe his plate with a piece of loaf bread, then put it in his mouth. "I guess it was about four this morning, somewheres 'round there. Before sunup, anyways. They rousted me out an' said I needed to come down to the station.

"So I went an' waited around an' waited around. Then fin'lly they come to talk to me — Ellis, it was, an' Peavey, too, who ain't too friendly. Anyways, my scarf was a-layin' on the table an' I was sure glad to see it. They never give it back, though, even when they said I could go.

"An', Miz Murdoch, I never woulda come to your house and bothered you, but they was too busy to drive me back to the mission an' your house was closer. It was icin' up out there, you know, and anyways, I figgered you'd want to know they found my scarf. I mean, you said they'd find it, an' I figgered you'd want to know you was right."

"I certainly did want to know," I said, "although I take no pleasure in being right in this case. Did they tell you where they found it?"

"No'm, just said at the scene of a crime. Or maybe they said *around* the scene of a crime. Something like that. I guess it coulda been just about anywheres."

Lamar was not being a whole lot of help.

"Well, tell me this, how did they know it was yours?"

"Oh, everybody knowed it was mine. They seen it enough, an' a couple of them boys was always askin' me if I got it on a trip to Scotland. Shoo." Lamar laughed and shook his head. "I ain't never been to no Scotland, an' they knowed that, too."

"So," I said with some relief, "they didn't identify it by getting your fingerprints from it?"

"Aw, shoot, no. They just knowed soon as they saw it whose it was."

I was feeling better and better, and almost got up to look for some cookies.

"But I heard 'em talkin' about finger-prints, now that you mention it, an' one of 'em said something like they couldn't get none off of a loose weave, but another'un said the label was a different kettle of fish, an' likely some would show up on it."

Well, that was a dash of cold water.

"On the other hand," I said in an attempt to come up with a reason to hope, "that scarf has been handled by any number of people, considering where it's been. I guess, though, that they'll take a special interest in the topmost prints — the most recent ones. Don't you think?"

"Maybe, if they think about it. But nobody's handled it lately but me an' them, so it won't tell 'em nothin' they don't already know. Which is a good thing 'cause their fingerprint man's out with the flu."

Well, that was cause for temporary jubilation. So I decided not to tell him that I had not only handled the scarf, I had specifically fingered the label. There was no reason to give him something else to let slip, although so far, he seemed to have kept my presence at the scene of the crime under wraps.

Wanting to confirm that, I approached the subject gingerly. "Lamar, did the deputies ask if anyone was with you?"

"No'm, they never did. All they wanted to know was what I was doing out there and how I got there."

"And what did you say?"

"I just said I got a ride out that way, 'cause I wanted to see how close my ole stompin' grounds was to where somebody got kilt. Then I told 'em how I used to hunt and trap back up in there, an' how I was a pretty good shot back then. Then I got kinda skeered for tellin' that 'cause I didn't know if that lady had got shot or what."

"No, she wasn't shot."

"I kinda figgered that out pretty soon 'cause they just laughed when I said I could shoot good. 'Course I ain't kept up with it, so I prob'ly couldn't hit Dick's outhouse now."

"Whose what?"

"Oh, sorry, ma'am, it's just a sayin'."

"Okay, let's go back over this one more time," I said, wanting all the reassurance I could get. "They know you were out there — in the vicinity, anyway — because they found your scarf. But they don't know that I was with you, right?"

"That's right, 'cause I didn't tell 'em. But they knowed somebody else was out there, 'cause I swore up and down that I didn't set off them lights an' sirens. An' you know I didn't, an' I know you didn't."

I sat up straight at that, quickly deciding not to correct him. Although, on further thought, he could've been right. All I'd done was press my forehead against a window-pane to get a better look into a dark room. Had that been enough to set off the alarms? Maybe it hadn't. Maybe that someone else — who by now I was convinced had been in the house — had set them off.

Feeling more hopeful, I went to the pantry and found a package of Oreo cookies.

"Help yourself," I said, opening the package. "Now, Lamar, have you given any thought to that light we saw? That's what drew us to the house in the first place. If we hadn't seen that, I would've just looked to see if there was a way down the hill, then gone back to the car and left. You wouldn't have had to run to the highway or lose your scarf or anything else. And, best of all, they wouldn't have known that we, I mean you, had been there."

"Oh, yes, ma'am, I heard the deputies talkin' 'bout that — they never think I'm listenin'. But they all went runnin' out there when the sirens went off an' they checked the house inside an' out an' all they found was a turned-on computer in that back room. You know how the screen'll light up when you touch something, then go out after it sets there awhile? Well, that's what it was."

"Then," I said, loudly enough to startle him, "that means somebody *was* in the house!"

I was so shaken by the confirmation of what I'd suspected that I didn't even wonder at Lamar's seemingly intimate knowledge of a computer. But I'd already concluded that Lamar was smarter than he sounded.

"Well, no'm," he said, shaking his head. "Not for sure, 'cause they was some trembles on the mountain back of them houses yesterday. That could've done it."

I knew that we occasionally had a few minor earthquakes in the area, which created havoc with dishes and knickknacks and so forth if they were near the edge of a shelf. So a minor heave of the earth miles away could very well jar a computer to life.

"But, Lamar," I said, "an earth tremble might light up a screen, but don't tell me it could turn a computer *on*."

"By dog, you're right about that!" Lamar's eyes lit up at the thought. "Don't that mean somebody was in there while we was out there?"

"It certainly does, and I want to know who it was. We didn't see a light anywhere else in the house, did we?"

He shook his head. "Not nowhere."

"So," I went on, "whoever it was must've known that house inside and out. I mean, to be able to move around in it in the dark, it had to be somebody who was familiar with it, don't you think?"

"I sure do, 'cause it was blacker'n pitch inside. Outside, too, pretty much."

We sat for a few minutes, thinking over what we'd seen and what it might've meant. I'd already come to my conclusion and waited to see if Lamar would come to the same one.

When he said nothing, I prodded him a little. "Who do you think it could've been?"

"Beats me," he said, as I almost threw up my hands. "But," he went on, "it couldna been no run-of-the-mill thief, 'cause we'd aheard him bumping into chairs an' things. See, you can't burgle a place you never been in before if you don't got a flashlight or some kinda light without making some noise."

"That's right! So who do you think it was?"

"Oh, that's easy. They pretty much always leave a deputy at a homicide. In case somebody wants to go messing around."

They Lord! Why hadn't he told me that before *we* went messing around?

"*Lamar!* I *asked* you while we were still in the car if a deputy would be there, and you said no."

"No'm," he said, shaking his head, "you asked me if I seen a deputy's car, an' I didn't. And, ma'am, I didn't know then what I found out later — that you was gonna go right up to that house. I tell you one thing, you got more nerve than I give you credit for."

"Thank you, Lamar," I said, recognizing the admiration in his voice. "I think."

CHAPTER 41

Lamar's eyes widened at the sound of crunching footsteps outside and the jingle of a key in the lock of the back door. I turned to look as the door swung open, and Lillian and Latisha, bundled to the eyeballs, walked in. They were both in heavy coats, mittens, boots, and headgear. Latisha wore a tasseled wool cap with a scarf wrapped around her head and face. Only her eyes were visible.

"Lillian!" I cried, getting to my feet. "Did you *walk* over here?"

"No'm," she said, quickly shutting the door, "we come in the car till it slide up against the curb. Then we got out and walked. It's slick out there."

"And cold," Latisha said, unwrapping her bright red scarf as Lamar eyed it with longing. "I almost froze my hiney off."

"*Latisha!*" Lillian cried. "I don't wanta hear that kinda talk."

"Yes, ma'am. I mean, no, ma'am, I won't say hiney no more."

"Lemme get that coat offa you," Lillian said, as she came out of hers. "Then you go on in yonder. You can watch Nickelodeon an' nothin' else. Miss Julia," she said, turning to me, "I hope you don't mind us just comin' on over. The phone don't work, an' my neighbor say they so many without power that we won't get it back till tomorrow night. An' maybe not even then. An' we already been cold and dark for more'n a hour."

"Of course not, Lillian. You know you're welcome anytime. Oh, and, Lillian, this is Mr. Lamar Owens. He, well, he was one of Sam's campaign workers, and the ice caught him off guard, too." No need to broadcast what else he'd been involved in.

Lillian gave him a warm smile, which Lamar returned with a nod of his head. "I better be goin'," he said, standing. "Now you got comp'ny."

"Sit right back down," I said. "You can't go out in this, and if Lillian can't drive in it, I sure can't. I'm afraid you're stuck with us, Lamar."

"Well, I don't wanta be no trouble."

"No trouble at all. We'll . . ." The phone interrupted me, and I hurried to answer it.

393

"Miss Julia?" Hazel Marie said shakily. "We're on our way over, if that's all right. Everything's out all over our street. The only thing working is my cell phone and the car. So far."

"You're driving?"

"Barely. The streets are so slick, we're hardly moving."

"Oh, Lord, Hazel Marie, be careful." I could just see Lloyd and the little twin girls being thrown around in a skidding car. "Come on as fast as you can. No, I don't mean go fast, but if you have to get out and walk, call me back. We'll come meet you."

After hanging up, I turned to Lillian. "If she has to leave the car, we'll have to go help carry the babies."

"I can help," Lamar said.

Before I could answer, Lillian looked around and said, "Somebody cookin' something?"

"Oh, my goodness," I said, running to the oven. "That's my supper. It's probably burned up by now."

Lillian moved me out of the way. "Lemme see." Taking my overcooked chicken pot pie out of the oven, she said, "It's a little crispy, but it's prob'ly all right. Dependin' on how hungry you are. I'll put another one in for you."

"No, don't do that. If it's edible at all, I'll eat it. I can't wait another hour." Actually, I was about to cave in from hunger, Roberta's quiche and pound cake long since gone and forgotten.

I ate it, sitting at the table with Lamar, who drank one cup of coffee after another and downed half a package of cookies as well. Lillian got Latisha ready for bed, but when she heard that Lloyd and the babies were on their way, she didn't have going to sleep in mind.

By the time I'd eaten everything except the burned crust, I was worried about Hazel Marie. "Lillian," I said, "they should be here by now. It's only four blocks, for goodness sakes. You think we should go look for them?"

Lillian went to a side window and, putting her hands up to the glass, said, "I think they already here. 'Least, I see some car lights out on the street."

And in they came, Hazel Marie carrying one heavily wrapped little girl and Lloyd the other, along with plastic bags full of whatever babies needed. It took forever to unwind all the blankets to reveal the little girls in their footed flannel pajamas. They blinked and squirmed in the bright kitchen lights, but, much to Latisha's dismay, Hazel

Marie and Lillian quickly started upstairs with them before they woke up completely.

"But I wanta play with 'em," Latisha wailed.

"In the morning," I said. "We'll need you to be the babysitter and play with them then."

"Come on, Latisha," Lloyd said, heading back to the library. "Let's watch television. Mr. Owens, you want to watch, too?"

Lamar glanced at me — for permission, I supposed. I nodded, and he happily followed them. I had introduced him to the newcomers, but Hazel Marie had been too busy to do more than smile at him, whereas Lloyd was instantly fascinated by my unusual visitor. It vaguely crossed my mind that I really didn't know Lamar Owens, and here I was putting him up for the night in a house with my nearest and dearest. Except for Sam, of course. I decided not to dwell on the little I did know of him — none of it salubrious — because I couldn't turn him out on such a night.

"We put them both in Lloyd's bed," Hazel Marie said when she and Lillian came downstairs. "And they went right back to sleep. I can hardly believe it."

"We put chairs 'gainst the sides of the bed so they don't fall off," Lillian said, going straight for the coffeepot.

"Come sit down," I said, "and let's figure out where we're all going to sleep. Lillian, you and Latisha will have your room, of course. Hazel Marie, can you sleep with the little girls?"

"Oh, yes, one or both of them crawl into bed with me most nights, anyway."

"Okay, we'll put a pallet on the floor for Lloyd. And I'll put Lamar on the sofa in the library. That'll work, won't it?"

Well, it would have if Coleman, Binkie, and little Gracie hadn't shown up. Coleman, in his uniform, apologized as soon as I opened the front door.

"Miss Julia, everybody's been called on duty tonight, so I've brought my family to you." He grinned. "I didn't want them to freeze, and you and Mrs. Allen next door are the only ones I know who have generators."

"Of course. I'm glad you came," I said, holding the door for them. "Come in, Binkie. And Gracie, how are you? Run on back to the library, honey. Lloyd and Latisha are watching television and Lillian is about to fix some popcorn."

There was a great shedding of coats, boots, and hats in the living room, accompanied by squeals of pleasure from the children and hugs of welcome between Binkie and Hazel Marie. I had a vague hope of finding a quiet place in the house to talk over my legal situation with Binkie, now that I knew about the back access to the Clayborn house. No need, of course, to tell her *how* I happened to know it. But since she was making an unheard-of house call, I might as well make use of it.

"Thanks, Miss Julia," Coleman said as he kissed his wife and headed for the door. "I'll try to rent that portable generator again — the one I had out on the sign. If I can get it, I'll pick up my girls in the morning." He stopped and smiled. "If we're not on for twenty-four hours. Just about the whole county's out of power, and sounds like half of the residents have had accidents. There's one right down the street here — somebody's car ended up on the sidewalk. Nobody in it, though."

"Oh," Hazel Marie said, "that was us. It just jumped the curb, and if it hadn't been for that telephone pole, we might've slid on into Miss Julia's front yard."

"I'll get it back in the street for you sometime tomorrow," Coleman said as he went out the door. "Y'all stay warm."

"Be careful," Binkie called after him.

With the children and Lamar in the library

watching television, the rest of us sat around the kitchen table to rearrange our sleeping plans. Lillian had popped corn for the children and offered sandwiches to anyone who was hungry. Lamar accepted, but the rest of us made do with coffee and cookies.

"Binkie," I said, "you and Gracie can have my bed. I'll put Lamar on a pallet in Sam's upstairs office, and I'll sleep on the sofa in the library."

"No, ma'am, you will not," she said. "I'm not about to take your bed. I'll sleep on the sofa, and Gracie can sleep on a pallet beside me. She'll love it."

"I wanta sleep on a pallet," Latisha said, having just come into the kitchen.

"Me, too," Gracie said, following her in.

"I do, too," Lloyd chimed in behind her.

"I tell you what let's do," Binkie said, accustomed as she was to taking charge. "Let's put all the children on pallets in the library, and I'll sleep on the sofa to supervise. How would that work?"

"Oh, that'll be good," Hazel Marie said, "if you don't mind sleeping on the sofa. But my girls better stay in bed with me. They'll be toddling all over the house if they wake up and can't find me."

So it was arranged, and Lillian and I raided all the closets, gathering quilts and blankets and pillows for those who would be sleeping catch as catch can.

She and I were in the upstairs hall when she lowered her voice and said, "Miss Julia, Latisha an' me can sleep on the floor, an' somebody can have our bed."

"No, Lillian, with this crew in the house, you're going to have your hands full keeping us fed. You'll need a decent night's rest in a decent bed." Then I leaned closer and whispered, "The only reason I offered mine is because I knew nobody would take it."

Just as we got downstairs, our arms loaded with the makings of pallets, the telephone rang. *Sam,* I thought, and hurried to answer it.

"Julia?" Mildred whispered. "You'll never guess who just showed up at my door asking if there was room in the inn."

"Who?" I whispered back, although there was no need for it.

"Emma Sue and your pastor."

"Oh, for goodness sakes, Mildred. I left word that they could come here, but, well, by now I have a house full. So I guess it's just as well they didn't."

"Well," Mildred said, "I was a little surprised they'd come to me, but I expect it was Emma Sue's idea. Anyway, I thought you'd get a kick out of your minister coming to my house."

"Uh-huh. How do you think she's doing?"

"Oh, I'd say there's a definite chill in the air. He tries to pamper and pet her, but she shrugs him off. Kind of touchy, seems to me, but I can't stand all that hovering, either. So she seems pretty normal to me." Then Mildred said, "Oops, got to go. They're coming downstairs."

I stood by the phone a few seconds after hanging up, thinking of how anxious Pastor Ledbetter must've been to keep his distance from me. Anxious enough, it seemed, to seek refuge with an Episcopalian, even though a member of his own church stood at the ready.

Well, I thought, *at least I know where he'll be as long as the power's out — right next door, and I'm not afraid of a little ice.*

CHAPTER 42

Looking in on the pallet-littered library before going upstairs, I knew that this night would be long remembered by the children. Too bad that the Pickens twins were too young to join them. Binkie had turned out all the lights, so that only the gas logs in the fireplace lit the room. Lloyd, Latisha, and Gracie had their pallets laid out on the carpet close to the leather sofa where Binkie was ensconced, propped up by pillows and covered by quilts. She was telling ghost stories by the flickering fire, and the children were clearly entranced.

Lamar was upstairs on the floor in Sam's office, the erstwhile sunroom that Coleman had once rented. After showing Lamar the hall bathroom, I had apologized to him for the lack of a bed.

Eyeing the quilt-padded pallet, soft pillow, and covering blankets that Lillian had placed on the floor for him, he'd said, "I've slept on the floor many a time, so it don't bother me. Fact is, that pallet looks better'n them cots at the mission 'cause it don't sink down in the middle. An' won't nobody be snorin' to keep me awake, neither."

Looking in on Lillian in her room, I thanked her for her help and wished her a good night. "You and I," I said, "are the only ones sleeping alone in a bed tonight."

"Yes'm, an' I aim to enjoy it."

We laughed together as I said, "Me, too."

I passed Lloyd's room on the way to mine, but refrained from tapping on the door for fear of waking the babies. Hazel Marie would probably have the worst night of us all, what with a tossing toddler on each side.

I closed the door of my bedroom behind me, relieved to have my guests satisfactorily dispersed in beds and pallets throughout the house, and looked with a twinge of guilty anticipation at my unshared bed. I missed my usual bedfellow, but was glad that no one else would be in it with me.

Walking to the side window, I peered through the glass toward Mildred's house. Her lights were still on, but it was dark everywhere else as far as I could see — no streetlights or traffic lights, even, and certainly no headlights. I wondered how my other neighbors up and down the street were faring. The town would open a few buildings with generators to house some of the elderly, the sick, and families with small children. And those with coal or wood stoves or fireplaces would welcome neighbors and friends. People would look after one another, I knew, but some would certainly spend a cold and hungry night.

"Oh, my goodness," I gasped, and pressed my face closer to the glass. Then I quickly turned off the lamps in the room and hurried to one of the front windows for a better view. Pressing my face close, I could hear the tick of falling ice outside the window.

All I could see was a swinging light aimed at the ground as somebody walked across the parking lot toward the church. Glancing up and down the street — or at least where I knew the street to be, for I couldn't see it — I looked for the lights of a patrol car, thinking a deputy might be making building checks. But I quickly discounted that, for they'd be too busy on a night like this for such routine calls.

Ah-ha, I said to myself, *it's Pastor Ledbetter, without a doubt, checking on the church.* I mean, who else could it be? Maybe he planned to turn the faucets on in the kitchen and all the bathrooms to prevent the pipes from freezing, because there was one thing you could say about the pastor — he took care of that church. It was, however, a little late to be worrying about frozen pipes — ice had been falling since mid-afternoon.

Well, maybe he'd had his hands full with Emma Sue. Maybe he'd been kept busy by looking after her or hovering over her, as Mildred had reported him doing. But Mildred didn't know how the pastor suffered from Emma Sue's migraines, and of course I wouldn't discuss such a thing with a non-Presbyterian.

When whoever was holding the flashlight went inside the church, there was no doubt in my mind that it was the pastor. I pulled an easy chair around so I could sit and watch what would happen next. Occasionally, I saw a glow through some of the windows in the Sunday school building, so I was able to mentally follow the pastor as he made his rounds.

While I waited for him to reappear, a possible plan began to form in my mind — what I should do was to start putting on layers of clothes and get myself outside to meet him on his return to Mildred's house. It would be a showdown at the O.K. Corral, or, more likely, given the insecure footing, a broken hip at the church parking lot.

I wasn't sure I wanted to risk it.

Nonetheless, I eased my door open and leaned over the banister to listen, wondering how many were still awake downstairs. They all were. I heard Lloyd and Latisha talking as they walked from the library to the kitchen for who-knew-what, and Binkie and Gracie laughing as they sang "This Little Light of Mine."

I'd never get out of the house without being seen, questioned, and talked out of arranging a chance meeting on an icy night. Somewhat relieved, I closed my door and went back to the easy chair to watch for the pastor's return. The ice might be preventing me from confronting him, but it was also preventing him from seeking a better hiding place than my next-door neighbor's house. *I know where you are, Pastor, and where you'll be in the morning.* I leaned forward, peering through the black night as I kept my silent watch.

My eyes got heavy after a little while, but I stayed at it, wanting confirmation that Pastor Ledbetter would go back to Mildred's and not go sneaking off somewhere else. What I wouldn't have given for one of those tracking devices I'd heard about — I'd slap it on him so fast it would make his head swim.

Of course if I ever got close enough to put one on him, I could go ahead and have it out with him right then and there, so all that thought proved was that I needed to go to bed.

Ah, I breathed, standing and peering closer, as the light from the flashlight appeared where I knew the back door of the church was. It lingered there a few seconds as I pictured the pastor locking the door. Then the light wobbled around a few times, then began to move toward the street. I could make out large boots moving cautiously in the round splay of light on the ice-covered pavement.

I gasped as the light suddenly flared up in the air, then dropped and rolled free. I could almost feel the impact as the pastor hit the ground. What if he'd broken something?

But no, the flashlight was picked up after a few seconds and began moving toward the street, but something was different. It looked as if the light were being pushed along the ground. I couldn't figure out what was going on, but then I did — the pastor, flashlight in hand, was crawling along the slick pavement.

Well, I couldn't blame him. It takes only one bad fall to forgo your dignity and get home the best way you can.

Assured that he hadn't broken anything that would slow him down, I was ready to consign him to Mildred and go to bed. But just as I almost gave up my watch, a brighter light — maybe something like the long, heavy one that Coleman carried — appeared from the right and moved quickly toward the pastor. Whatever it was cast a much larger beam of light, so that I could see that the new arrival knew how to manage ice, and probably snow as well, for, I declare, if the figure wasn't pushing himself along with a pair of ski sticks or poles or whatever they were. With little short skis on his feet, he was gliding along with that big flashlight attached to his body somewhere. I'd never seen the like.

I nearly pushed my head through the windowpane, I was peering so hard. I saw the newcomer help Pastor Ledbetter to his feet, then steady him to Mildred's driveway. Running to the side window to watch, I waited as the two figures seemed to stand talking, the glow of their flashlights outlining the lower parts of their bodies. What could they be discussing on a freezing night in the middle of Mildred's drive? After a few minutes, I saw only the smaller light go to the house, while the smoothly gliding, larger light disappeared down Polk Street.

I sat down on the side of the bed, practically winded, after watching . . . well, I wasn't sure what or who. One thing was for sure — whoever had come upon the pastor crawling across the street on his hands and knees certainly was prepared for getting around in a wintry landscape.

Who would that be? Why, someone who habitually exercised at night, and someone who was known to have lived in Switzerland, that's who.

CHAPTER 43

"Binkie," I said as soon as I stepped into the kitchen later than usual the next morning. I had not slept well, that long-legged skier having flitted through my dreams throughout the night. "As soon as you finish here, get a cup of coffee and meet me in the living room. I need a consultation."

She laughed and wiped cereal from the chin of one of the twins. With no high chairs at my house, she and Hazel Marie were feeding the babies on their laps.

"Okay," she agreed. "We probably need to go over a few things. But with the town in the shape it's in this morning, I expect the Clayborn investigation will be on hold for a while."

"Not for me, it won't," I mumbled, and waited for Lillian to dip up scrambled eggs onto my plate. "Have the children eaten?" I could hear Latisha ordering Lloyd and Gracie around in the library.

"Yes'm," Lillian said, "they eat awhile ago, an' now they in there making a fort outa the pallets."

"What about Lamar? Has he come down?"

"Done come and gone."

"*Gone!* He left in all this?" I waved my hand toward the frosted window.

"Yes'm. I tried to get him to stay, but he wouldn't. I give him a big breakfast, then he put two biscuits in his pocket an' say he see you when he got something else to tell you." She cut her eyes at me. "What you reckon he mean by that?"

"I have no idea, but I intended to find him a cap or hat of some kind before he left." I walked, plate in hand, to the table, wanting to forestall further questioning. "I hope he doesn't break his neck out there. Hazel Marie," I said as I sat at the table across from her, "did you get any sleep at all?"

"Oh, yes, I slept real well. And the girls did, too. Of course I had to move them every time I wanted to turn over, but we had a good night." She looked around as Lillian turned up the radio on the counter. "Is that the local station?"

"Yes'm," Lillian said. "The weather'll be on in a minute an' some news, I hope." She put the egg skillet in the sink, then turned

411

to us. "I been listenin' for a while, an' it still in the twenties out there. Nobody goin' to work this mornin', or to school, either. Everything closed 'round town, an' they tellin' everybody to stay home, 'cause nothin' gonna be meltin' anytime soon. But that *Mel in the Mornin'* been on the radio all night long. He spend the night at the station an' he kept on broadcastin' 'bout who need help an' where they was a wreck an' anything he could think of. They sayin' he ought to get a medal or something."

That brought out stories of happenings during previous meteorological events, such as storms, both summer and winter, the blizzard of '92, and so forth. Binkie, especially, had a store of tales relating to one or more of the deputies and the tight spots they'd gotten into — all from Coleman, I assumed.

I ate my breakfast and listened, but didn't join in. Aware of my growing edginess because *nothing was getting done* to clear the Clayborn case and, more specifically, *my name,* I couldn't just sit around talking and laughing while waiting for the ice to melt. It could be days before we got back to normal.

The cup of coffee I'd taken to the living

room with me was empty by the time Binkie came in with hers. I'd had time to sit and ponder my predicament as I listened to the five children playing, laughing, screaming, and running in the library. Thank goodness for thick walls. Maybe I didn't want a new house — they don't build them like they used to, anyway.

By the time I'd begun to wonder if Binkie was putting me off, I'd gone over what I wanted to tell her and to ask her, and had also decided that I needed to light a fire under her so she'd start demanding some results from the investigators.

And occasionally, in spite of my anxiety, to wonder where we all would've slept if Sam and I were living in the small, though perfect, house I'd once spent a morning daydreaming about. Vagrant thoughts come and go, don't you know, especially when you have to sit around waiting for someone.

"Sorry," Binkie said as she came in with a rush, closing the door behind her. "Had to get Gracie dressed and she wasn't happy about it. Okay," she went on, perching on the footstool by my chair, "I'm here for a consultation. What do you want to talk about?"

"Binkie," I said, taken aback, "what do you think I want to talk about? My legal

413

situation, of course. I want to know just what the investigators are investigating, and how far they've gotten. I want to know if they still suspect me. And I want to know the autopsy results, which you haven't seen fit to tell me. I had to learn about that from somebody else." I didn't tell her who.

"And," I went on, "it might interest you to know that I've found out a few things that would — with the proper presentation — deflect suspicion from me. I mean, *I've* been busy working my case, and I want to know what you've been doing."

"Miss Julia," she said softly, as if I needed to be pacified, which I did. "It's only been a few days, and the autopsy results just came back Friday afternoon. *Late* Friday afternoon, and they're inconclusive. Ms. Clayborn was killed by a blow to the head — actually, more across the temple than on the head itself. Although there was also a cut over the wound — which may or may not have been caused by the same weapon, which, by the way, hasn't been found. The only other trauma was a large bruise on the forehead. But no defensive wounds or anything else, except a few things thrown around the kitchen, which might indicate an attempt to escape her attacker. According to the husband, nothing was stolen, and she had no enemies. Now," Binkie said, putting her hand on my arm, "a forensic team from the State Bureau of Investigation will be here today if the interstate is open, so we're waiting to see if they find something that our team missed. We just have to be patient."

I was not appeased. "You, maybe, but not me. Have you looked out the window lately? If Sam can't get here from Raleigh, how do you expect a forensic team to make it from the same place? And, Binkie, there're a lot of things you don't know, but even worse, I doubt that even the investigators know them. For instance, do they know how easy it is to get to the Clayborn house *without* going through the front gate and having your license number taken down? And do they, or you, know that somebody was in the house the night before last turning on a computer, because it didn't turn on by itself no matter what the Richter scale says? And what about the strange, compulsively exercising man who's been running past my house late at night, and here he was again last night, *skiing* past, if you can believe that."

"Skiing? How?"

"Don't ask me. All I know is what I saw, and that's what he was doing. Helped Pastor

Ledbetter out of the middle of the street, too. Who, by the way, spent the night at Mildred's with Emma Sue, and, if you ask me, they need to be questioned, too. They've been acting in uncommonly strange ways."

"I heard he'd taken Emma Sue to Winston-Salem for treatment."

"I heard that, too. But if he did, it was the fastest treatment on record, because they were back here practically the following day. If, that is, you believe Norma, who rarely knows one day from the next. But that's beside the point, Binkie. I happen to know that the deputies are in possession of some evidence found in the vicinity of the Clayborn house — but not *in* it — and I want to know what they've deduced from that. And I want to know how someone could get in and out of the Clayborn house without setting off the burglar alarms."

"Well, for one thing," Binkie said, still centering on what I considered trivia, "we don't know that the house has an alarm system."

Believe me, it does, I wanted to say, but instead said, "*All* the houses in Grand View Estates have alarm systems. Homeowners' requirement." And said it as if I knew what I was talking about.

"Well," Binkie said, "be that as it may, let

me assure you that the deputies on the investigative team are as good as they come. And when the SBI forensic team gets here, I think we'll see some real progress." She patted my arm again, still in her pacifying mode. It still wasn't working.

"Now, Miss Julia," she went on, "I know this has been hard on you, but you can't let it get to you like this. It's normal to think up all sorts of wild and crazy scenarios when you're under stress, as you understandably are. And I know how easy it is to put the wrong interpretations on perfectly normal occurrences. But you have to leave it to the experts — they know what they're doing. I think it might be a good idea for you to talk to Dr. Hargrove. He could give you something for your nerves that would make all this waiting around easier on you."

"There is nothing wrong with my nerves." The nerve of *her* to suggest such a thing. "It's my life I'm worried about. And I assure you that I don't intend to spend the rest of it in the Atlanta pen. Nor do I intend to sit around in a medicated haze while everybody else piddles around taking their time to clear the innocent and convict the guilty. Whoever it is."

"All right, all right, I understand," Binkie said, but I wasn't convinced that she did. "I should've explained things a little better, so let me tell you what will happen. After the SBI forensic team finishes, and if there's still no clear indication of who or what caused Ms. Clayborn's death, there may be an inquest. Everyone remotely connected to the crime will be questioned as material witnesses in a courtroom setting, and a determination of what happened will be made." She stopped while I pictured being questioned in a public courtroom versus a private interrogation room. I didn't like the comparison. "That's if," Binkie continued, looking carefully at me, "the investigators don't come to a conclusion first.

"Now, Miss Julia," she said, pushing herself to her feet, "I want you to stop worrying about this. I'm looking after your interests, and I assure you that no one seriously considers you a suspect. The only thing," she said, then hesitated before continuing. "Well, they're trying to figure out how you got blood on your hand. You didn't get it from the puddle under her head — that hadn't been disturbed. There was a smear or two in some droplets on the floor, but not enough to account for the transfer on the counter. See, Miss Julia, there was a clear, unmistakable bloody print of your palm on the edge of the counter above the dishwasher."

"I explained that!" I cried. "I reached up over Connie to hold on to the counter to pull myself upright. It was the only way I could get up."

"I know, and so do they. It's just that they can't figure out where or how you'd gotten blood on your hand *before* you reached up and smeared it on the counter."

"Well, Lord, I don't know. Maybe I put my hand down to steady myself while I was squatting beside her. Oh, my goodness, Binkie, I was in such a state, there's no telling what I did. I didn't even know I had blood on my hand until I got to the car."

"Well, that's one of the issues that they'll turn over to the SBI. The only other question that nags the investigators is why you visited Ms. Clayborn the day she died — that's never been answered to their satisfaction. Especially since they know from all the ladies they interviewed that you disliked her. That being the case, it doesn't seem reasonable to them that you would go to see her. Of course," Binkie said, with what she thought was a conspiratorial smile, "they don't understand the social etiquette that requires a lady to be courteous and gracious even, maybe especially, to someone she simply can't stand."

Uh-huh, I thought, *and how do I make them understand the ins and outs of social etiquette when being gracious had been the last thing on my mind when I visited Connie Clayborn?*

A piercing scream from the library made Binkie jump to her feet. "I'd better see what's happening," she said, hurrying to the door. "They may be killing each other."

A poor choice of words, I thought, given the circumstances, and continued to sit and think over what Binkie had said. But mostly to think of what she hadn't. For instance, she hadn't asked any details about that runner or skier or whatever he was, and she'd very effectively veered away from discussing the Ledbetters' possible complicity. And she hadn't even asked how I knew about a back entrance to the Clayborn house or how I knew about a computer going off and on — clear evidence, it seemed to me, of an unknown — and not even looked-for — agent of Connie's death. And that scarf so unfortunately found at or near the scene? She'd not asked one question about that, either.

Why hadn't she? Maybe it was because she knew more than she wanted to let on at this stage of the investigation, especially about my bloody palm print on the granite countertop. But, more likely, I reluctantly decided, it was because she hadn't believed me. She thought that I was dreaming up wild and crazy scenarios because of my nerves.

Well, Ms. Binkie Enloe Bates, we'll just see about that.

Chapter 44

Inquest, I thought, and braved the pillow fight in the library to find the dictionary. On my way back to the living room, I heard the clatter of a snowplow and looked out the window to see a truck strewing sand or salt or both on the street. That was an encouraging sign that the weather might be improving. So I sat down and looked up the definition of *inquest:* a judicial inquiry of some matter, usually before a jury.

I closed the book and leaned my head back against the chair. The inquiry conducted by Detective Ellis alone had been bad enough, and it hadn't been improved by the presence of either Lieutenant Peavey or Binkie. To think I might now have to endure a public inquiry as to my actions, motives, and thoughts was enough to chill my bones.

I got up and checked the thermostat. Then I went to the front window and saw that a light snow was falling. My hope for better weather might have been premature. I shivered and thought how nice it was to have everybody safe and warm inside, but how much longer I could put up with a fully occupied house was another matter. And how much longer I could stay cooped up without freedom of movement was an even bigger matter. How tantalizing it was to know that the Ledbetters were only a few, though highly treacherous, steps away.

Did I dare take those steps? Yes, I had to. I had to have it out with Pastor Ledbetter and, more than that, I felt I should warn him that he'd better clear the air before he was called to testify at a public inquest. If he was motivated into all his evasive actions by concern that others would know that he couldn't control his wife's mood swings, he'd be hard-pressed to keep that to himself on a witness stand. And more even than that, I wanted to know what he had to say for himself.

If, for instance, he was motivated into all his strange behavior by something worse than concern about his pastoral reputation, then, warning or no warning from me, he was on his own. I couldn't help him.

"Miss Julia?" Lillian stood at the door. "Miss Binkie and Miss Hazel Marie say they makin' lunch for the chil'ren, so I'm gonna go rest my eyes for a while. They say if you want hot dogs, come on to the kitchen."

I smiled and shook my head. "I think I'll pass. But you've given me a good idea. After I call Sam, I may need to rest my eyes, too."

Closing the bedroom door, I sat on the side of the bed and punched in Sam's cell phone number.

"I hope you're safe and warm in a hotel room," I said when he answered. "And not on the road somewhere."

He laughed. "I'm not on the road, believe me. It's bad down here, but the forecast says we'll get a few degrees above freezing this afternoon, so things are looking up. How is it up there?"

"The same, but we've heard nothing about a warm-up. But, Sam, don't let a few degrees above freezing tempt you to start out. The temperature is likely to drop tonight, and the roads will be worse than ever."

"I know," he said, "but I tell you, Julia, I've had enough of this hotel living. There're three others on the committee who're stuck here like I am, so we're going to try to play some bridge or poker or something to get through the afternoon. I miss you, honey, and I miss being home."

Hearing a hint of loneliness in his voice, I forced a little laugh. "You'd probably run out and look for a hotel room if you were here. I have five children having the time of their lives at the top of their voices, and four women, including me, who're just before going crazy with cabin fever. You're lucky to be out of it."

We laughed together, as he agreed that he might be in better circumstances than I. Then I gave him a rundown of who was here and how we'd slept the previous night, although I refrained from mentioning Lamar Owens. Once Sam was home, I would tell him all about Lamar and how helpful he'd been, although I might gloss over how and where he'd lost his scarf. In fact, if the scarf revealed no evidence of its handlers, I might just leave that out altogether. No need to bring up something that had no bearing on the case.

So after a few more personal comments to each other, we ended the call. I hung up with his warm voice still echoing in my head, thankful that he was safe, but wishing that the temperature would rise and the ice would melt so we could all get back to normal.

But since that wasn't in the immediate

offing, I got up and went to the closet. Finding nothing that I needed, I made a mental note to go shopping just as soon as I could get the car out. I stood by the hanging clothes for a few minutes, pondering what I'd seen through the open door of Lloyd's room across the hall on my way to my bedroom.

Opening the door to the hall, I listened to the voices from the kitchen. Then I tiptoed across the hall and lifted Hazel Marie's fur-lined, mid-calf-high, waterproof boots and tiptoed back to my room. Then I went to Sam's closet.

"Miss Julia!" Lloyd's voice came from the foot of the stairs. "You want some lunch?"

I hurried to lean over the banister. "No, honey. I'll get something later. I'm going to rest for a while."

"Okay, we'll be in the library when we finish. And, Miss Julia, it's up to thirty-two degrees outside, so the ice might start melting this afternoon. We can't go outside yet, so Mama and Miss Binkie know some games we can play. We'll try to be quiet."

"Have fun, honey. You won't bother me."

I slipped back into my room, satisfied that the crew downstairs would be well occupied, but on edge because if I was going to do it, I had to do it before the melting began. I knew for a fact that if the weather improved, it wouldn't be long before power was restored, and Pastor Ledbetter would be on the move again.

I undressed, wishing for long underwear, which I didn't have, but pulling on two heavy sweaters instead. Then, rummaging through Sam's hanging clothes, I brought out a pair of wool pants that he rarely wore. Pulling them on, I almost despaired at the fit. They didn't. I had to clasp a fist full of wool at my waist to hold them up, and even with that, there was an awful lot of material hanging down in the seat. Well, I didn't intend to turn my back on anybody, so I didn't worry about it.

Instead, I found one of my belts and, pulling the trousers up to my chest, fastened it around my waist and hoped that would hold them.

But there was a lot of leg material puddling around my feet — Sam was taller than I — so I pulled on Hazel Marie's boots and stuffed the extra material inside them. Looking in the full-length mirror — which was probably an unwise thing to do — I decided that I looked like an out-of-uniform paratrooper going AWOL from an airborne unit.

Heavy coat, Sam's huge fur-lined gloves, a

wool scarf — not a Burberry — wrapped around my head and neck, and Sam's fishing hat on top, I was ready to brave the elements and corner Pastor Ledbetter before the ice melted.

My intent was to slip downstairs and out the front door while everybody was in the kitchen eating lunch. I had my hand on the bedroom doorknob when I heard the crunching and crackling of tires on ice and snow and, hopefully, sand. Hurrying to the front window, I looked down at a patrol car sliding to the curb, the chains on its tires notwithstanding. Coleman got out, a heavy sack in his arms, and proceeded to sprinkle Ice Melt on my front walk and steps. Then he rang the doorbell.

A stampede ensued downstairs as all the children ran through the hall to see who was there.

"Daddy! Daddy!" Gracie sang out, and there was a hubbub of voices welcoming him.

I cracked the door to the hall so I could listen, then quickly closed it as I heard Lillian come out of her room and go downstairs.

With the children talking excitedly, telling Coleman about their night on the floor, I could see my plan of slipping out fading away.

Then I heard Coleman say, "No, we had a big lunch, thanks anyway, Lillian. I have to be back on duty at six, and all I'd like is a couple of hours of sleep in a warm place. Honey," he went on as I pictured him turning to Binkie, "there's not a generator available between here and Atlanta, so you're here for another night if Miss Julia won't mind."

Hazel Marie broke in. "Of course she won't mind. But, Coleman, you must be dead on your feet. Come on upstairs and I'll change the sheets in Lloyd's room. It's the quietest room in the house."

"No, don't change sheets for me. All I want is a place to stretch out."

Quickly shutting my door as I heard them all start up the stairs, I hurried to turn down my bed, thump my fist in the pillow, and hightail it to the bathroom. I wouldn't put it past someone to stick their head in my room to tell me that Coleman would be sleeping across the hall.

They did attempt to moderate their voices as they passed my door, somebody whispering, "Be real quiet. Miss Julia's sleeping."

Well, no, I wasn't. I was burning up in two sweaters, wool pants, coat, scarf, hat, boots, and gloves in the bathroom. So I shed the top layer and waited for the noisy parade to go back downstairs and leave Coleman and me to our peaceful naps.

CHAPTER 45

As the upstairs quieted down with the retreat of the stampede, I redressed and peeked out into the hall. Coleman's door was closed, and the only sounds were drifting up from the distant kitchen. I eased my door closed — as if I were sleeping soundly behind it — and walked softly to the stairs. Down I went, almost holding my breath, and slithered in Hazel Marie's rubber-soled boots to the front door.

Closing it as quietly behind me as I could, I stood on the porch and surveyed the snow-covered yard, Coleman's car at the curb, and the lowering clouds that darkened the afternoon. Then I approached the three steps to the yard, decided that the Ice Melt had yet to do its job, and sat down on the edge of the porch. Fearing broken bones and who-knows-what-else, I didn't dare attempt to walk down the steps, so I scooted in a seated position from one step to the other until I could safely stand. Holding on to the snow-covered boxwoods that lined the porch, I gingerly put one foot in front of the other, smushing through the snow layer onto the crackling surface of ice underneath, then decided that the better part of valor was to get down on my hands and knees. It was dangerous going, but I was intent on crossing my side yard, pushing through the boundary plantings and popping out onto Mildred's side yard, then progressing across her yard to finally come face-to-face with Pastor Ledbetter.

My only concern — well, not the only one but the one of the moment — was that Lillian would look out the window and see something like Bigfoot scooting across our yard on all fours.

Reaching the boundary between my and Mildred's yards, I poked my head out of the thick plantings of azaleas, forsythias, and laurels and, pulling myself up by a dogwood limb, finally got to my feet. Light streamed from the windows of Mildred's house onto the undisturbed snow as I looked around to determine the best way to approach the house.

Her stately home sat on a slight rise, so I faced a slick climb to the front porch. The first step I took upended me, and, while it took a minute to determine that nothing was broken, I decided that I shouldn't cross that wide expanse on my feet. So, just as I'd crossed my own yard, I crawled.

On hands and knees I went, reminding me of the pastor's trek to the same place the night before. No tall skier came to offer help, thank goodness. I headed for the large living room window that looked out over the side yard — how often I had sat in one of the Louis something-or-other chairs and gazed out that selfsame window. It was my intent to get to it, then, using the sill to pull myself upright, to carefully make my way to the front door by clinging to the side of the house.

Finally reaching the boxwoods, which Mildred loved as I did, lining the foundation, I pushed through them to the side of the house. Then, using the windowsill as a handhold, I pulled myself to my feet. And looked straight into Emma Sue's face.

Her mouth dropped open, then she shrieked loud enough to be heard on Main Street and jumped out of her chair — where she'd been watching the new-fallen snow, I guessed — and flew out of the room, screaming as she went.

I quickly — well, as quickly as I could — sidestepped toward the front, holding for dear life to the side of the house. I could hear the uproar inside as Emma Sue sounded the alarm. Mildred screamed, "What is it! What is it! Ida Lee! Call the police! Hurry!" And a lower voice, the pastor's, undoubtedly, trying to calm a hysterical Emma Sue.

"Mildred!" I yelled, banging against the side of the house as I scrambled along. "It's me! Don't call the police, it's me!" Then, hearing Mildred call for her shotgun, I shrieked, "And don't shoot, either!"

That didn't help, so, slipping and sliding on the packed ice next to the house, I finally reached her columned front porch. Which was also covered with ice. Down I went on hands and knees, crawling as fast as I could to the door to cancel the call for help from the cops.

Reaching the door, I stretched up to ring the doorbell, then banged on the door, yelling, "It's me, Mildred! Let me in!"

The door swung open and there stood Mildred, the shotgun her daddy had given her in one hand. "What in the world? *Julia?* Is that you?"

"*Yes, it's me!* Who did you think it was?" I scrambled for a handhold on the jamb to help me rise, but my energy was spent. "Help me up, Mildred. I can't make it."

Between her and Ida Lee — mostly Ida Lee — I was able to get to my feet. "My deep apologies for my unorthodox arrival," I said in a regal manner, ignoring the astonishment on their faces. "But, really, Mildred, I didn't expect to be greeted by a gun stuck in my face."

"Well, I didn't expect you to come calling in that getup, either," Mildred sputtered. "I mean, you are *unrecognizable*!" And she started laughing and couldn't stop.

Ida Lee, bless her heart, took the shotgun from Mildred's hand before she lost complete control, propped it in a corner, then took my arm. "Come in, Mrs. Murdoch. We're so glad to have you." Ida Lee knew how to treat an unexpected guest, no matter how inappropriately dressed.

I stepped farther into the large foyer, then realized that Sam's pants had suffered some slippage, so that the legs were now blousing around the tops of Hazel Marie's boots. So I took off the boots and rolled up the pants. I did the adjusting while looking around for Emma Sue and Pastor Ledbetter. "Where are they?" I demanded. "I've not risked a broken leg, hip, or neck to have them slip away from me again."

"Who?" Mildred asked, red-faced from all the laughing.

"The Ledbetters. I know they're here, Mildred. You told me they were."

Sobering up, Mildred looked around. "Well, they were here a minute ago. Ida Lee, did you see where they went?"

"No, ma'am, I was too busy disarming you."

Under different circumstances, I would've laughed at that, but right then I was too anxious to prevent another escape by the pastor.

"Well," I said, taking charge, "let's round 'em up. Ida Lee, you look in the dining room and the kitchen. Mildred, take the living room and sunroom, if you will, and I'll clear the upstairs. Herd 'em in here, and don't let them escape." I headed for the stairs, behaving as if the house were mine, while totally ignoring the rights of the homeowner.

But neither questioned their assigned tasks, probably because, for one thing, Mildred's weight hindered her from a rapid climb up the stairs and she avoided them when she could.

I wasn't too agile myself, but the urgency I felt to confront the pastor propelled me up the stairs and through a quick glance in each of the many bedrooms, sitting rooms, and baggage rooms on the second floor. I would've searched the attic as well, but the door was locked.

Hurrying back downstairs, I called, "Did you find them?"

The answer was no, for both Mildred and Ida Lee stood in the foyer looking up at me with no sign of either Ledbetter.

"I don't know where they could've gotten to," Mildred said, frowning. "Ida Lee, you didn't find them?"

"No, ma'am, there's no sign of them. It's all very strange."

"Oh, my," I moaned, leaning against the newel, "if he's gotten away again, I don't know what I'll do." I could just see me down on all fours chasing the pastor down the sidewalk.

"What's going on?" Mildred asked — it was her house and she had a right to ask. "Why're they hiding and why're you after them?"

"Not them. *Him.* Because, Mildred, he got me in this mess, and he's going to get me out. And because," I said darkly, "I'm putting him on notice that I am not taking the fall for him."

Mildred threw up her hands. "Well, I don't know what you're up to, Julia, but he's your pastor so I'll stay out of it. I've never understood you Presbyterians, anyway."

CHAPTER 46

I wasn't about to explain Presbyterianism to Mildred at that particular moment. I had more pressing matters to tend to.

"Think!" I urged. "They have to be in the house somewhere. Where could they be?"

Ida Lee's face lit up. "The elevator," she whispered.

"Yes!" I said, turned to take up the hunt, then stopped. "Where is it?"

Mildred led us around behind the staircase, then pointed to a door that looked normal enough except for the call button on the wall beside it. The three of us stood looking at it.

"Is it up or down?" I whispered.

"It's down," Ida Lee whispered back. "We would've heard it if it had gone up."

I stood back. "You do the honors, Mildred. Push it."

She did. A motor hummed and the door opened with a jerk before sliding smoothly back. There stood Pastor Ledbetter with Emma Sue pushing away from him.

Mildred, always the thoughtful hostess, said warmly, "Oh, there you are. Look, Julia has come over for a visit, so we can have a nice little chat. Would anyone care for tea?"

The pastor cleared his throat, ushered Emma Sue out of the elevator, and, without a glance at me, said in ministerial tones, "Emma Sue's had quite a fright. She needs to lie down. Come, Emma Sue, I'll help you to bed."

Emma Sue didn't come. The pastor put his arm around her and urged her toward the door. "Larry," she said, shaking him off, "will you please stop pushing me around!" She stared at me. "Julia?" She gave a tentative smile, then began to laugh. "I don't mean to laugh at you, but you don't look anything like yourself."

"Oh, she doesn't mind," Mildred said, leading Emma Sue to a chair in the sunroom. "I laughed at her, too."

I didn't care. I was staring at Pastor Ledbetter, waiting to get him alone to have it out with him.

"Then," he said, drawing himself up, "I'll leave you ladies to it. I'll be working on my sermon for Sunday." And he began to walk away.

"As I'm sure you've heard, Pastor," I said, giving him every chance to have a private discussion, "I've been wanting to speak with you."

"I'm sorry, Miss Julia. This is just not a convenient time. The weather, you know, and Emma Sue's condition. Why don't you make an appointment for sometime next week when my schedule permits? Norma will make one for you."

He was trying to put me off *again*.

"No," I said, preparing to lay him low. "We'll talk right here and right now if that's the way it has to be. I've been trying every way I know how, Pastor, to tell you that the promise I made to you is no longer in effect, so take note here and now. That promise has gotten me in more hot water than I can stand, and it's put me in a position of withholding evidence in an official investigation. So I'm through. I'm not going to remain silent any longer. It's only fair — even though you've not been fair to me — to warn you so you can go in for an interview before I start talking. After that, you may or may not have a chance to confirm what I'm going to tell them, because they'll hunt you down like a dog, and do it a lot better and a lot faster than I've been able to do."

The pastor looked pained, and lowering his voice, he said, "Please don't upset Emma Sue. She's not well." Then in a normal tone, he went on. "My goodness, the weather has us all on edge, hasn't it? I suggest we talk about this later."

"Later? Later, when you've had time to run and hide like you've been doing ever since Connie Clayborn's body was found?"

Mildred perked up. "What?"

"Larry?" Emma Sue said, looking from him to me and back again.

Pastor Ledbetter patted the air with his hands. "Not now, Miss Julia. It's not a good time."

"Actually it's the *only* time, because it's the first time I've been able to hem you up. Now, here's what you're going to do. You are going *first thing in the morning* to see Detective Ellis at the sheriff's department, and you're going to tell him the reason I went to visit Connie Clayborn."

"Well, let's not get ahead of ourselves, Miss Julia. That's a matter for prayer for both of us."

"Good! You have all night to pray about it, but you better get yourself down there in the morning and set things straight. Because, Pastor, that's what I'm going to do. I am going to tell everything I know. And if you're not there to back me up, I will not only tell Detective Ellis, I will tell everybody else, including LuAnne Conover — and you know what that means — that *you* sent me to Connie to get her to apologize to Emma Sue, whose condition was reflecting badly on you. It'll be all over town by nightfall."

"What?" Mildred asked again.

Emma Sue looked up at her husband. "Why, Larry? Why would you send Julia to see that woman?"

"It was for you, Emma Sue," he said. "All for you. I asked Miss Julia to act as a mediator to reassure you, to make you feel better. The Clayborn woman had undermined your self-confidence so much that you were suffering a spiritual crisis. I thought . . ."

Emma Sue sprang to her feet, her hands in fists by her side. "You're *always* making plans for me. And now you thought by going behind my back and setting up some *intervention* that you'd fix things, didn't you? What else were you planning for me? A group session where you would *facilitate,* just as you always do? Wouldn't that be a feather in your cap."

"No, Emma Sue," I said before the pastor could speak. "You have it wrong. He didn't want anybody to know how deeply you were affected by Connie's criticism. Your reaction showed that he couldn't rule his own house — First Timothy, chapter three, verses four and five, as cited to me. Look it up. He was protecting you, that's true, but he was also protecting his reputation. He wanted your reaction to Connie's criticism kept quiet, and I foolishly went along with it, thinking I was being helpful. That's why I had to promise not to tell anyone, and that's why I'm now in big trouble with the law."

Emma Sue swung around to stare at her husband. Her face reddened and she seemed to grow in stature. "You were *ashamed* of me? That's what it was, wasn't it? And still is, isn't it? That's why you wouldn't listen to that doctor in Winston-Salem who recommended a psychiatrist. That's why you brought me home and said that the Lord would deal with me. And what else did you plan for me, I ask you? A quiet stay in an institution where I wouldn't embarrass you?"

"Emma Sue . . ." the pastor began. "You aren't thinking straight. You don't understand."

"Oh, yes, I am, and oh, yes, I do. You think more of what other people think than you do of me. Well, let me tell you something." And she walked right up to him and got in his face. "I'm through being your assistant pastor, through with committee meetings, and teaching Sunday school, and covering dishes, and calling on the sick, and volunteering for everything you dream up, and being in church every time the doors are open. All I want to do is plant flowers and dig weeds and prune and mulch and fertilize and watch things grow. That park is my Garden of Eden, and there'll be no snakes in the grass there, whether it's Connie Clayborn — bless her heart — or *you*.

"And another thing," she said before he could get a word in edgewise, "I *am* going to see a counselor — I'm going so I can learn how to live with you. And furthermore, I'm going to let everybody know what I'm doing." She swished around and began to walk out of the room. Then she stopped and turned back. "And furthermore than that, you're going to pay for every session I have. And I intend to have a lot of them." Then she left, and we heard her stomping up the stairs.

I wasn't the only one laying down the law.

I stood outside Mildred's house on my way home. I'd just gingerly gotten myself down her wide steps onto the snow and ice of the lawn and was hesitating before striking off across it. The sconces beside her door —

powered by the generator — lit the porch and cast a golden semicircle across the front yard.

I stood there thinking over the scene I'd just left, wondering why I wasn't feeling better about finally confronting Pastor Ledbetter.

I hadn't wanted to do it in front of Emma Sue, much less in front of a member of another church, but he had refused to talk to me alone. So it was his own fault.

Well, maybe not. I'd been so hot to tell him off, especially after chasing after him for days, only to find him hiding in Mildred's residential elevator, of all places. It beat all I'd ever heard.

But I hadn't brought up my niggling suspicions about someone using the access road before I got to the Clayborn house by way of the main road on that fateful day. I hadn't been able to bring myself to do it. I would leave that to Detective Ellis, if it occurred to him.

But I still didn't feel good about what I'd said, spilling it all out before an audience. A small one, but still. A Christian minister deserved respect, and I had withheld it. By the time Emma Sue had flounced off, the pastor was left looking bereft and deflated.

Then I mentally shook myself. He was going to look worse than that by the time I got through, come morning. It was going to be every man for himself, or, in my case, every woman for herself. I was tired of holding back important information concerning the death of another human being. If Detective Ellis wanted to know why I visited Connie, I was going to tell him, from *a* to *z*, exactly why I did, including my own eagerness to tell Connie off.

But I'd given the pastor fair warning, so I just wasn't going to feel bad about it any longer.

I started walking, avoiding Mildred's paved drive, which would be slick with ice, by picking my way along the side of it. The snow seemed mushier, and my feet in Hazel Marie's boots broke through the underlying ice with little trouble — a good sign, it seemed to me. So, rather than pushing my way back through the way I'd come, I headed for the sanded street, where walking would be more secure. The temperature might have been rising, but the sky was lowering and the afternoon was fast growing dark.

As I got to the road and stepped over the mounded snow and ice left by the snowplow, I realized I was hearing the rhythmic thuds of a runner's feet on the gritty street.

Oh, Lord, the night runner was out early. Well, I'd about had enough of him, too. So, with the comfort of having a sheriff's deputy nearby — even if he was asleep — I kept walking toward home. No more cowering in the bushes, too afraid to stick my head out. I was just before clearing the air, coming clean, ratting out my pastor — whatever you want to call it — to Detective Ellis, so I might as well take on the night runner, too.

He turned the corner without slowing down and headed not to the other side of the street, as he usually did, but straight toward me. I stopped and waited as he came closer. My first impulse was to scream my head off and hope Coleman wasn't a sound sleeper.

Wearing one of those all-over latex suits like a scuba diver or a luge racer, the runner's lanky frame ate up the yards, the feet, and the inches until he stopped, breathing heavily, right in front of me.

I looked him in the face and saw nothing but deep-set eyes and wet wool rings around his nose and mouth. My breath caught in my throat as he pushed up his ski mask.

"Well, Mrs. Murdoch," Stan Clayborn said, his chest heaving as he caught his breath. "Did you find what you were looking for at my house?"

CHAPTER 47

"How did you . . . ?" I started, then stopped, determined not to let him put me on the defensive. He had a lot to answer for, himself. I drew myself up, felt Sam's pants slide from under my belt, and clamped my elbows against my waist.

Lifting my head in defiance, I said, "I certainly did. Did you?"

"It's my house. I had every right . . ." He stopped, just as I had, realizing that he'd given himself away.

"That's quite possible," I agreed, "unless your house was still an active crime scene. And assuredly it was because the SBI hasn't been there yet. And I remind you, Mr. Clayborn, I was not *in* the house, messing with or destroying evidence, as apparently you were. And," I continued in case he had messing with me in mind, "I remind you that a patrol car is parked right over there and the driver of same is within easy ear-shot."

He turned his head to glance at Coleman's patrol car, then looked back at me. "I was there," he said quietly, all belligerence gone from his voice, "to commune with Connie, to reconnect our harmony one last time. I've been distraught without the connection we had. But I have to accept that she's joined that great River of Time, and the positive energy she'd left in the house would soon fade away in its flow. I had to be there before it was gone. The Universe was calling me."

"The what? *How*?"

"Never mind," he said, shaking his head at my ignorance. "You wouldn't understand."

He was right. I couldn't think of one Bible verse that had to do with such a phenomenon — trees that clap their hands, yes, but not a vocal universe.

But then, returning to his first question, he asked, "So it *was* you out there, creeping around my house. What did you expect to find that nobody else had found?"

"Don't belittle my efforts, Mr. Clayborn. I had to take matters into my own hands because the investigators had me in their sights. I had to see if someone could access your house by coming in on that fire lane. In other words, get there without being written up by the gatekeeper. And anybody could. In fact, I expect that's the way *you* came in Saturday night, otherwise you couldn't have been there to do any kind of communing, no matter who was doing the calling."

Still breathing deeply, he had nothing to say, so I went on. "And I'll have you know that I had no intention of going near that house when we first got there. It was only when we saw that strange glow in the back room that we decided to check it out. What was it, anyway? A computer you left on?"

He nodded. "I heard your car and saw you come down the hill. I didn't know who you were — thought somebody was breaking in after seeing the obituary. I waited in the hall to catch you at it and didn't think about the computer."

"Well, see, if it hadn't been for that light, we would never have come so close. So it was you who drew us there. All we were interested in was if it was possible for somebody — *anybody* — to have gotten to Connie unseen. And they could've." I stopped, waiting for a response that didn't come. "That was the way you came in, wasn't it? So there'd be no record of it?"

Looking down, he nodded and, in a choked voice, said, "That night, yes. All I wanted was one last word with her."

You poor thing, I thought. If he was hearing voices from the universe pouring out through a computer, he was certainly deserving of pity.

Then he lifted his head, that ski mask pushed up above his eyebrows, and looked at me. "But, Mrs. Murdoch, I did not kill my wife."

"Well," I said, hitching up Sam's pants again, "that's between you and Detective Ellis. But, Mr. Clayborn, tell me this. I'm interested in just how you use a computer to commune with someone who's gone on before, even with the universe involved. I know that modern means of communication can reach people around the world, but it's news to me that it can reach someone in *the other* one."

His mouth twitched in a semblance of a smile. "I don't use a computer for that. It was Connie's laptop and I was checking her e-mails to see if they would tell me anything. They didn't — she'd just gotten it — which is why the cops didn't take it, I guess.

"But," he said grimly, as he drew himself up a few more inches. "Who was with you? You keep sayin *we,* and I thought I saw someone else sneaking around. How do I know the both of you weren't trying to break in?"

"Because I just told you we weren't. I was there on a purely fact-finding mission, so don't get on your high horse with me. Detective Ellis will soon know all about it, including not only who was with me — a man, by the way, who is well known in law enforcement circles — but that you also were there doing who-knows-what. So be prepared.

"And," I went on, feeling myself on a roll, "while we're clearing the air, why do you find it necessary to be running and skiing around *my* house? I don't like it, Mr. Clayborn. I don't like seeing someone half-dressed pounding down my street every night that comes around. What's so interesting? What's on your mind? Are you checking on me? Are you trying to intimidate me into making a confession? Well, if you are, let me tell you something — *I* didn't kill your wife, either, and you can just find yourself another place to run."

Just then the power came on. Up and down Polk Street, the streetlights lit up, as did all the houses around us.

"Well, hallelujah," I said, looking around.

Stan Clayborn looked around, too.

"People will sleep warmer tonight. We should all be thanking the Universe for putting things right."

"I'll thank Duke Power, if you don't mind, since they're the only ones I'm in touch with. Now I've got to go inside. It's cold out here. But, Mr. Clayborn, I don't want to see any more sprints past my house from now on. You worry me."

"I'm sorry. I didn't intend to cause you any concern. I'm staying with a coworker not far from here until they let me back in the house. I run this way because I like this street. The grand old houses are beautiful — the kind that I admire. Connie and I spoke often of this street, although she," he said, with no undertone of criticism, "preferred a more modern style of architecture."

"I know she did," I said with more understanding than he knew. "She told us all about it at that lovely coffee she had last week." *And gave us her plans for demolition and reconstruction of our grand old houses while she was at it.* I thought it, but kept the thought to myself. By this time, I'd been laying down the law right and left to anybody who needed it, and I was tired.

I slipped back into the house through the front door, heard the sounds of activity throughout the house, and hurried as fast as I could up the stairs and into my bedroom.

Closing the door behind me, I quickly came out of my cold weather garb, including Sam's downward-creeping pants and Hazel Marie's toe-crimping boots. I had just slipped a cardigan on over my dress when Hazel Marie knocked on the door.

"Miss Julia? I hate to wake . . . oh, you're up. The power's back on, and I'm going to take my crew on home."

"You're welcome to stay as long as you want, Hazel Marie. Maybe you should give your house a chance to warm up."

She grinned. "I'll just have to keep the girls bundled up until it's warm. They've gone through all the diapers I brought, so I'd better get home before accidents start happening. Oh," she said, turning her head to look down the hall, "Coleman's up, and I think Binkie and Gracie are leaving, too."

"I'm coming," I said, and then as if I'd just noticed them, I went on. "I found your boots in here. One of the children must've been playing with them."

"Probably so. I think they've played with everything else in the house."

By another hour or so, I'd seen them all off

to their homes and I was left by myself in an empty house. Lillian and Binkie had moved chairs back to their places and put away toys and games, while Hazel Marie had folded up pallets and put sheets in the washing machine. I kept telling them to leave it all, that we'd straighten the house later, but Binkie said, "We made the mess, we'll clean it up."

I'd much rather have gotten her off to myself so I could tell her what I'd learned and what I intended to do come morning. All I'd been able to do in the midst of bundling up the children and getting things ready to leave was to tell her that I wanted to speak to Detective Ellis first thing in the morning.

"Not a good idea, Miss Julia," she'd said. "Let's don't volunteer anything. The SBI will surely be here tomorrow, and when their report comes back, you'll probably be called in. Let's wait and see."

"But, Binkie," I'd said, starting to tell her that I was ready to come clean. I didn't get to finish. Gracie was crying because she didn't want to leave, and Coleman was calling for Binkie to hurry because he had to go on duty.

But maybe it was better that I kept it to myself for a while longer. I had the night to consider exactly what I would do. As I sat alone in the library, I thought over the events of the afternoon. I'd cornered the pastor, renounced the terms of my promise, and told him to be prepared because it was all coming out. My obligation to him was over.

And I'd also stood up to the night runner, who turned out to be exactly who I'd suspected. And I had come to the conclusion that anybody who was getting messages from the universe was too far off in the stratosphere to take up arms against his wife. Daft people are usually too preoccupied to engage in vicious crime.

I suddenly sat up straight, though, as it occurred to me that he and Connie had not been in as perfect a harmony via the music of the spheres as he would have me believe. He valued old buildings; she wanted to bulldoze them. Could a man get mad enough over architectural designs to bludgeon his wife? It didn't seem likely, but I'd certainly pass my thoughts along those lines to Detective Ellis. Whatever he thought of the Clayborns' bones of contention, I would be out of it. All I wanted was to clear my name and erase it from his list of suspects.

CHAPTER 48

And pursuant to that determination and before I changed my mind or somebody changed it for me, I called the sheriff's office in spite of the late hour and asked to speak with Detective Ellis. It seemed to take forever for him to come to the phone, and when he finally did, he sounded rushed and harassed.

"Yeah? This is Ellis."

"Detective, this is Julia Murdoch. I know you're busy with much more important matters, but I need to put my mind, and yours, at rest before I go to bed tonight. I want to come in and see you in the morning. I'm ready to confess."

Dead silence. Then in a soft voice he said, "You are?"

"Yes, I've put it off long enough. Will you have time to see me about eight o'clock?"

"Mrs. Murdoch, I will *make* time. In fact, I can send a car for you right now."

"Oh, no, don't bother. I'm going to bed, and if you knew what kind of day I've had, you'd understand why. See you in the morning, Detective." And I hung up, satisfied that I was about to clear my conscience and my name, and would most likely make his day as well. I slept like a baby.

The phone woke me a little after six the following morning, which ordinarily would have aggravated me no end. But it was Sam telling me that he was checking out of the hotel and would soon be on his way home. That was worth being rousted out of bed before daylight, so after urging caution on the interstate, I got up and began to dress for the day.

What does one wear to a confession? I knew exactly what to wear to a tea, a coffee, a soiree, a dinner party, to church, a funeral, a wedding, a reception, to go shopping, pay a visit, go to lunch, work in the yard, or just piddle around the house. I was, however, at a loss as to suitable attire for an official confession. Not, I assure you, that I had never confessed to anything before. Not at all, because I enumerated my sins of omission and commission every night of my life, but I doubted that a flannel gown and robe would be an appropriate costume for meeting with Detective Ellis.

So I settled for some woolen pieces and serviceable shoes, then went downstairs to plug in the coffee. And I guess that every time I did that from then on, I would recall unplugging Connie's pot, as she was no longer able to do. I took that memory as a reminder to be grateful for the little things in life, no matter how routine or seemingly unimportant they might be.

Lillian and Latisha came in, stomping snow from their boots and shedding coats and gloves.

"No school again today, Miss Lady," Latisha announced, dropping her book bag. "If this snow stick around till June, look like we'll be out till next September, too."

"I don't think you can count on that, Latisha," I said, smiling at the thought.

"You up mighty early," Lillian said, addressing me. "Latisha, you go on in yonder an' make me a picture with your color crayons. On a piece of paper, not on nothin' else."

"I know. I know." And, picking up her bag, she started toward the library. "I 'spect I'll need a snack pretty soon, though."

Lillian rolled her eyes, then asked what I wanted for breakfast.

"Just the usual, thank you," I said. "I have

a busy morning ahead. I want to talk to Binkie first, then I'll be going to the sheriff's office and confess what they consider my misdeeds — although I consider my reticence in revealing certain privileged information indicative of the moral high ground."

"You what?"

"I merely intend to clear up a few minor matters that seem to have loomed large in Detective Ellis's mind, that's all."

"Miss Binkie know what you doin'?"

"I'm going right now to call her."

And I did, only to get Gracie's babysitter, who said that Binkie had already left to prepare for a court case due to be tried later in the day. Obviously, I thought, court did not run on the public school schedule, else it would call a snow day and lawyers and judges could color pictures, like Latisha, or make themselves available to their regular clients, like me.

So I showed up at the sheriff's office without my attorney, but right on time, just as I'd promised Detective Ellis. I am a woman of my word, which had been consistently proven throughout the Clayborn investigation, and which, I might add, had thus far proven to be of some detriment to me.

Detective Ellis greeted me in a gracious,

even solicitous, manner, ushered me into the interrogation room, inquired after my health, offered coffee, and quickly entered the usual information into his recorder.

"Now, Mrs. Murdoch," he said, an eager glint in his eyes, "tell me in your own words just what happened when you went to see Ms. Clayborn last Tuesday."

"Oh, I've already told you that. And in great detail, too. In fact, I told it to you twice, and nothing's changed. Everything having to do with my actual visit happened just as I said."

"But," he said, frowning, "I thought you wanted to confess."

"I do! That's why I'm here. You see, Detective, I know that it's been bothering you that I've been less than forthcoming about my *reason* for visiting Mrs. Clayborn. So I'm sure you'll be happy to hear that I have now pronounced as null and void any promise I may have made heretofore concerning that reason, so I consider myself free of any moral restraint whatsoever."

"Uh, run that by me again?"

"I told the one to whom I had made a promise *not* to tell that I was going to tell. Which is what I am now doing."

"You are?"

"Yes. You see, Detective, ideally he

would've released me from that promise on his own, especially when keeping the promise not to tell put me in such an uneasy position with you. Instead of stepping up to the plate, though, he avoided me at every turn, and the more he avoided me, the less I felt obliged to keep my promise." I stopped and considered that for a minute. "I tell you, I have had a moral struggle about to whom I owed the greatest obligation — to you, who wanted me to tell, or to him, who didn't. The only way to solve it was to track him down and tell him I was going to tell — you know, to warn him. It was the least and the best I could do under the circumstances. So I have now done that and formally renounced my promise of silence, and I'm ready to tell you what you've been wanting to know."

"I am more than ready to hear it, believe me."

"All right, here goes, and I hope the Lord forgives me if I've made the wrong decision. I've already told you that I called Connie Clayborn the morning of that fateful day, but what I didn't tell you was that it wasn't to thank her for her previous invitation, as I led you to believe. I called her because I'd been *asked* to." And I went on to tell Detective Ellis about Emma Sue's sad decline as she grieved over the town park and about Pastor Ledbetter's increasing concern about her. "He asked me to attempt to get Connie to apologize for her scalding criticism of Emma Sue's efforts on the park. Which was all well and good because Connie *should* have apologized. She went way over the line in what she said, and it just stabbed Emma Sue to the heart.

"Not literally, of course. But then, when he started in on the possibility of Satanic influence, I began to have second thoughts about getting involved."

"Satanic?" Detective Ellis perked up at that.

I waved my hand in a brushing gesture. "Oh, I discounted that right away. Connie was just ill informed and insensitive to the feelings of others, that's all. Poorly brought up, too, I would imagine. Anyway, I thought I could do some good by talking with her, not only to relieve Emma Sue's distress but also to help Connie fit in a whole lot better than she was doing on her own. But, Detective, here's the heart of my confession."

"Oh, good," Detective Ellis said, his shoulders sagging.

"I *welcomed* the request to speak to Connie because I wanted to give her a taste of her own medicine. I'm sorry to admit this because it reflects badly on me, but the truth of the matter was that I *longed* to tell her how cruel she'd been, how unthinking and unkind. So, with the mission I'd been given, I had the perfect opportunity to cut her down to size by letting her know how unlikely it was that she'd ever be invited to join the garden club or the book club or even to be invited for dinner anywhere."

"Oh, my," Detective Ellis murmured.

"Yes. So, you see, I harbored ill will toward her because I'd had as much to do with that park as Emma Sue had, and I was deeply offended by Connie's criticism. But, Detective, I never got to say another word to her after we hung up that morning. She was gone by the time I got there that afternoon. She never knew my real feelings."

"Okay, then," Detective Ellis said with something like a sigh, "let me get this straight. You went to see Ms. Clayborn because Mr. Ledbetter asked you to, and he asked you to because his wife's feelings were hurt, and you were glad to do it because your feelings were hurt, too, and you wanted to hurt Ms. Clayborn's feelings. That about it?"

"Not quite. You're not getting the underlying factors, Detective. It was more than just a few women's hurt feelings, as you imply."

464

I stopped, breathed deeply, and plunged ahead. "I hate having to tell on people, Detective. I hope you understand that I take no pleasure in exposing the secrets of others. But the motive of Pastor Ledbetter in sending me to Connie was his deep concern that his ministry was being compromised by his own inability to snap Emma Sue out of her depression. His situation is addressed in either First or Second Timothy — the exact reference escapes me now — so he was, in a sense, fighting to sustain his irreproachable standing within the church. And besides," I went on, cringing as I piled onto my own pastor, "he grew up in Abbot County and may have known about the fire lane behind the Clayborn house."

Detective Ellis sat straight up. "Huh," he said.

"Well, but Connie's husband also obviously knew about it, too, having lived right below it for some time. And in spite of his noticeable grief for his wife, epitomized by his attempt to commune with her by way of leftover positive energy *in the house* while it was still a crime scene, all was not in perfect harmony within that marriage."

"No?" Detective Ellis's eyes widened at the news.

"No. Mr. Clayborn told me on what I

hope was his last night run by my house that he and Connie agreed on everything except architectural design and . . ."

As the door suddenly opened, I looked up. Sergeant Coleman Bates stuck his head in, gave me a brief nod, then said, "See you a minute, Detective?"

Detective Ellis stood, scooped up his notes and his recorder, and started to leave. "Have a rest, Mrs. Murdoch. I won't be long."

So I waited, but rested hardly at all. Coleman had barely acknowledged me, which I put down to his official manner. Still, his serious demeanor had done nothing to reassure me, even though I'd now told everything I knew, including my heretofore untold motive for visiting Connie, the harsh feelings I'd held toward her, and the suspicious ones I still harbored toward her husband and my own pastor.

They say that confession is good for the soul, but if that were so, why, after revealing all that had burdened me, was I not feeling so good about having done it?

CHAPTER 49

After several lonely minutes, the door swung open and Coleman came in, Detective Ellis right behind him, and Lieutenant Peavey stopping in the doorway.

"Miss Julia," Coleman said, putting his hands on the table and leaning toward me. "You don't have to do this — you may want to consult your attorney or you may not want to do it at all — but I'm asking you to bear with me and help me conduct a little experiment. You know I've been off for several days, so I've just had the opportunity to study the crime scene evidence — the forensics, the scene drawings, the investigators' notes, the statements that were given, and so on. There's a big question mark in the notes that, with your help, I want to try to answer."

"Why, Coleman, you know I'll help any way I can."

"Okay. Here's the problem: you left a

partial finger- and palm print in a smear of blood on the granite countertop above the head of the victim. The assumption has been that you got the blood on your hand from one of the puddles or spatters on the floor or on the victim, then transferred it to the countertop. I'd like to see how that happened. Would you be willing to show us exactly what you did when you walked in and found Ms. Clayborn on the floor?"

"Well," I said hesitantly, my eyes darting around, "I'm not sure I can recall *exactly* what I did. I was in a state of shock when I realized that she was no longer with us, and I was kind of operating on instinct or impulse or something. More or less."

"We understand that," Coleman said in a kindly tone, "and this is all unofficial — no notes and no recordings will be made. I just want to see if what I suspect will prove to be true, and whether it will or not, either way, it will not damage you or your testimony."

"Well," I said again as I looked into Coleman's honest eyes, "I trust you, Coleman, so I'll do whatever you want."

"Good. Let's walk down to the lab." He took my arm and led me out into the hall, where I saw a number of deputies gathered around, Lieutenant Peavey towering over all. We led the convoy halfway down the hall and turned into the department's laboratory. A wall of cheap kitchen cabinets with black Formica countertops, centered by a sink with rust stains, ran down the right side of the room. The flock of deputies crowded into the other side.

"Okay," Coleman said, stopping me short of the cabinets. "Deputy Caine, please assume the position." There was a murmur of laughter as a woman deputy carefully lowered herself to the floor, where I saw that an outline of Connie's body had been drawn in chalk. Deputy Caine was about Connie's size and, with Coleman's help, she arranged herself within the outline. And as she did, my mind flashed back to what I had found, and I could almost see Connie again as she lay half on her stomach, one side of her face with its one eye staring ahead, one knee pulled up, and one shod foot sticking out beyond the end of the cabinets.

I blinked away the association, noting to myself that Deputy Caine was clad in a dark navy uniform consisting of long pants and boots, and not clunky shoes and a dress that was hiked up to reveal pink nylon step-ins — which I doubted Deputy Caine would have had on even if Coleman had gone so far as to explicitly recreate the scene by exposing her undergarments.

Coleman crouched beside her, adjusting her position in small ways, a nudge here and a nudge there, then he looked her over. "Comfy?" he asked.

"Just get on with it," she told him.

"All right," he said, standing and looking around the expectant audience. "We've got to use our imaginations a little here. This cabinet right here," he said, pointing to the door above and to the side of Deputy Caine's head, "represents the dishwasher, which is located on the right side of the sink cabinet both here and in the Clayborn kitchen. Notice that the victim's head is pretty much aligned with the join between the dishwasher and the next cabinet. See that, Miss Julia?"

I nodded, trying to visualize a stainless steel dishwasher door instead of a stained plywood cabinet. "I see it, but I can't swear to it."

"That's all right. We can, because measurements were taken and drawings were made, and I've reproduced them here. Now, Miss Julia, you come over and squat down beside the victim in the same place and position as you did that day. Then I want you to go through the motions — as well as you remember them — just as you did then."

He stepped back and I stepped forward, reluctantly, I admit, for I had no real desire to go through those awful minutes again, even if I could recollect my exact movements.

"Well," I said, "I know I squatted down beside her. Like this." And I carefully adjusted my feet near, but not touching, Deputy Caine and resumed the position I'd taken as well as I could, in spite of creaking joints and aching muscles. "I called her name, then I touched her shoulder. Like this." Deputy Caine's shoulder was soft and warm, not at all like the feel of Connie's shoulder. "Then I pulled down her skirt tail, which I now know I shouldn't have done, but at the time I was trying to save her some embarrassment, not knowing that she no longer cared about such things." I went through the motions of pulling down a skirt.

"And," Coleman asked, "you were still crouched beside the body?"

"Oh, yes, I hadn't moved an inch and my limbs were letting me know it, too. But there was so much blood coming from under her head and so many spatters around that I was very careful not to move around in them. But then, just as I realized that Con-

471

nie was actually dead, the power went off and the lights went out." I shuddered, swept again by the fear I'd experienced in those moments.

"So what did you do when that happened?"

"I had only one thought, and that was to get out and away. Squatting there beside a dead acquaintance in the dark, I heard what I thought was a shuffling movement, and I was scared out of my mind."

"We understand," Coleman said. "So try to react just as you did then. You heard something. You were frightened. Don't tell us. Show us what you did."

I closed my eyes and relived those frightful moments so that they seemed to be happening again and, in spite of having determined never to put such a strain on my protesting knees again, I put my right hand on the floor and reached with the other one for the countertop. By pushing with one and pulling with the other, along with a wrenching of stiff joints and quivering muscles, I managed to gain my feet and turn toward the crowd of deputies, ready to flee the scene as I'd done before.

"See that!" Coleman said to the onlookers. "That's what I thought happened. Show us your hand, Miss Julia."

I turned both hands up and, to my surprise, my left palm and fingers were smeared with a dark powdery substance. "What did I do? What is this?"

"Fingerprint powder," Coleman said, a smile of satisfaction on his face. "It'll come off." He handed me a paper towel.

Turning to the deputies, he went on. "Miss Julia has just shown us what I think happened. Forensics checked every spatter and pool of blood in that kitchen, looking for where her hand picked up the blood and then transferred it to the edge of the counter. But they didn't find anything, because she didn't transfer it. She just happened to take hold of the countertop at the exact spot where Ms. Clayborn's head hit when I think she fell. And since the countertop is black granite, Miss Julia wouldn't have noticed the blood. So when she grasped the counter edge and pulled on it to stand up, the blood got smeared to look like a transfer. And I'm convinced the medical examiner can prove that the impact of the victim's head on the edge of that granite counter both fractured the skull and caused the cut across the wound."

"She *fell*?" I asked in wonderment. "Nobody killed her?"

"That's what I'm thinking," Coleman

said. "And a second look by forensics may prove it." Turning aside, he said, "You can get up now, Deputy." And Deputy Caine got to her feet in one swift, graceful movement — so different from my awkward rise.

"One more question, Miss Julia," he went on. "When did you close the dishwasher door?"

"Close it? I didn't close it. It was closed when I got there."

"Right. Now, here's the thing," Coleman went on. "When the first responders got there, the dishwasher door was closed — not locked, just closed, and nobody questioned it because the only fingerprints on it were Ms. Clayborn's. But a second, more careful look turned up a small smear of blood on the *inside* of the door near the corner. I'm suggesting that Ms. Clayborn had climbed onto a chair — there was one overturned — and perhaps up onto the counter itself to reach the high cabinets. Somehow or another, she slipped and fell, hitting her head on the sharp edge of the counter, then bouncing off the corner of the open dishwasher door. From there, she fell to the floor into the position we found her, and I'm suggesting that the impact of her head on the corner of the door caused the second wound on the forehead — the bruise — and also caused the door to spring closed when she fell to the floor. I think we can prove that by seeing what the door does when it's given a fairly heavy lick at the same spot."

Even though I was still in a daze of awe and confusion at Coleman's proposition, and still wiping black powder off my hand, I could see the nods and smiles among the deputies. It made sense to them and even to Lieutenant Peavey, who had not just a smile but a grin on his face. Case solved.

"How did you figure all that out?" I asked as I stood with Coleman at the door leading out of the sheriff's office. I was just before leaving for home, having been assured that neither I nor anyone else was a suspect in the death of Connie Clayborn.

"From watching you crawl out of my tent and using me as ballast or leverage or whatever to get to your feet. In other words, I saw that you needed help of some kind to get up, and when I read your description of what you did that day in the Clayborn kitchen, it just made sense that you'd reach for something to pull yourself up with." He smiled with well-deserved but unassuming pride. "Just paying attention to detail was what it amounted to."

"More than that, Coleman, more than that." I pressed his hand, gave him a grateful smile, and started to open the door. "Oh, I almost forgot," I said, turning back, "will you be seeing Lamar Owens anytime soon?"

"Without a doubt."

"I want to make sure he has a hat or scarf or something. You lose a lot of heat through your head, you know. If you'll see to it, I'll repay you for whatever you get."

Coleman smiled. "We'll find him something. Don't worry about it."

"Oh, one more thing, Coleman." I stood with my hand on the door, ready to leave but still troubled by questions. "How can you be sure that Connie Clayborn fell? She could've been pushed or thrown against the counter, couldn't she?"

"Could've, yes. But remember, she wasn't a small woman, so think of what it would take to push or throw her with enough force against the counter to cause the kind of wound she had. And remember — well, you may not know this, but the autopsy showed no bruises or handprints or other evidence that would've been there if someone had grasped her and thrown or pushed her. I know you thought you heard somebody in the house, but they found no evidence of anybody. There'll be an inquest, I expect, but it's looking accidental."

"Well, I guess it's a relief that no one is getting away with murder. But, I declare, Coleman, I wish you'd come up with this several days ago. You would've saved a lot of wear and tear on my nerves."

He laughed. "Yeah, well, I was sign sitting. But the guys would've gotten it sooner or later."

I wasn't too sure about that, but I thanked him again, wished him a good day, and, finally, walked out the door of the sheriff's department — a free woman, thanks to him.

I stopped beside my car, a sudden thought blooming in my mind — Roberta had said all along that Coleman should've been on the case. Maybe she wasn't as balmy as I'd thought.

I left then, but on my way home a few questions raised their ugly heads. What was Connie's husband really doing in his house the night that Lamar Owens and I had also shown up there? Communing and computing just didn't seem answer enough. And speaking of Lamar, what had happened to his beloved scarf, begrimed though it was, but also laden with my fingerprints? Coleman had not mentioned those fingerprints, so had they not been found, or had the deputies decided that the scarf had no bearing on what they were thinking at the time was a murder case?

Furthermore, were the deputies still looking for who or what had set off the house alarms? Or would Lamar's scarf give them a reason to assume that he'd been the likely burglar who'd been scared off by the lights and sirens? I'd hate for him to be blamed for something that had essentially been my idea and, thus, my fault, even though Lamar had never seemed the least concerned about the possibility of lengthening his arrest record.

I would watch out for him, though, and if the presence of that scarf near a crime scene came back to haunt him, I would confess to my sudden urge to wash the filthy thing, and I would also confess my part in our trek along the fire lane. Until and unless that happened, I decided, I would just keep it to myself. But even if it did come up, all they could pin on me or him concerning that fiasco was a misdemeanor trespassing charge, and I had a good lawyer. When I could find her.

Turning onto Summit Avenue, I began castigating myself for having suspected Pastor Ledbetter — how could I have done that? And why had I beaten myself to a pulp over keeping his secret when it hadn't amounted to a hill of beans? For days I'd let myself roil around in a state of turmoil over telling on him or not telling. But that's what comes from being a person of high moral character, and I guessed I'd do it again given the same circumstances.

I turned off Summit onto Polk, then made a left turn into my own driveway. My heart sped up at the sight of Sam's car, and I hurried inside the house. The kitchen was empty — maybe Lillian had made a tactful retreat — so I hurried through it calling my beloved's name.

He met me in the hall, and let me just say that we had quite a nice reunion. It took some time, however, after we were seated together on the leather sofa in the library, for me to tell Sam all that had happened in the few days, which I readily admit seemed much longer, that he had been gone. Sam was highly impressed with Coleman's acuity in being able to turn a murder into an accident, all because he'd seen an aged woman struggle to her feet. And Sam was delighted to hear about Lamar Owens — at least the part he played in the events that I chose to tell.

As for the night runner, Sam, like me, wasn't so sure that the man had chosen our street on which to run simply in order to admire the gracious homes along the way. We decided that it was more than likely that Stan Clayborn really had suspected me of some complicity in his wife's death and was keeping an eye on me. I shuddered at the thought, but felt safe enough with Sam home and Lieutenant Peavey satisfied with the conclusion of the Clayborn case.

As for Pastor Larry Ledbetter — well! Sam was irate at our pastor's unconscionable behavior toward me, and he even went so far as to spring to his feet, ready to track him down and forcibly express his displeasure.

"It's all right, Sam," I said. "Really it is. He's more to be pitied than condemned. His heart was in the right place, wanting to take care of Emma Sue and to preserve his position in the church — we really can't blame him for that. He just had too high an opinion of that position and got his priorities wrong."

I drew Sam back down beside me and held his hand. "The only thing that I *would* blame him for," I went on, "is the way he treats Emma Sue, but she pretty much put him in his place at Mildred's. I just hope she'll stick to it. Anyway, he wanted to take Connie down a peg or two — as did we all — but he turned out to be the one who got taken down, which might prove the best thing that could've happened."

"Well," Sam said, pulling me close, "I intend to let him know that I don't appreciate the untenable position in which he put you. And I'll tell you something else, Julia, this is the last time I'm leaving you alone. From now on, when I have to go somewhere, you're going with me. You get into too much trouble when I'm gone."

"Yes, but I manage to get out of it, at least so far. Mainly because, I readily admit, of having friends in high places." I leaned my head against his shoulder, comforted by having him home. "But I missed you, Sam. I really missed you."

After a while, Sam said, "Hold on a minute. I have something for you."

He went out into the hall and returned with a professionally wrapped package. "I hope you like it, honey. We didn't have time to look around much, but there was a nice shop next to the hotel. So I brought a gift for my sweetheart."

I quickly unwrapped it, deeply appreciative of his thinking of me while engrossed in discussions of judicial appointments, visiting with old classmates, and lunching with the governor. I carefully folded back the tissue paper under the lid, and there was

Sam's thoughtful gift — the last thing I would've ever expected.

"Oh, Sam," I said, pulling it out to its full length and admiring its softness and distinctive design. "A Burberry scarf! How did you know it's what I've always wanted?"

ABOUT THE AUTHOR

Ann B. Ross holds a doctorate in English from the University of North Carolina, Chapel Hill, and has taught literature at the University of North Carolina in Asheville. She is the author of fifteen previous novels featuring the popular southern heroine Miss Julia. She lives in Hendersonville, North Carolina.

The employees of Thorndike Press hope you have enjoyed this Large Print book. All our Thorndike, Wheeler, and Kennebec Large Print titles are designed for easy reading, and all our books are made to last. Other Thorndike Press Large Print books are available at your library, through selected bookstores, or directly from us.

For information about titles, please call:
  (800) 223-1244

or visit our Web site at:
  http://gale.cengage.com/thorndike

To share your comments, please write:
  Publisher
  Thorndike Press
  10 Water St., Suite 310
  Waterville, ME 04901